The Fox
and the
Flame

Kassandra Flamouri

Willow Root Books

For Zoe, my little lioness.

Author's Note

Kingsgarden is a beautiful, magical place, but no world is perfect. There are some darker elements to this story, so I have a few content warnings, just in case. I've included everything I can think of in the list below, but if you come across something you think should be noted here, please let me know. I can be reached by email at flamourifiction@gmail.com or on Instagram (@flamourific).

Birth trauma (one scene)

Brief mention of sexual assault

Family death (on-page)

Child death (off-page)

My nurse used to tell me nightmares are both the fruit of our sins and our punishment for them. She must be right, because I have always had one great nightmare and one great sin. Both haunt me—one by day, and one by night.

This is what I see. What I have always seen, night after night.

I stand over Kingsgarden like a giantess, with one foot planted in the northern reaches and one on the shores of the southern sea. My hair tangles in wisps of cloud, and the whole sky crowns my head, studded with sparking stars.

I look out over the breadth of the Garden, the domain that was never meant to be mine: the City of Lilies spilling out of the great lake to the east, the City of Orchids circling my right foot, and the City of Ferns tickling my left. The City of Sage sprouting from the vast Indigo Plains, the City of Pine nestled deep in the great northern forests. All the known world, spread at my feet. And, at my back, the City of Roses. Thorns prickle, softly at first, then harder.

The thorns bite into my skin, burning across my back. For a moment I stand, paralyzed with dread, then turn. A figure swathed in flames claws its way out of the roses, ripping away the clinging ropes of thorns and flinging them away to burn. Once free, the figure tips its face to the sky and lets out a cry like the roar of a wildfire.

The figure begins to move, and the vaguely human features coalesce into a girl made of light and flame, with molten skin and fiery hair. She takes one step, then another, graceful and terrible in equal measure. She pauses, poised on the tips of her toes, then leaps into the air with her arms and legs extended like wings.

The fire girl lands in a burst of flame and ash, making me choke and cringe away from her. But, if she sees me at all, she pays me no mind. Sparks trail behind her as she dances across the Garden, setting cities and villages ablaze with each footfall while I watch, helpless to stop her.

Finally, she stops and walks back to me through the flames. Tears of fire flicker down her face, echoing my own. She takes my hand, and together we watch my kingdom burn.

Chapter One

"An eleven-year-old made me do it," is, I suppose, never a good excuse when you're seventeen and presumably old enough to know better. It's especially flimsy when the eleven-year-old in question is a poor tavern keeper's daughter and you're the princess of Kingsgarden, who *definitely* should know better. Has that ever stopped us?

It has not.

I have long since accepted that the most I can do is mitigate the damage. For example, I did succeed in persuading Jessa that jumping off the roof was not the optimal method of field-testing her flying suit, and the incident with the soup would have been much worse if she'd been left entirely to her own devices. But on this occasion, faced with a simple matter of eavesdropping, tragically weakened as I am by an empty belly and yet another night's sleep lost to nightmares, I am powerless in the face of Jessa's will... and, it must be admitted, my own curiosity.

Still, I try.

"We shouldn't be here," I whisper as we crouch beside the kitchen door. "This conversation is clearly private. Anyway, we're supposed to be reviewing amphibian anatomy."

"That can wait," Jessa whispers back. "This can't."

"I don't have much time today," I insist. "The reconstruction ceremony—"

"Shhhh," Jessa says, flapping her hand at me. "I think it's that stupid shelter guardian again."

I frown. What is a guardian doing here? The nearest shelter is on the far eastern side of the Lower City. The network of group homes are a long-standing project of the House of Light and Shadow, an extension of their belief that beauty's ultimate manifestation is one of strength. For nearly twenty years now, they've been establishing safe havens for those with no one to care for them: orphans, childless elders, citizens suffering from illness or infirmity... and widows. A smile spreads across my face as I begin to suspect what business a shelter guardian might have with Jessa's mother. Pia will eat him alive.

"If she catches us, I'm blaming you," I tell Jessa.

Jessa grins and passes me a few mugs and a rag.

"In case she catches us," she whispers, then raises a finger to her lips.

"I am losing patience with you, Master Yoren." Pia's voice is polite but sounds somehow frayed at the edges. "As I have told you before—on multiple occasions—how I conduct my business is none of your concern."

"But it is *not* your business," replies a male voice—Master Yoren's, I assume. Something about the depth and tone of his voice sounds contrived, like a boy playing at being a man. "That's the point."

"My husband's business, then," Pia says. "The business that I run and have run for the last six years. The business of feeding hungry people who are likely wondering where their supper is because I'm back here and not out there feeding them. This business. Whatever you want to call it, it's still none of yours."

"It is not your place, woman!" Yoren's voice rises and cracks, making Jessa grin.

"Whether it is or isn't, it's not your place to say," Pia says. "I am a widow. I have every right to continue my husband's work. The king's law says so."

"Just because it's legal doesn't make it seemly," he says hotly. "You ought to be in the shelter, caring for other unfortunates and being cared for in turn. The

House of Light and Shadow was magnanimous enough to start a shelter in this very neighborhood, and yet you scorn our good works."

I hadn't heard about a new shelter in the neighborhood. It must be very new. That would explain the man's zeal—he needs recruits.

"I scorn no one," Pia says. "I appreciate your... enthusiasm, Master Yoren. And, of course, I respect and honor the House and all those in your care. Surely you must realize that there are those whose need is greater than mine. How can it be right to take up the House's time and resources when I'm doing perfectly well on my own? I have work that I enjoy and a good income to provide for myself and my daughter. I won't scorn that or my husband's name by throwing it away."

"But you must—"

"No one can tell me what I must do save the king and my husband. The king hasn't said a word, and my husband is dead," Pia snaps, finally losing her temper. "I am a widow, with a widow's rights. One of those rights is to call the City Watch to remove you from my premises—a right I am more than willing to exercise, so I suggest you leave. Now."

Yoren curses, and Jessa and I scramble away from the door just in time to avoid him as he storms through. I catch only a brief impression of pimples, red hair, and equally red ears before he disappears in a swirl of robes. Jessa and I stare after him for a moment, then jump as the scrape of a chair being pushed back signals Pia's approach. Jessa snatches up a pitcher of ale and makes a dash for the nearest patron, while I rub furiously at my mug, blessing Jessa's foresight. Pia appears in the kitchen doorway, her face like thunder. When she sees me, she opens her mouth as if to demand what I'm doing behind her bar. Then she blinks and smiles warmly.

"Ari." Pia smiles, but the skin around her eyes looks pinched and tight. "I'm glad you're here. I need to speak with you, and the waiting was agony. You've finished your lesson?"

"Not exactly," I say.

"Take a break, then," Pia says, her eyes flicking to Jessa. "If I wait any longer, I'll burst. Come to the kitchen with me for a moment."

"Um," I shift guiltily. "Mightn't—um, someone—hear us in the kitchen? If they were to listen at the door? Hypothetically."

"Hypothetically," Pia says, raising her voice and fixing Jessa with a look that promises untold depths of punishment, "that person would regret such a breach of privacy. Intensely, and for many weeks to come."

Jessa pouts and turns away, her shoulders hunching against the force of Pia's glare. I follow Pia into the kitchen, wondering whether Pia knows Jessa and I were snooping before and only cares that this next bit stays a secret, or if she doesn't know and will be furious when she finds out. The thought makes sweat bead under my arms.

"Get away from that, you little monster," Pia snaps, shooing a fat tabby cat away from the enormous kettle of stew bubbling on the hearth.

Nettle, Jessa's cat, yowls and stalks away, his tail stiff with offended dignity. I offer my hand, and he pushes his head into it.

"So, what is it?" I ask, gathering Nettle into my arms.

His solid weight is comforting against my chest. When Pia doesn't answer right away, I pull Nettle closer.

"Jessa is growing," Pia finally says. "And I must find a place for her."

"What do you mean?" Unease creeps over my shoulders. "She has a place right here."

"I've spoken to a Temple representative," Pia says. "They'll take her on a contingent contract, but only if she enrolls by the end of the year. They say she'll be too old to learn, otherwise. They say she may be too old already. She's nearly twelve, and her Gift is beginning to manifest. That dratted cat follows her everywhere."

Pia casts a dark glance at Nettle, as if it's his fault Jessa's Gift as a Beastspeaker has begun to bloom.

"But—but she *can't*," I sputter, dropping Nettle in my horror. "A contingent contract? She could be scrubbing pots for the rest of her life!"

"That's no worse than what she'd get here with me." Pia closes her eyes as if in pain. "At least this way she has a chance at a better life."

"It's a chance in a thousand," I say flatly. "Jessa likes the arts well enough, and she does have a real knack for drawing, but... "

I trail off. The Temple of Graces trains acolytes in the five Divine Arts: Music, Dance, Sculpture, Painting, and Poetry. Some choose to also train in the more worldly arts of physical pleasure and physical defense. They become Companions to grace the halls of whatever household they choose, and those households pay well for the honor. But only a handful in every rising class are accepted as Initiates, and fewer still as Companions. Those who fail to earn their Mark or don't wish to become Initiates return to their families or find work in the City—but only if their families have paid the staggering cost of their tuition.

Pia doesn't have that kind of money, obviously. The only way Jessa will receive the Temple's training, room, and board is with a contingent contract. The Temple will extend Jessa a loan, and, once she's initiated, the loan will be forgiven in its entirety. But, to *be* initiated, she'll first need to pass a grueling set of tests and trials. If she fails, she'll end up working off her debt in the laundries or the kitchen.

Jessa's chances of earning her Mark are depressingly, vanishingly slim. Though she is bright and vibrant and curious, her passion is for animals and natural philosophy, not the arts. She'll never make it.

I shake my head. "Only the truly devout earn their Initiate's Mark, Pia. You can't fake a vocation."

"I know that," Pia says sharply. She sighs again. "I know, Ari. But what am I to do? You know how she is. She won't be happy as a tavern maid. At least as an acolyte she'll have another few years to find something she can live with." Pia gives a laugh that's equal parts sardonic and despairing. "And the Temple has more eyes and more hands to keep her at her work than I do."

"She can come to the palace," I say. "I've said it before. She can be tutored by the same scholars who tutored me."

"And then what?" Pia demands. "Assuming she doesn't get herself arrested, she'll never be more than your maid, doing the work of a thrall."

"She'd be working like a thrall for the Temple, too," I point out. "That's the whole reason they offer contingent contracts. They don't allow thralls on Temple grounds, so they need human labor."

"That is both disrespectful and untrue, Princess," Pia says, scowling at me. "Anyway, at least there she'll have a fighting chance. And you don't know—she's young. She might find her passion. She just needs time, and the Temple can give her that."

"What she needs is a proper school," I say. "Like the House of Light and Shadow's academy."

Pia shakes her head. "They'll never accept a girl."

"I know! But if we could open our *own* academy, one for girls—"

"But we can't," Pia says. "You asked, and the king said no."

"He said he didn't have the money," I correct her. "He didn't say no."

Pia snorts. "He's your brother, and he dotes on you. Of course he didn't say no."

"It's just the money," I insist. "Every spare coin goes to the reconstruction debt."

Pia winces at the reminder that the Honeysuckle Rose Tavern, like every other building in the Lower City, was rebuilt with the king's own coin after an earthquake leveled the whole district six years ago. That's how I met Pia and Jessa. Pia's mother, Maja, was my nurse. She and Jessa's father were both killed in the earthquake, and I pestered my brother until he took me to see Maja's family. I brought them daisies.

Even now, a lump rises in my throat at the memory of Pia standing in the rubble, with Jessa weeping into her mother's apron. By the look on Pia's face, she's remembering, too. I didn't mean to dredge up something so painful, but maybe it will work in my favor. I press on eagerly.

"You know as well as I do how much the king cares. If I could come up with my own funds, he'd say yes."

"And how are you going to do that?" Pia demands. "Have you uncovered a fortune since last year, or the year before? Be honest with yourself, Princess—and with me. A dream is all well and good, but that's all it will ever be unless you act on it. And you haven't acted." She overrides my protest. "I don't blame you, child. If you haven't acted, it's because there was no reasonable action to take. But we must accept that this school of yours is never going to happen."

My eyes sting. She's right, of course. I've been dreaming about a school for girls ever since I was denied entry to the House's academy as a young girl myself. But maybe that's all it can ever be—a dream. And, anyway, what right do I have to object to Pia's plans for Jessa? I believe what I said about Jessa's chances of earning her Mark, but in the end it's her mother's decision, not mine. And I have no better alternative to offer.

"I'm sorry," Pia says gently. "But it must be done."

"No, *I'm* sorry," I say, blinking away tears. "Pay me no mind. You must do what you think is best."

That's not how I feel, but I know it's what I'm supposed to say, even if it hurts.

I swallow hard. "I think I should go. Jessa will know I'm—I'm upset. And I can't lie to her."

"I understand," Pia says. "But you'll be back, won't you? It would break Jessa's heart if you left us for good."

"Of course," I say, shocked out of my heartache for a moment. "I would never abandon her. Even if I'm not—if I can't—"

My throat closes, and Pia grips my shoulder.

"Come on, then." She leads me back into the dining room. "Jessa, time to bid Ari farewell for now. She isn't feeling well."

"But we haven't finished our lesson!" Jessa cries, then registers the second part of what her mother said. "Are you sick, Ari?"

I look at Pia, helpless.

"Her courses have come on," Pia lies smoothly. "You'll know how unpleasant and inconvenient it is soon enough."

Jessa wrinkles her nose. "Don't remind me. You'll be better by tomorrow, though, right?"

I give a weak smile. "I hope so."

"Good," Jessa says. "You can bring me more scrolls."

"Jessa," Pia sighs.

I squeeze Pia's arm. This time a smile comes more easily.

"Of course I will," I say. I keep hold of Pia's arm as I head for the door.

I should just hug her and leave. Jessa is her daughter, her responsibility. I should leave her in peace to make whatever choice she feels best, without any interference or false hope. But I can't.

"Please, don't make any decisions yet," I whisper. "Just... give me some time to think."

Pia's lips purse. "I won't say anything to the Temple, or to Jessa. Not yet. But you'd best think of something soon."

I look back at Jessa, who seems to be comforting the still-disgruntled Nettle. He lounges in her arms, his eyes narrowed to slits as she scratches under his chin. I can't bear the thought of her risking her future with a Temple contract. I want to tell Pia not to worry, that she can count on me to find a solution. I'm the Rose Princess, after all, a royal daughter of the Garden. I should be able to make such a promise.

But I've never been much of a liar.

"I'll do my best," I say instead.

Pia looks at me with sad, steady eyes. "I hope it's enough, Ari. I truly do."

"Yes," I agree with a wobbly smile. "So do I."

Chapter Two

I find my guard, Rowan, lounging against the stone wall of the tavern and polishing his boot-knife. He's hidden among the climbing roses and honeysuckle for which the tavern is named, but I know where to look. A rose petal falls into his messy brown hair, making me smile in spite of everything. But something of my distress must still linger in my face, because Rowan's gaze sharpens when he sees me.

"What's wrong?" he asks.

"I just... Pia had some bad news," I tell him. He opens his mouth, and I shake my head. "I don't want to talk about it. Is that a new knife?"

"Yes," he says, frowning at the blade.

"What happened to the old one?"

"Lost it." At my raised eyebrows, he sighs and adds, "To Luca. I bet him he couldn't beat me in two out of three bouts."

I try again to smile. "Well, that was stupid of you."

"Evidently," Rowan says sourly.

My half-brother, Luca, is the best in the king's guard with any blade, be it sword or knife or eating tines. Something Rowan knows as well as I do but occasionally chooses to forget.

"So what happened?" Rowan asks.

"I don't—"

"Want to talk about it," he finishes. "You said that. But if something's happened, I need to know."

"It's nothing to do with you," I say.

Rowan grins, poking me in the ribs. "Did Pia finally cut you loose? I've never understood why a sensible woman like her would allow her daughter's head to be filled with madness and fluffery twice a week."

"It's not madness and fluffery," I snap, stung. "It's history and mathematics and—and it's none of your business. Come on, we're probably already late."

Rowan makes a face. He's looking forward to today's ceremony as much as I am—that is to say, not in the slightest. But he's bound by duty to stay by my side, and I'm bound by duty to do as my king and eldest brother commands. So off we must go, even though all I want is to hide under my covers and cry.

It makes me feel guilty, as so many things do. Costi—King Miocostin, as he's known to the rest of Kingsgarden—was just trying to be kind. Even when his councilors objected, he insisted on including me in the ceremony today. I didn't have the heart to tell him that I'd rather clean chamber pots with the thralls.

I look back at the Honeysuckle Rose. What I wouldn't give to just stay here. If only I could turn back time. If only I had my own money, my own power, and not just a title. But there's no use in wishing for impossible things.

"Let's go, then," Rowan says, holding out his hand.

I take it and we slide out of the Honeysuckle's shadow, joining the colorful stream of humanity flowing toward Market Square. No one notices us. Such is Rowan's Gift, a Shadowfoot's stealth and silence. He can move through a crowd in broad daylight, completely unnoticed. The effect isn't as strong when he's towing me along, but it's enough to let us move safely about the City.

It's the only reason I'm allowed out with just one guard, and that in turn is the reason I allow said guard more liberties than a princess might otherwise. Rowan needles me mercilessly as we walk, determined to uncover the cause of my distress. Ordinarily, I appreciate his dedication. When I was thirteen and he was fifteen, he hid a bucketful of eels in a boy's bed because that boy wouldn't stop trying to kiss me. Horrible Hadrian never recovered. To this day, he blanches at the sight of them, even grilled and served on a platter. I may or may not have made it a point to request eels whenever he and his father dine with us, but that's neither here nor there. Well-intentioned or not, I've had enough of Rowan's digging.

"Rowan," I say. "Shut up. As your princess, I ask you—no, I *command* you. Shut. Up."

"I'm just saying—"

"Rowan."

He sighs. "Fine. Enjoy the scenery, then."

"I always do," I reply with a sniff.

The City of Roses is famed throughout Kingsgarden for its beauty. Most credit the Upper City and Midtown for our reputation, but the Lower City has always held my heart. Its wood and stone buildings cluster together in hodge-podge of styles and sizes, most overgrown with ivy or moss, with flowers spilling from windowsills and bushes exploding from every spare corner. Many of the bushes and hedges include comically ugly faces peeking through the branches, stone statues meant to ward off unlucky spirits.

Defacement of public property is so common—and far too skillful to be considered actual defacement—that the perpetrators hardly bother to hide their activities. Torch poles are carved with flowers and animals, and the mismatched cobblestones have been swapped and rearranged to form swirling designs so that every street is a work of art unto itself.

In the original plans for the reconstruction, everything was to be done in the precise, pristine style of the Upper City. But there was such an outcry that Costi directed the builders to recreate the buildings and neighborhoods as exactly as possible, though of course some modifications had to be made in order to protect the buildings from future disasters. But I think the builders succeeded in recapturing the spirit of the Lower City. It's still odd and disjointed, perfectly imperfect. I adore every inch of it.

The scenery changes subtly as we get closer to Market Square. Gardens become more regimented, and the buildings feature more marble than quartz or granite. More and more of the beauty on display appears to be dependent on Light—on magic. Water features, enchanted by the House of Light and Shadow, disappear into nothing or loop endlessly back on themselves. Illusions of brightly colored birds flicker overhead. Fantastical, magically crafted plants march along the street in careful rows.

Only the Temple grounds are entirely natural. The spectacular blooms are cultivated by Greenloves, citizens Gifted with an affinity for plants. Most are also acolytes, painters and poets who draw inspiration from the beauty of the gardens.

I pause before a miniature replica of the Temple, complete with tiny columns of pinkish stone that somehow manage to capture the sweeping scope of the original. The Temple has always made me uneasy. Our faith teaches us to revere the beauty in the world and in ourselves—but the Temple's conception of beauty is so narrow! There's more to beauty than aesthetics, or even moral goodness. What about the elegance of a mathematical formula or the beauty of logic, of understanding?

The House of Light and Shadow sponsors an academy, but they value the intellectual arts as an avenue to power and achievement rather than something beautiful in its own right. Aside from the shelters, they have no official presence in the City, thank the stars. They sequester themselves in their drab and dreary pile of rocks atop the cliffs, immersed in their mysteries and finding beauty in strength and excellence.

I sigh, running my hand over a tiny replica of the Temple's spires. So many dismiss the wonder of our histories—the fact that we *have* histories, even! They never think of how amazing it is that we can hear the words of the dead and catch a glimpse of their world through simple parchment and ink.

Sometimes it feels like Jessa's the only one who understands, who feels the same joy that I do at the sight of a stack of scrolls or the sense of peace that comes from disappearing into one's own head. The rest of the world might think me odd and unfeminine, but Jessa understands... for now. What will she think—*how* will she think—after eight years in the Temple's care?

Rowan, miraculously, obeys my command to hold his tongue. He leaves me to my own thoughts all the way to Market Square, speaking only to point out the cluster of councilors and assorted nobles standing behind the dais where my brother will deliver his speech. I sigh and make my way toward them, taking my place beside Councilor Norrin Prosper. The lines around his crinkled blue eyes deepen as he beams at me, seeming genuinely pleased by my presence. His gray hair is tied back in a neat little knot at the back of his head, secured with a jaunty little pin in the shape of a rose.

I can't help but smile back, though a pang of bitterness steals some warmth from the gesture. Norrin, a well known eccentric, would tutor Jessa if I asked—and if Pia would agree. But Pia's pride is a fearsome thing. Even if I could assure her that Jessa wouldn't end up a maid, Pia would never accept anything she saw as charity.

I can't make such a promise, in any case. Princess or not, educated or not, I have no more power or freedom than I did before Norrin took me under his academic wing. But that's not Norrin's fault, so I try again to smile.

"Hello, Norrin."

He squeezes my hand. "Arismendi, welcome. A beautiful day for a beautiful celebration, is it not?"

"It is," I agree, looking out over the mass of spectators.

Market Square is always packed with folk from all over the City, but today it's bursting at the seams. The array of color is dizzying—the color of clothing, of faces, of hair and eyes, of language. Children are held aloft or perched on their parents' shoulders, straining to see the stage erected in the center of the square. All around me, accents and dialects clash as the crowds chatter and shout with excitement. Everyone seems to have something to say.

Except, of course, the thralls. They drift silently after their masters or bear ladies and lords aloft in litters, their faces blank and empty. I've always found thralls eerie in their perfection: creatures like men and women, indistinguishable—at first—from citizens of the Garden. But a second glance will tell anyone that they aren't quite human. They move and breathe and eat, but it's only a facsimile of life. They lack that subtle spark of knowledge and awareness that makes people... well, *people*.

Thralls have no minds, no voices, no souls. They're empty shells made in our image, dolls animated by Light. What makes thralls so valuable is their dual purpose: They make useful servants, yes, but they also generate Light. The raw energy of their bodies is converted into magic by some means known only to a very few. Thralls are the lynchpin of the House's financial and political might, and the secret of their creation is guarded more closely than any religious mystery.

Today, I feel almost like a thrall myself: helpless, powerless. Voiceless. The feeling only intensifies as a hand lands on the small of my back. I turn and find myself face to face with Hadrian Prosper—Horrible Hadrian, of bucket-of-eels fame. He's not even looking at me. He's laughing with one of his equally horrible friends, using me as a prop to bolster his reputation.

As if his reputation needs any bolstering. Hadrian looks like he was spawned by Beauty herself, with shining golden hair and eyes as blue as the summer sky. He carries himself like the lord he is, with his head high and his shoulders thrown back. His manners are elegant, his speech refined, his attire impeccable. The sweet stench of wealth oozes out of his every pore. Which, I assume, is the reason men and women alike routinely throw themselves at his feet.

Hadrian has never seemed to grasp that I don't find him irresistible. The idea that anyone might think him less than perfect is, as far as I can tell, incomprehensible to him. I consider calling for Rowan, who would be only too happy to explain to Hadrian—in detail, with physical demonstration—just what we think of rich dandies and their airs. But that would upset Norrin, who is by some paradox of nature both one of my favorite people and Hadrian's father.

So I grit my teeth against Hadrian's presumption and focus on more pleasant things, like my brothers' arrival. Costi strides through the crowd with Luca just behind him, shaking hands and kissing babies like the seasoned politician he is. Though barely thirty, he has ruled Kingsgarden for over a decade. Ever since our father's death, he has poured all of himself into caring for his people, with special attention to his occasionally wayward siblings. Even before Father died, it was mostly Costi who raised us, with our father ill and our mother long dead.

Shame floods me at the thought of my mother, as it nearly always does. I push the feeling away, focusing on Costi. He stands at the podium in front of me, squaring his shoulders as he so often does before making an address. Luca plants himself like an oak at Costi's side, a picture-perfect guardsman save for the fox curled at his feet.

Luca is a Beastspeaker like Jessa, Gifted with the ability to commune with animals. The fox, Kirit, is Luca's latest rescue and my favorite. Kirit is sweet, funny, and wickedly smart, and far more pleasant company than the ornery old hound who previously attached himself to Luca.

Luca's Gift is unusual, not only because it's stronger than most in the City but because Luca is also a Lightcrafter. I've found that those who learn to use Light tend to forgo their natural Gifts, relying instead on the more predictable and powerful magic offered by Lightcraft. Luca cultivates both, which I've always thought very wise of him.

Costi, on the other hand, has always leaned into his Gift. He knows a few charms, but even those he mostly uses to shore up his abilities as a Honeytongue. His talent lies in persuasion and charisma. A useful Gift, for a king.

They're powerful men, my brothers. Good men, too, fiercely loving and honorable. If, as a woman, my possessions and person must be legally controlled by men, I could do a lot worse than Costi and Luca. No one else, thank the stars, has any personal or legal claim on me. Certainly not Horrible Hadrian, whose proprietary grip grows more infuriating by the minute.

Hadrian is breaking the rules. I feel I should be able to do something about it, but everything I do always seems to be wrong, even if I'm in the right. And Costi is about to begin his speech. Unsettled though I am by Pia's news and now Hadrian's advances, I can't bear the thought of spoiling this day for Costi, for the City. Today marks the anniversary of the Catastrophe, and with it the long-awaited completion of the Lower City's reconstruction. It took six long years and all the crown's money—more than that, even—to re-build these homes and streets and businesses, and I can't make a scene and ruin it for everyone.

So I do nothing. Unless teeth gritting counts. But I don't count it, because it accomplishes nothing. Much like Hadrian, who is preening and puffing himself up as if he's personally responsible for the project's success. The thought makes me grind my teeth even harder. The only thing Hadrian can take credit for is having a rich father.

Norrin Prosper isn't simply wealthy. He's disgustingly, unfathomably wealthy. But he's also kind and just, two qualities that are unusual in a rich man—and qualities he does not share with his son. Norrin was the only one of Costi's councilors to contribute to the reconstruction fund. The rest did nothing but moan and wail about the expense, and yet here they all are, smugly patting each other on the back. Hadrian, the most pompous of all, is apparently feeling smug enough to include me in the back-patting.

"Darling Arismendi," Hadrian murmurs in my ear, and my skin crawls at his closeness. "I wish you would accept my offer of a thrall, if only to arrange your hair and press your clothes. A woman of your station must reflect and enhance the beauty of whatever space she finds herself in. You were made in Queen Amari's very image, Arismendi. You must give that image all the honor and care it deserves. Graces keep her, what would she say if she could see you so disheveled?"

I glance down at the tail of my red-gold braid, which I've been twisting and sliding between my fingers, and at my rumpled dress, which actually *had* been pressed this morning but which is now wrinkled and streaked with dust from crouching on a tavern floor.

Perhaps my mother *would* be ashamed to be seen with me. She was famous for her beauty and grace. But she was even more famous for her good heart and gentle piety.

"I like to think she'd remind you that true beauty lies within as well as without," I say, taking a step away from him. "The Temple teaches us so."

"One is nothing without the other," Hadrian says firmly. "At least let me cast a glamour to put some color in your cheeks and remove those unsightly circles under your eyes. You look *ill*."

His brow furrows, but I know from long acquaintance with his character that it's an expression of distaste for my defects rather than anxiety for my wellbeing.

"I appreciate your concern," I say, looking away to hide my own distaste. "But no, thank you. Glamours make me itch."

At this, Hadrian laughs. "Darling Arismendi, they do no such thing. If you'll only allow—"

"But she doesn't allow. She just said so."

Hadrian jumps at the quiet voice and finally—*finally*—takes his hand from me as Rowan appears at his shoulder, seemingly from nowhere. Relief floods me. I smile up at Rowan, who has evidently reached the limit of his ability to stand by while Hadrian is being an ass.

"This is no concern of yours, Shadowfoot," Hadrian sniffs, smoothing his vest down and moving as if to reclaim the space at my side.

"On the contrary," Rowan says, and plants himself directly in Hadrian's path. "What concerns the princess concerns me as well. It's my job. And, in this case, my pleasure."

"You will have neither pleasure nor employment for much longer, if I have anything to say about it," Hadrian says coldly. "And I will, sooner than you think."

Rowan, thankfully, does not rise to the bait. He just stands there with his arms crossed, staring at Hadrian like he's a grotesque but mildly interesting beetle. For a moment, I think Hadrian might hit Rowan—well, maybe not *hit*, exactly. I'm not sure Hadrian actually knows how to punch a man. As a child he had a certain fondness for slapping and kicking, and right now he looks like he'd very much like to do both. But he just sneers at Rowan and turns back to his friends.

"Hadrian," I mutter, shaking my head in disgust. "You'd think he'd have gotten tired of his little game by now."

Hadrian has been playing at courting me since I was seven and he was eight. As might be expected from someone dubbed Horrible Hadrian, his idea of courting leaves much to be desired. I met him for the first time when Norrin agreed to teach me sums and the rudiments of rhetoric. I can recall all too vividly the way his nose turned up as he scoffed at my 'delusional frivolity'.

"You won't need any of that when you're married to me," he said.

I ignored him then, and I ignore him now. But Rowan is still watching Hadrian, his gaze troubled.

"Ari, I think—*ouch*."

Rowan glares down at the fox standing on his boot. Kirit grins back, baring sharp, white teeth. There's a small tear in the knee of Rowan's trouser leg where Kirit must have nipped him. I look up and direct a frown at Luca's rigid back. He doesn't turn, his message having been clearly delivered. With a start, I realize Costi has already begun to speak. And Kirit is leaning in for another bite of Rowan's leg.

"Alright, alright," Rowan mutters. "I'm going."

As seamlessly as he appeared, Rowan is gone, disappearing into the crowd as only a Shadowfoot can. I shake my head and run my braid through my hands once more, trying to concentrate on what Costi is saying.

His speech is a masterpiece, I must admit. He takes a grim story of death and chaos and spins it into a lovely tale of resilience, courage, and the love and trust between the king and his people. He's a master of words, my brother, a Honeytongue through and through. You can't hear him speak and not find yourself touched, enraptured by his words and voice. Which isn't to say that any of it is a lie—the story is true.

It's just not the whole truth, because politics rarely allow for such luxuries. I understand that. I do. The world is imperfect, and even a king is only human. Costi does what he can, and what he must. I don't *blame* him, exactly, for the details missing from his story.

But the careful phrasing and sanitized truths still bother me. For example, he says that half the City was destroyed in an earthquake, and that's true. But I can't forget that the 'half' in question was the entirety of the Lower City, while

Midtown and the Upper City were left nearly unscathed. Or the fact that it wasn't chance or accident that left the Lower City decimated while the more affluent neighborhoods sustained barely any damage at all. *Those* buildings had long since been magically reinforced, protected by charms and amulets infused with Light.

The mages of the House of Light and Shadow could have applied the same reinforcements to the Lower City any time they liked. But they hadn't, and, when the earthquake came, not a single shed remained standing past Market Square. The House mourned the loss along with the rest of the City. They erected a couple of monuments to honor the dead and offered up their prayers for the bereaved, but when Costi asked for their help in the reconstruction, their aid looked more like extortion. Knowing my brother would not leave the Lower City unprotected a second time and believing he had no other recourse, the House had presented a proposal riddled with absurd fees. You could practically smell the gleeful avarice in the ink. But—ah, Costi's reached that part of the story.

"A collection of manuscripts was found," Costi says, and the pride in his voice fills me with a confusing mix of warmth and resentment. "It was discovered that in ages past, our land was often plagued by earthquakes. But despite the near constant convulsions of the earth, buildings rarely fell. How could this be, in an age that pre-dated the widespread use of Light? The answer was mechanical, not magical. Our ancestors employed simple yet ingenious methods to protect and stabilize their buildings. As time went on and the quakes abated, these methods were lost to history... until they were re-discovered six years ago."

Cheers rise from the assembled councilors, and it spreads to the crowd. My jaw aches from clenching it so hard. I don't mind Costi taking credit; someone has to, and he has more claim than most. It was his effort—and his money—that turned the idea into a reality, after all. But what had the councilors done except get in his way at every turn, complaining endlessly about the risk and shoving the House's reports and proposals under his nose? The only one who did anything remotely useful was Norrin, and even his contribution was barely a drop in the well of Costi's debt.

"A historic day, is it not?"

Hadrian is back, bending down to shout into my ear. I wince and try to shift away, but his hand is at my waist, holding me in place.

"I've always admired your devotion to the king," he says, giving me a tender-eyed look that I've seen little girls give puppies. "Though I must question his judgment in allowing your presence here today. These ceremonies can be quite tedious, and it's nothing to do with you, is it? I'm sure there are far more productive and pleasant uses of your time. Like preparing a trousseau."

I close my eyes and take a deep breath, praying for strength. "Hadrian, I have no need of a trousseau."

"It's happening, my love," he says, treating me to a grin that shows every one of his gleaming white teeth. "I've spoken to my father, who will speak with the king. It's time for us to wed."

All I can do is stare at him, rendered temporarily mute by outrage. Then I recover and jerk myself out of his grip.

"Don't be ridiculous," I snap. "You—"

"You're right, of course," Hadrian says contritely. "I should not have spoken of it here. I will attend you after supper and give you the proposal you deserve."

He gives me one more squeeze and resumes an ostentatiously attentive stance as Costi continues his speech. I can't listen. Even Costi's voice can't reach me now. My mind is caught up in knots, each one a tangle of frustration and fury. It's all too much. Hadrian's intention to marry me—now apparently real and imminent—his assumption that I will acquiesce, Jessa's future as an indentured servant, and my brother's rock-blasted speech.

Yes, a collection of manuscripts was found. Yes, ancient methods of construction were discovered. But by whom? *By whom?* It wasn't Costi. It wasn't Norrin or any other scholar. It certainly wasn't Hadrian, who would rather spend his time at the theater or wine houses than go anywhere near the scroll rooms.

It was *me*. Just a girl, barely older than Jessa is now, armed with nothing more than a question and the drive to find an answer. But no one would ever acknowledge that openly, even if such an outlandish story were believed. A girl, even a royal one, is only good for one thing in Kingsgarden: service to a man. As a daughter, a sister, a wife, a mother. The idea that she might have something more to offer her community, to her country, is apparently so intolerable that even a king must obscure the truth with tricks of rhetoric.

Costi insisted on including me in the ceremony as a gesture of gratitude, an attempt to give me some sliver of the credit I deserve, but I don't feel thanked. I don't feel valued. I feel angry and bitter and trapped in a world that defines me by my sex. A world in which a man like Hadrian feels perfectly justified in speaking to me as he did, as if our marriage is a foregone conclusion. A world in which Jessa could lose her freedom, her whole future, because her only path to a better life lies with the Temple and its contingent contracts. A world I want no part of and never did.

But what other world is there?

Chapter Three

When the ceremony is finally over, I slip away before Hadrian can snatch at me again. Rowan reappears at my side, scowling over his shoulder at Hadrian.

"I have to get out of here," I tell him. "*Now.*"

"That may be difficult," Rowan says, frowning as he looks for an escape route.

The audience in the square now looks like a bubbling kettle, with streams of people flowing in a dozen different directions. It will take forever just to make it to the other end of the market, never mind all the way to the King's Terrace.

Rowan takes my hand. "Luca's townhouse is just a couple of streets over. And it looks like he has the same idea, look."

I follow Rowan's gaze to Luca, who's ushering Costi toward a small side street with the help of a few other guards. Kirit sits on his shoulder, safe from stomping, careless feet.

"Let's go, then," I say. "Before we get trampled."

I give heartfelt thanks to the Graces for Rowan's Gift as we slide through the crowd—not quite effortlessly, but easily enough. Though people still press and jostle against us, we can be as rude as we like. No one can see us, and so no one can complain about an elbow to the gut.

Still, my nerves are dangerously frayed by the time we reach the little townhouse Luca inherited from his mother. We know little about her, just that she was a widow when Father met her and that she died soon after Luca was born. I've always wondered what happened and how my mother felt about it. By all accounts, she loved Luca like her own for the short time she had him. Just two years... and then I came along.

The thought adds a layer of anguish to my already seething emotions as we shut the door behind us. I lean against it and run my braid through my hands, trying to calm myself. It doesn't work.

"You're going to rip your hair out by the roots if you keep that up," Rowan tells me. "Did Hadrian ask what I think he asked?"

"He didn't ask me anything," I say. "He informed me. That absolute *ass*! How could he possibly think I would ever agree to marry him?"

Rowan raises his brows. "I imagine it didn't take much effort. He's never been denied a single thing. Why should he expect to be denied now?"

I scowl. Rowan is right. Norrin, though an eminently wise and judicious man, has a blind spot the size of a draft horse when it comes to his son. When we were children, Hadrian never thought anything of demanding whatever he wanted in any given moment. Sweets, clothes, toys, thralls... everything he desired, he received. And it didn't stop as we grew older, either. He's never lacked for fine wine or art or women. He can be charming when he chooses, and if that ever fails, I'm quite certain the depth of his purse makes up for it. Whatever the reason, he always seems able to attract and retain companionship for however long he wants it.

I never thought much about it—I never thought much about *him* if I could help it. But now, it seems, I'll have to. Now, the prize isn't sweets or rare artworks. It's me.

But it isn't *me,* exactly, that he wants. He complains often enough about my lack of pride in my appearance, my manners, my interests, even my freckles—all six of them, clustered high on my left cheek. They upset Hadrian so much he once petitioned Costi to have them permanently removed with some special paste cooked up by the House of Light and Shadow.

No, I can't believe Hadrian cares one whit about *me* in the personal sense. What he's after is my position. My title. My stomach clenches, and I can't tell if the sensation is born of fury or fear.

The door opens again, revealing Costi and Luca. They blow in with a gust of wind, laughing uproariously at something. Something I suspect is more than a bit off-color, judging by the way they stop as soon as they see me.

"Seeking sanctuary?" Costi asks, dropping a kiss on my head. "I don't blame you. It's a mess out there. Still, I think it went rather well."

He looks at me hopefully, and I try to smile.

"It was lovely, Costi."

"So why do you look like you just swallowed a live eel?" Luca asks, peering at me.

"Funny you should mention eels," Rowan says.

"Hadrian says he's going to marry me," I tell Costi, trying not to let it sound like an accusation. "He said Norrin is going to speak to you about it. You'll tell him no, won't you?"

Costi tugs my braid. "Of course, foxling. I promised, didn't I?"

Relief washes through me. Costi swore on Father's grave that he would never force me into marriage. But that was a long time ago, and a marriage alliance could buy him a substantial amount of support, not to mention money. A princess would fetch a tidy sum for a bride price.

"You'll still need to hear Hadrian's proposal, though," Costi says. "I won't insult the Prosper family by denying the boy before he even speaks to you."

My stomach sinks. "I have to?"

"So what if you do?" Luca asks. "Just say no."

"And don't feel bad about it," Rowan adds. "You shouldn't be embarrassed just because he can't take a hint."

"I'm not *embarrassed*," I say. "I'm—I don't know. Worried. Norrin has been so kind to me, and he'll be so hurt."

"Norrin will understand," Costi assures me. "And so will Hadrian, if he knows what's good for him. Just be firm and clear, and don't let him make you feel small. You're a princess."

"That's precisely the problem," I say. "If I weren't a princess, he wouldn't give me a second glance."

"An occupational hazard, I'm afraid," Costi says, his tone regretful. "I've been fending off young ladies and their mothers for the last decade at least."

"And you've never found any of them... interesting?" I ask.

Costi's romantic prospects—rather, lack thereof—is a topic of such speculation and gossip that it reached even my ears. And if *he* were to marry, it wouldn't be seemly for anyone to even think about marrying me for at least another year or two.

"I have plenty of time," Costi says. "And so do you, little fox. Don't let anyone tell you otherwise. Now, if you will all excuse me, I'm going to go have myself a little holiday."

"By which he means he's going to work in my study rather than his own," Luca says drily.

"No councilors in your study," Costi says, and disappears down the hallway.

"He's a good brother." Rowan says, his face uncharacteristically serious, almost wistful as he gazes after Costi. "A good king."

"The best," I agree.

"How rude." Rowan shakes himself and pokes Luca. "Hear that? You've been outranked as a brother."

Luca rolls his eyes. "As if that's anything new."

Kirit scampers over and leaps into my arms. I grin.

"Nonsense. Both—" Kirit yaps, and I cuddle him closer. "*All* my brothers are the best."

"Ari, this is no time to start acting like a lady," Rowan says. "Go on, tell him how second rate he is. You need to practice for Hadrian."

"I will do no such thing," I say.

"He's right, actually," Luca says. "Let me have it. I'm an upstart thug born to an upstart whore—not even a proper Companion. Just a loose woman who tried to ensnare a king."

"Stop it," I say sharply. I hate it when Luca talks like that. He tries to hide his shame behind jokes, but I know he feels the weight of his illegitimacy. It hurts him.

"I'm not going to insult you," I go on. "And I'm not going to insult Hadrian, either. I'm just going to be clear and firm, like Costi said. I can do that and still be civil. For Norrin's sake, at least."

"Not with Horrible Hadrian," Rowan says. "He'll never believe you're serious. Your only hope is to insult him so badly that his pride will force him to retract the proposal."

"Stop," I say again. "You aren't children anymore, and neither is he."

Rowan scoffs. "So he's a large horse's ass instead of a small one."

"And now he has no nursemaid or tutor to smack him with a rod," Luca agrees. "Hardly an improvement."

"You're not helping," I say, glaring at them. "I'm trying to be positive."

"Better to be realistic," Luca says. "If we don't prepare you, he'll drag you into a betrothal while you're busy trying to say 'no' nicely."

"Thank you," I say sourly. "Your faith in me warms me to my bones."

Luca grins and flicks my nose in the way he knows I hate. "Good luck."

Then he too disappears into the house. Rowan looks at me, his brows raised.

"Want to raid Luca's storeroom? I bet there's still some of that fancy cheese."

"No," I say. "I need to think. Or not think. I don't know."

Rowan opens the door and looks outside. "The rush seems to have passed. Would a walk help?"

"It will, actually," I say, brightening. "Let's go for a long, *long* walk until Hadrian forgets about me. It shouldn't take him long—lots of pretty girls in wine houses, and that's where he'll be come sundown."

"A long walk it is, then," Rowan says, and bellows our plan in the general direction of the kitchen.

Luca bellows back in acknowledgement, and we set out. At first, we wander in companionable silence with no particular destination in mind. But after a while, Rowan starts needling me again.

"Are you going to tell me what happened this morning?" he asks. "It can't be worse than Horrible Hadrian."

I sigh. "No, it's not worse than Hadrian. At least, not for me."

"What's *that* supposed to mean?" Rowan demands. "Ari, did you kill someone?"

"That's not funny," I inform him, giving him a dark look. After a moment, I say, "Pia wants to send Jessa to the Temple on a contingent contract."

Rowan cocks his head, puzzled. "Why is that bad news? It would be quite an opportunity—provided Jessa has enough sense to take advantage of it."

"It's not a matter of good sense," I say. "Temple life is a divine calling. You can't just *decide* to hear Beauty's voice whispering in your ear."

"But you can decide to work hard and succeed anyway," Rowan replies. "It just takes discipline."

"I'm not sure that's true, at least not at the level the Temple requires. And besides, what kind of life is that?" I shake my head in sorrow. "She deserves better."

"Very few people get what they deserve, Ari," he says softly. "Good or bad."

"I don't accept that," I say. "I can't."

He sighs. "Then I'm afraid you'll be disappointed very badly and very often."

"I'm well aware of *that.*" I glare at him. "You think I haven't been disappointed a thousand times already?"

"I'm just saying—"

"I know you're *just saying*," I snap. "That's the problem. You *just say* whatever comes to mind without stopping to think about how you say it or if you should say it at all. Stars forbid you pause to consider that I've already heard whatever it is you're *just saying*—or, perhaps, thought of it myself."

Rowan's face grows red, and he scowls. "Well, if you know so much already, O wise and discerning one, you must have some magic solution to alleviate poor Jessa's suffering. Do share it with this unworthy servant."

"And let you patronize me some more?" I snort. "No, thank you."

He says nothing more, and neither do I. The silence grows spiky as we go on, heading deeper into the Lower City. With neither pleasant company nor conversation to keep them at bay, my troubles descend like vultures. Around and around I go inside my own mind until my head feels like it's being split open with a hammer. I stop walking and sigh, rubbing my temples. This would all be so much easier to deal with if I'd gotten any amount of decent sleep last night.

"I need to rest a while. By myself," I add as Rowan opens his mouth. I point at a secluded courtyard, where a wide fountain burbles merrily among half-wild shrubbery and flowering trees. "I'll just sit there. There's an armory around the corner. Go get yourself another knife."

"What for?" Rowan asks, but he looks tempted.

"For your next doomed wager," I say. "Or whatever. You and Luca have always given the impression that one can never have too many knives."

"That's true," Rowan says. Still, he hesitates. "You'll stay right here? You won't run off and get yourself kidnapped or murdered to spite me?"

"I promise," I say, rolling my eyes. "Now, go away so I can think."

Rowan disappears in the flicker of an eye. I sit on the edge of the fountain with a deep sigh, staring into the water as if I'll see the solutions to my problems swimming about like fishes. I'm not worried about Hadrian so much, not any-more. As unpleasant as the experience will surely be, it really is straightforward. I'll say no, he'll be offended, and we'll all have to deal with his snit for a while, but life will go on.

Jessa's dilemma, on the other hand... I don't know. There has to be something I can do for her. Being my maid wouldn't be so bad, would it? I'd make sure she had the best of everything—tutors, dresses, food, entertainment. She'd lack for nothing.

Except the company of children her own age. Except a position of honor or an opportunity to *do* something with her education. As Pia pointed out, Jessa would be alone. The palace is staffed almost entirely with thralls, with only a few humans in honored positions like head cook, garment mistress, steward—jobs that require judgment and creativity. People would laugh at a human maid.

For myself, I don't care, but if they laugh at me, they'd do worse to Jessa. They'd think her simple-minded, maybe, fit only for a thrall's work. Or worse, they might think her my honey-bee, despite her age. Gossip that the princess has taken a child lover wouldn't just be embarrassing. It would be disastrous for my family—for Costi's reign. As much as I hate it, Pia is right: A contingent contract is Jessa's only option. Unless I can think of something better.

I'm so deep in thought that I don't realize I'm not alone—not until a hand lands on my shoulder.

Chapter Four

I startle, whipping around so quickly I nearly fall into the fountain. A young woman stands before me, her vibrant dancer's costume blazing against the pale white and pink blossoms of the cherry tree behind her. Dark curls tumble around a deep brown face so beautiful the force of it strikes me like a slap to the face, leaving me dazed.

A slight smile curves her lips as she regards me, her eyes crinkling in amusement at the corners. The color of those eyes catches me off guard, the bright cinnamon-copper color a sharp contrast against her dark skin. Her sleeveless tunic reveals long, lithe arms taut with muscle. My eyes, roving over her features, snag on a rune decorated with swirling roses just below the hollow of her throat. It's the Mark of an Initiate. Below it, another, smaller rune dangles from the end of a rose's stem. I gasp. She's not just an Initiate. She's a Companion.

"Forgive me," the girl says, taking a step back. "I didn't mean to scare you. I just thought you looked troubled."

"What are you doing here? You're a Companion," I say without thinking, then blush. "I'm sorry. That was rude."

"Not rude," she disagrees. "A bit blunt, maybe, but a fair question. I was born in this district. It doesn't hold many happy memories, I admit, but I like to come here sometimes to think and remind myself where I come from, how far I've traveled."

She smiles, but I can't find it in me to smile back.

"I'm sorry to disturb you. I'll just... go."

She cocks her head. "You're not disturbing me. And you were here first, anyway."

"Right." I say, scooting over as she sits beside me. "That's true."

I stare at her, at a loss. Perhaps I shouldn't have sent Rowan away. The City being a supremely safe place, his primary job as my bodyguard is to facilitate escapes from conversations like these. A serious look and a murmured "This way, Princess" is usually all it takes. I don't know what to say to this girl. So I just give an awkward little wave and rise to leave. But she isn't done with me yet. The Companion catches my hand, looking me over with her copper eyes.

"Don't go," she says. "I didn't mean to chase you away."

I bite my lip. It's a bit odd, isn't it, the way she's behaving? Paradoxically, I find myself relaxing. If she acts oddly, then maybe it doesn't matter if I do, too.

"What did you mean, then?"

She shrugs. "To help, I suppose. I thought perhaps we could help each other."

"How?" I ask, curious now.

"When I was young, this fountain was said to possess certain powers."

"Let me guess," I say. "It grants wishes?"

"Not exactly," the Companion says. "Sells them, maybe. Or barter. Yes, I suppose it's barter if no coin changes hands."

If she's trying to catch my attention, she's succeeding. I have no idea what to make of her, but I'm intrigued. It's only after I sit down again that I notice she hasn't released my hand.

"What's the trade, then?"

"A secret," she says. "But it takes two people. You can't really tell a secret unless there's someone to tell it to, can you? I'll give you a secret if you'll give me yours. Maybe the magic will work for us."

It occurs to me that spilling my secrets, which after all are royal ones no matter how trivial, might not be the most prudent course of action. But this isn't just any stranger. She's a Blessed Sister of the Temple, sworn to serve the people. And, well...

"I could use a wish right now," I admit with a rueful laugh.

"Excellent." The Companion raises her brows, a small smile playing around her full lips. "So. Will you make some magic with me?"

I blush. A Companion makes more than one kind of magic in the course of her work. Did she intend the double meaning? Her smile grows, and so does the heat in my cheeks. She's definitely teasing me.

"Certainly," I say, lifting my chin.

Her smile widens into a delighted grin. She takes my other hand and turns toward me so that our knees nearly touch.

"What now?" I ask. "I don't even know your name."

"I think it adds to the mystery, don't you?" she says, her eyes sparkling.

I grin. "Yes. You go first, then. What's your wish?"

"No, no, no," she says, shaking her head so that her curls bounce against the smooth skin of her cheek. "That hasn't been paid for yet. We have to tell our secrets first."

"Any secret?" I ask.

"It depends on the size of the wish, I suppose," she says with a shrug. "I imagine a bigger wish demands a bigger secret."

"It wouldn't do to underpay," I agree.

"Alright, I have mine," the Companion says. "Are you ready?"

"Quite."

She hesitates, her playful manner falling away. "I'm a Dreamwhisper."

Her eyes flick to mine, perhaps to gauge my reaction. I can understand the impulse. Dreamwhispers are mistrusted and reviled nearly as much as Spirit-walkers, for much the same reasons. Dreamwhispers can enter a sleeper's dreams and manipulate them—the dream and, if the Dreamwhisper is skilled enough, the person. But I can't imagine this beautiful, peculiar person using her Gift for ill.

"How does it work?" I ask. "Can you enter anyone's dreams?"

The tension in her face melts away as she smiles again. She tilts her head back and forth. "It depends. If I know a person well, if there's a connection, I can reach them from afar. Not very far, mind you, but I don't have to be in the same room as I would with a stranger or acquaintance. But the first time, I usually need to touch the person, no matter who it is."

"Fascinating," I murmur. It makes sense, though. The stronger the connection, the stronger the effects.

"It's a useful Gift for my line of work," she remarks, and her grin grows wicked. "I leave my patrons well satisfied."

"So you don't actually... " I let the thought trail off, blushing again. Stars, will my face ever return to its normal color?

"Not usually," she says with a shrug. "I couldn't do half so much for them awake as I do while they sleep. But I don't mind a tumble if he's handsome—or kind, or funny, or otherwise attractive enough to make it worthwhile. You know how it is."

"I don't, actually," I mutter. "I'm not—I've never—"

"I see," she says, peering at me more closely. "You're a lady. I suppose your family is saving you for the marriage market."

I wince. "Not exactly."

"So why not take a lover?" she presses. "Or a honeybee?"

"No one ever wanted me, I suppose," I say, trying to make it sound like a joke. But it's the truth, and it stings.

Many girls, forbidden to risk their virtue and marriage prospects by passing their time with boys, satisfy their curiosity and their bodies' needs with each other. It's tolerated, if not openly endorsed, in the Lower City. It's less common in Midtown and the Upper City, or maybe the girls just do a better job of hiding their activities. I wouldn't know. I don't have any friends among the unmarried ladies of the King's Terrace with whom to even discuss such things, much less engage in them myself.

"What a shame," the Companion murmurs. "It's surely somebody's loss."

I blush. Again.

"So," she says, brisk now. "That's my secret. What's yours?"

I consider this. I really only have one, and it's nearly the same as hers.

"My Gift," I say. "My Gift is a secret, too. I'm not a Dreamwhisper, though."

She gives me an appraising look. "Spiritwalker?"

"No."

"Hmm." She studies me, tapping her chin with her finger. "Lightfinger? A well-born lady picking pockets would be rather unseemly. Or is it something embarrassing? I once knew a girl who could belch longer and louder than a man twice her size. Not very useful, but certainly impressive."

I laugh bitterly. "I wish that were the problem."

"So what is it?" the Companion asks. "What's your Gift?"

She leans forward, full of warm curiosity and a spark of playful complicity, like we're accomplices in some secret adventure. Between Hadrian's romantic aspirations and Pia's catastrophic news, I was already desperate to escape my reality. Now this beautiful stranger with flower petals falling softly into her hair is here, inviting me into what feels like a dream. It feels good. Safe. Feelings, as I know too well, can be deceptive—but right now, I don't care. Maybe it's wrong, maybe I'll regret it later... but I trust her.

"As far as everyone but my brothers are concerned, my Gift is for reading and learning." I wrinkle my nose. "As if that's the only way a girl could be a scholar. As if a girl can't simply be intelligent and motivated."

Her brows shoot up. "A scholar! My, my, you are full of surprises. But go on. What's your real Gift?"

I look down, a lump rising in my throat. I've never told anyone what my Gift is, not even Costi, though he knows perfectly well. He was the one who realized what it was in the first place. But he's never spoken of it, and neither have I. I've never wanted to, either. But now I'm tempted, not only by my new friend's honesty but by the promise, however ridiculous, of a wish. I do have a wish, and it's a big one. Will my one secret, my deepest shame, be enough to win me a school for Jessa? I take a breath, then speak.

"I foretell death. But not all the time, and not soon enough to do anything to stop it. It's my curse." Before I can stop myself, the words burst out of me. "It's—my punishment."

"Your punishment!" The Companion draws back and looks at me in astonishment. "What can you have done to deserve a punishment such as that?"

I don't answer, and she smiles tentatively, perhaps trying to lighten the mood. "Did you read too many books? Set your parents' library on fire?"

"No," I say hollowly. "I killed my mother."

She opens her mouth, then closed it. Shame floods me. The playful, dreamlike mood of our meeting has disappeared, replaced by a thick, awkward silence. My new—and soon to be erstwhile—friend glances away, then back, then at her lap. The lump in my throat thickens. Why did I say that? I'd already told my secret, I didn't need to say anything more. And now I've ruined everything.

But then the Companion takes my hands and looks me in the eyes.

"You can tell me, if you want," she says.

I look at her, taken aback. "You're not—it doesn't make you uncomfortable?"

She gives a small laugh. "It makes me plenty uncomfortable. But I can see that it's hurting you, and I'd rather be uncomfortable than stand by while you're in pain."

I blink rapidly. "I think that's the kindest thing anyone has ever said to me."

"You need to raise your standards." She squeezes my hands. "So. Will you tell me?"

"I'll tell you," I say softly, but it takes me several long moments to begin. "My mother died because of me. I've known it most of my life—but not all of it. When I was little, I didn't really understand. I knew she was gone, of course, everyone told me so. But I never really thought much of it. I didn't know what I was missing. Lots of people don't have mothers. I thought it was normal. And I thought... well, everyone said she was gone, but I didn't know what it meant, not truly. I thought she just wasn't *there*. I thought I might meet her one day.

"But then my father died, and my brother explained what dying meant. He said I'd never see father again. Never. But even then, I didn't really understand. 'Never' didn't mean anything at first. But then a moon went by, then two, and I missed Abba so much. Then I started to understand. And I started asking questions and wanting to know more about death. I visited the butchers and found rats killed by the palace cats or drowned in water troughs. I learned that death doesn't just happen—it's caused by something. It had never occurred to me to wonder how my mother died, because I didn't know enough to ask. But once I did... Nurse tried to tell me it wasn't my fault, but it was. Of course it's not the same as, I don't know, stabbing someone with a knife, but nothing can change the fact that it was I who killed her. I got stuck, and neither Gifted Healers nor Lighthealers could get me out. They had to cut me out of her belly, and she died."

The Companion bites her lip, rubbing her thumbs over my knuckles. "Being the cause of something and being at fault for it aren't the same thing."

"Aren't they?" I give a hollow laugh. "The result is the same. My mother is dead, and my Gift is tainted with death."

"It isn't the same thing at all," she says firmly. "And I'm sure you know that."

I don't say anything to that. She's right. I *do* know it—most of the time, with most of my heart. But even on my good days, I can't escape the knowledge that my mother died so that I could live. Even if it wasn't my fault, even if I don't have to atone, I *do* have to make her sacrifice worthwhile. The trouble is that the rest of the world seems to think the best way to do that is to just look pretty and be quiet.

"Well, our wishes are duly paid for," I say, trying to regain the sense of light-hearted mystery that we shared before I ruined everything. "Do we share those, too?"

She looks at me steadily, her brows drawn and her lips pursed. But she doesn't say any more on the subject of my mother, and after a moment, her face clears.

"Yes, we do." She waves a cautioning finger at me. "You must take care with the wording. And, above all, you must be sure of what it is you really need. You might think that you want to marry the handsome fellow you met at the market, but he could turn out to be cruel or stupid. Better to wish for a calm heart or good judgment, something like that."

"Is that what you're wishing for?"

She shakes her head. "I'm still thinking. Anyway, I went first last time. You tell me what you're wishing for."

"I'm not sure," I say. "There's something that I want—desperately—but it's like you said. So many things could go wrong."

"What is it?"

"A school," I say softly. "There's a girl I know. She's clever and capable and just wants to learn—everything. I've been teaching her what I know, but it's not enough. Her mother wants to send her to the Temple on a contingent contract. But you would know better than anyone that only the truly devout are initiated. Jessa is many things, but devout is not one of them. She has almost no interest in the Divine Arts. She'll never make it."

The Companion bites her lip. "The Temple has always made a point of not turning anyone away, but I've sometimes wondered whether it's more cruel than kind to let someone sign that contract, knowing that they're likely going to fail. I'm sorry."

"It's certainly not your fault," I say with shrug. "If it's anyone's, it's mine. I've been dreaming about opening a girls' school for years, but I never acted on it. If I had... "

"So act on it now," the Companion says, her eyes lighting up. "I think it's a wonderful idea."

I shake my head. "It's too late. Jessa's mother has made up her mind. And, anyway, there's no money for a venture like that. I asked my brother last year."

"And is your brother the only person in this city with money?" she asks, raising her eyebrows.

No, he isn't. The King's Council is full of rich, influential men. But the thought of asking the Council to fund a girls' school... they'd laugh themselves silly. Or, worse, explain in kindly, patronizing detail all the reasons girls are unfit to pursue the intellectual arts. The very thought makes me sick.

"It sounds like what you need is a sharp eye for opportunity," the Companion says. She gives me a shrewd look. "And maybe a little courage."

"That would be two wishes," I point out.

"Well, you gave two secrets," she says. "I'd say you earned an extra wish."

"Alright, then," I say with a nod. "Courage and a sharp eye. What's yours?"

"Clarity, I think," she says, her expression clouding. "I've been offered a position... an opportunity. And I'm not sure I want it. It's a great honor and a chance to do good, but it's also an enormous responsibility."

I wait expectantly, but she doesn't say anything more. She gazes into the water, her face pensive. I watch her, quite as mesmerized by her as she appears to be by the water. She's unlike anyone I've ever met—engaging and warm, utterly without pretension. And honest. She didn't deflect my awkward and unintended vulnerability or offer false reassurance, as a stranger is entitled, even expected, to do. Instead, she accepted the discomfort and offered genuine compassion in return. The thought so warms me that it almost overcomes my regret over the incident.

"Yes," the Companion says, shaking herself. "I wish for clarity."

"I wish for courage and a sharp eye," I say. I look at her. "Is that it?"

"Not quite," she says. "Now we drink from the fountain."

She dips her hand into the water and brings it to her lips. I copy her, though with far less grace. Water splashes across my skirts and hers, making her laugh, but there's no malice in the sound.

"Sorry," I mumble, wiping my chin with a rueful smile. "So... it's done?"

"It's done," she confirms.

I bite my lip. I don't want our meeting to end. I want—what? To see her again. Yes, definitely that. But how? Where? When? Growing up half-wild with Luca and Rowan as I did, there was never any need for me to seek out companionship. How do other girls go about making friends? But then, this Companion isn't like any girl I've ever met. Perhaps she wouldn't mind... perhaps I could simply... ask her. But she'll need to know who I am, first.

"I should tell you," I say. "I'm—"

"Not supposed to be hanging about in secluded corners with strangers." I squeak in surprise as Rowan appears beside me. "Not that I suspect you in particular of anything nefarious, Sister, but still." To me, he says, "You do remember that it's my job to protect you, don't you? That I left you alone against my better judgment as a special favor to you, and that if anything had happened, your brothers would have me executed?"

"Luca couldn't execute you," I point out. "He's a bastard."

"Which will be a great comfort when Miocostin commands his bastard brother to behead me," Rowan says sourly. "I'm sure it will be much less agonizing if the order comes from the king rather than my best friend."

The Companion is staring at me. "Luca... Miocostin. You're—you're Princess Arismendi!"

I hang my head. "I was about to tell you. I'm Ari. This is my guard, Rowan. Rowan, this is—my, um, friend."

"The sun shines on you, Sister." Rowan gives her a brief bow, but he's still focused on me. "You might like to forget that you're a princess, but I'm not allowed to."

He takes my arm and urges me away from the fountain.

"Stop that," I mutter, straining to turn back to the Companion. "I'm sorry, I—"

"Don't worry," she says, the smile returning to her lips. "I have a feeling we'll meet again, Princess."

"Goodbye," I say, taking one last look at her lovely face.

Just before Rowan pulls me around the corner, she calls, "Wait! Arismendi... Ari."

I twist, breaking free of Rowan's grip, and turn to her. "Yes?"

"I hope your wish comes true." She reaches for my hand, and I give it to her. "When it does, come find me."

I bite my lip, suddenly anxious. "How, when I don't know your name?"

Her smile is brilliant as she presses our palms together, fingers splayed. "My name is Sadra."

"Sadra." I let my fingers slide through hers and squeeze gently. "I'll find you."

"Promise?"

"Promise."

As Rowan hustles me away, it occurs to me that I've made two promises today, and I have no idea how I'm going to keep either of them.

Chapter Five

Rowan doesn't speak to me for nearly the entire walk back to the Terrace. I don't mind. I'm still buzzing from my odd encounter and the pleasure of making a friend. After a while, however, he looks over at me and snorts.

"You," Rowan says, "are a fool."

I blink at him, confused. "What?"

"You've never shown the slightest interest in anyone, and you decide *now* is a good time to go all cow-eyed?" he demands. "And over a Companion, of all people! I hate to break it to you, but they don't hire themselves out to women."

"Don't be ridiculous," I laugh. "I don't want to hire her. I just...I think she could be my friend."

"I'm not enough? You wound me."

I look at him sharply, afraid for a moment that his feelings really are hurt, but all I see is lingering annoyance. I grin at him, relieved.

"Yes, I can see the blood seeping around the edges of that stick up your—"

"Don't be vulgar," Rowan chides. "It's unbecoming."

"If I'm vulgar, you have only yourself to blame," I tell him. "Maybe if I'd had a Companion for a friend instead of only you and Luca, I would be more ladylike."

"And maybe Hadrian wouldn't have waited so long to sink his claws into you," Rowan says. "Lest you forget what you have to look forward to."

"How kind of you to remind me," I say sourly.

"Watch out," Rowan says, pulling me to the side as one of the councilors—Orean, I think—passes by on a litter born by thralls.

It's almost too bad Rowan pulled me out of the way. Hadrian's proposal would have to wait if I were trampled by thralls. On the other hand, they've provided Rowan with a new target for his ire. He glares after them, muttering something about "lack of courtesy" and "public menace" as he checks to make sure he didn't hurt my arm. His concern takes the edge off my irritation with him. It must have given him a fright to find me alone with any stranger, no matter how respectable.

"I'm sorry I scared you," I say. "I promise I would have stabbed her first at the slightest hint of danger."

"Thank you," he says dryly. "I am completely reassured. Come on, then. You have a proposal to suffer though. Tarry any longer, and you'll miss it."

"What a tragedy that would be," I mutter.

Rowan grows more cheerful as we approach the Terrace Gate, teasing me and anticipating Hadrian's impending rejection with unseemly glee. I just smile and keep walking. Normally, this is my favorite part of the walk home. I love the Terrace Gate—which isn't a gate at all, really, just a wide rocky outcropping that hides the opening into the ravine known as the King's Terrace. The stone is covered with intricate, ancient carvings. Some depict figures from the Garden's history and legends, but most are simply beautiful: roses, of course, and other flowering vines; swirling designs reminiscent of water and fire; butterflies, dragonflies, doves, kites...all lovely, but made somewhat less so by the knowledge of what awaits me inside.

I sigh at the cool breeze that greets us as we pass through the Gate, bringing with it the heady perfume of thousands of flowers and the fresh scent of river water. All around us, councilors' villas seem to grow out of the sides of the ravine, spilling down the narrow valley like a wave of exquisite architecture and horticulture.

The palace lies at the far end of the ravine, its two wings bisected by the waterfall known as the Mare's Tail. Bridges cross the gap in a series of elegant arches, shimmering with iridescent light—and Light. Generations of Lightcrafters have left their mark, both for protection and design. The result is a marvel of beauty and power shining like a beacon in the mountains' shadow.

But it's still home, no matter how grand, and the tension in my shoulders eases just a bit as we enter the courtyard. Soren, the palace steward, greets me with a deep bow. I smile in greeting and start to move past him, but he stops me with a gentle hand.

"I've been instructed to inform you that Lord Hadrian Prosper is waiting for you," he says.

Something in his voice makes me suspect that those instructions came from Hadrian himself. And not very politely, if I'm not mistaken.

"Where?" I ask with a sigh.

"Balia's Bridge," Soren replies.

I scowl. Balia's Bridge lies at the base of the falls, spanning a wide pool nearly hidden by a perpetual mist. No one uses it because it's impossible to cross without getting caught in the spray. No one but me, that is. It's my favorite spot in the Terrace, as Hadrian no doubt knows. For a moment, I imagine what it would feel like to receive a proposal of marriage there, in my favorite place. If the proposal came from someone other than Hadrian, it would be unbearably romantic. But it *is* Hadrian, and it feels as though he's systematically ruining every lovely thing in my world with his greed. That's what this is all about, after all. He doesn't want *me*. He wants a princess. A prize.

"Well," I say grimly. "I suppose I'd better get this over with."

"Let's go, then," Rowan says, squaring his shoulders.

"*I* will go," I say. "This is going to be unpleasant enough without an audience."

Rowan frowns. "I don't like leaving you alone with him."

"He won't hurt me," I say. "He wouldn't dare."

"Still, take this just in case." He tucks a slender knife into my sash. "If he lays a finger on you, cut it off."

"With pleasure."

I leave Rowan in the courtyard and go to meet my fate.

Hadrian is waiting for me at the Mare's Tail, as promised, leaning elegantly against the bridge's rail. A faint glimmer around his body signals a charm of some kind, likely something to keep the mist from mussing his clothes or hair. He straightens at my approach, beaming so widely I can see each and every one of his gleaming white teeth. I smile weakly in response.

"Hello, Hadrian."

"My dear Arismendi." He takes my hands and kisses them, letting his lips trail over my knuckles. I shudder. "You can have no doubt what I wish to say—to ask you."

"None at all," I say glumly.

"I have always admired you for your loyalty to your family and your gentle nature," he goes on, oblivious. "But this last year, you have simply...blossomed. The beauty of your form caught my eye as your inner beauty caught my heart. I...forgive me, I've never..." He looks down with a deep sigh, and even I can tell it's pure affectation. "I've never felt this way before. I...I love you, Arismendi."

Oh, *vomit*.

"Hadrian, please stop," I say. "I must—"

"I cannot!" he cries passionately. "You must allow me to express the depths of my love. I cannot live without you, Arismendi. I must ask you—no, beg you—"

"Hadrian!"

"—to be my wife."

No. A simple word for a simple sentiment. In this moment, it's all that is called for—rather, all that should be called for. But that's not how things are done. Costi will expect better from a member of the royal family. And Hadrian... all the careful phrasing in the world likely won't soothe his pride, but I have to try.

"I am...honored," I begin, but I falter immediately. "I..."

I look away, playing for time, trying to think of something to say that won't offend him badly enough to affect my relationship with his father or his father's relationship with my brother. But I needn't have worried. Hadrian can always be counted upon to fill a silence with his own voice.

"I don't mean to boast, of course," he says, his voice exuding smugness. "But you must know that the Prosper line is the most illustrious in the Garden, after your own. If any man is worthy of the Rose Princess, it is I."

I have to fight to keep a grimace of distaste from my face. "Hadrian—"

"And there are more practical benefits to consider," he goes on, oblivious. "My father is the richest man in the Garden, more wealthy even than—forgive my impertinence—your brother, the king."

He's right. The Prosper family has supported the House of Light and Shadow from the beginning and has profited immensely from the relationship. Hadrian will one day inherit some of the largest, most prosperous auction houses in the kingdom. And that's to say nothing of the dividends he'll receive from the family's share in the thrall trade.

"I can give you anything—everything—you could ever desire," Hadrian says, sweeping his arm out to encompass this invisible 'everything.' "Name it, and it's yours."

My first impulse is to reject the offer, certain that I'll never be tempted to take anything from his clammy, grasping hands. But then it hits me that there *is* something, something I want badly enough to pause and think. As I told Sadra, and Pia before her, all that's standing in the way of my school is an exorbitant amount of money. And here is Hadrian, offering me just that. Accepting the offer means accepting *him,* of course, and the very thought makes my skin crawl. But what about Jessa?

"Arismendi?" Hadrian prompts, a flicker of annoyance crossing his face.

"Forgive me," I say slowly, my mind racing. "I'm just—a bit overwhelmed."

His face softens. "Of course. I would expect nothing less from a young woman of your gentle sensibilities."

"I need time," I tell him. "To think, to consult my brother."

"My father has spoken with the king already," Hadrian is swift to assure me. "We have his blessing."

"Still," I insist, ignoring the bald-faced lie. "This is not a decision to be made lightly. I will not marry without hearing my brother's counsel and receiving his blessing myself."

"Have mercy, Arismendi," Hadrian says. He still holds my hands. He kisses them again, his puffy lips sucking at my skin like a pair of leeches. "I burn for you."

He releases my hands, and I barely resist the urge to scrub them against my skirts.

"I'll try not to take too long," I say. "But you must be patient."

"But, my love—"

"I won't be rushed or pushed into this, Hadrian," I say firmly. "If you really want me, you'll wait."

He heaves a sigh, his whole face pinching together. *What* in the name of all that is beautiful is that expression supposed to be? He might possibly be trying to look mournful and woebegone, but it looks more like constipation to me.

"Very well, then," he says with a slight bow.

"Thank you." I try my best to sound polite, but I'm already backing away. "I'll give you an answer as soon as I can."

As soon as Hadrian is out of sight, I hike up my skirts and dash into the palace. In the corridors, Lightglobes bob in the corners like tiny swarms of fireflies and skim across the ceiling like stars. On a normal day, the gentle glow soothes me. But today, I can't be soothed. My thoughts race and tumble together, each contradicting the next.

If I marry Hadrian, I can use the money from my bride price to fund the school. Well, I suppose *I* won't, personally. I'm the bride—of course the money won't come to me directly. It will go to my brother, my guardian. But Costi will use the money for the school if I ask him to, I'm sure of it. And what then? The Council will object that the money should go to pay the crown's debts from the reconstruction, and they wouldn't be wrong. So I'll make the school a condition of the marriage. The wedding will be held only after the school opens, with funds set aside for its maintenance.

But—no, this is mad. *I* am mad. Marry Horrible Hadrian with his caterpillar lips, his soft hands, his panting greed? The prospect makes me physically ill. And afraid. When I marry, my husband will become my legal guardian. He'll have complete control over my life, from the clothes I wear to the food I eat. I'll have some protection as the king's sister, but even Costi's influence would be limited if I left the City. Could he forbid Hadrian from taking me away? Probably, but not without cause.

Taking a husband would be dangerous enough, even if he were a man I liked and trusted. And Hadrian is a far cry from either of those. He's vain and arrogant and fake, and he would take far too much pleasure in having control over another person. As children, he lorded his station over boys of lesser families and slapped servants and thralls for minor missteps just because he could. He tried to do the same to Rowan, until Luca taught him better.

I hesitate at the door to the scroll room, where I'm sure to find Norrin at this time of day. I stand there for several long moments, arguing with myself. There's no reason not to just go in there and ask him. This is in fact a small stroke of genius on my part, a gamble I can't lose. If Norrin says no, I have a perfectly good reason to reject Hadrian's suit, and in such a way that he can't blame me. If Norrin says yes…but do I really want him to say yes?

No, part of me screams. But I force myself to think of Jessa, pushed into a life she doesn't want because she has no other choices as a low-born girl. I have a choice, through no merit of my own. I have a choice simply because I'm a princess, because a wealthy man desires me… and maybe because I made the right wish. A sharp eye for opportunity. Well, here's my opportunity, and all I need now is the courage to act on it. Courage—my second wish. Did I truly earn it, as Sadra said?

There's only one way to find out.

Chapter Six

Five minutes and many deep breaths later, I push open the door to the palace scroll room and march inside. As I hoped, Norrin is sitting at a table, a Lightglobe hovering over his shoulder to illuminate the scroll before him. Ordinarily, I would wonder what's on the scroll before anything else. But not today.

I take one more steadying breath and say quietly, "Your son has asked me to marry him."

The door to the scroll room slams shut behind me, as if to punctuate my declaration. Norrin looks up, a quizzical expression on his wrinkled face.

"What, just now?"

I can't help making a face. "Yes, I've just left him."

Norrin smiles. "And what did you say? Have you come to tell me that I will have another daughter?"

"It depends," I say slowly, sinking into the chair opposite him.

"It depends?" Norrin's smile fades into a puzzled frown. "On what?"

I fiddle with the tassel on my skirt. "Well... on you."

Norrin squints at me and sighs. "My dear Arismendi—"

"Please don't call me that," I say, shuddering. "You sound like Hadrian."

"Well, I am his father," Norrin says. "And you *are* very dear to me."

"You know I prefer to be called Ari."

"You prefer to forego the honor due your person and your rank," Norrin replies. "But someone must remind you of your worth, and if that person must be me, so be it. Now, *Arismendi*, tell me what on earth this is about, and start from the beginning."

I sigh. "I don't even know where the beginning is."

"Take a moment to organize your thoughts," Norrin says, rising to his feet with the scroll he was studying. "Think about what you want from me, and then ask yourself what I need to know in order to understand why you want it—and why I should give it to you." He taps my head with the scroll. "I will return this to its home, and, when I return, you will be ready to make your case. Whatever it is."

I take another breath, and this one steadies me. This is what Norrin taught me to do, what I want to teach Jessa to do: think critically, use logic to attain my goals and improve my circumstances.

"While you're there," I say, looking up at Norrin. "Can you bring back the scrolls my brother used to rebuild the lower city after the Catastrophe? The architectural texts."

Norrin shoots me a keen glance but doesn't question me. He merely nods and disappears among the stacks, leaving me to consider what I want, what Norrin needs to know in order to understand why I want it, and why he should give it to me.

When he returns, I motion for him to spread out the scrolls. I rummage for a moment until I find the bundle I want: A detailed collection of diagrams and instructions on construction methods from an era rife with earthquakes.

I tap the scrolls and place them in front of him. "You remember these, don't you?"

"Certainly," Norrin replies with a nod. "They saved the treasury, these scrolls. After the earthquake, the House of Light and Shadow wanted to charge a fortune to reinforce the new buildings of the lower city with Light. Your brother's children and grandchildren—their children, even—would have been burdened with the debt. And then the king unearthed these scrolls and found a way to protect the new buildings without Light, using nothing more than practical, logical construction."

I nod. "Well, I think this is the beginning... because my brother didn't find these texts. I did."

Norrin's eyes widen for a moment, then he laughs. "That explains a great deal. I never did understand how he found them, when I could swear he was all but chained to the Council chambers. It was *you*... How splendid! If I recall, it was around that same time that he began calling you his little fox. Not just for the color of your hair, eh?"

At this, I can't resist rolling my eyes. "It's not even red. It's yellow."

"It's a little red." Norrin leans back and studies me, his arms crossed. "I suppose I shouldn't be surprised, considering your Gift."

I squirm. As I explained to Sadra, nearly everyone believes my Gift to be for reading and learning, and Norrin is no exception. I hate lying to him, but as a child, I was too frightened and ashamed of my Gift to reveal it. Now, after so many years of letting him believe the lie, I have even more to be ashamed of. I have long justified the deceit by telling myself that it isn't a *total* lie. In a sense, my Gift really is the root of my thirst for learning, for it has made me keenly aware of the consequences of ignorance.

On the night of the earthquake six years ago, I woke screaming in terror a full five minutes before the quake hit. I'd been having nightmares for days, gripped by some nameless horror I couldn't identify. I had taken to sleeping in my brothers' rooms, too frightened to sleep alone. It was Costi, therefore, who made the connection between my night terrors and the earthquake. It reminded him, he said, of the way I had wept as a little girl in the days preceding our father's death.

"My nurse was in the lower city that night," I say now, my heart squeezing at the memory. "She died in the quake, like so many others. I didn't understand why it was only the Lower City that collapsed. Costi said it was because the palace and villas are reinforced with Light. But only some of the upper city buildings are reinforced, did you know that?"

"I didn't at the time," Norrin replies gravely. "But I realized it soon after, yes."

"I thought it was odd," I go on. "Everyone was so shocked by the quake. It was the first quake in fifty years, and no one remembered the one before that. No one knew what to do about it. It scared me, and it made me think—what else might happen that we didn't know to prepare for? So I started reading about the earthquakes of the past, and I found something curious. In the last quake, only a few buildings collapsed. But they were—"

"The newer buildings," Norrin finishes for me. "I remember. I was only a boy at the time, but I remember. The builders were fined for negligence. It was quite the scandal."

"Negligence," I repeat. "Exactly. The report I read criticized the builders for abandoning the 'old ways.' But he didn't say what those old ways were, so I kept reading and found accounts from an era marked by frequent, violent quakes. But the reports of collapsed buildings were far, far fewer. I found the scrolls explaining their construction methods soon after. I showed them to Costi, and he took them to the Council."

"And presented your work as his own," Norrin says with a tiny frown.

"Of course," I say grimly. "Not one of them—except you, maybe—would have listened to a twelve year old girl. But do you see? In order to protect ourselves, in order to grow and thrive, we have to *know* things. You taught me to read and study and look for answers, and it saved the Lower City. Think of what other girls could do if they were given the same chance."

"Arismendi, what are you saying?" Norrin peers at me. "You've laid your foundation, now tell me plainly."

I brace myself. "I want to open a school for girls."

Before he can say anything, I rush on, "There are so many girls in the City who don't even know how to read. Their only choices for education are expensive private tutors, which most can't afford, and the Temple, which only the richest can afford without contingent contracts. They shouldn't have to sign their lives away to get an education. Girls don't even have the option of apprenticeship. Think of what they could accomplish if they had the opportunity to learn and grow. What have you been telling me for the last ten years?

Cultivation of the mind is as important to a civilized society as the cultivation of crops. How can we call ourselves civilized when half the population is barred from such cultivation?"

"An interesting notion," Norrin says, and my jaw clenches.

It's *interesting*, is it, the idea that women do in fact count as people? Not, say, *painfully obvious*? But now is not the time to pick apart Norrin's word choice. I hold my tongue and watch Norrin, waiting for him to respond. He takes his time, leaning back with a thoughtful, distant look in his eyes. Finally, his gaze returns to me.

"What does this have to do with Hadrian's proposal?" he asks.

I close my eyes and spit out the words before I can lose my nerve. "You know I don't want to marry your son, and he only wants to marry me because I'm a princess. But I'll do it, if you give me my school. I know it will be horribly expensive, but there it is. That's my price, and I think it's a fair one. I *am* a princess, after all. With our families bound by marriage, you would be second only to the king in power and influence."

I can't bring myself to speak the most compelling advantage out loud, but Norrin must be aware of it already: Miocostin is thirty years old, still unwed, and, as far as anyone can tell, intends to stay that way. If he dies without an heir, it could very well be my child who ascends the throne. Norrin's grandchild, if I were to marry Hadrian.

"There might be other advantages as well," Norrin muses. He drums his fingers against the table, studying me. "A high-profile, unorthodox, charitable endeavor... Yes, there are possibilities there. And there is a precedent. It was Queen Amari who mobilized the House of Light and Shadow to build the city's shelters for women and children. She oversaw the project from its inception."

"So... you'll help me?" I ask, hardly daring to hope.

"Yes." Norrin slaps the table and nods to himself. "Yes, I shall. Let us go to the king and bring him our good news." He takes my hands in his and squeezes them, beaming. "Welcome to the family, Princess."

I take a deep, shaky breath. "It's not done yet, Norrin. We still need Costi's approval."

Norrin beams. "How could he not approve? This is splendid, my dear. Just splendid!"

"Splendid," I echo wanly. "Indeed."

Chapter Seven

My mother's portrait gazes down on us as Norrin and I enter Costi's study. Her smile is gentle, beatific. Her hair is red-gold, like mine, but hers seems to blaze in a way mine never has. My father's portrait hangs beside hers, stern and strong, with sharp, clear green eyes that seem to see right inside you. Queen Amari and King Costaran, who ruled the Garden together in love and harmony—until I came along.

My brother sits below, a perfect blend of the two, both in personality and appearance. He has our father's dark hair and broad shoulders, and our mother's kind brown eyes. He's as conscientious as our father and compassionate, like our mother. Unusually—unwisely—compassionate, or so some of his councilors say.

He's a good man, my brother. I've always known it. He would have been well within his rights to despise me for causing the death of our mother, but instead he cherished me. My first memories are of riding on his shoulders with my fingers buried in his dark curls and screaming with laughter as he tossed me into the air. Even when our father died and he became king, he always had time for Luca and me. He raised us as well as our father would have done—better, even, and we love him for it.

But that care has taken its toll, and Costi's black hair is shot with gray. His eyes are tired and serious, and he laughs less and less with each passing year. I can only hope that my marriage will have the added benefit of easing his burdens. Norrin isn't the only one who seeks closer ties to the crown, and Costi has already denied countless requests for my hand even in the face of growing resentment from the council.

"Little fox," he greets me when Soren, the steward, announces our arrival. "Councilor Norrin. What a pleasant surprise. Have you come to save me from these trade agreements?"

"In a sense, my king," Norrin says with a smile. "We have some happy news to share with you."

"Oh?" Costi shoots me an alarmed glance and gestures to the chairs before his desk. "Sit, please."

I take my seat and clutch at my skirts with sweaty hands. Stars, I'm going to be sick. Can I really do this? My stomach bucks, rolls, then settles. I take a breath. Yes, I can. I must. For Jessa.

"Give me your news, then," Costi says. "Though I somehow doubt it's truly happy. My sister looks most unwell. Little fox, are you going to vomit on my desk?"

"No," I squeak. I clear my throat and try again. "No. I'm fine. I've agreed to marry Councilor Norrin's son."

Costi gapes at me for a moment, then rearranges his face into an expression of calm curiosity. "Why?"

As quickly as I could, I explain Jessa and Pia's dilemma and my plan to open a school.

"Pia," Costi says. "That's the woman you met during the Lower City's construction. Your nurse's daughter, isn't she?"

"Yes," I say. "But it's not just because Jessa is Maja's granddaughter. All girls deserve a chance to learn."

"I know, little fox," Costi says. "And I agree with you, as I agreed with you when you asked me for funds last year. But even without the House of Light and Shadow's fees, the cost of rebuilding was substantial. We have many debts to repay."

"I know," I say quickly. "I know. That's why I've asked for Norrin's help. He's agreed to fund my school in exchange for the marriage alliance."

Costi's eyes shoot to Norrin. "Is that so?"

"It is, my king," Norrin says with a bow. "I will pledge twenty thousand gold pieces."

I nearly fall out of my chair. "Twenty *thousand*—"

Norrin smiles. "A royal sum for a royal bride."

"But—but that's twice what any other man would dream of paying," I gasp. "Are you sure? The other councilors will think you're mad."

Norrin shrugs. "What does it say about my wealth—and the success of my business ventures—that I can part with so much gold with ease? Fear not on my account, Princess. In any case, we will need every flake of that gold and then some. Twenty thousand should keep your school going for, oh, ten years, I should think. After that, you will need to apply to the crown for funds once more. It is my hope that by then you will be able to demonstrate the practical value of your school and its impact on the City's citizenry."

"And it's *my* fervent hope that our debts will be paid by then," Costi adds with a sigh. Then he frowns at Norrin. "You have so much ready to hand?"

"Not all at once, no," Norrin admits. "But we don't need the entire sum all at once, do we?"

"No," Costi says. "But still, it's easy to offer money that doesn't yet exist."

Norrin draws back in surprise. "Do you doubt my word?"

"Of course not," Costi says, raising a placating hand. "But things happen. Mercantile bargains may be broken or dissolved, but marriage vows may not."

"What do you suggest, then?" Norrin asks stiffly. "I cannot divine the future, as you say. Nor can I deliver twenty thousand marks as a lump sum."

"I ask only that the wedding take place after the school opens," Costi says, the same safeguard that I'd considered. "With enough gold to run for at least a year. And a contract outlining future payments, of course, with appropriate collateral in the event of default."

"That is fair," Norrin agrees, though he doesn't look happy about it. "I must admit, however, that your lack of faith pains me."

"I have utmost faith in *you*, Norrin," Costi says softly. "But you are not a young man, and ten years is a long time."

A look of mingled pain and sadness crosses Norrin's face. But he doesn't protest. He may hold certain delusions about his son's character, but even he can't deny the likelihood that Hadrian will abandon the project as soon as he thinks he can get away with it. I bless my brother for his ability to state the uncomfortable and somewhat offensive obvious without consequence. Being a man—and a king—holds certain advantages.

"Very well," Norrin says. "Arismendi shall have her school and a contract in hand before she comes to the wedding altar."

I reach out and clasp Norrin's hand. "Thank you, Norrin. You don't know what this means to me."

"I have some small idea," he says, and squeezes my fingers. "And it gives me great pleasure to play a part in this venture."

Costi smiles and leans back, satisfied. "I, too, am pleased that you've found a way to make this happen, little fox. But are you sure?"

"I am if you are," I say, peering at him worriedly. "Your councilors won't like the idea."

"Let me worry about that, foxling." Costi rises and kisses my forehead. "They'll make some noise, but they'll get over it. Marriage, on the other hand, doesn't just blow over. You must be certain."

I draw a shaky breath. "It was going to happen sometime. At least this way I'll get something out of it."

"Come now, Arismendi," Norrin says with a sardonic smile. "It's not so bad. Hadrian is handsome and courteous, and marginally less stupid than most rich young men."

No, Hadrian isn't stupid. I could almost forgive him his faults if he were.

"He is young," Norrin says, his voice filled with compassion—and hope. "He still has time to grow up... especially with a woman like you at his side."

I nod mutely, unable to speak. Costi leans against the desk, his arms crossed as he and Norrin go on to discuss the arrangements to be made and how they will present their agreement to the Council. Councilor Orean, especially, is sure to make a fuss as he's apparently on the warpath already about some proposed tax. I retreat into silence, pummeled by doubt.

Hadrian—my price. My prize. I've won… but it doesn't much feel like victory. Have I truly done right? I've kept my promise to Jessa, but at what cost to my brother, and myself? I'm not so worried about Norrin. He'll benefit enormously from a marriage alliance with the crown, and he can be trusted to weigh that benefit against the blow to his coffers and his reputation.

But my brother loves me. He would do anything for me. Has he really thought this through? I can't ask him. I can't question the king's judgment in front of a councilor, even one as trustworthy as Norrin. And even if Costi is acting rashly, he'll never admit that he's making a mistake in making me happy. But I have another brother, one who won't hesitate to tell me if I'm being silly or selfish.

"We can announce the betrothal to the public at Balia's Banquet," Norrin is saying. "The people will love it."

"What?" I blink rapidly, trying to force my attention back to the present conversation. "Balia's—"

Costi, too, is frowning. "Isn't that a bit soon? That gives us little more than a moon's cycle to prepare."

"Many hands make light work," Norrin says cheerfully. "And many gold coins buy many working hands."

"The Banquet would be… thematically appropriate," Costi says, considering.

I stand abruptly. "Will you excuse me?"

"Of course, little fox," Costi say. As I turn to go, he catches my hand. "Preparations will move quickly. If you change your mind, you must tell me at once."

I nod, my throat tight and dry. "I will. Thank you, Costi."

I smile and bow my head. I exit gracefully, like a lady, with careful steps and squared shoulders. But the moment the door clicks shut behind me, I run.

Luca is in the practice yard drilling the palace guards. It's a small space, barely large enough to be called a yard, but it's just right for a palace guard barely large enough to deserve the name. There isn't much to guard against on the Terrace, after all. Even so, Costi insists on a high level of expertise. Luca is in charge of training new recruits, and he evaluates and drills the veterans as well.

The veterans hate that a stripling of nineteen is authorized to judge their skill. They say he's nothing but a jumped-up bastard—and a Beastspeaker, no less, barely more than a beast himself. In the beginning, they also grumbled that his position was due to his relationship with the king rather than any merit of his own, but those grumbles at least faded after Luca fought every single one of them and won.

Still, I know Luca feels the weight of their resentment as well as the pressure of his position, so I hide in the shadow of a dogwood and watch from behind its trunk. It wouldn't do to disturb his concentration. One mistake could prove disastrous to the tenuous authority he's won. But I'm anxious to speak with him, and it seems like an age until Luca finally dismisses the guards. I emerge from behind the dogwood and he smiles, his look of stern concentration melting away.

"Hello, foxling," he says, swiping his sleeve across his face. "Everything alright? You look like you're about to vomit on my shoes."

"I'm not going to vomit," I sigh. "Not on a desk or your shoes or anywhere else."

Luca blinks. "I appreciate that. Though I don't have a desk handy, in any case."

I cross my arms with a scowl. After a moment I ask, "Where's Kirit?"

"Um." Luca looks around, squinting. "Ah. There."

I follow his pointing finger and find the fox basking in the sun with his belly up and his tongue lolling out.

"Kirit," I call. "I need you."

The fox flops upright like a flailing fish and runs to join us, leaping into my arms with a yap of greeting. I catch him with practiced ease. Luca's forehead crinkles with worry as he studies me, and I cuddle Kirit closer.

"Like that, is it?"

I nod mutely and bury my nose in Kirit's soft fur.

"Hello, little brother," I murmur. "Have you been good?"

"He stole Councilor Orean's belt-purse," Luca says, uncorking a water flask.

I pull my nose out of Kirit's ruff and smile down at him. "Well done. Did you give it back?"

"He hid it," Luca says. "And he won't tell me where. He says he's saving it."

"Saving up for a big purchase, are you?" I ask Kirit, and give another wobbly smile. "You can get me a wedding gift."

Luca chokes, lowering the water flask. "A *what*?"

Tears fill my eyes. My throat squeezes painfully, making me gasp.

"I think I did something bad," I whisper.

"You didn't." Luca stares at me in horror. "Ari, tell me you *didn't*."

I close my eyes. "I did. I'm marrying Hadrian."

"*Why*?"

The story spills out of me, words tumbling out in a barely coherent rush. Luckily, both my brothers are well practiced in deciphering what Luca long ago termed "sisterbabble."

"So, to summarize," he says. "You've sold yourself into a marriage contract, which gets you the money you need for your school but puts Costi in a questionable political position. And, of course, obliterates any possibility of happiness for you."

"Yes, exactly." I chew on my lip. "Have I gone mad? Hadrian will become my master in the eyes of the law. He could take me away."

"You don't need to worry about *that*," Luca says. "If Hadrian mistreats you, I'll carve out his liver—" Kirit yaps, and Luca nods seriously. "And Kirit will eat his liver. And Costi—well, if Hadrian is lucky, it'll be a swift beheading."

I giggle in spite of myself. Luca smiles and goes on, "You won't have to go anywhere if you don't want to. And if you do go, our spies will go with you to be sure you're safe. If you're not, or if you're unhappy, you can come home. Costi will make sure of it."

I let out a breath, my fear easing. It isn't anything I didn't already know, but it helps to hear it said out loud. But the relief is touched with sadness.

"I'll never get to be with someone I love, though." Before Luca can say anything, I wave the words away. "It's alright. Girls like me don't get to marry for love, we always knew that. What about the questionable politics, then? Am I a terrible person for putting Costi in such a position?"

Luca shrugs and begins stripping off his wrist guards. "I suppose that depends. Were you just making it all up? All your reasons for wanting to educate girls, I mean. Do you not really believe that it will benefit the City and the kingdom?"

"Of course I do," I say, then bite my lip. "But... I'm afraid my motivations aren't—I don't know. Pure, I suppose. I've dreamed of this school for so long, ever since the House Academy rejected me. What if this is more about me and my unfulfilled wishes than about helping people?"

"But your wishes weren't unfulfilled," Luca points out. "You got your education. In fact, you got a far better education than you would have gotten at the Academy."

He's right. I know he is. And yet I'm still plagued by doubt and a peculiar shame I can't quite put my finger on. But Luca does, and he drags it out with typical bluntness.

"I know you've always felt responsible for Queen Amari's death," he says. "And you think you have to atone for it. Is *that* the impurity of motive you're worried about?"

I don't speak for a moment. When I do, my voice is steady.

"I don't *feel* responsible," I say. "I *am* responsible."

"An infant isn't responsible for anything, Ari," he says, grasping my shoulders.

I barely hear him. "It's true. I do want to atone. I want my mother's sacrifice to mean something. But that just brings us back to selfishness, doesn't it? It's still about me and my feelings, not the girls. Not the Garden."

Luca sighs and gives my shoulders a little shake before releasing me. "Alright, let's say—purely for the sake of argument, because you're being ridiculous—that your motives *are* impure, and you're actually being selfish. So what?"

I let out an incredulous huff. "What do you mean, 'so what?'"

"Just that," he says. "What does it matter? If it's true that a school will help these girls and also help the kingdom, what does it matter if your reasons are selfish? It's still a good thing." His gaze turns gentle. "And... would it be so terrible if it also brings you some joy? Or fulfillment, or whatever it is you're looking for? You're allowed to want things for your own sake. Your mother didn't give you *her* life, Ari. She gave you yours. She'd want you to live it for yourself, not just for your family or your people."

I stare at him, shocked into silence by the tenderness and sincerity in his voice. After a moment, Luca clears his throat and says briskly,

"Enough of this. Your brain is just spinning because you've made an enormous investment, and now you're responsible for it. But it's done. The only thing you can do now is make sure the investment pays off. Can you do that?"

I swallow and nod. "I can do that."

Luca raises an eyebrow. "That wasn't very convincing. Try again, little fox. Or are you going to give up and keep hiding in the scroll room for the rest of your life?"

"Ass." I stamp on his foot, making him double over with a curse. Kirit gives me a reproachful look and wiggles out of my arms. "I can do this. I *will* do this."

"Much better," Luca says through his teeth. "Go and get me a few new toes, while you're at it."

Chapter Eight

I don't sleep at all that night. Question after question spins through my mind—questions I'm certain Pia is going to ask me the minute I tell her the school is going to open. Her skeptical face hovers in my imagination, shooting each question with the force of an arrow.

When will the school open? Where will it open? Who will teach the girls, and what subjects? How many girls? And *which* girls? How am I going to recruit them? What will their schedule look like? Will they have the opportunity to visit their families, and will transport be provided? How will their progress be measured? What support can I provide them after they leave and try to establish themselves in business or find work? How *exactly* will the education I'm providing help them in the real world? Who will oversee the school and ensure the quality of education? How will disciplinary issues be resolved?

Around and around it goes, my thoughts churning like the pool at the base of the Mare's Tale. The worst part is that I *do* have answers to a lot of the questions. I'm just not sure they're good ones. Who am I, after all? I'm not an expert on pedagogy or philosophy or business. I'm not an expert on anything.

By midnight, I'm nearly crying with frustration and exhaustion, so over-whelmed I find myself longing for the more familiar torture of my nightmare. I toss and turn, then pace my chambers, then sit at my desk and fill my slate boards with scribbled notes. Wipe them clean. Start again. Pace. Trip over a fallen scroll and crack my head against the bed post. Get back in bed and cycle through everything again, but this time with a headache.

Dawn comes, and I drag myself from my bed with a strange mix of reluctance and relief. I'm exhausted both mentally and physically and want nothing more than to sleep, but sleep won't come until I have a plan. So I have to make one.

I pull a sheet of parchment from the chest beside my desk and sit down, running a hand through—or rather into—my tangled hair. Is Norrin awake yet?

Do I care?

Well, yes. But not enough to go back to bed and let Norrin remain in his. I grab a stick of charcoal and scribble a note, being careful not to let the letters smudge. Lightnibs are cleaner, but you have to know at least something of Lightcrafting to activate them. Maybe it's hypocritical of me to allow such a gaping hole in my own education, but I just don't like Lightcrafting. Most people I know use Light for silly, useless things. Illusions in place of cosmetics, moving things that could be moved by hand just to show off. It always seems to be far more about status than utility. And, of course, dealing with Light means dealing with thralls.

There's a guard posted outside my door, as usual. Not Rowan, though. He's likely training with Luca at this hour, or possibly honoring the Graces at the Terrace's small sanctuary. This guard must be new. I know all the guards, and I don't recognize his face.

"Excuse me, Guardsman… " I trail off.

"Sammon," the guard supplies.

"Guardsman Sammon." I hold out my note. "I need this delivered to Councilor Norrin."

"Certainly, Princess." Sammon reaches out and seizes the arm of a passing thrall. "Deliver this note to Councilor Norrin."

The thrall takes the note and starts to turn away, his—its—face pale and listless, like all thralls. Before it can leave, I pluck the note back.

"Mistakes happen," I say by way of explanation. "You know how thralls are. They need to be trained to do specific tasks. Maybe this one knows where to go, but maybe not."

It isn't as if the thrall can tell us, after all.

"It would be safer for you to deliver it, Sammon," I say. "I don't want it going astray."

Sammon frowns. "I'm not to leave my post, Princess."

I sigh. "Of course. Come on, then. I'll deliver it myself."

Outside, a fine mist shrouds the Terrace. Here and there shafts of sunlight pierce the mist to gild leaves and petals. I turn down the covered lane that will take me to Norrin's villa. Pale stone crunches and shifts underfoot, loud in the silence. I'm probably the only one awake right now aside from the guards and thralls. It's soothing... but also a little lonely. A wave of longing for the Lower City washes over me. Though I'm well aware of the struggles they face, Pia and Jessa's life sometimes fills me with yearning, even envy. Despite their troubles, they're happy together. They laugh more than they shout, they sing more than they cry. They know their neighbors, and their neighbors know them.

My neighbors know the Princess by name and sight—and by their own gossip. But they don't know *me*. I'm closer to the guards and cooks and other professionals on the Terrace. They're open about what they want from me, and their needs are simple, reasonable. A staffing crisis, a supply emergency, the occasional sick child in need of care. With the glaring exception of Norrin, my brother's councilors ignore me completely, and their wives and daughters long ago gave up trying to cultivate any sort of relationship with me. I just don't know how to talk to them. If I say the wrong thing, pay too much or too little attention to the wrong person, it could be disastrous. Safer to stay out of the game than play the part badly and make Costi's life more difficult than it has to be. Especially now.

As we approach Norrin's door, Sammon reaches past me to knock. I suppress a sigh. A princess can't even knock on a door herself. Or speak for herself.

"Princess Arismendi requires an audience with Councilor Norrin," Sammon says, puffing out his chest.

Norrin's steward, a man named Cressen, gives me a concerned look. "Certainly, Princess. If you would care to wait in the inner courtyard?"

"Thank you, Cressen."

Cressen leads me through the house to the inner courtyard, where a small table stands beside a gilded fountain. I take my seat, and Sammon takes up a post in the shadow of one of the courtyard's columns.

"Councilor Norrin will join you directly," Cressen says. "Shall I order some refreshment in the meantime, Princess?"

"No, thank you, Cressen."

Cressen bows and hurries away. I stare at the gilded fountain, which likely could fund my school for years all on its own. No one—*no one*—is as wealthy as Norrin Prosper. I'm lucky that the richest man in the Garden is an intellectual and humanitarian. And, I suppose, a father with a son of marriageable age, even if that son is a snob and a dandy. Ugh. What would I have done if Hadrian had never been born, as I've so often wished? Proposed to Norrin himself?

"No," I mutter. "Do *not* think about that."

"Good morning, Arismendi."

I squawk in surprise, nearly falling off my chair as Norrin takes his seat across from me. "Norrin! I'm sorry to trouble you so early. I just—I couldn't sleep, and I need your advice. About the school."

Norrin smiles. "You held out longer than I thought you would. I was expecting you last night."

"I wish I'd come," I sigh. "I didn't sleep at all."

"Tell me," he says, settling back with his arms crossed.

I release the torrent of questions and doubts like a windstorm, my hands flying and twisting in my hair until I'm finally out of words—and air. After a beat of silence, Norrin reaches out to pat my head, which now rests on my crossed arms.

"First, let me say that your questions are necessary ones, and I am pleased and proud that you have thought of so many," he says. "But second, let me remind you that they don't all have to be answered today. I believe the first decision to be made is the scope of this project. For your inaugural class, I would suggest eight to ten students... "

I lift my head, the tension fading from my shoulders as Norrin continues to speak and we trade ideas back and forth. This is exactly why I came to him. Talking things through together always brings clarity... even if the talks do tend to be rather lengthy. Two hours later, my stomach has unknotted enough to start rumbling. Norrin calls for food and drink, which appears with such speed that Cressen must have had it prepared and waiting.

But it isn't Cressen who serves us, of course. It's a thrall bearing the appearance of a middle aged woman. Despite the appearance of age, she can't be more than thirty. Thralls never live much past that due to the amount of energy required to artificially animate their bodies and generate Light. I shift away as the thrall leans in to place a dish of fruit and cheese in front of me. I can feel the buzz—or maybe the heat—of the Light coming off her in waves. Trained Lightcrafters can sense and use Light even when the source isn't in the same room or sometimes even the same house, but this close even I can sense it.

"Thralls make you uncomfortable," Norrin observes.

I hesitate, then nod. "Yes. Rowan's parents were killed by their thrall. It was compromised by a Spiritwalker."

"And is that all?" Norrin peers at me.

"Isn't that enough?"

"Certainly," Norrin says, popping a piece of cheese into his mouth. "But I suspect that it isn't the only reason."

I sigh. "I suppose not. It's just—they look so *real*. I can't look at them and not see a person."

"But they are not real," he reminds me gently. "They are dolls made flesh, nothing more."

"But they move, they eat, they sleep," I blurt, then blushed. "They follow directions. They learn, at least to an extent. How do we know—"

"How do we know what?" Hadrian saunters into the courtyard, motioning for Cressen to pull up a chair for him. "What have you two been discussing so intensely all morning? The benefits of joining our family, I hope."

"In a sense," Norrin replies with a fond smile. "But just now, we are discussing thralls. Arismendi's empathy has gotten the better of her, I'm afraid."

"Dearest, the creatures are manufactured, not born. They have no feelings with which to empathize." Hadrian sits beside me and takes my hand. "Though your kindness does you credit. It is one of your many enchanting qualities. Have you come to a decision regarding—"

The last thing I want to do is discuss my personal feelings and foibles with Hadrian, but if the alternative is discussing his proposal, I know which is the less disagreeable choice.

"The House of Light and Shadow doesn't tell anyone how they create thralls," I say. "What if—"

"What?" Hadrian scoffs. "A conspiracy? They've all been lying for the last two hundred years?"

"Alright, not lying," I huff. "But what if they're just wrong? How many people even now believe that animals don't have thoughts or feelings, simply because they've never met a Beastspeaker to tell them the truth?"

"And what does Lucoran say?" Norrin asks, raising his brows. "He's a Beastspeaker. Can he hear thralls?"

"His Gift works best with canines," I say. "He's alright with cats, not so good with horses. He can't hear mice or birds at all... but other Beastspeakers can. Maybe it takes a certain kind of Beastspeaker, or another Gift entirely."

"A fair point," Norrin allows. "But if in two hundred years no one has been Gifted with the ability to hear and speak with thralls, I think it's more likely because the thralls have nothing to say than because no one with the right Gift has been born yet."

"I suppose so," I say grudgingly. "I know it's probably silly. I just find them unsettling. If the House creates them, why can't they create something else? Something not—human shaped."

"Humans are beautiful," Hadrian says with a shrug. "And more useful in a city than horses or cows."

"I do hope you'll be able to reconcile yourself to it, my dear," Norrin say. "Otherwise you'll find being a part of this family most uncomfortable."

"What's this?" Hadrian asks. He turns and beams at me. "Am I to understand that you intend to become a member of this family? You will be my wife?"

"I will," I say, trying to look pleased for Norrin's sake.

"Though she drives a hard bargain," Norrin says with a wink.

"Details!" Hadrian seizes my hands and clutches them to his chest. "Whatever she wants, we will provide. Is that not so, Father? Oh, my dear Arismendi, you cannot know how happy you've made me."

I grit my teeth. What I wouldn't give to never hear the words "my dear Arismendi" pass his lips again.

"On the contrary," I reply, tugging my hands away. "I believe I understand quite well."

"Would you like to explain the terms of our arrangement, Arismendi, or shall I?" Norrin asks, a smile tugging at the corner of his mouth.

"Let us not sully this good news with talk of coin," Hadrian declares. "A lady need not concern herself with such things."

"Indeed," I say sweetly. I rise, ready to make my escape. "I suppose it falls to you, then, Norrin. I'll leave you to it."

"Not so fast, Princess," Norrin says. "Sit down, if you please. You mustn't run away from this. As my son will be your partner in life, so will he be your partner in business."

In an unprecedented moment of unity, Hadrian and I speak as one: "*What?*"

Hadrian gives an incredulous laugh. "A partner in business? Father, what on earth can you mean?"

"You promised Arismendi her heart's desire in exchange for her hand," Norrin says. "And what she desires most is a school for the young girls of the City."

"A school for *girls*?" Hadrian turns to me with that tender look I so despise. "Arismendi, surely you can't really expect—"

"A school is exactly what I expect," I say coldly. "Your father has promised funds for the initial investment and continued payments for ten years. You and I will wed only after the school has opened and both of you have signed a contract guaranteeing ten years of funding."

"But—but—" Hadrian flounders for a moment, looking absolutely flabbergasted. He turns to Norrin. "Father, this is preposterous! What will people say?"

"They will say that you are a rich and generous lord worthy of the name," Norrin says. "They will say that you are a man of vision and charity, and that you gave to the needy of your own accord."

For some reason I don't understand, this shuts Hadrian up. He fumes a moment longer, his jaw clenched, then sighs.

"Isn't there some other charitable endeavor you might consider?"

I stare at him in stony silence. He rubs a hand over his forehead. "Very well, then. I shall act as your agent."

"What?" I shoot to my feet again. "Norrin, I'm perfectly capable of doing the necessary work."

"Your abilities are not the issue," Norrin replies. "It is a matter of propriety. A lady of breeding does not enter into business agreements on her own. She does not make arrangements or sign contracts. She needs an agent."

"That's not true," I argue. "Pia—"

"Pia is a widow," Norrin says. "And a commoner. It's different."

"*How?*"

Norrin spreads his hands. "That's simply the way it is, my dear. If you want to get anything done, you will need a man at your side. What better man than your betrothed?"

"But—" I flick a glance at Hadrian, who's already rolling his eyes. "Forgive me for speaking so plainly, but Hadrian is hardly the advocate I need. He thinks it's a foolish idea. A woman's whim. He doesn't care if the school opens or not."

"You're wrong, my love," Hadrian says. "If we cannot wed until the school opens, you may trust that I will work tirelessly to see that it does."

I snort. "How inspiring."

"You don't need my sincerity." Hadrian shrugs, finally dropping his facade of an ardent lover. "Just my voice, and my signature."

"I suppose," I say dubiously, though I find his honesty refreshing.

Norrin smiles and reaches out to take our hands.

"This a good way to start your marriage," he says warmly.

"What, with vulgarity and extortion?" Hadrian grumbles.

"With honesty and cooperation," Norrin corrects him. "Such a seed might grow into something wonderful. A true match."

"Indeed," Hadrian says dryly. "Our hearts will sing in perfect harmony on our wedding day."

Though his skepticism isn't exactly flattering, it's better than gooey-eyed, false romance. And it's the first time I've found myself in agreement with him in... well, ever. So maybe Norrin is on to something, after all. We might never—no, we very likely *will* never—have a loving marriage, but perhaps there's hope for a respectful one.

I leave Norrin's household with a heavy heart. I should be pleased. As I said to Luca, I know better than to expect anything more from a political marriage. But still, a part of me grieves for the loss. If I ever find love, it will be doomed to obscurity, a shameful, dangerous affair that could ruin me. Will anything—any*one*—ever be worth that risk?

Rowan is waiting when Sammon and I return to my quarters. He's scowling, which doesn't surprise me. He also looks worried, which does.

"What's wrong?" I ask. "Has something happened?"

"You could say that." He nods to Sammon. "You're dismissed."

Sammon stiffens. "But, sir, my shift doesn't end until—"

"It ends now," Rowan informs him. "You are dismissed. Go, before I give you a citation for disobeying and disrespecting a superior."

"Yes, sir." Sammon reddens, then salutes smartly and strides off with his shoulders up around his ears. I can still see the rosy glow on the back of his neck as he reaches the end of the hall and disappears.

"That wasn't very nice," I observe, frowning at Rowan.

Rowan ignores me.

"Luca told me what you did," he says without preamble. "Tell me, are you insane or merely spiteful?"

"Spiteful?" I stare at him in bewilderment. "What on earth are you talking about?"

"I told you there was no way to help Jessa, so you had to go and betroth yourself to *Hadrian* just to prove me wrong?"

I laugh, surprising us both. But it's harsh, bitter laughter, born of disbelief and resentment rather than humor.

"Yes, I sold myself to a man I loathe just to prove you wrong," I tell him. "It has nothing whatsoever to do with helping Jessa or finally turning my lifelong dream into a reality. It's all about you, Rowan."

Rowan flushes, his face going even redder than Sammon's did. "Ari—"

"I don't want to hear it," I snap. "For once, just be quiet. You tend to your business and let me tend to mine."

"And where does that business take you today, Princess?" he asks stiffly. "To the City... or to Villa Prosper?"

"I've just come from Norrin's table, as it happens," I say, my voice cool. "Now I need to give Pia the good news. I just need my cloak, and then we can be off."

Rowan doesn't speak again the whole way to the Lower City. Though the silence is prickly and uncomfortable, it's better than his usual barrage of judgments and too-large opinions. Still, it sours my already sour mood even further. By the time we arrive at the Honeysuckle Rose, I'm out of sorts and off-balance. Unable to think of a more graceful way to break the news, I march up to Pia, plop onto a stool beside the customer she's serving, and say,

"It's done."

Pia gapes at me a moment, then snaps back to attention and thrusts a plate of chicken in sweet sauce into the customer's hands.

"What do you mean, 'it's done'?" she demands, already turning to take another plate of food from the counter behind her. "What did you do?"

"I got the funding for the school," I tell her.

"How?" Pia asks with narrow eyes. "What have you done?"

"I agreed to marry Norrin Prosper's son," I say, my stomach clenching as I force the words out. "The Prosper family will pay a bride price of twenty thousand gold marks, and all of it is going to the school."

Pia's jaw drops, and with it the mug of ale she was holding. She curses and bends, whipping a rag out of her apron. I lean over the bar and keep talking.

"I have a plan," I say quickly, as if I can convince her in the time it takes her to finish cleaning the spill. "We'll open next year, by late spring or early summer at the latest. To do that, we need facilities for ten students—I was hoping you would help me with that—and teachers and staff. Exactly what sort of staff we need depends on what sort of facility we secure. The curriculum will focus primarily on the intellectual arts: logic, history, mathematics, natural philosophy, and ethics. But the learning will be well rounded. The girls will get an overview of the Divine Arts, of course, and they'll learn business and economics. And they'll learn to defend themselves. They'll study for six years and come out of it ready to command their own lives and futures, and—" I pause and scowl at her, my hands on my hips. "Pia, stop looking at me like that. I did it. We're opening a school and *it's going to work.*"

Pia slams a new mug of ale down in front of the waiting patron and leans against the bar, looking winded. She bows her head and stands like that for a few moments, then looks up. Her brown eyes are intent on my face.

"How do I know this won't fall through?" she asks. "What if you change your mind tomorrow?"

"I can't," I say, my voice hollow. "Councilor Norrin and I have already spoken to my brother. The contract is being drawn up, and the announcement will be made in two days. There's no turning back now."

"And if I still want Jessa to go to the Temple?"

I draw back so abruptly I nearly topple off my stool. Jessa can't go to the Temple. I got the money. There's going to be a school. How can Jessa be subjected to the Temple now? *There is going to be a school.*

Yes. Yes, there is. A school—*my* school. With or without Jessa.

"Then I'll have one more chair to fill," I say. "This isn't just about Jessa, Pia. I'm going to see this through."

Pia gazes at me a moment more, then gives a brisk nod. "Alright, then."

"Alright?" I look at her suspiciously. "Alright, what?"

"Alright, Jessa can attend your school." She jabs a finger in my face. "And woe betide you if it falls through and Jessa misses her chance at the Temple."

"It won't." I seize the finger and pull it to my chest. "I swear, Pia. It's going to happen."

"Good." Pia tugs her finger back and jerks her head at the growing pile of dirty dishes at the end of the bar. "Now either get back to the Terrace or get to work and help me. Rowan, too, while we're at it."

I laugh, giddy with relief, and fetch Rowan from where he's been lurking in the corner. Shoulder to shoulder, we wash dishes until the lunch rush is through. Once the crowd has thinned, Jessa emerges from the kitchen.

"Ari!" Jessa cries. "I thought I heard you. Is everything alright? Are you feeling better?"

"More than alright," I say, pulling her into a hug. I grin at Pia over her head. "Can I tell her?"

"Tell me what?" Jessa demands.

"You're going to attend the princess's new school next year," Pia says.

Jessa's jaw drops, just as her mother's did. Though Pia tries to smile, I can see the lingering worry in her face. She's taking an enormous risk by putting her trust in me. I promised her a school, and I simply have to deliver. If I don't, the Temple won't take Jessa even she wants to go. She'll be out of options.

"A school?" Jessa breathes. "A *real* school?"

"Yes," I tell her. "A real school with real teachers, not just a bumbling princess."

Jessa draws herself up and frowns at me. "You're not bumbling. You're the smartest person I know."

Warmth floods me, and my eyes prick with unexpected tears. Rowan doesn't even laugh. Instead he reaches out and squeezes my shoulder.

"I think this calls for a toast," he declares. Without waiting for Pia, he pours four mugs of cider and passes them around. "To Arismendi."

Jessa throws her arms around me again, slopping cider down both our skirts. "To Arismendi."

In that moment, with Jessa laughing and crying into my shoulder and Rowan's peace offering in hand, I can't regret what I did. It's a good thing, a right thing. And I will see it through.

Chapter Nine

It's been three days.

Three days of pretending I'm sure. Three days of insisting to everyone, including myself, that I know what I'm doing, of refusing every opportunity to change my mind. But my time is running out. In just a few hours, Costi and Norrin will sign the contracts with the other Council members as their witnesses. No matter what I told Pia, it's not done yet. It's not too late. I could still change my mind. But once those contracts are signed and witnessed, it really will be too late.

I stare at my bedroom door, the dark, heavy wood a solid barrier between me and the world. There's a heavy bolt that I've never used before. I find myself wondering if there's one on the other side that I've never noticed. Maybe Rowan or Sammon should lock me in, just in case I snap and try to tackle Costi in the Council chamber or something.

Though I probably don't need to worry. Since leaving Jessa and Pia, I've hidden in my room, paralyzed with fright, all my feelings of pride and certainty lost in a haze of dread. Hadrian's smug face keeps floating to the front of my mind, and each time I'm forced to recall that I will be his wife. He will be my husband. Everything I have will belong to him, including my body. He'll expect heirs. He—*we*—will have to... no, it's too horrible. I can't think of it.

But I have to. Hadrian isn't the only one who will expect children from me. If Costi won't, or can't, produce an heir to the throne, I have to. Taking Hadrian to bed is an unavoidable certainty. But surely there must be a way to make it boring or unpleasant enough that he won't seek me out. Shadow and blight, what a depressing thought. But even more depressing is the fact that it gives me hope.

I curl up on the long couch beside my window and stare out, my head on my knees. A soft mist drifts through the Terrace, smudging the edges of the perpetually blooming dogwood and cherry trees. The green of moss and ferns shines in contrast, blazing against the white. And through the mist, something else blazes as well: a young woman dressed in red, with wild, dark curls.

"Sadra," I breathe, my face pressed against the glass.

Sadra! Sadra is *here*, in the Terrace. I can't believe my luck. But then... maybe it isn't luck. Maybe our wishes tied our fates together. Maybe we were meant to meet again.

Smiling at my fanciful thoughts, I throw a soft, gray gown over my night shift and shove my feet into slippers. Rowan jumps, cursing, as I throw open the door. The piece of wood he was carving falls to the ground. I rush past him and catch a little flash of red out of the corner of my eye as he brings his thumb to his mouth.

"Hey!" he calls after me. "Where do you think you're going?"

"Wherever I want," I call back.

"Not without a guard, you're not," he says, scooping up his knife and wood.

"Keep up, then," I yell over my shoulder.

I race down the stairs and through the entrance hall, ignoring the disapproving look of Soren, our steward. Rowan is likely just behind me, but, unsurprisingly, I neither see nor hear him. Outside, I look around wildly. Where is Sadra?

There. I spot her just in time to see the end of her sash flicker around the far end of the East Wing. Warmth fills me as I realize where she must be going: the Mare's Tail. She's heading for my favorite spot in the Terrace. Perhaps it *is* fated.

"Being ridiculous," I mutter.

"You certainly are," comes Rowan's annoyed voice from over my shoulder. "What on earth has gotten into you?"

"Be quiet," I say absently. "And stay here."

Rowan moves to plant himself in front of me, crossing his arms. "And let you wander on your own, clearly deranged? I think not."

I shoot him an annoyed glance. "We're on the palace grounds. There's nothing to guard me against here."

"There's that girl," he says, scowling in the direction Sadra went. "What's she doing here? She could be following you."

"I'm the one following her," I point out. "I liked her. I want to see her again, and you're *not* going to ruin it by lurking and glaring the whole time. Stay here."

"No."

I shrug and move forward, giving him a sharp kick in the shins as I pass. "Stay out of sight, then."

I make my way to the Mare's Tail with eager steps, peering through the swirling mist. My heart pounds in my chest, but I feel lighter than I have in days. Hope buoys me, filling me so that it seems to push almost painfully against my skin like an over-full wine skin. My breath catches as I step onto the bridge and see her. She's graceful even in stillness, leaning against the rail much as Hadrian did just two days before. But Hadrian was posing, manufacturing an air of elegant romance. Sadra is elegance itself, her face tilted back to receive the mist. Her poise is natural, unaffected. She exudes confidence—security. Is that just her, I wonder, or does it come from her faith?

"Sadra," I say softly, and she snaps upright with a soft gasp. When she sees me, her eyes widen.

"Princess!"

I wince, my lightness draining away. "Please don't call me that. I don't want to be a princess today."

"I wasn't aware it was optional," she says with a crooked smile.

"It isn't," I sigh. Then I force myself to smile. Having finally found her, I don't want to scare her away with my gloom. "What are you doing here?"

"Fulfilling my wish," she says. "I accepted the position I told you about."

"Oh," I say, scrutinizing her face. "So... is this an occasion for congratulations or condolences?"

She laughs. "A bit of both, I think. I've accepted Lord Orean Glory as my patron. For the time being."

"Orean!" I wrinkle my nose. "I see."

"Exactly," Sadra says with another laugh. "What about you? Did your wish come true?"

"It did," I say, my little cloud of gloom thickening around me.

"Both wishes?" Sadra asks shrewdly.

"Yes," I say. "I found both an opportunity and the courage to take it. But it came with a cost."

"A steep one, seems like," Sadra observes. "You look like you've been sentenced to death."

I made a face. "Almost. I've agreed to marry Hadrian Prosper."

"And you don't like him?"

"You wouldn't, either," I assure her. "He's... Well, you'll see for yourself soon enough, if you're staying in the Terrace."

"I'm sure I will," Sadra says. "He's that bad?"

"Worse. But his father is going to fund my school."

Sadra goes quiet for moment, then peers up at the stone statues carved into the rock beside the waterfall. "That's Balia the Blessed, isn't it?"

"Yes," I say without looking. Balia and I are old friends.

"A fitting guardian for this place," Sadra says. "And for you."

"How do you mean?"

"She knows about sacrifice," Sadra says. "I think she would honor the one you're making."

I look up at the statue. The features are worn, almost indistinguishable from the surrounding stone. But if you look closely, you can see her: an old woman cradling a baby in her arms. She is Balia, the queen who sacrificed her life to save the child she had spent so long trying to conceive. Sadra probably meant to be encouraging, to bolster my courage by comparing it to Balia's.

But I don't know. Balia's sacrifice represents humility, selflessness, gentility, tradition. What I'm doing flies in the face of all those things. People will say I've forgotten my place and that I'm going to lead young girls to do the same. They'll say it's an act of pride and willfulness, that I'm spitting on tradition by taking girls from their traditional roles. They'll call my students—assuming I find any—shameless and uncouth. What would Balia think of my dreams?

What would my mother? Would she be proud of me, or would she be ashamed that I would risk her legacy and tarnish our family's name? Even now, years after her death, people speak of my mother as if she were a saint. They call her peerless, the perfect lady, Balia's Most Blessed. Will my school, my dream, dishonor her memory?

I don't know—but Sadra is still waiting, looking at me hopefully.

"Thank you," I tell her. "Balia is an example to us all."

I spend the rest of the day thinking about Sadra, wondering when I might see her again, and I fall asleep thinking about her, too. When the fire-girl appears in my dreams and takes my hand, I find myself wishing she were Sadra.

I wake the next morning in a disorienting haze of unease and longing, then confusion. There's shouting. It sounds like it's coming from Costi's study, but who would dare shout at the king?

The king's brother might. But Luca is always so careful, so concerned for Costi's reputation and his own. Luca is a king's son the same as Costi, but he'll never be entitled to anything. Luca has always been determined to prove to the world that he earned what he has.

He's fighting a losing battle, of course. No one will ever believe that he really deserves any of it—his position in the Guard, the house in Midtown, not even the clothes on his back. Everyone will always believe that he owes everything to our brother's generosity. But that doesn't stop him from trying to prove them wrong. He's the perfect soldier, the perfect citizen. He would never risk the fragile shield he's built for himself—unless someone else were about to.

Concerned, I hurry down the corridor to Costi's study and, ignoring the two guards stationed outside, push open the door. Inside, Costi and Luca are glaring at each other, their faces red and their jaws and fists clenched. I have but a moment to marvel at the resemblance between them, which isn't always so apparent, and then they're at it again.

"I won't do it," Luca hisses.

"You will." Costi slams his fist on the desk. "Blood and ash, you will do this, Lucoran, because I am your brother and your king, and I am giving you an order."

"An order that will *ruin me*," Luca yells. Two bright spots stand out on his cheekbones. "And you—this is a mistake, Costi. They'll say—"

"Since when do you care what people say?" Costi scoffs.

Luca stares at him. "Are you joking, or are you really so far above us all that you can't see how things are—how they've always been?"

"What are you talking about?"

I wince. As much as I love Costi, I can't blame Luca for the incredulous laugh that bursts out of him... or the hurt that flashes across his face as it does.

"If you don't know, I don't think I can explain it to you." Luca finally notices me leaning against the door and gives a bitter little smile. "Ah, little sister. Right on time. Perhaps you can enlighten our brother. Stars know he's more likely to listen to you."

Luca brushes by me and slams out of the room, leaving me to stare at Costi in shocked silence. Costi avoids my eye, shuffling the parchments on his desk. I step forward and take the parchments from him.

"Are you going to tell me what that was about?"

Costi drops into his chair, massaging his temples, then his face. I say nothing, waiting as he breathes into his hands. When he finally surfaces, I think I see—no, I have to be mistaken. Those can't be tears in his eyes.

"Costi, what's going on?"

He smiles weakly. "Nothing, little fox. Luca's just being obstinate."

"About what?"

Costi studies me for a moment, then sighs. "Danner is retiring as Captain of the Guard. I mean to appoint Luca as his replacement."

I stare at him. "But he's only nineteen."

"Do you doubt his capability?" Costi raises an eyebrow. "You know as well as I do he's the best swordsman we have."

"But that's not all a Captain is, is it?" I ask slowly. "The Captain leads the Guard, gives orders. In wartime, the Captain becomes a general."

"And you don't think Luca can do that?" Costi asks.

"Of course he can," I say. "Luca knows what he's doing. But just because an order is given doesn't mean it will be obeyed."

"It will be if the alternative is a flogging," Costi counters, his face growing dark.

"But is that the way you want the King's Guard to operate?" I ask. "The Captain of the Guard is the highest rank with the highest honor, and there are men in the Guard who have served you longer than Luca has been alive."

"Luca is the best candidate," Costi says stubbornly. "He has the skills and instincts of a commander."

"But not the experience." I shake my head. "I hate to say it, but Luca is right. It's a mistake. The men already resent him, some of them even hate him."

Costi scoffs again. "Their pride is hurt that a younger man has the skill and talent they don't."

"A bastard," I correct him quietly. "Their pride is hurt that a bastard has the position and authority they don't."

"It doesn't matter that Luca is a bastard," Costi says. "It's not like the old days. Father—"

"Father made it legal to recognize and raise a bastard," I finish. "Because he wanted Luca, and because Mother insisted. But Father was a king, and Mother, from what you've told me, was an unusually compassionate woman. But in the rest of the City, bastards are still left on the steps of the Temple and the House's shelters. Maybe some are taken by their fathers, but their mothers are cast out with nowhere to go. If the baby is lucky, he grows up never knowing he's illegitimate because if people find out, he'll never have a family of his own. No one will wed their daughter to a bastard if they have a choice. The shame is still there, Costi. A law can't change that."

"But the way I treat a bastard might," Costi says. "If what you're saying is true, then how can I expect my subjects to treat bastards decently if I don't do the same myself—for my own brother, for rocks' sake?"

"Elevating him at the age of nineteen and passing over the veterans of your Guard isn't treating him decently," I say flatly. "Your men will say it's nepotism, and they'll be right. It would be hard for them to swallow even if he were legitimate—even if he were their prince. The fact that he's a bastard will be like rubbing salt in the wound."

Costi gets to his feet and turns away, his hands on his hips.

"I hear what you're saying," he says. "And maybe you're right. But it has to be Luca."

I frown. "Why is that?"

"I trust Danner," Costi say, turning back. "He's intelligent and capable, and, more importantly, he's devoted. Honorable. Jash and Voss—those veterans you're so concerned about—they're not. They've gotten lazy and complacent, and, no matter what you or Luca may think, I'm not blind. I see how they treat Luca. I thought it was because he's young. I didn't think—but it doesn't matter. If they don't respect my brother, they don't respect me. How can I trust men like that to guard my family? I need someone who can be everything Danner is and more, someone completely loyal." He scrubs a hand over his face. "I need him, Ari. I need my brother. He's the only one I can trust to protect us."

A chill creeps over my shoulders. "Are we in particular need of protection?"

"Maybe," he says, a shadow passing over his face. "The Council is... displeased."

I bite my lip. "Is it the school?"

"Not exactly," Costi says. "Though that's part of it. I plan to institute a series of taxes to help defray the cost of rebuilding the Lower City as well as other projects for the public good. It's like you said—it's in everyone's interest to care for *everyone's interests*. Stars know I've tried to care for all my people, but I can't do it all myself. Those on the Council need to pay their fair share."

"And they don't agree." I let out a sharp breath through my nose. "Of course."

"Norrin believes that they'll open their purses of their own accord if he provides an example for them to follow," Costi says. "He says their pride won't allow them to do otherwise."

My stomach plummets to my feet. "How long has Norrin known about these taxes?"

"A few months," Costi says. "I broached the idea at the turn of the year. All the final payments were coming due to the builders, and I was applying for another letter of credit, and I thought—the Council enjoys all the honor and power that comes with ruling a kingdom, and they should also share in the responsibility. Norrin agrees, but he doesn't think they need to be forced into it."

"I imagine he was eager to show you he was right," I say.

Costi nods. "He promised to help with the debt and more. Any opportunity he could find, he said."

"And I gave him one," I say hollowly. "I thought... I thought he believed in me. In what I'm doing."

"I'm sure he does, little fox," Costi says, then he makes a face. "But I won't pretend that's the only reason he agreed to fund the school."

I laugh a little. "It's so—*Norrin*. In one swoop, he gets not only leverage to advance his political agenda but a princess for his son. And I can't even be mad at him for it, because he's also a good man doing a good thing."

"I don't know," Costi says. "I think you can be a little mad. He could have agreed to help without the betrothal."

"He could have, couldn't he?" My mouth twists, then I shake myself. "Is it working, at least? Are the other councilors donating to worthy causes on their own?"

"No," Costi says flatly. "They're meeting with each other instead of me and muttering about tyranny."

"And that's why you need Luca."

Costi sighs. "And that's why I need Luca."

"How can I help?" I sink into the chair opposite him. "No public announcements have been made yet. If the school is part of the problem—"

"Stop it," Costi says, reaching across the desk to take my hands. "This not your fault or your problem, foxling. You're doing a good thing, and I want you to keep doing it. I really believe that this school is good for the people and the City, and I'm so proud you've found a way to make it happen. Don't worry about me, alright? Just enjoy your victory, and then get to work."

"I will," I promise, though a cold weight has settled in my stomach.

He smiles and squeezes my hands. "Good. I'll do the same, and it will all come right in the end."

I want to believe him, but I leave with the sick feeling that my school—my dream—has created a weapon for my brother's enemies to use against us. But I've gone too far now to turn back, even if I wanted to. If I back out, it will make Costi look even worse... and it will break Jessa's heart. And mine.

Costi is right. The only thing I can do is make absolutely sure the school is a success, so that's what I'll do.

Chapter Ten

On the morning of my betrothal banquet, I wake with my stomach in knots. This is it. Balia's Moon will rise tonight, and her banquet will also be mine. After today, my fate will be sealed. There will be no going back. I pick at my breakfast of bread and fruit, but each bite makes the pain in my stomach worse. Rowan's face, when he arrives with a note, does nothing to ease my disquiet. His mouth is set in a thin line, his jaw tight.

"What's this?" I ask, knowing he won't ignore a direct question.

"From Hadrian," he replies shortly and resumes his station by the door.

I shoot him an annoyed look. *I'm* the one being sold like a cow at market today, not him. What right does he have to sulk?

I sigh. About as much—or as little—as I do, I suppose. No one sold me, after all. I made the bargain myself. My mood, already less than ideal, sours further as I read Hadrian's note.

My dear Arismendi, I am looking forward to this evening more than I can say. From tonight on, you will represent the Prosper family as well as the royal family, and I trust that you will conduct yourself as a lady worthy of both. This, of course, must include proper attention to your personal attire and appearance, which—forgive me—I have observed to be a particular weakness of yours. To that end, I have taken the liberty of assigning you a personal thrall. My sister, Ismeni, was kind enough to provide you with a gown, as you likely have nothing suitable in your own wardrobe. A seamstress will attend you to fit it properly. Ismeni has directed me to ask you—rather, to implore you—not to spill anything on it.

My face burns. Really, everything burns. With anger, of course, but also with shame. Never in my life have I felt so small, like a grubby child. This is what my betrothed thinks of me. It's nothing I didn't know already, but Hadrian's opinion never mattered before. He was never in a position to dictate my wardrobe or conduct. But as my betrothed, he now has every right to expect such things from me. As my husband, he will have both the right and the power to enforce those expectations.

I crumple the note in my hand and move stiffly to the window, where I stand with my arms wrapped around myself. Tears press against the back of my eyes hard enough to make my head throb. But I don't let them spill over. I can't. If I start crying, Rowan will feel obliged to do something about it, and that "something" could very well land him in prison.

So I say nothing, do nothing, until the promised thrall and seamstress arrive. The seamstress, at least, is warm and pleasant. And fast, stars be thanked. She flutters around me with her pins and knotted strings, chattering about the banquet and reminiscing about her own daughter's marriage. Not ten minutes later, she shucks me out of the gown and sits in the corner to make her alterations.

A thrall steps forward with a small basket of hair pins and thread, her eyes on the ground. Gritting my teeth, I take my seat and sit in tense silence as she—it—arranges my hair in an intricate series of braids and then moves on to my face, dabbing strange creams and powders on my lips, my eyelids, my cheeks. Her touch is light and sure, and yet somehow distant. Absent. It makes me shiver.

I shake off my unease. There are bigger things to worry about, like the fact that my intended husband believes me to be a bumbling infant and that his family apparently shares that opinion. I was already anxious, for this is my first time serving at Balia's Banquet. The Terrace will be packed with citizens from every reach of the City of Roses, all eager to enjoy a night of food, drink, and finery. The ladies of the Terrace don simple clothing and serve the guests, humbling themselves as Balia once did.

The story goes thus: After the Conqueror died of his wounds, his wife Balia and their son were held hostage by rebels from the outlying Cities. In an attempt to placate her captors, Balia served them a lavish feast with her own hands and begged them to spare the life of her son. They agreed to spare her son, the rightful king, but sentenced her to death to appease the former rebels and satisfy their need for blood—though they called it justice.

They paraded Balia naked through the streets to her beheading. At first, they laughed and jeered, but soon they found themselves impressed by Balia's courage and shamed by her dignity. By the time her head fell at their feet, they were overcome with remorse. They honored Balia with ten days of funeral games and pledged themselves to protect and guide her son alongside the former king's advisors until the boy came of age. Balia was ever after revered as a paragon of everything a woman should be: loving, selfless, dignified... and, above all, humble.

If it weren't for the betrothal, I might have actually enjoyed the feast in Balia's honor. After all, it's the one banquet at which I'm allowed to forgo the itchy, unfamiliar, awkward dresses that I have been stuffed into on every other formal occasion in living memory. But the betrothal *is* happening, and it's supposed to be a surprise, a bit of drama to curry favor with the masses and—hopefully—gain their support as I begin working toward my decidedly less than humble goals.

My shoulders hunch as I imagine all the things that could go wrong. But then, Hadrian is so fussy he'll find something to complain about even if everything is perfect, so there's really no point in worrying. I take a deep breath and force myself to straighten. The seamstress catches my eye and gives an approving nod.

"That's it," she said. "Head up, shoulders back. Firm but supple, like a willow. That's how a lady carries herself. Queen Amari had the knack of it, right enough. She was a joy to watch. No matter what she was doing, she held herself like a Grace on earth."

"I wouldn't know," I say sadly, but she doesn't hear.

"Here, now." The seamstress stands, shaking out the gown with a sharp snap. "Let's get you into this. Move, you."

The seamstress flicks the thrall's hands away from my face and takes her place. The thrall falls back to the corner, where she stands with her hands folded in front of her, awaiting further orders.

The seamstress helps me into the gown and spends a moment fussing with the sashes that hold it in place. Hadrian's sister chose well. The gown is simple, as is appropriate for Balia's Banquet, but the fabric is rich and heavy, draping over my bony frame in a way that emphasizes my curves. Rather, makes it appear as if I *have* curves. And it's so *soft*. I might actually last the whole evening in this. I smooth a hand over my hip and take a tentative step. The swish is nowhere near as grating as that of my other dresses. It's almost pleasant.

"Turn, please, Princess," the seamstress says, and I do. After a few moments' inspection, she beams. "You look just like your ma. Lovely, Princess, just lovely. Young master Prosper won't be able to keep his eyes from you."

I wince.

"I must leave you now," she says. "Balia's blessings on you today and on your wedding day."

"Thank you," I tell her, though as far as I'm concerned, Balia can keep her blessings—and the babies that come with them.

The seamstress flits about, gathering up her supplies as I muster the courage to look in the mirror. When I finally do, I gasp.

There in the mirror stands a lady. A princess. People always say I look like my mother, but I never saw it. Not until now.

The fabric of my gown, though soft and simple, shimmers with tiny accents embroidered with gold thread and tiny, almost hidden, pearls. I move closer, peering at my hair. My hair usually looks sort of dull, with no true color of its own but something that can't decide whether to be blond or red. But now it positively glows red-gold, like a candle flame or a sunset. The green of my eyes seems more vibrant and sharp, like Luca's. Like Father's.

"Did you cast a glamour on me?" I ask the seamstress, almost accusingly.

She laughs. "No, Princess. The only magic here is that of a well-fitted gown, a bit of paint, and your own beauty."

"I... I didn't know I had any," I say, touching my face. "Not like this."

"You have plenty, Princess," she says with a gentle smile. "Though I'd advise you to keep your fingers off your face, or you'll smear the paint and likely smudge it on your gown, as well."

I snatch my hand away, my face burning under the paint. Hadrian might be a boor, but he isn't wrong. When it comes to acting like a lady, I *am* a bumbling infant. And if I'm not careful, the whole City is going to know it before the evening is over.

When I am finally permitted to leave the palace, I find the Terrace transformed into a wonderland of lights and music. Enchanted lantern flies and swallows swoop overhead, glimmering with Light. Every tree, shrub, and flower stalk is in violent bloom, perfuming the air with a heady mix of freesia, lavender, lilac, and, of course, rose. Then the wind turns, and the scent of roasting meat and spices hits me full in the face along with the sounds of laughter and song. A pack of children dashes by, shrieking with delight, each with pastries clutched in their fists and jam smeared across their faces.

I smile wistfully, remembering how I used to haunt the kitchens with Rowan and Luca. In the weeks following my father's death, I made myself Luca's shadow. Even at eight, he knew every nook and cranny of the palace. Every hidden room, every secret passage. More importantly, he knew all the palace guards and their rotations. Those we couldn't avoid, we charmed and wheedled into pretending they hadn't seen us when Maja came looking.

Luca and Rowan were happy enough to let me join them as long as I could keep up. So I kept up. My tiny legs grew strong and sturdy, and I traded my skirts for an old pair of Luca's trousers. With my hair under a cap, even Maja was hard pressed to recognize a princess under my veil of dirt and general grubbiness.

But those days are long gone, and it looks like my days of quietly working alongside the steward and cooks are going the same way. I raise my hand to an enchanted butterfly and let it settle on my finger. Last year, and the three years before that, I had a hand in preparing the Terrace for Balia's Banquet. Not the Lightcrafting, of course, I've always been hopeless at that. Nor the food or decoration or any of the finery. Artistic endeavors, too, are beyond me. But I'm as capable of fetching and carrying as anyone else, and I *am* good at seeing what needs to be done and then doing it. I liked helping. It made me feel like I wasn't just—*existing,* useful only as an object to be admired.

Not this year. This year, the banquet took shape without me. This year, I'm the entertainment.

"Ari," a voice calls, and I turn to see Costi and Luca emerging from the palace doors.

"Look at you!" Luca takes my hand and twirls me around in a circle. "You're lovely. Who knew?"

"I did," Costi says staunchly, and kisses my cheek. "Well done, foxling."

"It wasn't my doing," I feel obliged to admit. "The dress is a loan from Lady Ismeni."

"That was kind of her." Costi studies me more closely, his eyes flicking over the gown, my hair, my face. "She has good taste."

Luca scoffs. "When did you become an expert on women's fashion?"

"Well, am I wrong?" Costi demands, gesturing to me. "She looks perfect."

"Let's just go," I say, a hollow feeling in my stomach. "We don't want to keep our audience waiting."

"Wait." Costi lays a hand on my bare arm, holding me back. "Ari, are you sure you want to do this? It's not too late."

I shake my head, suddenly blinking back tears. "Of course it is. We've agreed. Norrin has agreed. The arrangements have been made."

"But nothing has been signed," Costi insists. "I didn't save the contract for tonight just to put on a show for the crowd. I wanted to give you a way out. But after tonight... "

I close my eyes. After tonight, I will be tied to Hadrian for the rest of my life. A betrothal contract is a sacred bond. Unbreakable, barring death or treason. Socially, I'll be as good as his wife. The only difference from marriage, as far as I can tell, is that Costi will have to repay my bride price if I die before the wedding. And, of course, the consummation must wait until after the wedding, thank the stars. A small difference, but an important one.

"Are you ready?" Costi asks.

I take a breath. "I have to be, don't I?"

"Ari..."

"Stop." I hold my hand up and wince away from another offer of escape, which I'm terribly afraid I might be tempted to accept. "I have to marry somebody, and my chances of finding a true love match are small."

"But not none," Luca says quietly.

"Not none," I admit. "But I have this opportunity to do something good—something great. I won't let it go just to gamble on finding love later."

As I say the words, I know they're true. If it's not Hadrian, it will be someone else. And even if I did find someone I loved, or could grow to love, that wouldn't make it right to give up on my school. How could I be happy knowing I'd been too selfish and cowardly to follow through on this—transaction—this exchange that will allow me to do so much good for Jessa and who knows how many other girls in the City?

"I have to do this," I whisper.

Costi nods, his face grave. "Let's go, then. It's nearly time."

I swallow and wipe a trickle of sweat from my brow. Though the evening is as mild and fresh as anyone could hope for, I feel like I'm burning from the inside.

But it doesn't matter how I feel. It's time. I take Costi's arm and let him lead me through the crowd. Luca and Rowan—where did he come from, and when?—walk before us, parting the sea of laughing, shouting, drinking citizens. I keep my eyes on the ground, suddenly sickened by all the color and motion. The people evidently take my posture as demureness, because they throw flowers at my feet and yell things like "Balia smiles on you, Princess!" and "Good girl!" My head spins, and my breath comes fast. But I keep going, clinging to Costi's arm and putting one foot in front of the other.

Then we're on the small stage erected against the wall of the ravine, just inside the Terrace Gate. Hadrian is already there with Norrin, staring down at me with an expression both smug and covetous. I stumble on the first step, and Rowan's hand slips under my elbow. I take his hand and Costi's. Luca steadies me at my waist, and together they all but carry me forward. My legs are shaking, rubbery, as if my bones have turned to jelly. Darkness nips at the edges of my vision, and there's a strange pressure in my ears, like they've been stuffed with fabric. I can't hear what Costi's saying—something about great honor being bestowed upon the Prosper family, and trust—and now Hadrian is talking about the joining of great families. Costi releases me and steps forward to an ornate table displaying a scroll. The contract, I realize dimly, and I look away rather than see my life signed away. A moment later, I feel Luca give me a gentle push toward Hadrian.

I take one step and gasp as the stage seems to tilt under me. I stop and wait for it to steady—or, perhaps more accurately, for Rowan to leap forward and steady *me*. But he doesn't, nor does Luca or Costi. I have to do this on my own.

"Ari!"

It's a faint sound. The voice is small, young. I scan the crowd and—there. Jessa is skipping across a table laden with food, nimbly avoiding the many hands grabbing for her. A small, incredulous laugh escapes my lips, and my head clears. Jessa needs this. Jessa needs me. I can do it.

I square my shoulders and take the last few steps to Hadrian's side. He offers me his hand, and I take it.

"The sun shines on you, my lord," I say, pitching my voice to carry as best I can.

"And on you, my love," Hadrian replies.

I grit my teeth, and the crowd sighs as one. Then they burst into applause as Hadrian pulls me into a deep kiss. I stiffen and instinctively try to pull away as his tongue forces its way between my teeth. But I have no leverage so close to his body, and I can do nothing but wait, numb, as his hands travel across my sides, my back.

When it's over, I paste a smile onto my face because that's what the crowd wants. And, perhaps more importantly, what my betrothed certainly wants. It's done, now.

I belong to him.

Chapter Eleven

I descend from the stage on Hadrian's arm, but I let go almost immediately. He lets me. The men of the Council converge on him, pounding him on the back and clasping his hands. Costi, too, receives his share of congratulations. His smile is broad and easy, but I don't think I imagine the glint of fury in his eyes as he claps Hadrian on the shoulder. No one pays any attention to me.

"That swine," Rowan growls into my ear as Hadrian laughs heartily at something Orean just said. "I'll kill him."

"It's done," I say with a shiver, trying not to notice the speculative glances Hadrian and Orean send my way. "And if you kill him, I don't get my money."

He makes a face. "True."

"Rowan, I need to get out of here," I tell him. "Cover for me?"

He looks around and points to an opening in the hedges nearby, a pathway left purposely dark to encourage the mingling of guests in the courtyards.

"There. I can give you five minutes," he says.

Good enough. I duck beneath a swath of dangling vines and leave the courtyard behind. I need to be alone, if only for the five minutes Rowan can successfully hold off my brothers.

I come to rest at the cliff face. Heedless of my white dress, I lean against the moss-covered stones. Cool dampness seeps against my back and shoulders, but it does nothing to cool the fire in my chest. My whole body shakes with it. I shift uncomfortably, shaking my hands out as if I can physically cast the fury from my body.

"Princess?" a soft voice calls. "Ari?"

I freeze, my breath catching.

"It's me. Sadra." Sadra appears, her face barely visible in the gloom. "Oh dear. I came to make sure you're alright, but you're obviously not."

"I'm fine," I say, but the tremble in my voice betrays me.

"Nonsense," Sadra says. "Anyone with eyes can see you're not."

"Which is why I wanted to be alone," I say. I don't mean it to sound harsh, but it does.

"You're right," Sadra says, withdrawing back into shadow. "Forgive me."

"No, wait." I push myself off the wall. "*I'm* sorry. I didn't mean—I just wasn't expecting anyone. I've been longing to see you again, and now here you are. But—what *are* you doing here?"

"I was commissioned to dance," Sadra says. "By a woman named Marsali."

"She's the banquet coordinator," I say. "She has good taste."

"She told me I came highly recommended," Sadra says, looking at me with a small smile.

I blush. "I might have mentioned that a new dancer was in residence on the Terrace," I admit.

"That was kind," Sadra says, moving closer. "Thank you."

"I was happy to do it," I say. "It was the only useful thing I was able to do."

"Silly, you should hear what people are saying." She leans against the wall beside me. "This is the best banquet in living memory, and it's all down to you—and that kiss."

I turn away, suddenly blinking away tears.

"It *was* the kiss, wasn't it?" Sadra says, pushing off the wall and coming around to stand in front of me. "Do you truly hate him that much? It's just a kiss."

I sniff. It probably does seem silly to her. After all, she does much more than kiss the men she contracts with.

"I don't like him," I say. "In fact, I rather detest him. But that's not what—that's not why I—" I flounder, my face flaming. "It's just... He did it just for the spectacle. He doesn't even want me. I know he doesn't."

"How do you know that?" Sadra cocks her head. "Have you asked him?"

"Hadrian has a type," I say. "And I'm not it."

"Oh? What's his type, then?"

"Proper ladies," I say. "Graceful, charming, well spoken. Beautiful."

"I find you very charming, actually," Sadra says. "Beautiful, too."

I give a skeptical snort.

"You doubt me?" Sadra asks, feigning offense. "How dare you question my judgment—I, who have spent my life studying beauty."

I smiled weakly. "You're kind to say so."

"Well meant lies are still lies," Sadra says. "And I'm an honest woman."

"Then I won't further impugn your honor." I sigh and tip my head back against the stones behind us. "I just feel so stupid and—and dirty. And angry. I feel like he stole something from me."

"Stole what?"

"It's silly."

"So? Tell me anyway. What did he steal?"

I blush again, grateful for the dark. "My first kiss."

"Oh. That isn't silly," Sadra says after a moment. "And it wasn't your first kiss, either."

I cock an eyebrow and look over at her. "Were there other kisses that escaped my notice?"

She scoffs. "That wasn't a kiss; it was an assault. A wet and sloppy one."

I laugh bitterly. "Well, he'll have his opportunity to improve upon the first attempt, once we're wed. My first kiss will be his, one way or another."

"Not if you beat him to it," Sadra points out. "You only have one first kiss. You can give it to whomever you please."

"Who, then?" I ask with a grimace. "My pool of admirers is rather shallow, I think you'll find."

"You only need one," Sadra says. "And I'm happy to volunteer."

For a moment I can't speak as shock wars with curiosity. I peer at her, trying to catch her expression in the gloom. "You're teasing me."

"Am I?" she asks with a grin.

She shifts forward, her eyes sparkling. Her body has barely moved, but now the space between us feels charged and tight.

"What if I said yes?" I challenge.

"Then I would kiss you right now," Sadra says. "And thoroughly enjoy it, too."

I laugh. She can't be serious. But a strange sort of defiance comes over me, and I find that I don't want to back down. I don't want to be the quiet one, the shy one, more a frightened rabbit than the fox my brothers named me. For once I want to be bold, daring. Her face is but a hand's span from my own, and the scent of cinnamon is on her breath.

"Kiss me, then," I say.

I cross my arms and wait, still so sure that she must be playing that, when it comes, her kiss freezes me in place. My eyes widen, then flutter shut as Sadra's lips move over mine. Then, so gently I almost don't feel it happening—except I feel *everything*, from the touch of her fingers to her hair brushing my cheeks—she unwinds my crossed arms and twines her fingers through mine, stepping forward to close what little space was between us. She's my height almost exactly, and we fit together as if made for one another.

Heat blazes through me at the thought. Paradoxically, it makes me shiver. I feel like I'm burning and drowning and falling, all at the same time. A soft whimper escapes me, a sound so foreign I almost look around for Kirit. Sadra sighs in answer, her body softening against mine.

"I've been dying to do that," she whispers, touching her lips to the little cluster of freckles on my cheek.

"I didn't think—I never thought—" I take a shaky breath, trying to marshal my spinning thoughts. "Why? I mean—why me?"

"Why not you?" Sadra traces my lower lip with her finger, a hungry look in her eyes that makes my pulse quicken in response. "Do you truly think so little of yourself?"

"I suppose I must," I murmur, wishing I were brave enough to kiss her finger as I want so badly to do.

"Then I'll have to teach you better," she replies. She leans in, but before our lips can meet, Luca's voice cuts through the darkness.

"Ari," he calls. "You can't hide forever. Costi needs to speak with you."

Panic flashes through me as Luca's footsteps draw closer. He can't see me like this. Other girls might take a honeybee, but not a princess. Certainly not on the eve of her betrothal! Finding mutual education and pleasure in another girl is a practice widely accepted, or at least ignored, throughout the City. But only until one or other of the girls is ready to take her place as a wife and mother. Then she's expected to put girlish indulgences aside. A princess, Costi would say, must be above such things. And after tonight, I'll be constantly on display, a public commodity for anyone—everyone—to judge.

"Sadra," I say. "I—"

But she can already see it in my face. She silences me with a fleeting kiss and whispers in my ear, "I'll find you again."

And then she slips away like smoke, vanishing into the deep shadows of the garden.

Chapter Twelve

She's singing. The fire girl. She wanders from City to City, tearing up roses and lilies by the roots and setting them on fire with her tears. And, all the while, she sings a sad, haunting song in a language I can't begin to understand. Yet there's something soothing about the melody, a cadence and contour to it that makes me think it's a lullaby.

It's a bit ironic, I suppose, to find a lullaby in a nightmare. More ironic still, the lullaby does its job. I lie with my head pillowed in a pile of ashes and rose petals and listen to the fire girl's voice and the crackle of flames until I can't distinguish one from the other—or maybe they were one and the same all along.

And I sleep.

I wake in an uneasy haze, still unsettled by my dream, last night's banquet, Hadrian's kiss. His assault, as Sadra put it. And Sadra. Sadra most of all. I don't know what to make of her or her kiss, and I don't try. Instead, I go in search of Costi and find him in his study. But he isn't alone. Norrin and Hadrian rise as I enter, their faces expectant. Irritation spreads through me, prickling and hot, like a rash. Haven't they taken enough of my attention and peace of mind for the time being?

I take a breath. They are both a part of my life now. I agreed to this—I *asked* for this. So I fix a gracious smile on my face and nod in greeting to them both. Norrin takes his seat once more, which I note is behind the massive oak desk, right beside Costi's. He clasps his hands before him, his face stern. Hadrian stands before the desk, scowling.

"Is something the matter, Costi?" I ask, frowning.

"I wanted us all together to talk something over," he says. "To make sure we're all aware and in agreement in regard to our respective duties and responsibilities. What is expected of us and, most especially, what is *not* expected."

"I agree," Hadrian says, drawing himself up. "Arismendi's behavior—"

"What!" I gape at him, too surprised to be offended. "What did I do?"

Hadrian rolls his eyes. "You can't just disappear like—"

"Hadrian," Norrin says gently. "You are in the presence of your king."

"I—of course," Hadrian says, flushing. "Forgive me."

Costi stares at him long enough to make him squirm. When he speaks, his face and voice are positively glacial.

"It is not Ari's behavior I wish to discuss," Costi says. "It's yours."

Hadrian's mouth pops open. "My king! What—"

"Hadrian!" Norrin cries, looking—unreasonably, in my opinion—shocked at Hadrian's audacity. "You will speak when the king speaks to you, and not before."

"Yes, Father," Hadrian mutters.

"Costi," I venture. "What is this about, exactly?"

"I want to talk about what happened last night," he says. Then, seeing my blank look, he adds, "The kiss."

"*Oh.*" Relief washes over me, accompanied by a rush of love for my brother. "Thank you, Costi. I appreciate that."

Costi gives me a fleeting smile, then pins Hadrian with his gaze once more. When Hadrian keeps his mouth shut, Costi nods, leans forward over the desk, and speaks very quietly.

"I need you to remember something, Hadrian," he begins, "Fully and completely. You must remember that you are not yet my sister's husband. You have none of a husband's conjugal rights. For your father's sake, I am willing to give you the benefit of the doubt so far as your intentions went." Here he eyes my betrothed with distinct disfavor. "Perhaps you are simply young and eager to wed, as my friend suggests. My sister is indeed a lovely girl. But you will not treat her so again. Though she will be your wife, she remains my ward until the day she takes her vows. Touch her again without her express consent and I will have her released from the betrothal and you publicly whipped."

Hadrian stiffens. "My king—"

"You have something to say?" Costi asks, raising an eyebrow. "Still? My goodness, it must be important."

Norrin closes his eyes.

"I only wished to express my deep affection for the princess," Hadrian says. Red stains his cheeks. "Surely—"

I make a strangled sound somewhere between a snort and a growl.

"My dear Arismendi," Hadrian blusters. "Surely you know how I—"

Costi makes a small sound, and Hadrian subsides into sulking silence. Costi turns his attention to me.

"I understand why you disappeared last night," he says. "I don't blame you, and I'm not angry. However."

My stomach sinks. "However?"

He regards me unhappily, tapping a finger against the desk. "Hadrian does have a point. There were many who wished to see you and speak to you last night, many who craved your attention. It was an opportunity to gain favor with the people you intend to help and gain their trust, not to mention the potential donors to your cause among the Terrace folk. But that opportunity was squandered because you were not there."

I nod, swallowing against the lump in my throat. He's right, of course. I should have had better control over myself.

"It's not fair for me to say this," Costi says softly, "But I must. You cannot conduct yourself the way you have in the past. I let you grow up without the burden of your title because I wanted to spare you its weight, but now I fear I've only denied you the tools you need to carry it. You never learned how to engage with society, how to talk to people."

"I know how to talk to people," I say indignantly. "Just not—"

Costi nods again. "Not these people. But they're the ones you're going to need on your side, little fox."

"So... " I focus very hard on a spot above Costi's head, trying not to see Hadrian smirking out of the corner of my eye. "So teach me. I can learn."

"I can't teach you to be a lady, foxling," Costi says. "But Norrin thinks he knows someone who can."

"Who?" I ask, though I have a suspicion.

"My daughter," Norrin supplies. "Lady Ismeni."

I sigh. "She did give me a very nice dress to wear last night."

"You wore it well," Norrin says, his face crinkling with a fond smile. "Ismeni was delighted."

"I'm—I'm glad," I say, forcing myself to smile back. "And I'll be very grateful for her help. When do we begin?"

"Today," Costi says firmly.

"Today," I echo, my stomach sinking even further.

"She's waiting for you in the garden."

"This is an excellent idea," Hadrian declares. "How clever of you to think of it, Father. If anyone can turn Arismendi into a proper lady, Isi can."

Norrin winces. "Hadrian."

"What?" Hadrian protests. "I'm being encouraging."

"Hadrian," Norrin says again, his eyes closed. "Do shut up."

Ten minutes later, I find myself not in the gardens but in the archives. I *intended* to meet Ismeni, truly, but before I even made it down the corridor, Soren appeared with news of a dispute between two orderlies tasked with cataloguing a newly acquired collection of manuscripts. In my defense, I did consider—briefly—that Ismeni was waiting for me, but Soren shouldn't have to deal with something like this when there are so many other things that require his attention.

"I thought the ultimate decision should be yours, Princess," he whispers to me as the orderlies snipe at each other. "Or Councilor Norrin, but he's still in conference with the king. *I* certainly don't know which scrolls should go where."

"You did right, Soren," I assure him. "Poor organization is how manuscripts go astray. If this is the collection I'm thinking of, it took far too long to acquire for us to take any chances."

"Thank you, Princess," he says, looking relieved. "I'll leave you to it, then."

I take a deep breath, steeling myself, then wade into the fray. At first the orderlies merely stare at me, then each rushes to defend his position. I listen politely, forbearing to point out that they are both entirely wrong. The archives are and have always been organized by subject, then time period, then author, and I see nothing in the scrolls they show me that suggests any ambiguity in categorization. A few gentle reminders and suggestions are enough to resolve the matter.

Once the scrolls are safely ensconced in their new homes, I let out a deep sigh of relief, making a mental note to speak to Soren about reassigning these particular orderlies. I turn to go, but a tall, auburn-haired lady stands in my way.

"Lady Ismeni," I say, taking a step back in surprise. "I—um, was on my way to see you. I just had an, um—"

"Emergency?" Ismeni suggests with a slight smile.

"Yes."

I study her. Ismeni is Hadrian's sister, but she's rarely at Villa Prosper. The poor lady is married to Councilor Orean—the same councilor who has apparently hired Sadra as his Companion. But there's no time to wonder about what Ismeni might think about that. She's watching me with polite interest, clearly waiting for me to say something.

"I'm, ah, ready now," I say sheepishly.

"Good," Ismeni says. "Come, let us walk in the gardens, and we can talk."

I let Ismeni hook her arm through mine and follow her out to the palace gardens. We stroll for several long minutes in silence, and with every step I wonder what I'm supposed to say, or if I'm supposed to say anything. Ismeni, howeevr, seems perfectly at ease. She floats along with an elegance and grace I'm sure I'll never match. Finally, she speaks.

"So," she says. "The announcement has been made. The contracts have been signed. You are to be my sister."

My stomach clenches at the reminder, and I have to work hard to keep a straight face.

"We are overjoyed to welcome you to our family, Princess. But my father believes—and I must say, I agree—that you are in need of female companionship and guidance." She pats my hand. "Through no fault of your own, of course. But the fact is that you lack the skills and knowledge to conduct yourself appropriately in society. I'm here to change that."

It's nothing I don't already know. I was just told as much, at length. But it still stings. And it worries me. It wasn't only shyness that kept me from court life. In the early years of Costi's reign, I saw how men and boys suddenly wanted to be his friend. I sat with him when this political intrigue or that came to light, and he discovered that those he thought he could trust were only using him to push their own agendas. True friendship, I learned, is a sheer impossibility on the Terrace. Everyone wants something.

"Your husband is often at odds with my brother," I say, trying not to sound as suspicious as I feel. "And you've never sought me out before. I can see why Norrin might ask you to do this, but why would you agree?"

"My husband may not always agree with the king, but he'd be a fool to spurn an opportunity to build closer ties," Ismeni says, a smile touching her lips. "But that's not why I agreed. I agreed because I think I can help you, and I want to. Need there be more to it than that?"

"From what I've seen, yes," I say. "But if Norrin thinks you're the best choice, I'm sure you are, whatever your reasons."

"A glowing endorsement," Ismeni laughs. But she quickly sobers and squeezes my arm gently. "You can trust me, Arismendi. Queen Amari was my greatest source of solace and guidance after I lost my mother. I hope you'll allow me to pass on some of that guidance to you."

A dart of sadness strikes my heart. My mother was beloved by everyone—a mother to everyone, or so it seems. Everyone but me... and I have no one but myself to blame for that.

I swallow the lump in my throat and nod. "Thank you, Lady Ismeni. When do we start?"

"This very moment," she says. "Forgive me, Princess, but you walk like a little boy. Keep your back straight, but relax your hips. Take smaller steps, like this."

Ismeni spends an hour correcting my gait as if I'm a horse in training. Everything about the way I move is wrong, apparently. The angle of my shoulders, the tilt of my chin, the placement of my hands and fingers. My carriage must scream royalty, Ismeni informs me, and an hour's hard work wins me little more than a whisper.

"We have much to do," Ismeni concludes, frowning at me as I walk toward her for what feels like the thousandth time. "I must leave you now, Princess. But a seamstress will attend you this evening to measure you for new gowns."

"What's wrong with my gowns?" I ask irritably, my patience frayed by Ismeni's lesson.

Ismeni sighs. "Everything, Princess. Everything."

Chapter Thirteen

Two weeks pass in a blur of lessons with Ismeni and an avalanche of new gowns, new people, and new responsibilities. Soren, our steward, has always asked me to do things—find an answer or a person, dictate a letter. But now he wants my *opinion*, too. So do Kora and Perrin, the palace's head cook and culinary Lightcrafter. What should be served for dinner? Who should be in charge of hiring new kitchen staff?

"You're a lady now, foxling," Costi says when I mention it, somewhat unnerved by the change. "The chatelaine of the Rose Palace. You're in charge."

"Of the color of the drapes and whether to serve the meat in white sauce or red," I grumble.

"Don't look down your nose at it," Costi tells me. "It's a real job, and Soren has generously taken it on in addition to his other duties until you were old enough to step into the role. It's time to help him shoulder the load."

I go to bed duly chastened and dream of the fire girl, as I do every night. But when I wake the next morning, she's still there. I gasp and jerk away from the face that hangs over me. For a moment, I could swear my bed is on fire along with the woman sitting beside it. But then the flames recede, and I see that the blazing light is only the morning sun. The fire girl's face resolves into one that I know—not well, but well enough to recognize her. It's Lady Ismeni.

I take a few more breaths and lie still until the panic fades, then look around. A few shafts of weak sunlight slant through the window, and the birds are singing their usual morning song. It can't be long after sunrise. But Ismeni seems perfectly alert and at ease, elegant as always with her auburn hair expertly arranged. A dark-haired thrall hovers at her shoulder with her head bowed and hands clasped before her.

"Lady Ismeni," I croak. "You are in my bedchamber."

She smiles. "I am, Princess. We have much to do."

"And it couldn't wait until after breakfast?"

"No, as it happens," Ismeni says. "You lack the requisite tools to progress any further. We must rectify that immediately."

"The seamstress already came," I tell her. "Several times, in fact."

Ismeni laughs. "I'm not talking about dresses, child. You need a thrall." Seeing me flinch, she goes on, "My father has informed me of your aversion. And I want you to know that I understand. I felt the same way as a child. It's difficult not to—they look so much like us that we can't help but project our humanity onto them. I did the same with my dollies. I had one named Tilli that I loved more than life itself."

I look at her in surprise and sit up, propping myself against the pillows. "Luca made a cloth dog for me out of an old pillow. I called her Flower."

"A dog," Ismeni says thoughtfully. "I suppose that's not surprising, considering Lucoran's Gift. Let me guess. You worried that Flower was secretly alive and suffering because you weren't feeding her or playing with her or loving her enough. You took her everywhere and slept with her in your bed so she wouldn't get lonely. Maybe you felt guilty when you dropped her or got her dirty?"

Ismeni is eerily close to the mark. I never felt guilty for getting Flower dirty—Luca assured me that dogs love getting dirty—but I felt like a murderer when Flower's worn seams finally split and she fell apart. I look at Ismeni and give a tiny nod.

"And you came to accept that Flower wasn't really a dog, did you not?" Ismeni asks gently. "You grew out of it."

I nod again, though something inside me screams that it's not the same thing at all.

"You'll grow out of this, too. You just need more exposure." She gives my knee a brisk pat. "And that exposure begins today. A shipment of thralls has just arrived from the north, and we will attend the auction."

"Today?" I ask. "But—"

"Today," Ismeni says firmly. "Your thrall will need, at a bare minimum, two weeks of intensive training with a specialist before it will be of any use to you. You must see, then, that we have not a moment to lose."

Apparently moments spent in sartorial deliberation aren't considered wasted, because Ismeni spends an hour at least rummaging through my clothing chests looking for something that doesn't look like, in her words, either a museum relic or a rumpled bed sheet. Finally, she settles on a pale blue gown that, based on other discarded choices, I would have thought would fall into the bed sheet category but is somehow different enough from the others to be acceptable.

"This fabric is heavier," Ismeni explains when I point out her hypocrisy. "The way it drapes over your bust and hips changes the overall impression completely. And with the right accessories—" She snaps shiny brass cuffs around my wrists like shackles and stands back. "It's actually quite lovely. Different, but so are you. Everyone knows that, there's no point in trying to hide or deny it. Better to accentuate your difference and turn it into an asset."

I'm still wondering whether I should be offended by this as she herds me out of the palace, with Rowan on our heels. For once in his life, he has been rendered speechless. Perhaps having Ismeni around isn't without its advantages.

The auction is a lavish affair, with a reception housed in a marble monstrosity of a building. Ismeni tows me through the crowd like a dog on a leash, chatting animatedly with an unending parade of men and women dressed in the finest silks and linens I've ever seen. Everywhere I look, I see beautiful faces set in complacent, serene smiles. They're all so at ease with themselves and each other, completely sure of their places. I quail. Is this what I have to compete with—what I have to become? I tug self-consciously at my gown, which has somehow gotten smudged with jam though I haven't so much as looked at any of the food being served. The gesture catches Ismeni's attention, and her gaze snaps to the small dot of red.

"Mind yourself, dear," she murmurs, pressing a finger to the spot. It disappears with a tiny flare of Light. "There. You know, if you hadn't scared off your last Lightcrafting instructor, you'd be able to take care of things like this. I must speak to my father about resuming your lessons."

I wince. "Oh, don't—"

"And another thing," she goes on. "We've met no fewer than four women with both the time and means to be of use to you. If you want your school to succeed, you'll need more than my father's gold. That, after all, will eventually run out. When the time comes to petition the crown for more funding, you will need the Council's support. *These* are the kinds of men the Council aims to please—friends, relatives, business and social associates. You would do well to begin cultivating contacts among their wives."

"But how?" I ask, my gaze darting from one elegantly attired lady to the next.

"You can begin by saying hello."

Ismeni pushes me toward a cluster of women.

"Remember, you're a princess," she says. "You have nothing to fear from them."

Nothing except looking like an utter fool. But Ismeni is right. I'll have to get used to this, so I might as well start now.

I spend the next hour making light conversation with what feels like every woman in the room. All the while, sweat trickles between my breasts and down the small of my back. But I don't make a fool of myself—or if I do, I'm too inept to realize it, which I suppose is some comfort.

"How much longer?" I ask Ismeni wearily as we pause for refreshment.

"A while yet, though the bidding will begin soon. Be careful with that," she adds as she handed me a crystal cup filled with pomegranate juice.

I drink slowly, both to avoid spills and to hide my dismay. A vicious headache has settled into the base of my skull, and my feet throb in my too-tight shoes. It's ridiculous—I've spent far longer on my feet helping Pia at the Honeysuckle Rose with no pain at all, but here I feel like my every limb is in danger of snapping clean off.

I nearly weep with relief when an unctuous-looking man in red robes invites the assembled guests—rather, customers—into the garden, where the auction will be held. I take a deep, steadying breath. One step closer to escape. The worst is still to come, but perhaps there will be chairs, at least.

There aren't. It takes another half-hour of mingling before the thralls are brought out, and the sight of their pale, blank-eyed faces saps what little remains of my strength.

"I can't do this," I whisper to Ismeni.

Her brow furrows. "My dear, whatever do you mean?"

"They just look so *alive.*" My breath comes faster. "I can't do it. I can't."

Ismeni gives me a swift hug. "Yes, you can. Because they *are* alive, at least in a sense, and they would be helpless on their own. You will give one of them a place and a purpose. Some call me silly, but I believe it's our responsibility to provide for their welfare as best we can. Think of it as a pet."

"A pet that looks just like any of the girls who might be my students," I reply through my teeth. "I think I'm going to be sick."

"Not just like," Ismeni disagrees, pinching the soft skin on the inside of my arm. "Now, you must take hold of yourself. Look at them. Anyone can see they're different. Less. Alive, yes, but less than human. They require shelter, guidance, protection. You can give them that."

I study the thralls and can't deny that every one of them looks lost and pathetic, as if it would starve if someone didn't tell it to eat.

"Alright?" Ismeni asks.

I nod weakly. Guidance. Protection. That doesn't sound so bad. The man in red calls for attention, and the buzz of conversation quiets.

"My lords and ladies," he calls out. "For centuries, our ancestors relied on the abominable practice of slavery to meet the citizens' demand for labor. Until the

House of Light and Shadow provided an alternative, a triumph of Lightcrafting and compassion: the thrall. Shaped like men and women, with all the attending physical capabilities but devoid of emotion or spirit. They do not suffer, do not grieve. They are the perfect servants, beautiful in their simplicity. Our offerings today are suitable for young ladies of discerning taste: lovely of form, biddable and trainable. We will begin with this flame-haired beauty. What am I bid?"

The red man pulls a thrall forward. Her fiery red hair tumbles loose about her face, contrasting beautifully with the milky pallor of her skin.

"Charming," Ismeni murmurs, considering. "But I think not. Her coloring won't quite complement yours."

To my left, a portly man murmurs something to his companion. Both men chuckle, turning lascivious grins on the thrall. One of them calls out a bid. Bile rises in my throat. But then another bid is called, and another, until the thrall finally goes to an elderly woman. The young girl at her side squeals with delight and rushes forward to guide the thrall away, cooing over her prize all the while.

A girl—a thrall—with dark skin and corkscrew curls goes to the merry-faced lady with whom Ismeni and I shared spiced meat pies inside the auction house. A freckled one is sold, then one with rosy cheeks and a figure that looks like it was once plump.

"Which one do you want?" Ismeni whispers. "Surely one has caught your eye."

I shrug. "No. What about you?"

"That one," Ismeni says promptly, pointing to a slender thrall with dark hair and delicate features. "She'll look precious with my Dove."

I make a noncommittal sound of agreement and shift in a vain attempt to ease the pressure in my feet. How does the House decide what new thralls will look like? Are the thralls sculpted, somehow? I shiver at the thought of an artist elbow deep in flesh and blood instead of clay. The image is ridiculous, of course, but how *are* thralls made?

The next thrall is brought out, and a strange hush falls over the crowd. Confused, I focus on the thrall and realize that she—it—is the most gloriously beautiful creature I've ever seen. A waterfall of golden hair falls to her waist, fine as spun silk. Even at a distance, I can see her eyes are a clear, icy blue. Her blank face is smooth and serene and still, like a statue in truth. Beside me, the portly man and his friend are all but salivating at the sight of her.

"By Beauty herself," the portly man mutters. "That's it. That's the one. I must have it."

"For your wife, of course," his friend says dryly.

"Of course," the portly man says. "But surely the best gift is one we both can enjoy. Twenty gold marks!"

The red man beams. "Thank you, my lord, an excellent opening bid."

"No," I whisper.

"Twenty-five," another calls out. Another man—if anything, he looks even more disreputable than the portly man, flushed and eager.

"Twenty-eight!"

"Thirty!"

Men! All men, and I'll eat my shoe if a single one of them actually wants this girl for his wife or daughter.

"Fifty gold marks," I cry without thinking.

"Arismendi," Ismeni whispers, looking pained. "I don't think this one is appropriate for you."

"Fifty," the red man repeats after a shocked silence. "Very generous, my lady. Do I have fifty-five?"

"Sixty," the portly man barks, glaring at me.

I glare right back. "Sixty-five."

Ismeni sighs as if in resignation, then squares her shoulders and faces the portly man with a dazzling smile.

"Lord Bion, surely you don't mean to deprive the princess of her prize?"

Ismeni doesn't shout, doesn't even seem to raise her voice, but her gentle reprimand draws the entire garden's attention. The portly man jerks back as if struck, then peers at me. His eyes widen.

"Princess, forgive me," he stammers. "I didn't recognize you."

I only stare at him, unprepared for the abrupt change in his demeanor. I have no notion at all of what to say, so I don't say anything. That seems to work just as well.

"Sixty-five marks, then, to the Rose Princess," the red man cries, after a moment's uncomfortable silence. "Congratulations, my lady."

My stomach drops. It's done. The thrall is mine. As I step forward to claim my property, strength drains from my legs until I think I might collapse. My hand trembles as I reach for the golden-haired thrall. I can't do it. If I put my hand on her and feel the warmth of her skin, I won't be able to remember that it's a doll in my grasp, not a girl. I turn the reach into a gesture to follow me, which the thrall does without even a flicker of reluctance. Without a flicker of anything.

"I'm sorry," I whisper, too low for any but her to hear.

A beaming clerk waits for me in an antechamber, his freckled face creased in a smile.

"Congratulations, Princess," he says. "An excellent choice indeed. Come, sit. I have information you must hear."

I sit on a padded bench and smooth my hands uncertainly over my skirts. But I jerk as the clerk seizes the thrall and, quite without warning, hikes up her skirts. She doesn't even flinch.

"Here," he says, pointing to the star-burst pattern burned into her hip, "is the brand of the House of Light and Shadow. It isn't only a mark of origin. This brand is what allows a thrall to produce Light. I hope you'll forgive me for burdening you with the technical details, but I wish you to understand the importance of this mark. The brand absorbs the energy produced by the thrall's body and concentrates it into usable Light. It is imperative that this brand never be damaged or removed. If you wish to imprint the thrall with your own sign, the iron must be placed elsewhere."

"I don't—that won't be necessary," I mutter, sickened at the thought.

"Very well. There is another caution I must impress upon you," the clerk goes on. "A thrall is a great asset to your household and station, but ownership of a thrall does carry some risk. You must be vigilant. Watch for any signs of unusual activity or expression—a smile, a tear, disobedience or independent action, any sign of humanity. Our mages have done their work well. It is easy to forget that they are not human, especially for a tenderhearted lady like yourself. But you must remember that thralls have no spirit, no soul, no intellect. If a thrall acts as a human, it's because a human is pulling the strings. You especially must exercise caution, as close as you are to the king. If you see anything that causes you disquiet, send for the House of Light and Shadow immediately."

I shiver, thinking of the stories I've heard all my life of Spiritwalkers invading a thrall's body and using it for ill. Rowan's own parents were killed by one such villain.

"Do you understand, Princess?" the clerk asks, finally letting the thrall's skirts fall.

"I understand." I swallow and force myself to look at the thrall, who stands impassively even with the clerk's hand lingering possessively on her hip. I look away. "Are we done here?"

"Ah." The clerk coughs delicately. "There is yet the matter of payment, Princess."

I bite my lip. I'm not sure how much coin Ismeni brought, but I know my bid was far higher than anything she would have expected or accounted for. Still, as people constantly seem to be reminding me, I am a princess. Surely that must count for something.

"You will send the bill to the palace, will you not?"

"Not for a purchase such as this," the clerk replies. "We require assurances of liability. Signatures."

"But the money you don't require right this moment," I press. The clerk still hasn't taken his hand from the thrall's body.

"No, but—"

"Then show me where you require my sign," I say. I pull a rose pendant from inside my dress. "I have my seal here."

The clerk stares at me as if affronted. "You are a lady. I require your agent's seal and signature."

"Why?" I demand, truly annoyed now. I want to slap the clerk's hand away from the thrall. More importantly, I want to leave this place.

"A woman cannot be held accountable to a contract such as this, being ill-equipped to make financial decisions," the clerk says stiffly.

"That's ridiculous," I say with a snort. "Women make financial decisions all the time. They buy property, run businesses—"

"I should hate to argue with you, Princess," the clerk says. "I cannot release this thrall into your care without a qualified seal and signature."

"Arismendi, what is taking so long?"

I turn and sigh in relief as Ismeni swept into the room with the dark-haired little thrall in tow.

"This—man—says I can't sign for my own property," I huff.

"It isn't *your* property," the man says coolly. "The king is your guardian, and so the thrall belongs to him."

At this, my anger threatens to bubble over. "I don't even want the stupid thing, but I'm told I must have a thrall of *my own*. The ownership is intended to be mine."

"Nevertheless, legally—"

"Do not trouble yourself," Ismeni interrupts, her voice firm but offset—or perhaps augmented—by a sweet smile. "Our guardsman will provide the sign and seal. Go and fetch him here, if you please. He's just outside."

The clerk frowns. "A guardsman, my lady? But—"

"My brother, then," Ismeni says, impatience creeping into her tone for the first time. "He'll be at the warehouse with my father...the owner of this auction house."

"Oh." He blinks once, twice, then the color falls out of his face. "*Oh.*"

"Take your time," Ismeni says with a sweet smile. "We'll wait."

The clerk turns and hurries away, almost running. I throw myself down on a bench, more annoyed than ever. Ismeni sits beside me and carefully arranges her skirts.

"We are fortunate for a small delay," Ismeni says, her voice low. "I wanted to speak with you before anything is signed. Are you certain this is the thrall you want?"

I sigh in exasperation. "I don't want a thrall at all. This one will do."

"Then perhaps you'd consider exchanging it for another?"

"Why?" I ask, curious now in spite of myself.

Ismeni is silent for a long moment, then speaks with a certain reluctance. "She is... very well crafted. Whatever woman she was modeled after was very beautiful."

"So?" I shoot her an amused glance. "Surely you don't think I might become jealous of her beauty."

"There is Hadrian to think of," Ismeni goes on, looking at me as if she expects me to grasp some hidden message.

I sigh again, more deeply this time. "Ismeni, please speak plainly. I'm too tired for veiled words."

Ismeni lets out a sharp breath through her nose. "Wicked child. You force me into vulgarity, and I do not appreciate it. Very well, then. Such beauty may tempt your husband to take the thrall to his bed instead of his wife."

For a moment, this doesn't seem like such a bad thing. But then shame floods me. No matter what anyone says, I simply can't see a toy in place of a girl, and the idea of sending another girl unwillingly to a man's bed in my place fills me with disgust.

"I can't believe that was your intent," Ismeni says. "Though some women do encourage such behavior. My father hopes—as do I—that yours will be a happy marriage. It will be difficult. I won't deny that. My brother is... spirited. Distractions like this beauty will only make it harder to cultivate the bond between you."

Until now, I haven't given much thought to the more personal aspects of my impending betrothal. I haven't let myself, not wanting my courage to desert me completely. But with our agreement now public, I'll be expected to spend more time with him. Talk to him. Dance with him. And, eventually, wed and bed him.

"What am I to do, then?" I ask. "You say I must have a thrall, and they were all pretty."

"Not as pretty as this one," Ismeni says. "Lord Bion sought this one for himself, as you know. He's willing to exchange—"

"No." I stand up. "No. You suspect that my husband might use this thrall for his own pleasure, but I *know*—and I think you do, too—that Lord Bion intends the same. We'll take our chances with Hadrian."

Ismeni looks pained. "Arismendi, I think this is a mistake."

"Maybe it is," I allow. "But for better or worse, the thrall is now under my care."

"Arismendi—"

"No."

I look at the thrall and accept the awful truth.

"She's mine."

Chapter Fourteen

Hadrian arrives sometime later with Norrin at his side. Norrin greets us with a kiss on his daughter's cheek, then mine. Hadrian ignores us. He walks around my newly purchased thrall, looking her over and nodding enthusiastically to himself. To my relief (and, I think, Ismeni's) his attitude is one of professional appreciation, without the lecherous avarice I saw in Lord Bion. Finally, he steps back and beams at me.

"An excellent choice, darling," he says. "I commend you."

"Yes, well done," Norrin agrees. "You've taken your first step toward becoming a lady, and I have taken the liberty of arranging your first step toward becoming a school-mistress."

I frown. "What do you mean?"

"You need premises for your school, do you not?" Norrin says with a smile. "I've scheduled a few tours and interviews for you to begin your search."

"Really?" I hug him impulsively. "Thank you, Norrin. When do we begin?"

"This afternoon," he says, laughing as I gasp in delight. "What, did you think I would try to hold you back? Procrastinate and hope you get bored or change your mind? My dear, you wound me. I want you to succeed. I hope, in time, you will come to truly believe that."

"I do," I say quickly. "Of course I do, Norrin. I just—I don't know, I thought it would take more time."

"It will take plenty of time," he says, shaking a finger at me. "That's why you must begin at once. In fact, you really ought to go now. Ismeni and I will deal with the thrall. Hadrian, if you would—?"

Hadrian, who has been inspecting his sister's purchase, looks up. "Hm? Oh, yes." He hands me a note and goes back to his inspection. I take the note and open it, revealing what appears to be a list of names and places.

"Lord Joram," I say, squinting at Norrin's cramped, messy handwriting. "But he's the House Premier, isn't he? What are we meeting with him for?"

"The House of Light and Shadow has rooms and outbuildings that they may be willing to rent," Norrin explains. "As well as young mages who may be willing to teach."

"I see."

I bite my lip, trying not to let my unease show, but Norrin knows me well.

"Just go and have a look," he says. "See what he's willing to offer. You have several appointments this afternoon, so you needn't feel pressured to agree to anything. In fact, I would strongly advise you not to make any agreements at all today. Just gather information and impressions, and, if you can find them, additional leads."

"Yes." I let out a breath, and my nerves settle somewhat. "Alright. I can do that."

"Of course you can, my dear." He pats my shoulder. "Come and tell me about it later. For now, I must bid you farewell, or you'll be late."

Hadrian, finally done with his examination of the thralls, takes my arm with a proprietary air that makes me grind my teeth. "Yes, come along, darling."

Hadrian tucks my hand into his elbow and tows me away, through the crowd of customers and onto the street where Rowan has been waiting. When he sees Hadrian, Rowan's face twists into a scowl. I sigh. Hadrian's company is going to be uncomfortable enough without Rowan antagonizing him. He doesn't even have to say anything. Rowan has a peculiar talent for irking people without saying a single word, and I have no doubt he'll be exercising that talent to its fullest extent today.

"Where are we off to, Ari?" Rowan asks, his glance daring my betrothed to object to his familiarity.

Hadrian, thankfully, only looks away with a disdainful sniff.

"The House of Light and Shadow," I tell him, and his brows lift in pleased surprise. "We're looking for premises to house the school."

I show him Norrin's list, and his brows all but disappear into his scalp.

"You're trying to see all these today?" he asks. I nod, and he sighs. "Well, we'd best get started then."

"You seem familiar with the route, Rowan No-name," Hadrian says as Rowan leads us up the steep path to the House. "Did they let you sweep the floors as a boy? Clean the privies?"

"Rowan studied there with Luca," I say, frowning. "He graduated with distinction."

"I am astonished that their standards have fallen so low," Hadrian says. "I must have a word with the Premier."

I dart a glance at Rowan and wait for the retort that must surely come. Everyone knows Hadrian was tutored privately because he was too soft and spoiled for the rigors of the House's academy. But Rowan merely smiles and keeps walking. A moment later, I see his fingers twitch and flex against his thigh, and Hadrian falls flat on his face in the dirt.

"Careful, my lord," he says blandly as Hadrian picks himself up, face burning. "The path is just a bit uneven through here."

I bite my lip, not daring to look at either Hadrian or Rowan. If Costi were here, he'd want me to say something diplomatic and gracious, perhaps even chastise Rowan. But Costi isn't here, and Hadrian is a pompous snot who had it coming.

My smile fades. He's a pompous snot I promised to marry, and making sport of him isn't going to make that any easier.

What to do? I can't apologize or make Rowan apologize himself, and not only because Rowan would rather eat a bucket of rotted eels. Any sort of apology would force Hadrian to admit that Rowan had gotten the better of him and thus increase the insult. But doing nothing doesn't seem like a good idea, either.

Blight, how does Costi manage this diplomacy nonsense? I kick a stone off the path and watch as it clatters off the edge of the cliff. The House looms above us atop the ridge, its blocky towers flanking its sides like an eagle's wings. The impression of menacing strength only grows as we climb higher. By the time we reach the gates, I feel as small and insignificant as a gnat.

"It's the casting, what you're feeling," Rowan murmurs as he ushers me through the gate. "The House preaches strength above all things. Power is woven into every pebble of this place. It takes some getting used to."

I rub my arms, looking around at the stern gray walls and even sterner faces. Does Norrin really think this a suitable place for young girls? How can anyone learn anything in a place like this? Everything is so hard, so rigid... and cold. But that isn't fair. Up here, outside the protection of the Terrace, the natural chill of spring prevails. No doubt the House mages believe the comfort of a constant climate is a weakness.

I turn to Hadrian. "I'm not sure—"

But he isn't listening.

"There's the Premier," he says, and strides forward to greet the lord and master of the House of Light and Shadow.

Premier Joram is a large man. He always seems to take up just a bit more space than is comfortable, both with his body and his presence. His belly is round and tight, like a drum, and his shoulders, though heavily padded with fat, are broad. His gray hair is pulled back in a tight knot, his face framed by a well-groomed beard.

"Princess." Joram greets me with a deep bow. "You honor us with your presence."

"The honor is mine," I say, fighting the urge to look to Rowan for direction. "I appreciate how busy you must be. We won't take up much of your time."

"Nonsense," Joram says. "It's not every day the Rose Princess arrives on our doorstep. And young Hadrian! I haven't seen you since you were a boy. Your esteemed father tells me your instruction in the Craft has been superb despite your absence from these halls."

"No expense was spared," Hadrian assures him, his chest puffing ever so slightly.

I catch Rowan's eye-roll out of the corner of my own eye and step on his foot in warning.

"This way," Joram says. "Lord Hadrian, there are several projects in particular I wished to show you which I think you and your father will find most interesting."

Throughout the whole of the tour, neither the Premier nor my betrothed speaks a single word to me or makes any reference to the school. If I had any interest in the House as a site, I would have been enraged. As it is, I'm merely irritated at the time Hadrian is wasting quizzing Lord Joram about a new avenue of research. Something about a more cost-effective method of manufacturing amulets. Amulets emit Light, as thralls do, but not as much. An amulet also wears out after a few months, where a thrall's body generates Light as long as the thrall lives. On the Terrace, there are so many thralls that there's Light everywhere, for anyone to use. But those in the Upper City and Midtown carry amulets if they can't afford a thrall.

"Rowan," I whisper as Hadrian and Joram pore over a set of scrolls spread across a table. "Do something."

"Says the princess to her lowly guard," Rowan mutters. "You do something."

"Says the guard to the woman in a house of men," I retort. "You forget, guardsman. A lady of standing never speaks for herself. It isn't *seemly*. Just get us out of here, will you?"

"As my princess commands," he says, and clears his throat. "My lords, forgive me. The princess has a number of appointments to keep today. We must take our leave."

"So soon!" Joram gives me an oily smile. "The time has gone too quickly in your pleasant company. You must visit us again, when you have more time to spare."

I can't think of a single thing to say in response to this absurd falsehood, and so I merely nod. "Thank you, Lord Premier. For your time."

If not your attention, I add mentally. I certainly received none of that. But it doesn't matter. Jessa will never set foot inside these walls.

But if not here, where? I fish the list out of my pocket and frown. All three buildings are in the Upper City, right in the thick of the theater district—the loudest, busiest sector of the City. That won't do at all for a place of learning. Norrin wouldn't put them on the list without a reason, though, and I don't want to look as if I'm spurning his help.

I sigh and tuck the list back into my belt-purse, then realize that it was probably rude to turn my attention away from Lord Joram so completely and without acknowledging his response. But I needn't have worried. He and Hadrian are deep in conversation once more, leaving me to trail behind them as we make our way back through the labyrinthine halls.

My step quickens as we approach the outer gates. Stars, get me out of this place! But as we cross the courtyard, the gates fly open and a red-robed mage strides through, followed by a contingent of guards dressed in black and white—the House's colors. At least ten guards have swords and spears trained on a mousy-looking man who stumbles forward on bleeding feet, his chest heaving. His eyes are bleak with exhaustion and despair, but something in his gaze and the set of his jaw makes me shiver.

"Princess, look away," Lord Joram says, looking genuinely distressed as he ushers us in another direction. "I hope you'll forgive us. Spiritwalkers don't work around our schedules, I'm afraid."

"Of course," I murmur, surreptitiously peering around Lord Joram's bulk. "Does this happen often?"

"Our investigators are very diligent, Princess," he says, not answering my question. "And our guards are well able to keep these criminals in check once captured. You have nothing to fear."

"Not exactly the environment you're looking for, is it?" Rowan murmurs.

I grimace. "Definitely not."

So we leave the House and descend into the City, where Hadrian insists on stopping to inspect his father's auction house and then for a drink at the most expensive wine house he can find. The tours are a disaster, each building more unsuitable than the last, and all somehow even worse than the House of Light and Shadow.

All through the final tour, Hadrian and the building's owner laugh together about the absurdity of the project and the foolishness of women. By the time we're through, my jaw aches from the strain of keeping my mouth shut. A muscle is twitching dangerously in Rowan's jaw, and I'm half tempted to let him do whatever horrible thing he's so obviously longing to do to Hadrian. Norrin might still give me the money if his son dies in a tragic accident that can't be traced to me or mine. If anyone can cover up a bloody murder, surely a Shadowfoot can.

But I can't let him do that.

Surely not.

"I could be wrong," I say as we leave the last building. "But I imagine our position as buyers would be taken more seriously if you didn't openly mock the work we're trying to do."

"I was establishing a rapport," Hadrian replies, and patted my arm. "Leave the business dealings to me, darling. It's what I'm here for."

With effort, I resist the urge to remind him that he is to act as my agent, and as far as I'm concerned an agent's role is to be quiet and provide a signature where I decide a signature is needed.

"Indeed," I say through gritted teeth. "In any case, our business seems to be concluded for the day, so I suggest we return to the Terrace."

"Yes, we must ready ourselves for tonight's banquet," Hadrian says, brightening. "You know, in the future it would really be best if I made these outings alone. We are quite behind schedule."

At this, Rowan's composure breaks and he lets out an incredulous snort.

"You have something to say?" Hadrian inquires icily.

I shoot Rowan a look, and he shoots me one right back.

"No, my lord," he says, with exaggerated politeness. "Not a thing, my lord."

I sigh and rub my forehead. "Let's just go, shall we?"

Rowan bows and indicates the King's Road with a sweep of his arm. "This way, my lady, my lord."

Hadrian gives him a look of intense dislike and strides past him. I punch Rowan's shoulder as hard as I can.

"Ow! What was that for?"

I glare at him. "You are *not helping*. Can you please try not to make this harder than it has to be?"

"Can you try not to act like such a mouse?" he returns. "You're letting him treat you like a thrall!"

"I need him on our side," I say. "I can't do this on my own."

"You could if you weren't a princess."

"But I *am* a princess," I remind him, not without bitterness. "I need an agent to get anything done, and Costi and Norrin both say he's it."

"The king could change his mind," Rowan insists.

"And where would I be then?" I demand. "Hadrian is going to be my husband. Even if he's not my agent, he's going to be in my life *for the rest of my life.* I've given up any hope of a happy marriage, but a productive one may still be within my grasp. I'd like to preserve that possibility."

Rowan looks away, angry, and I fight down my own anger. What right does he have to be angry over something that is happening to me when I am denied the luxury? For a moment, I hate him—and my brother, and Norrin, and whoever decided that 'well-bred' has to mean 'helpless'.

"Come on, then," Rowan says finally, and turns away.

I move to follow, but a flicker of red catches my eye. *Sadra*—she's across the street, staring at me through the crowd. The wind catches the tail of her bright red sash, blowing it across her body and her curls across her face. She grins at me with a spark in her eye that seems to fly straight into my chest and ignite.

"You go," I find myself telling Rowan. "Cover for me."

"Not a chance," he says, following my gaze. "It's not safe."

"I'll be fine," I said. "Sadra is a Temple Companion. She can defend me as well as you—maybe even better."

"I was talking about me and the young lord, actually," he says. "As you're so concerned for his welfare."

"You can control yourself," I say. "I believe in you. Cover for me, please?"

Heat creeps up my neck and into my face, and Rowan looks again at Sadra. "This is the same Temple Companion I found you giggling with? The same Companion who was so concerned for you the night of your betrothal that she spurned Lord Orean to go after you?"

"Did she?" I ask, absurdly pleased.

Rowan rolls his eyes but gives me a little push. "Just go."

"Thanks."

I squeeze his arm and dart across the street.

"Hello," I say breathlessly.

"I hoped you'd see me," she says, a shy smile spreading over her face. "And that you'd come. I thought I probably shouldn't interrupt."

"Next time, you should," I say. "Nothing would please me more."

She laughs. "The courtship is off to a thorny start, I take it."

"You could say that. Though to be fair the thorns aren't all his."

"Whose, then?" She cocks her head. "I can't believe they're yours."

"No, not mine," I say, though I almost wish they were. "My guard, Rowan. He's my brother's best friend and feels entitled to air his opinions more freely than he should."

"Ah," Sadra says. "Is it jealousy, do you think?" Seeing my incomprehension, she adds, "Does he want you for himself?"

"Want me—no, of course not!" I frown. "At least, I don't *think*... rocks, I hope not. That would be terrible! Do you really think he might?"

"No," Sadra says with a grin. "I mean, I suppose it's possible, but I just wanted to see what you thought of the idea. For my own selfish reasons."

My skin, already flushed with her nearness, blazes with something halfway between fear and excitement. I try to muster something clever to say in response, but my tongue has gone heavy and hot, like the spicy sausages Luca loves to buy from street vendors. Sadra gives me a cheeky grin.

"You're enjoying this, aren't you?" I ask when my tongue has finally remembered its purpose.

Her grin widens. "Oh, immensely. I could happily spend the rest of the day making you blush. But I shall take pity on you and ask you instead what brought you into the City today."

I don't mean to tell her everything, but I do. She already knows about Jessa and Pia, if not by name, so I tell her about my hopelessly unproductive afternoon, which leads me backward to my horrible morning at the auction house, then further backward to Costi's directive that I learn how to be a lady, then even further backward to my deal with Norrin, then forward to my fears about Hadrian's role in my future, then sideways to Costi's struggles, and then somehow to Luca and Rowan and our childhood running amok on the Terrace. By the time I finally run out of words, I feel as if I'd poured my entire life into her ear.

"I'm sorry," I say. "I didn't mean to—"

"Sorry!" Sadra shakes her head. "I don't know when I've heard a more interesting story. I always thought this school of yours was a wonderful idea, and I want to help."

"I don't know what to say." I look away, flustered. "Do you truly—I mean, are you sure?"

"Of course! I want to help." She smiles. "Truly and sincerely."

My answering smile feels silly, too big for my face. But somehow, I don't care.

"I might have some ideas about a building for you," Sadra goes on. "I'll look into a few things and keep my eyes open. And if you need anything, just say the word."

"How?" I ask, then blush. "I mean, how can I send word to you? You live in Villa Glory. You're Companion to Councilor Orean. I can't just write to you. People will talk."

"Ah." Sadra frowns, then fishes a piece of jade out of her pocket. "Put this in the pool at the base of the Mare's Tail at sunrise, and I'll know to meet you there at sunset. I have one, too, and I'll do the same if I come up with anything."

I take the jade piece, which is actually a smooth disc carved with the figure of a rose. The tiny thing fills me with such joy, I could happily stand here all day just staring at it. But I've already fallen too far behind Rowan and Hadrian—not to mention behind schedule.

"Thank you," I say, folding my fingers protectively over the disc. "It means more than I can say. But I'd better go."

Sadra smiles. "Goodbye for now, then."

Reluctantly, I make my way up the wide, grand way of King's Road. After only a few dozen steps, however, I turn and look for the telltale splash of red. Sadra is still there, watching me even as I watch her. She raises her hand in farewell and slips into the crowd, but not before I catch sight of the words on her lips.

See you soon.

Stars, I hope so.

Chapter Fifteen

My thrall—rocks, even thinking of it makes me sick—isn't in my rooms when I return, nor anywhere in the palace. Apparently Ismeni sent her directly to some facility where thralls are trained to serve. The reprieve is a relief after such a taxing day.

But the next day is just as taxing, and the next even worse. Every lead on a school building turns into a dead end. Every day brings a new smirking face, a new mocking comment veiled in soothing platitudes. Hadrian, who is meant to support me in my efforts, smirks and chuckles right along with my detractors. It's maddening. It's humiliating.

But not surprising.

The Rose Moon comes and goes, and spring warms into summer. My thrall returns to me with the name Sparrow, which I can only assume is an (entirely vain) attempt to downplay her beauty. Her presence in my life is as uncomfortable as I imagined it would be, but it's not without advantages. Preparing for banquets, for instance, is much faster and easier than it was before. So I do my best to ignore my misgivings and focus on my mission.

Norrin, far from discouraged by our lack of progress in finding a home for the school, advises me to simply keep looking and turn my attention to the next task: teachers. My first step, he says, is to prepare a list of desired qualifications and questions in preparation for the interview process. I make the mistake of mentioning it to Jessa, who of course has so many questions and so many opinions that her weekly lesson feels a bit like standing under a waterfall.

"How many teachers will there be? Will you be teaching any lessons? You have to teach at least one, it's your school, you can't—"

"Jessa." I reach over the table and pinch her lips shut with my fingers. "I am *trying* to teach you a lesson right now. Can we focus on that? Please?"

"How can I?" Jessa cries passionately, pulling away. "There's so much happening, and I want to *know*!"

"There's nothing to know," I say. "I haven't even started interviewing candidates yet. I promise, the moment there's something to tell, I'll tell you."

"Can I interview the teachers with you?" she asks. "It would be helpful to have a student's perspective, wouldn't it?"

"Absolutely not," I say. "We're lucky *I'm* even allowed to be there."

Jessa frowns. "But it's your school. And you're the princess."

"I'm a woman," I say, trying to keep the bitterness out of my voice. "And that means my very presence makes negotiating more difficult, but I can't let Hadrian do it on his own. So, no, you can't come. What you can do is focus and get through this manuscript."

Jessa pouts but eventually settles down enough to absorb what the writer of the manuscript has to say about the difference between a lie and a falsehood. Before I leave, however, she insists on writing out her own list of qualities and criteria to guide my hiring decisions. She doesn't let me leave until I review it, either.

"Smart," I read, "Patient, kind, helpful, good at listening... believes in us and what we're doing."

"It's a good list, isn't it?" Jessa asks, her voice anxious. "We don't want anyone without all of those, do we?"

"It's a good list," I say around a lump in my throat. "It's a really good list, Jessa. I'll do my best."

The moment I return to the Terrace, I send word to Hadrian and Norrin that I want to begin our search in earnest and that I would like some guidance on where and how to find suitable candidates. When I hear from Norrin, I find that he took that to mean that I wanted him to do the work himself. Within days, he has arranged for a full day of interview appointments, all with recent graduates of the House Academy looking for positions.

"They won't be the cream of the crop, exactly," he warns me. "But this is quite an unconventional endeavor, and we can't expect to compete with more established schools for the best candidates."

"How encouraging," I mutter.

"Stay positive," Norrin says. "You might find someone unconventional himself. Someone who thinks and sees beyond the confines of the House and has suffered for it, who would be grateful—excited, even—for an opportunity to do something different. You might find someone wonderful."

"I might," I allow, though inwardly, I add, *But I doubt it.*

Hadrian and I set off once again for the House of Light and Shadow, with Rowan as our guard. Luckily, no one falls in the dirt this time, though there is some sniping. I don't know how much more of this I can take. Surely Costi must see that Hadrian is just plain unsuitable as an agent. Far from bringing us closer, the endeavor has simply made me certain that I am going to be miserable in my marriage—which makes me all the more determined to see my project through, so I'll have something good in my life once I'm handed over to my boor of a husband.

The House steward greets us this time, the Premier being otherwise occupied. He leads us to a stark, plain chamber that Rowan says is used to greet guests. Other Terrace dwellers might be put off, even offended, by the lack of comfort, but I don't mind. Austerity is the way of the House. Beauty in simplicity, strength. I take no issue with their overall philosophy or aesthetic, just with their attitude toward the "weaker" sex. No matter what Norrin says, I know how today's interviews are likely to end.

I'm right. One candidate after another comes and goes with barely any discussion at all. I get the impression they only showed up as a favor to Norrin, or to avoid any semblance of offense to the king, my brother.

But then there's a young man who stays for more than five minutes and actually listens to me when I explain what I want of him. My heart lifts, and I begin to hope that maybe Norrin was right. Maybe I've found someone who fits that last criterion on Jessa's list. Maybe there *is* someone special hidden away here in this barren fortress. What was his name? Kern, that's it.

"What sort of curriculum are you planning?" Kern asks, leaning forward in his chair.

"Mathematics, history, and natural philosophy will form the core," I say, before Hadrian can speak. "I consider economics to be a natural extension of mathematics, and students will combine their historical studies with exercises in rhetoric and written composition. They will receive some instruction in the divine arts, of course, as well as self-defense." I ignore Hadrian's eye-roll and focus on Kern.

"And Lightcrafting, I presume," Kern prompts.

"Oh—yes, certainly," I say, belatedly realizing that of course a House acolyte would expect as much. Blight, I'll have to find a thrall for the school, or there will be no guarantee of Light to craft with.

"I'll do it," Kern announces, and I give a cry of delight. "For thirty marks each moon."

My cry turns into a gasp. "*Thirty—*"

"Thirty seems reasonable enough," Hadrian agrees.

"Reasonable!" I round on Hadrian, furious. "The House begged your father to teach at the Academy, and their best offer was twenty."

"Well, it's quite a different situation, sweet one," Hadrian says, and his patronizing tone makes me want to stab him where he stands. "We must account for the extra work. It will be quite difficult, after all. One can't expect girls to grasp the material as readily as young men would. Not to mention the damage to Kern's reputation. It's only fair to compensate him."

Kern smiles at Hadrian. "I'm glad you understand, my lord. It's an interesting proposition, to be sure, but it *is* a risk."

"I see," I say icily. "Well, thank you for your time, Kern. We'll be in touch."

"You're making a mistake," Hadrian warns me as we descend the trail into the Terrace. "You should have made him the offer on the spot. He'll think better of it, now, and refuse you when you ask—or ask for more money."

"I'm not going to ask," I say. "Thirty marks! It's ridiculous. And I'm not hiring anyone who thinks teaching girls is beneath him."

Hadrian laughs. "Then you'll never hire anyone at all."

I want to argue, or hit him, or maybe have Rowan hurl him over the edge of the cliff. But I can't—not only because Costi wouldn't approve, but because I'm afraid he's right.

Is this how it's going to be? Can I only succeed by making morally question-able compromises and giving my students less than they deserve? But if that's the case, what will this school actually be teaching them? That they should accept scraps and let their values bend when it's convenient?

No. No, there has to be another way, and I'll find it. I just need some time and some thought. And maybe a snack.

And so I find myself a snack and take some time to think, and then I get to work. I spend the next three days talking to the ladies of the Terrace and Upper City, gathering names and addresses for the private tutors who teach their daughters. Then I write to those tutors and explain what I want and what I'm willing to give in return. But then a week goes by, and one by one the tutors send in their replies and regrets. They can't possibly leave their current students, they say, not for any money—and certainly not for what I'm offering, which is significantly less than what they make from private clients.

My one consolation is Sadra, who meets me at the Mare's Tail when I leave the jade piece, just as she promised.

"I hope you need something that I can help you with," she says as we lean against the mist-damp rail of the bridge. "None of my ideas for the school building came to anything, I'm afraid."

"Do you know any teachers?" I ask hopefully. "The only person who has shown even the slightest interest is a House mage, and he's asking for *thirty marks* per moon, just because the students are girls. He thinks he needs to be compensated for the extra work and damage to his reputation. Can you believe it?"

"Sadly, I can," Sadra replies with a humorless laugh. "We get those types in the Temple, too." She puts on a sanctimonious face and a deep, smug voice. "'Well, male dancers have more power and more difficult maneuvers, so of course they get paid more.'"

"What!" I gasp in outrage and sit up. "And the Temple Mother allows this?"

Sadra shrugs. "She can't control what citizens are willing to offer. And she can't negotiate directly, either. Not legally. She's a lady of standing, like you."

"I hate it," I cry so passionately I surprise even myself. "This notion that just because I have breasts, I can't possibly know what I'm doing, that I'm not fit to do things for myself."

"I do, too," Sadra says with a weary shrug. "But this is the world we live in."

I peer at her. "You don't really mean that."

"No," Sadra says. "But shouting about it does no good. You have to do something—usually on the sly."

"But what can I do?" I ask miserably.

Sadra cocks her head. "Quite a lot, if half of what I've heard is true. Tell me again what you're planning to teach these girls?"

"Logic, mathematics, economics, history, composition, rhetoric, natural philosophy, the divine arts, and self-defense," I rattle off.

"And you've been teaching your Jessa such things all along, haven't you?"

I bite my lip. "Jessa said that, too. But I'm not—"

"Not what?" Sadra presses. "Not capable? Not qualified? Do you know the material or not?"

"Mathematics are my weakest point," I say. "At the rate Jessa is going, she'll need a new teacher within a year. Natural philosophy even sooner, but if she had to she could continue largely on her own if I find her appropriate material to work with. History, composition, and rhetoric would be no trouble, nor would self-defense—I can make Rowan do that." I gave a snort of laughter. "Forget about the divine arts, though. I'd be a disaster."

"It opens up a lot of options if you're not looking for one person who can do everything," Sadra said. "It'll cost you one way or another, whether it's your time or your money, but if you end up with good quality, at least it'll be worth it, right?"

"Yes, it would." I consider her. "You received training in the other arts as well, didn't you? Enough to provide a foundation?"

"I did," Sadra says, her face falling. "And I would love to teach, but I have… other commitments that I can't neglect. I'm sure we could recruit someone, though. Lady Ismeni, even. I've heard her sing, and she's not like most Catchsongs I've met. She doesn't just rely on her Gift. Her technique is flawless."

"Alright, then," I say decisively. "I'll teach history, composition, and rhetoric, and Rowan can see to the self-defense. I'll ask Ismeni about the Divine Arts. I could make do with the rest if I needed to, at least until we find somebody suitable. Though I *would* like to find somebody straight off, if only to ease some of the load." I make a face. "Costi and Norrin will never let me out of my social duties entirely."

"You're probably right," Sadra says. "But I think they can be persuaded to bend a little. So. Between you, Rowan, and Ismeni, that just leaves the numerical arts. Much more manageable."

"Maybe I should be casting an even wider net," I muse. "Proper teachers clearly aren't interested, and I'm tired of chasing them. But there are a lot of working people with the skills I need, even if they don't have teaching experience. I'll speak with Pia about it and see if she knows anyone good with numbers."

"Perfect," Sadra says with a grin. "Have I helped?"

"You have," I tell her. "It's so nice to have someone to talk to about this. Someone who really wants to help me."

"Doesn't the king? Councilor Norrin? Your guard?"

"It's different," I say with a frown. "Costi has more important things to worry about, and Norrin keeps *doing* things instead of helping me do them myself.

Rowan is helpful, in his way, but he helps because it's his job, not because he agrees with what I'm doing and wants to do it, too. I like talking to you about this. It's like—like having a friend."

"It's not *like* having a friend," Sadra disagrees. "It *is* having a friend. I like you, Ari."

"But you don't *like* me," I say before I can stop myself, then blush so deeply my face feels scalded.

Sadra gives me a grin balanced on a knife's edge of sly and sensual. "Don't I?"

"You haven't tried to—I mean, I thought you might want to—" I break off and look away, trying to marshal my thoughts.

"Want to what?" Sadra asks, her grin widening.

I take a deep breath and then face her again. "I thought—I hoped you might want to kiss me again."

"I do," Sadra says simply.

"Then... then why haven't you?" I force myself to keep my eyes on her face, though every nerve screams to look—or run—away. "You could have left your jade coin. No one comes here but us. You could have kissed me again."

My courage runs out, and I drop my gaze to her hands.

"I could have," she agrees. "But I was waiting for you."

"Why?" I look up, shocked.

"Maybe it's because you're a princess, and I was intimidated," she says, shifting toward me. "Maybe I was afraid to take you from your work. Or maybe I just wanted *you* to kiss *me*." She leans in close and trails a finger across my knuckles. She's so close that her curls tickle my cheek as she goes on, "I'm a Companion. It's my job to take charge. To make my patron feel wanted. Maybe I want to feel that for a change. Or maybe... "

"Maybe?" I ask breathlessly.

"Maybe I like seeing you squirm," she finishes with a grin, pulling away. Then she shrugs. "Or maybe it's all that rolled together. And also the fact that your position means a misstep on my part could cost me my head. In any case, I'm afraid you're in charge from here, Princess. If you want something from me, you'll have to ask for it."

I gulp, my face flaming once more. "That might be difficult."

"Will you try anyway?" she asks, softly now, almost pleading.

I look up, and I see her blush for the first time. My heart pounds as I reach out and take her hand.

"Yes," I say. "I'll try."

Chapter Sixteen

Sadra and I are reluctant to part. But part we must, she to fulfill her duties as Orean's Companion, and I for my lady lessons with Ismeni. I try not to think too hard about either Sadra's duties or my own as I make my way to the palace gardens. Ismeni awaits me on a small bench, arranging a bouquet of flowers in her hand. She looks up with a smile as I approach.

"Sit with me," she says. "How is your charm work?"

"Nonexistent," I say, taking my place beside her. "I know how to sense Light, but I stopped going to my lessons before I ever learned to do anything with it."

Ismeni's brows draw together. "I knew you were unskilled, but I thought—well, never mind. We'll start at the beginning." She plucks a petal from one of the roses in her bouquet and holds it out to me. "You're going to make it float."

"How?" I resist the urge to lean away from the petal—and the task.

Ismeni cocks her head. "However you like. A skilled mage can affect objects, even people, around him with his will alone. Most of us, however, require tools and tricks to focus our intentions. I like to sing."

I make a face. "I'm—um, not very good at singing."

"You don't have to sing," she says with a smile. "But perhaps a rhyme?"

I shrug. "I suppose."

Feeling silly, I repeat after her the simple couplet: *Rose bud, rose bud, fly to my will. Rose bud, rose bud, yield to my skill.*

Nothing happens.

So I try again, and again. And again.

"Is this really necessary?" I ask, rubbing a hand across my forehead. "Surely if I really need Light for something that badly, I can hire somebody."

"There are a thousand little things you'll need to do that will be faster and easier with Light," Ismeni says sternly. "And even if you hire other practitioners, you need to know what can and can't be done, what's worth doing, and for how much. Managing a household is real work, Arismendi, and you need the right tools if you expect to do a good job. A lady isn't merely pretty and obedient. She must be capable. Your mother knew that, which is why she studied diligently with the best Lightcrafters the Garden had to offer."

I stifle a groan, then inwardly chastise myself for my snobbery. She's right, of course. So I try for another quarter of an hour until my head feels like it's going to split open. Ismeni finally relents, floating the rose petal away with a flick of her finger.

"You'll be able to do that and much more," she promises. "It just takes a little time and practice. Which you will do every night before bed. Agreed?"

"Agreed," I mutter wearily. I rub my eyes, then look at her. "Ismeni, can I ask you a favor?"

"You know I am yours to command, Princess," Ismeni says easily, gathering up her bouquet.

"You aren't," I say. "Friends don't give commands."

Ismeni looks up, startled, then smiles warmly and pats my cheek. "You are sweet. What is this favor, then?"

"I've decided to teach at the school myself," I say. "Not everything, but some subjects. I can't possibly teach the Divine Arts, though."

Ismeni starts to laugh, then turns it into a polite cough.

"Forgive me, Ari."

I wave away her apology. "I need someone with a firm grounding and a kind heart, and I think you'd be perfect. Well—Sadra suggested it first. She said your technique is flawless, that you don't rely only on your Gift."

"Sadra said that?" Ismeni asks, looking surprised. "Interesting."

"Yes," I say, looking at her curiously. There's something odd in her face—a tightness. It takes me a moment to realize what it means. "You don't like her?"

Ismeni smiles crookedly. "It's difficult to like the woman who shares your husband's bed."

"But... " I hesitate, unsure if we're close enough that I can say what I mean to say without giving offense. "Forgive me, but I've always gotten the impression that you don't really like him, either."

"I don't," she says, far more bluntly than I'm used to. "And in many ways I'm grateful that he has someone else to satisfy his desires. But it still stings to know I've been set aside—that no matter how beautiful or accomplished or dedicated I am, my husband has never and will never truly value me." She shook her head with a sad little laugh. "You're too young yet to understand... and I hope you never have to."

She goes quiet for a moment. I do too. I wasn't expecting such vulnerability from her. She always seems so poised and gracious, the perfect lady. But if there's one thing I'm coming to realize from my forays into Terrace society, it's that nothing is what it seems on the surface.

"So," Ismeni says briskly, shaking off her brief melancholy. "You want me to teach at your school."

"Yes." I bite my lip. "Will you? It would mean so much to me."

She sighs. "I wish I could say yes. Truly, I do."

"But?"

"Orean... " Ismeni looks away, her lips pinching. "I don't like the man—in fact, I rather despise him—but he *is* my husband. And he would be... displeased."

I wait for her to elaborate, but she doesn't. I push down my disappointment and consider the position she's in. Is Orean already 'displeased' with her for spending so much time with me? I've known for some time that Orean has nothing but disdain for my brother and his rule, but is he so petty that he would hold his wife's friendship with me against her? Can he punish her for it?

Yes, of course he can, and that's his right as her husband. He can dictate how she spends her time, and with whom. Perhaps he doesn't exercise that right because I'm the king's sister, and it isn't—yet—politically expedient to show Costi any disrespect. But if Orean ever does decide it's worth the insult, he could forbid Ismeni from seeing me, or from leaving the house at all. He could express his "displeasure" any way he liked, and no one would stop him.

"Ismeni," I say softly. "Am I making a mistake?"

She looks at me quizzically. "What do you mean?"

"Marrying Hadrian," I say. "Marrying at all."

"The king will protect you," Ismeni says, just as softly. "You know that."

I shake my head. "Even a king can't live forever. What if something happens to him?"

"I don't know," Ismeni says. "But, my dear… if it's not Hadrian, it will be someone else. You are a princess. Your marriage would never have been a question of 'if', only 'when' and 'to whom'."

"I know," I say miserably. "I know that. I thought I could do it. I thought Hadrian could change, or that I didn't really know him. But… I do know him, and he hasn't changed."

Belatedly, I remember who Hadrian is to Ismeni. Blood rushes to my face.

"I'm so sorry," I say, wringing my hands in my skirts. "I shouldn't be saying these things to you, of all people. And you've been so kind to me—"

"Ari, I'm well aware of Hadrian's shortcomings," Ismeni says dryly. "I am his elder sister, am I not?"

I search her face. "I haven't offended you?"

"No, dear," she says with a smile that soon fades. "I know who he is, and I like to think I've come to know who you are. Yours will likely never be a close match. But it's done." Ismeni tucks a stray lock of hair back into the mass of curls and braids at my neck. "Unless… you're not really considering breaking the betrothal, are you?"

For a moment, I'm overwhelmed by the urge to shout, *Yes! Yes, I changed my mind. I'm not going to marry him.* But I can't do that. I'm so, so close. Jessa is depending on me, and going back on my word now would be disastrous for Costi. Ismeni, too, is wrapped up in this. She was born a Prosper, and both she and her husband stand to gain, politically and socially, from my marriage to Hadrian. She's supposed to be preparing me for my new role as the lady of Villa Prosper. If the marriage doesn't happen, Orean could blame Ismeni. How would he express his displeasure then?

"No," I say. "No, I can't—I mean, I don't want to call it off. I'm sorry. I'll be fine. Everything will be fine."

"It will," Ismeni agreed. "You're doing a wonderful thing, Ari, don't forget that." She hesitates. "I can't promise it will be enough, not all the time. But it's not nothing, and that's more than many of us can hope for."

For the first time, I wonder if the girls of the Lower City aren't the only ones in need of rescue. I'm terrified of marriage with good reason, and I have the protection of the king himself. Women like Ismeni are at the complete mercy of their husbands, with no recourse at all. Suddenly the school seems far too small, a single drop to assuage the thirst of thousands.

"I'm sorry I can't be more involved," Ismeni says. "But I'm sure I can help find someone suitable. My old tutor, for instance—she stopped teaching on the Terrace ages ago, but your little project is novel enough that she might be interested. Shall I ask her?"

"What would I do without you, Ismeni?" I sigh.

"What we all do, my dear," Ismeni says with a faint smile. "Endure."

Chapter Seventeen

A few days later, Soren arrives with a note from Pia summoning me to the Honeysuckle. My eyes widen as they skim over the message, my heart pounding with excitement. I return to one line and read it three more times, just for the pleasure it brings.

I have your teacher.

I leap to my feet and yank open the door, fully intent on running the whole way to the Lower City. But before I can so much as step into the corridor, a small explosion of fur and kisses greets me. I stumble backward under Kirit's enthusiastic greeting, laughing in spite of myself. Luca follows and steadies me, plucking the wiggling fox out of my arms. He tucks Kirit firmly under his own arm and fishes a handkerchief out of his pocket.

"Save it," I say, wiping my face on my sleeve and peeking past him. "Where's Rowan? He's not sick, is he?"

"No, he's just doing me a favor," Luca says, his voice glum. "I needed a break from Costi."

"What's Costi done?" I ask with a frown. "Is he still pressuring you about the Captaincy?"

"Sort of," Luca admits. "I already agreed—we both know it was inevitable. In any case, I'm Captain. But now he's trying to tell me how to *be* Captain. I know he's just trying to help, but... "

"*But*," I agree, taking his arm. "I'm sorry. Well, I can require the Captain's services whenever you like. Just say the word."

"Thanks, foxling." Luca pats my hand. "Where are we off to?"

"The Honeysuckle. Pia has a friend who she says is a perfect candidate for our mathematics teacher. Someone named Calan."

Luca smiles warmly. "That's wonderful, Ari. Do you think she's right?"

"Only one way to find out," I say, and all but drag him out of the palace.

Pia's friend isn't there yet when we arrive. Jessa and I wait at the bar, attempting—with very little success—to work through a manuscript filled with illustrations of animal anatomy. Jessa pops up every minute or so to run to the door and peek out. I, too, have difficulty sitting still. Kirit, ever helpful, alternates between baiting Nettle and running madly around the tavern begging for scraps while Luca tries in vain to contain his small companion's enthusiasm. Pia just shakes her head and keeps serving cider and soup to whoever wants it.

"Someone's coming!" Jessa cries from the door. "Mama, what does this person look like?"

"Oh, you'll know him when you see him," Pia says with a slight smile. "He's hard to miss."

"What does that mean?" Jessa demands. "Is he hideously ugly? Or unbearably handsome? Does he have one leg? What?"

But Pia only smiles. To my surprise, a slight blush touches her cheeks.

"Pia," I whisper delightedly. "Do you *fancy* him?"

She swats me with her towel, her smile disappearing. "Don't be ridiculous, girl. Jessa! Come back here and get back to work."

Jessa comes back to the bar, dragging her feet and looking over her shoulder.

"You, too," Pia says to me, fixing me with a gimlet eye. "Focus."

"Right," I say, squaring my shoulders. "Jessa, sit down and look at this frog liver."

With a monumental effort, I marshal my energies and throw myself into the lesson. Jessa eventually settles down, and we're both engrossed in an explanation of amphibian respiration when a shadow falls over us. I look up and nearly fall off my chair in alarm. Before me is the largest man I've ever seen. He towers over us, and I could swear his head brushes the ceiling. His muscles bulge through his shirt, and every inch of visible skin is covered in tattoos. Jessa looks up, squeaks, and really does fall off her chair. But she's up again in an instant, gazing up at the man with wide, adoring eyes.

"You're *magnificent*," she gasps. "Are you Calan?"

"I am," he replies gravely. "You must be young Jessa. And Princess Arismendi?"

I nod dumbly, rendered mute by the giant before me. Kirit, of course, has no such reticence. He prances right up to Calan and yaps, planting his feet on Calan's shin, which is as far up as he can reach.

"Who is this?" Calan asks, his face lighting up with delight.

"Kirit," Luca supplies, joining us. "I hope you'll forgive him, Master Calan. He's young."

"You must be Lucoran," Calan says. "The King's Beastspeaker... and Captain, I hear."

Luca's smile turns stiff. "Indeed."

"It's a great honor to meet you all," Calan says with a small bow. His voice is calm and deep, but surprisingly soft for such a large man. "I think it's wonderful, what you're doing for the City's girls."

"You'd be the first man to say so, aside from my brothers," I say. "Do you really believe that?"

"I do," he says firmly. "May I sit?"

"Um." I blush. "Of course. Please, do."

"I'll get cider," Jessa says, and rushes off. "Luca, help me."

"So," Calan says, sitting beside me as Jessa pulls Luca behind the bar. "You're opening a school. Tell me about it."

I launch into the speech I've given so many times by now I have it memorized. Calan stops me halfway through.

"That sounds very reasonable," he says. "But I meant—I suppose I meant, tell me why you're opening a school."

I blink and give him a suspicious look. "Why? Do you think it's something that *needs* to be justified?"

"I don't think that," Calan says calmly. "If I did, I wouldn't be here. I want to know about your motivation, personally. Why you? Why the princess?"

"Why not me?" I counter. "Any woman can have a brain, want to use it, and want the same for other women. It's only luck that I *am* the princess and can do something about it. And since I can, I think I should."

Calan nods. "Good. Now, I understand you're looking for someone to teach the numerical arts."

"Yes," I say. "Pia said that you have the skills I'm looking for, but she didn't elaborate. Could you, please? Elaborate, that is."

"I have the skills," Calan replies. He hesitates, his eyes growing guarded. "But I'm not sure how much elaboration I can provide. My background is... unusual, and not something I'm willing to discuss, even with a princess. Perhaps you could examine my skills instead—give me a trial and satisfy yourself of my abilities."

I furrow my brow. "You aren't a criminal, are you?"

"I am not," Calan says, but with an edge that somehow makes me very aware of the careful phrasing in the present tense.

I chew my lip. Pia wouldn't have recommended him if he were violent or dangerous. But it would be a risk to hire someone with a questionable past. If anything goes wrong, it could damage the school's reputation to the point of failure. It could damage Costi's reputation, too. But surely a good man—and I'm sure he *is* a good man, if he has Pia's favor—deserves a second chance?

I can always say no later. There's no point in worrying about it before I find out if his grasp of figures is up to scratch. But how? I prepared questions for an interview, not an audition. I think for a moment, then call to Jessa for a slate and chalk. She brings it and serves the cider while I write.

How many years does Grace give a man? A beardless child one-sixth of his life, another twelfth while whiskers grow rife. One-seventh more before marriage begun, five years more for a daughter or son. Alas, cruel fate and the cold take the child four years before the man's grave is compiled. The child lived half the years of the man, who lived how many years of the Graces' great plan?

It was one of the first real number riddles Norrin gave me, and, I think, a good initial test. If Calan can't solve this, there's no point in questioning him further. I offer the slate and chalk to Calan. He takes them and reads the riddle, then gives a small chuckle and makes a few marks. I cut my eyes at the slate, straining to see what he's written without being too obvious about it. But I can't make out what he's doing at all. He seems to be filling the slate with nonsense scribbles. Then, far more quickly than I would have thought possible, Calan speaks.

"Eighty-four years," he says, setting down the chalk.

"How did you do that so quickly?" I ask, flummoxed. "Can I see your work?"

Calan hesitates, something like fear passing over his face. Then he smiles and hands over the slate.

"You won't recognize the marks," he says, almost apologetically. "It's my own system. You'll often find my methods unusual, I'm afraid. But they're effective."

"Can you use them for shape-theory as well? Angulars?" I ask.

"I can," Calan replies. "Shall I show you?"

"Yes, please," I say eagerly.

We sit for over an hour as I quiz him on various areas of mathematics and logic. By the end, my head is spinning with excitement. His methods are like nothing I've ever seen before. It's amazing—and very clear that Calan's ability far exceeds my own. He's also patient and kind as he explains his procedures and marks, with no hint of arrogance or condescension. When Jessa comes back with the cider and jumps into the conversation, he takes it in stride and includes her without batting an eye. He doesn't talk down to her but explains things and answers her questions with warmth and calm competency. In short, he is an excellent teacher.

But he's such a puzzle! One that could blow up in my face if anything goes wrong. Costi would never approve. It's too great a risk. But Calan has so much to offer—not only knowledge, but that something extra that only great teachers possess. Norrin has it, and I think I must have a little, too, or Jessa wouldn't have put up with me for all these years.

"Why do you want to teach?" I ask finally.

"Why not? Do you think it's something that needs to be justified?" He quirks an eyebrow at me, teasing me with my own words.

"It shouldn't be, but I've found that it is," I say, though I smile to acknowledge the joke. "I've interviewed many men over the last few weeks, and most think teaching girls is beneath them. The rest are only willing to teach highborn girls, and only for exorbitant fees."

"I'm a skin artist now," Calan says, motioning to the tattoos on his arms. "But I wasn't always. I don't often think—I don't like to remember what I've lost. But this brings back the good bits, makes me feel like I have something back. And... I have a daughter."

Warmth fills me. "And you want her to attend the school?"

"Yes," Calan says softly. "With all my heart."

"What's her name?" Jessa demands. "Do you live in this neighborhood? Why haven't I met her—or you—before?"

"She's very shy," Calan says. "But she wants to learn. She'll be a good student for you, if you'll take her."

"Of course we will," I tell him. "She'll be very welcome, won't she, Jessa?"

"Of course!" Jessa cries. "Can I meet her now?"

"Perhaps not just this moment," he says with a laugh. To me, he says, "Do I pass muster?"

I hesitate. Calan has ghosts in his past, and his unwillingness to talk about them makes me nervous. He's an unknown, which makes him a risk. I should say no. Or, at the very least, I should speak with Costi before I make a decision. But I can't believe that this brilliant, gentle man poses any real threat. He's perfect for the position, an utter miracle. I won't find another teacher like him, not if I spend the whole year searching.

I glance at Jessa to gauge her reaction and find that she's not even paying attention to us anymore. She's scribbling madly on a fresh slate, using the new system Calan taught us.

"Beautiful," she whispers to herself, then shoots to her feet. She stares into space for a moment, breathing hard, then shrieks, "MAMA. You have to see this!"

Calan and I laugh as Jessa dashes away. Then Calan turns to me and prompts, "Princess? Am I hired?"

In spite of the risk, in spite of good sense, I find a grin spreading across my face.

"Yes," I tell him. "You're hired."

Chapter Eighteen

The thrill of having finally made some tangible progress has me floating on a cloud all the way home. I am, in a word, euphoric.

At least, until Rowan brings me rudely back down to earth. He pokes his head into my room to let me know he's taken over for Luca again, but then he catches sight of the manuscripts strewn across my desk.

"What are those?" he asks.

"Treatises on pedagogy," I say happily. "I've been trying to find time to read them for ages, and I think I deserve a treat now that I've—"

"Of course you do," he says. "But do you have time for all that? As I recall, preparing for a banquet is a rather lengthy and laborious process for you."

"Banquet?" I ask blankly. "What banquet?"

"Councilor Orean's sister," he replies, with the tiniest wrinkle of his nose. "Sima, or whatever her name is."

"Cimari," I say, my heart sinking.

I'd forgotten. Councilor Orean's younger sister came to the Terrace nearly two years ago to be presented to Terrace society. Many young ladies do, and some stay in order to make marriage alliances or simply enjoy all that the City of Roses has to offer. Cimari never did either but spent all her time holed up in

Villa Glory practicing Lightcraft. The news that she was to marry Premier Joram surprised no one, though I was and still am a bit disturbed by her eagerness to wed a man old enough to be her father.

But I still have to go, and I have to make myself pretty for the happy couple. It is indeed a lengthy and laborious process, as Rowan was kind enough to remind me, even with Sparrow. I spend the whole time wishing I didn't have to go until I remember that a banquet hosted by Villa Glory will surely feature the resident Companion as the night's entertainment. The thought of seeing Sadra gives me the energy I need to finish my preparations, and, by the end, I'm fairly certain I won't embarrass anyone. Sparrow is putting the final touches on my hair and face paint when a knock sounds. I motion to the door. Sparrow silently crosses to open it, revealing Hadrian.

"Good evening, my dear," he says, sweeping a gallant bow. "You look lovely."

I shoot a glance at Rowan for confirmation, unsure whether Hadrian is mocking me or not. Rowan leans around him and gives me a brisk nod. I smile in relief. Perhaps tonight won't be a disaster. For the first time in my life, I actually *want* to look pretty. Which has nothing whatsoever to do with my intended husband, of course, and everything to do with a certain Companion.

"But what is this?" Hadrian murmurs, stepping around me and into my rooms.

"Hadrian," I protest. "You shouldn't be in my rooms."

He ignores me. Of course.

"Your thrall has been returned to you," Hadrian observes, walking around Sparrow and looking her over appreciatively. "It looks as though she's settling in well."

"Yes," I say unenthusiastically. "So I've been told."

"She'll make an excellent addition to our household."

Rowan and I share a look. Evidently no one has told Hadrian that I have no intention of leaving the palace after we wed. But that conversation will have to wait.

"We should go," I say. "We're already late."

"We're supposed to be late," Hadrian says easily. "We'll be the highest-ranking guests there, after the king."

I purse my lips. He sounds far too pleased about that fact. But there's no point arguing with him. He was a vain, insufferable boy and has grown into an even more insufferable man. This is just who he is as a person, and I have to learn to accept it.

"Let's not be *too* late," I say. "We don't want to miss the food."

If he hears the barb in my words, he gives no sign. He nods seriously.

"Orean lays the best table in the whole City," he says. "There's a rumor going around that there's to be a roast peacock."

I hold back a snort with difficulty. Don't people have anything better to talk about? But then, I suppose it's better to gossip about dead birds than live people.

"Let's go find out, shall we?" I suggest.

"Certainly, my sweet."

Hadrian turns away from Sparrow with a dazzling smile and offers me his arm. I take it, suppressing a sigh, and we set off.

I've never been inside Ismeni's villa, and I'm curious to see what her home looks like. When we arrive, I find nothing grand but rather an immediate impression of understated elegance. I'm not surprised, not in Ismeni's home. Despite the warmth of the braziers and the soft glow of Light, however, I don't think I'm imagining a chill—something in the anxious pinch of the steward's face and the distant smile on Ismeni's. A stab of sympathy strikes my heart. How miserable must she be, that I can see none of her normal warmth here in her own home?

"Welcome," she says, bowing her head to us both. There is grace in the gesture, but no life. "My husband is most eager to greet you, Hadrian. If you'll follow Baran?"

We follow the steward deeper into the villa, offering small, polite conversational tidbits to each other like little cakes. Hadrian seems to be enjoying himself, but I'm so hungry, I can't stop thinking about *actual* little cakes.

"Is that... " Hadrian's eyes widen, and he drops my arm to inspect a statue lit by a fall of sparkling Light. "It is!"

"It's what?"

Curious, I join him and lean forward only to be thrust backward by Hadrian's outstretched arm.

"Careful," he said. "Serran Sun's work is priceless. This is one of perhaps three statues ever sold."

"Why only three?"

I frown, looking over the statue. It's made of marble, like countless other statues I've seen on the Terrace and in the City. It isn't particularly attractive, either, depicting a dying tree choked by vines.

Hadrian rolls his eyes. "Because scarcity fosters demand. This must have cost Orean upward of five thousand marks."

"Five thousand!" I scoff. "For an ugly tree and a license to boast?"

"Oh, I'm sure Orean could tell you all about the philosophical and artistic merit of the work," Hadrian says with a smirk. "But the pleasure of having something no one else does certainly adds a certain spice."

My jaw clenches as Hadrian's hand comes to rest on my waist. Baran clears his throat politely.

"This way, my lord, Princess. Councilor Orean is most eager to see you."

"Of course," Hadrian replies. "Lead on, my good man."

Orean greets us in the banquet hall. At least, he greets Hadrian. He ignores me completely. Hadrian doesn't bat an eye, accepting the precedence as his due. Such treatment isn't anything new. I should be used to it by now, but it still gives me a sour taste in my mouth. How in the heavens am I supposed to get anything done in this Grace-forsaken city if no one will even look at me, much less do business with me? With Luca or Rowan as my agent, I might manage, but not with Hadrian fighting me every step of the way. I can see why Norrin pushed for a partnership, but what was Costi playing at? I can't ask him, though, because Hadrian takes his seat—which should be *my* seat—at Costi's right hand. Luca sits on Costi's left, and Kirit announces his presence with a cold nose on my ankle.

"Tell me, how are the plans coming?" Costi asks, signaling a thrall to pour my wine.

Before I can reply, Hadrian leans forward, blocking Costi from my sight.

"Marvelously," he says. "I have a lead on a school building and am in discussions with several promising candidates for the teaching staff."

I grit my teeth, reach for my wine, then think better of it. Drowning my ire in wine won't help. Not in public, at any rate. I surreptitiously pull Kirit into my lap and focus very hard on the feel of his fur under my hands and his comforting weight across my legs. It makes me feel a bit better, but I'm still relieved when Orean finally takes the floor, his robes flowing behind him and his lips set in a beatific smile that doesn't suit his face.

"My esteemed guests," he begins. "It is my honor to host you all here in my home, but most especially the king and his family. I offer you only the best and most beautiful we have, in all things. Let us begin the evening with homage to the Graces. It is with great pride that I present my wife, Lady Ismeni, and my Companion, Sadra, of the Temple of Graces."

My heart lifts as Sadra appears. She looks stunning in burgundy and gold, her dancer's costume shifting and flowing around her body with each movement, revealing tantalizing hints of deep brown skin. Orean bows and retreats to his seat, leaving the women to their exhibition. Ismeni's voice rings out, capturing every ear in the room. That is her gift. She's a Catchsong, Gifted with a voice you can't help but listen to. Her song is captivating, compelling, irresistible... to most.

My attention is all for Sadra. She is more than compelling. She is... entrancing. Her every movement is sure and strong and—I flush—sensual. The feel of her skin under my hand comes back to me in a rush, and with it the memory of her breath mingling with mine. Warmth spreads from my chest outward... and downward. My face flames. I want to flee and find some quiet, dark place to regain my composure, but I can't move a muscle. When Sadra's eyes find me, I feel as if I'll burn up like a scrap of paper in a candle flame. She gives me a small, wicked smile that makes me squirm in my seat.

"Are you well?"

I jump as Rowan bends to whisper in my ear. He frowns.

"You're pink. And sweaty."

"Am I?" I say weakly. "Perhaps it's the wine."

"Right. The wine."

Rowan snorts, but he can't question me further. The Premier is on his feet now, talking about honor and duty and the joining of families. He drones on, and out of curiosity I wonder how long it will take him to introduce Cimari. But, alas, I am disappointed, if not surprised. Lord Joram concludes his speech with no acknowledgment of his bride beyond a few references to her fruitful womb and his future heirs.

At long last, he bows and takes his seat. Countless thralls spill into the banquet hall, bearing trays of food. Steam rises from each dish, coalescing into fantastical shapes and then swirling away into the eaves. Hadrian's roasted peacock appears, complete with feathers that blaze with unnatural color. No doubt the flavor has likewise been magically enhanced, but I barely taste it. I count down the seconds until the meal is over, and I'm out of my seat the second my plate is removed. Sadra will be waiting for me somewhere, I'm sure of it. But where?

The garden seems like a good place to start, and I make my way through the cheerfully lit corridors with eager steps. It takes me far longer than I'd like to find the garden in the maze of unfamiliar corridors, but I manage it in the end. The manicured flower beds and winding paths are as lovely as everything else in Villa Glory, but nothing makes it lovelier than Sadra's presence.

"Finally," she cries, popping out from behind a stand of lilac bushes. "I was beginning to think you wouldn't come."

"I'm sorry," I say breathlessly. "I couldn't get away, and then I got lost."

"Well, you're here now," Sadra says, taking my hand. "Will you walk with me? I have news."

"Gladly," I reply, my insides fizzing at the feeling of my palm against hers. "What news?"

"I visited the Cloisters yesterday with Mother Wenla, and I remembered that you were looking at the House's outbuildings," she says. "So I wondered if the Cloisters might have any that aren't in use, and I was right! There's one that used to house novices, but it's been empty for some time." She smiles ruefully. "Not many feel themselves called to a cloistered life these days, it seems."

The Cloisters! They would be perfect: quiet, removed from the bustle of the City but close enough for students to visit home on their rest days if they wish. And Temple initiates, though painfully narrow-minded in some ways, lack the oppressive arrogance of House mages and would be much less likely to sneer at young girls trying to better themselves.

"Do you think they'd be willing to rent it to us?" I ask Sadra.

"I can't promise anything, but I'm sure Sister Tilla would at least be willing to discuss it. Would you like me to arrange something?"

"Yes!" I squeeze her arm. "You are a miracle."

She beams.

I blush.

And then an annoyed voice cracks through the night. "*Arismendi.*"

"Hadrian," I mutter with a wince. "I have to go."

"Yes," Sadra agrees, but her voice is smaller than I'm used to, almost forlorn.

I leave her with heavy steps and a heavier heart. I want to turn back, to say something more. But Hadrian is suddenly there, looming out of the darkness and scowling at me.

"Where have you been?" he demands, catching my arm in a painfully tight grip.

"In the garden," I reply, trying unsuccessfully to pull my arm away.

"Yes, I can see that," he says irritably.

I crane my neck, my arm still caught in Hadrian's grip. "Where's Rowan?"

"I sent him away," Hadrian informs me. "You have no need of a guard here, surrounded by both our families. Whom you have gravely insulted, I might add."

"Don't be ridiculous," I snap. "There is no insult in stepping out for some air."

"For nearly an hour," he snaps back. "Your absence was noticed."

"Not by you, I'll wager," I retort.

"No," he says through gritted teeth. "By Councilor Orean and Premier Joram."

"Only through Ismeni, I'm sure," I say. "Neither of them has ever even—"

I break off with a cry of pain as Hadrian gives my arm a vicious squeeze.

"You will speak when I give you leave to speak, and not before," he says coldly. "It is high time you learned to conduct yourself as a lady should. And if the king will not teach you, then—"

"Then surely a lesser man would not presume to take his place," a cool voice cuts in. Sadra appears on the path before us, one hand on her hip.

Hadrian's face shifts in an instant, and he gives Sadra a pleasant smile. "Blessed Sister, what an unexpected pleasure. But this is a matter between my wife and myself."

"Your wife?" Sadra asks, raising one eyebrow. "Did I miss the wedding?"

Hadrian flushes so deeply I can see it even in semi-darkness.

"Regardless, Sister, this is a private matter."

"I'm not sure any man is permitted to have a private anything with the king's sister," Sadra says. "Not until the wedding, anyway. But what do I know of these things? Surely the king would know better. I think I'll go ask him."

She moves past us, hips swishing, and gives Hadrian's hand on my arm a pointed look. He snatches it back as if burned.

"I suppose I should return to the banquet, then," I say, rubbing my arm. "Since my absence is causing everyone such distress."

"Yes, let us not embarrass ourselves further," Hadrian says, giving me another dark look. Then he smirks. "Though I suppose I shouldn't complain if I find my betrothed messing about with a Companion. Learn well, my dear. I look forward to quizzing you on our wedding night."

I don't reply. I can't. If I open my mouth, I'll scream. Or retch, or both. Hadrian tucks my hand securely in the crook of his arm and leads me back inside, where everyone is still feasting and laughing. I look at them all and wonder if any of them are actually happy or if they're all simply pretending, trying to hide how miserable they are and snatching what small comforts they can, where they can.

This is it. This is what my life is now, and what it will continue to be. For the first time, I wonder if the school is worth it. Jessa wouldn't want this for me. If she knew… but it's not just about Jessa, I remind myself. I need to do this for my people. My city.

"I'm doing a good thing." I whisper it softly, like a prayer. "An important thing. I can do this."

I can do it. I can. Perversely, it's almost easier now to go through the motions of the banquet. Lost as I am in a haze of misery, I barely notice the other guests or their noise. Some speak to me, and I suppose I must reply, but I forget what I say as soon as the words are out of my mouth. But Hadrian seems pleased enough, and the only critiques Ismeni offers revolve around the drops of wine splattered on my skirt and the loose curls escaping from the pins in my hair. In fact, it's probably my best performance yet. The secret, it seems, is simply soul-crushing despair.

Easy.

Sadra finds me at the end of the night, and I'm dimly aware that her face is desperately unhappy. She pulls me into a secluded corner and speaks quickly into my ear.

"I can't bear it," she breathes. "Seeing you like this—with him—please, tell me what I can do."

"Do?" I frown. "What do you mean?"

"To help," she says. "Or—to be with you. Whatever you want."

I look away. I know what I want, but the thought of asking for it makes me break out in a cold sweat. Still, no one ever got what they wanted by waiting for it.

"I want to be with you," I whisper. "I want to be close to you, alone. Can you—is there any way? Guards are posted in the courtyard outside my window, but I could speak to Rowan… "

Sadra bites her lip, considering. "I don't think I can risk it, not that. But—" She takes my hand. "There's another way, if you trust me."

"I trust you."

The words come quickly, without thought. I *do* trust her... though perhaps I shouldn't. I've met her all of—what? Two times? Three? But to take them back would be not only cowardly but dishonest, and I won't lie to her.

"What do I need to do?" I ask.

At this, she grins. "Nothing. Just fall asleep, and I'll come to you."

I gasp. "You mean in my dreams. You can do that? Even from afar?"

"Yes. We—we have a connection now." She studies me, her eyes worried. "Are you afraid?"

"No."

Something flickers inside me, a tiny flame chasing away the dull shadows that wrapped my heart. I'd all but forgotten that Sadra is a Dreamwhisper. To have her walk in my dreams! How fascinating—and, I realize, how *intimate*. My face warms. Well, I wanted to be close to her. My heart begins to pound, and excitement floods my veins. Which could be a problem, I realize with dismay.

I look at Sadra, my eyes wide with alarm. "What if I can't fall asleep?"

"I'll wait," she laughs. "Count rose petals or something. I have faith in you."

That night, I dismiss Sparrow earlier even than usual and dive into bed, positively dying to fall asleep. I don't, of course. I lie awake for what feels like half the night. I try everything—counting petals, as Sadra suggested, reading books, stretching.

The irony is unbearably cruel. I normally dread the night, rife as it is with nightmares. But now that the one thing I want is to fall asleep, that very desire chases sleep away every time it draws near.

It's maddening, but I manage it in the end. One moment I'm wondering how I'll find Sadra, and the next moment I'm standing on a cliff overlooking the City. I feel no surprise. It seems perfectly reasonable to be poised on the edge of a hundred-foot precipice with a herd of horses. And not just any horses. These horses are blue and purple and pink, and some have wings. One clops up to me—definitely clopping, though its hooves barely skim the ground—and lets out a belling neigh. I jump back, startled, and teeter on the edge of the cliff for a moment that should be far scarier than it is. An answering neigh floats toward me on the wind. I right myself and spin around to look.

More winged horses skim across the rooftops of the City like butterflies, neighing and snorting and prancing in the air. Sadra sits astride one, her hair flowing in the wind like a dark waterfall. The City spreads below us, the light of the morning sun setting the rooftop gardens ablaze. But the City is empty. It's just me and Sadra, alone in the world. Once I see her, I realize that I'm dreaming. My excitement returns in full force, and a grin spreads across my face.

A horse as white as snow swoops down to land in front of me, and as it gets closer I can see it isn't white at all. Rather, it *is*, but it's not only white. Within the blinding whiteness are other colors, rippling waves of gold and green and blue. It makes my head hurt to watch, so I look into her eyes. They're dark as night, and as peaceful. She seems... kind. Far kinder than any horse I've ever met, but then I've only met my brothers' high strung war horses. They're fierce and swift, and I love them, but they aren't kind.

I place my hands behind the mare's wings and vault onto her back. Immediately, she takes to the air. Her wings pump with a power that seems at odds with her delicate build. We rise and rise into the sky. Sadra laughs and beckons me onward, perched easily atop her purple steed.

"Is this you or me?" I call. "I mean—am I dreaming this, or are you dreaming for me?"

"A bit of both," she yells back. "But who cares? Let's fly!"

As we soar over the City and into the clouds, I find myself staring not at the fantastical tableau below us or the sparkling horses darting in and out of the rays of sunlight but at Sadra. She doesn't need the streaks of rainbow light in her hair or a gown of cloud-mist to be beautiful. She is enchanting all on her own.

I still can't believe my luck, that someone like her wants to be with someone like me. That she thinks I'm funny when everyone else thinks I'm odd, that she thinks I'm beautiful when everyone else thinks I'm plain. It doesn't matter to the Terrace folk that I'm a princess. Well, not to anyone but Hadrian, who only wants to use me to advance himself. I'm quiet and awkward and have no style, and they long ago dismissed me as irrelevant—until I was betrothed to the richest son in the kingdom. But not Sadra. To Sadra, I was someone worth knowing, worth having, even before the betrothal.

That thought, and the knowledge that this is all a dream, gives me courage. I pull my legs up and lean forward so I can crouch on my horse's back. Wait, I tell myself. Wait until... now! I push off and launch myself at Sadra, knocking her off her horse. We fall through the clouds, laughing and tumbling end over end as we plunge to the earth. Our limbs and hair tangle around each other. Our lips meet, soft and fierce by turns, hands roving and searching. I can't tell which is more exhilarating—the fall or her touch.

The ground rushes up to meet us, but I have no fear. We pass through the grassy meadow as if it, too, were a cloud. Instead of black earth, we fall into a deep pool filled with stars. At least, that's what it feels like until I realize that the blackness isn't a pool but the night sky. We've fallen into the earth and right back out again.

"This is amazing," I murmur, my arms still locked around Sadra's waist as we drift in a circle.

"You're amazing," she counters.

There are stars in her eyes, and they look like little universes of their own as her eyes roam over my face. She smiles and brushes her thumb across my freckles.

"I love these. They're like a little constellation."

"You're the only one who thinks so," I say, a smile curving my lips. "Everyone else thinks they're a horrible blemish."

"Idiots, all of them."

I laugh, then let out a huge sigh. "I love it here. Let's never leave."

She laughs. "The waking world has its merits. You can only feel so much in a dream."

She kisses me in demonstration, and I see what she means. Her lips are warm, but not as warm as they should be. Our fall from the sky was thrilling, to be sure, but of course that's because the real sensation—blinding terror—was dulled by the dream.

"You're right," I say with a sigh, then teasing, added, "As always."

"No one's always right," she demurs, and her smile fades. "And the longer you go without making a mistake, the bigger the mistake tends to be when it finally finds you."

I bite my lip. "Is this... what we're doing... Are *we* a mistake?"

She pulls me close, and we spin weightlessly. "If it is, I don't care."

We fall silent after that. There's so much we could say—about the school, about Hadrian, about our future—but we just float in silence among the stars.

Chapter Nineteen

The next day, Sadra and I meet at the Mare's Tail at sunset. As lovely as she was in my dream, she is lovelier still in the flesh. Heat races over my body as I remember kissing her. The feelings are already fading, as dreams do. I want to kiss her again, desperately. But I lack the courage in my waking life, so I simply lean beside her on the bridge and smile idiotically.

"Hello," I say.

"Good evening," she says, and we stare at each other for a long, awkward moment before bursting simultaneously into laughter.

"Thank you for last night," I say finally. "I really...I mean it was very..."

I almost tell her about my nightmares and the heady mix of exhilaration and relief I felt upon waking and realizing that I had actually rested. But she looks so shy and hopeful that I can't bear to sour the mood.

"Helpful, I hope," Sadra says, biting her lip. "Or enjoyable, or at least novel."

"All of that and more," I assure her. If she only knew. "Can we... can we do it again? Sometime, I mean. If you want."

Her face lights up. "Whenever I can, and as often as you'll let me."

"So as often as you're able, then," I say with a grin. "Tonight?"

"Tonight," she promises.

She's as good as her word. She comes to me that night and the next, and the next. Each dream is more fantastical than the last, and blessedly, blissfully free of the fire-girl and her flaming tears.

The combined joy of restful sleep and Sadra's companionship gives me the strength to persevere in waking life, which is nowhere near as pleasant. As the summer goes on, my days fall into a pattern. In the mornings, Hadrian and I tour more properties without success, and, in the evenings, we attend feasts and banquets and intimate gatherings to forge the connections Norrin says are so critical to the success of both my school and our marriage. I'm not sure if we're any more successful in this arena, but I do think I'm doing an acceptable job of hiding both my boredom and my lack of social graces. At least, Hadrian doesn't complain about my conduct or appearance any more than he usually does, which I count a victory.

Still, when Sadra tells me one night that a Temple representative will be available the next morning to meet with me, I leap at the chance with a desperation that would be embarrassing if anyone but Sadra were to witness it. When I rise in the morning, I ask Soren to cancel any appointments Norrin may have arranged for me. I also pen a hastily written note to Hadrian, making vague references to women's ailments and not feeling well. Sparrow drifts away with the note, and I take the opportunity to dress myself for once, a luxury I've learned to miss. I'm finished long before Sparrow returns—empty handed, as Hadrian apparently didn't even bother to reply. But I don't mind, as his disregard means I needn't bother coming up with a better lie. Even so, I make sure to leave early enough that there's no risk of running into Hadrian on my way out. Which isn't terribly early at all, but Hadrian will likely be in bed well past noon if he spent last night the way he usually does.

I finish off my braid with a bit of jade ribbon that reminds me of Sadra's token. Which in turn reminds me of Sadra herself and our magical night together, which makes me grin like a fool as I flick the braid back over my shoulder. I collect Rowan from his post, and we make our escape. He fusses a bit at first about the abrupt change in schedule, but, when Sadra meets us at the Terrace Gate, she gives him no opportunity to sulk. She positively sparkles, chatting animatedly, telling funny stories, and drawing stories from us in return. I suspect she may be putting in a special effort to endear herself to Rowan. I suspect also that it's working. By the time we reach the Cloisters, his gait and demeanor have relaxed enough to make him seem almost pleasant.

Sister Tilla meets us at the gates, her face plump and motherly. Her rosy cheeks look like little apples as she beams at us and ushers us through to the Temple Cloisters. Which, as I thought would likely be the case, are nothing like the House of Light and Shadow. Though perched similarly on the ridge overlooking the Terrace and the City, they have none of the House's grim, suffocating air of *seriousness*. The Sisters are quiet, but it's a serene sort of silence, and occasionally broken by odd vocalizations or chimes. Seeing my puzzled look, Sister Tilla chuckles.

"Here at the Cloisters, we delve deep into the Divine to understand its roots. We try to answer questions like the true nature of sound—how it works, how it changes, where it really comes from, how it is received."

I blink. "Not... by your ears?"

"Is a sound really in your ears?" Sister Tilla asks. "Or is it in your head? The Temple Mother once told me of a man she treated who swore he couldn't hear a thing but would turn his head in response to a clap or a click. Not every time, but enough that it couldn't be chance. And how does sound travel from one person's voice to another person's ear—and on to the mind, if that's truly where sound lives?"

"And the other arts?" I ask, intrigued.

"Oh, I could keep you here all day telling you everything," Sister Tilla says with a laugh. "But let's see... Sister Fawnya is investigating the ligaments of the knee and the recovery rate of injured dancers. Brother Ansam has made great strides in color theory. Brother Hodin has—"

"Shall we have a look at those outbuildings?" Sadra breaks in hastily, and I reluctantly agree, though in truth I'm fascinated by the Cloisters' work. Excitement builds in my chest. This is it. This is the right place. Bless Sadra. Bless her a thousand times.

We wind through the Cloisters, a clean but somewhat disorderly collection of buildings constructed of stone and wood. Some are smooth and elegant, some intricately carved, some just odd (some sort of experiment in aesthetics, perhaps?). But throughout the tour, I sense nothing but peace and purpose. And *quiet*. It's perfect, and by the time we reach the outbuildings, I've made up my mind.

"Here we are," Sister Tilla finally says as we round a bend in the path. "There are enough rooms to house dormitories and classrooms. There's a kitchen and refectory, as well. But it's—well, as you can see, it's a bit run down."

My heart falls to my feet. "A bit rundown" is an understatement. The building, though large, is in shambles, nearly overgrown with vines. Several of the windows are shattered, and some are gone entirely. The door has come loose from its hinges and slumps precariously against the frame.

"There's nothing wrong with the building structurally, is there?" Sadra asks, turning to Sister Tilla. "It could be... spruced up a bit, couldn't it?"

"Oh, yes," Sister Tilla assures us. "There are some repairs that will have to be made, certainly, but the integrity of the structure is in no way compromised."

"It'll cost you, though," Rowan observes. "Even just clearing things out and fixing up the exterior. Are you sure you want to allocate funds for this?"

I bite my lip. The real answer is *yes, definitely* but I need more information.

"How much would the Temple take for them?"

"Five hundred marks for a year's use, I should think," Sister Tilla replies tranquilly, as the bottom drops out of my stomach. I turn to Rowan. "And how much do you think it would take to make the buildings usable? Any idea?"

Rowan frowns. "You'll want a mason's estimate, but I would assume about the same amount. Maybe a bit less."

Too much. That's too much. But this is the place. I know it in my bones.

"What if you could raise the funds?" Rowan asks, surprising me. When I look at him, he shrugs defensively.

"Half the galas and banquets we've been going to were to raise funds for one thing or another," he says.

"Were they?" I ask, bemused. "I didn't realize."

He snorts. "Of course you didn't. You always spend the whole time counting down the minutes until you can leave."

"He's right," Sadra says, her eyes sparkling. "You could get people to donate. Throw a good enough party and they'll give you whatever you want."

I do not like where this is going. My stomach twists at the very thought of playing hostess with Hadrian on my arm. But, as objectionable as I find the mental picture, it occurs to me that if I need to weasel money out of my rich neighbors, there is surely no one better suited to do the weaseling than my unbeloved husband-to-be. Blight, did I make a mistake in leaving him at home today? I'll have to tell him I was lying about being ill, and where I've been, and what the fundraiser is for. Well, I'll just have to find a way to smooth it over. Surely a bit of groveling isn't too high a price to make my school a physical reality?

"Well, Costi will be happy, at least," I sigh.

"Exactly," Sadra says enthusiastically. "You're taking the initiative, doing princess-ly things. I bet he'll make a big donation himself."

"Even though he shouldn't," I mutter with a pang of unease. Costi's money troubles are only worsening, even with Norrin's support. I *have* to make this school a success. I can't let him down.

"Alright," I say. "I'll do it. Let's have a party."

Chapter Twenty

As much as I don't want to leave the peace of the Cloisters or Sadra's company, I know there's no sense in putting off the inevitable. Rowan and I bid Sadra goodbye and go straight to Villa Prosper. Our walk—or maybe just Rowan—is unusually quiet. I am lost in my thoughts, logic and emotion circling each other like a pair of angry dogs. The thought of spending more time with Hadrian makes me want to vomit, but I don't see a way around involving him. For one thing, Norrin made it clear that Hadrian is to be my partner in this, and he will definitely have something to say about it if I plan a large, public event without my betrothed. For another, I need guests for this to work, and Hadrian can get me some. He might be vain and pompous and insufferable, but he's also connected to all the wealthiest men on the Terrace and in the Upper City.

Rowan finally breaks the silence as we approach Villa Prosper.

"Are you sure you want to do this?" he asks.

"Of course I don't," I say with a grimace. "But I want that building, and I'll do what I must to get it."

Rowan nods and raps on the door, his face unreadable. Cressen ushers us in and informs me that Hadrian is still abed, which surprises no one.

"I'm sure he won't deny you an audience, Princess," Cressen assures me, showing us to a small parlor. "I'll just go let him know you're here."

Rowan takes up his station at the parlor door. I settle into a chair and run my fingers over the gilded wood. I should have waited. What am I going to say to him? How am I going to convince him to bring all his fancy friends and then convince them to fund the restoration of a derelict cloister outbuilding meant for a girls' school? He just wants the school to open so he can marry me. He doesn't care about making it a success. He doesn't care if the girls actually learn anything. If it were up to him, he'd open the school in a public latrine.

Hadrian enters with his usual flair, arms outstretched. I rise to meet him with a sigh and let him take my hands.

"My dear Arismendi, what a pleasant surprise." He kisses my cheek, letting his lips linger just a moment too long. "I thought you were ill, and yet here you are. Did you miss me that much, darling? I'm flattered."

There's no reasonable response to such a statement, so I waste no time trying to find one.

"I found a building," I say instead. "But it needs some work, and it will take more money than we accounted for. So—"

"Wait a moment," Hadrian says. "We already have a building."

I stared at him. "What? No we don't."

"We do as of last night," he informs me. "I made a deal."

Last night? I can guess where and how that deal had been made. Hadrian goes on, beaming at me as if he's done something marvelous.

"A client of ours has a property in the Lower City that he's been trying to offload. I gave him a better price than he had any right to expect."

I cross my arms and try to stay calm. "Where in the Lower City?"

The slight hesitation told me all I needed to know.

"Honey Row?" I ask, naming the brothel district. "Or maybe the Midden?"

"It's not *in* the Midden," Hadrian says. "But—nearby, yes."

I groan. "Hadrian! The Midden? There's only one place in the City that's genuinely unsafe, and that's it! No. My school is not—"

"It is," Hadrian says, scowling. "I already agreed."

"Well, *un*-agree," I snap. "The school is going to be housed at the Cloisters—as soon as I raise the money for repairs."

"Arismendi, I can't go back on my word." Hadrian speaks gently, as if to a child. "It isn't honorable."

"Your honor is not my responsibility," I say, and I am shocked—but not displeased—at how cold my voice is. "And the school is not yours. You had no right to make such an agreement without my consent."

"No right!" Hadrian forces a laugh. "My dear Arismendi, I will be your husband."

"You are not my husband yet," I remind him. "And if you don't fix this—*today*—you never will be."

He glares at me furiously. "I will not be dictated to by a woman."

"Then you forfeit the marriage alliance," I declare. "The terms of our arrangement are very clear. We will not wed until the school opens, and the school will open where and when *I* decide."

"What's this?" Norrin strolls into the room, his arms full of scrolls. "Trouble, my dears?"

"Yes," I snap, too upset to pretend. "Hadrian is trying to ruin any chance of success for my school."

"My dear Arismendi," Hadrian sniffs. "You are hysterical. Just calm down."

My vision goes red. Norrin hastily sets his scrolls down on a nearby table and ushers us both into his study.

"What happened?" he asks.

"Arismendi has been having difficulty securing premises for her school," Hadrian says with a shrug. "So I did it for her. I was only trying to help."

"The Midden," I spit, too angry to get a complete sentence out. "*The Midden.*"

"What?" Norrin peers at me worriedly. "What about the Midden?"

I cast a poisonous look at Hadrian. "Ask him."

Norrin sighs. "Hadrian?"

"I bought a building in the Lower City," Hadrian says. "For an excellent price. And it's not *in* the Midden."

"But close by." At Hadrian's nod, Norrin frowns. "Hadrian, that is not a neighborhood suitable for young girls."

Hadrian scoffs. "Why not? I'd wager a good many of Arismendi's prospective students live on the same street."

"Maybe," Norrin allows. "But that is what she—*we* are hoping to change, is it not? We want to help them better themselves. And that will be difficult to do if the girls remain surrounded by the squalor into which they were born."

"It will be difficult to do in any case," Hadrian says dismissively. "If not impossible."

"We won't know what's possible and what's not if we don't try," Norrin says firmly. "I'm sorry, my son, but I must agree with the princess. You have erred. Egregiously."

Hadrian scowls. "Fine, then, I've made a mistake. I'm sorry."

"You're sorry?" I stare at him, then Norrin. "That's it? He's sorry?"

"What else do you want?" Hadrian huffs.

"I want you to fix this!" I cry. "I want you to dissolve the contract."

"*Is* there a contract yet?" Norrin asks sharply.

"No," Hadrian says after a brief hesitation. "But I gave my *word*—"

I make a sharp gesture, cutting him off. "You gave me your word, too. You agreed to act as my agent and help me carry out my plans—*my* plans. You promised to help me, Hadrian, and all you've done so far is undermine me and get in my way."

Norrin winces and murmurs, "Arismendi, mind yourself. Such words are unbecoming of a lady."

I expect Hadrian to seize on this opportunity to remind me of my place, but it seems I've pricked his pride sufficiently to demand a response.

"Get in your way!" he blusters. "You have no idea what it takes—how hard I've been working to make this blighted school happen for you. I spent the better part of the week in negotiations to get you this building at a decent price, and now you want me to renege on the agreement?"

I open my mouth to point out that he himself said the seller was happy to part with the building, which likely is little more than a shack, but Norrin lays a hand on my arm and gives me a stern "let me handle this" sort of look.

"You're in a difficult position," he tells Hadrian. "But Arismendi didn't put you there. Speak with the seller. Explain that circumstances have changed, make your apologies, and walk away."

Hadrian scowls, his jaw working. Finally he mutters, without looking at me, "I'll do my best."

"When?" I demand.

"Tonight," he snaps, now glaring at me. "Is that permissible? *Princess?*"

"If that's the best you can do," I say coldly, glaring right back.

Norrin sighs. "Let's just have some tea, shall we?"

Chapter Twenty-One

Even Rowan doesn't protest when I ask him and Luca to accompany me into the City that evening. He knows as well as I do that "I'll do my best" likely means "I'll do nothing whatsoever" as soon as Hadrian is out of his father's sight. If I could, I would cancel whatever arrangement he made myself, but the only way to get to the seller is through Hadrian. I don't even know the miscreant's name.

I doubt that Hadrian will allow me to accompany him or speak to the seller myself, and so my best chance is to follow Hadrian in secret when he goes to meet the seller tonight—and I do believe he will go, if only to avoid lying to his father outright. If he succeeds in breaking his ridiculous agreement, wonderful. If he doesn't, I'll do it for him. And if he tries to stop me, Rowan and Luca will beat him to a bloody pulp and leave him dying in a gutter.

"Won't you?" I demand as we don ragged cloaks and slouchy hats, our disguises for the evening.

"With great relish," Rowan assures me.

"With great discretion," Luca corrects Rowan, ever the voice of caution. "But yes, also with a certain amount of relish."

"Good," I say shortly, and stalk out of the room with the boys on my heels like two great guard dogs and Kirit gamboling ahead.

We install ourselves in the shadows around the City side of the Terrace Gate, pretending to be a trio of gambling beggars and waiting for Hadrian to appear. Kirit, far too boisterous and recognizable, is banished to play in the nearby gardens. A pair of young ladies pass through the Gate, then a cluster of off-duty guardsmen, then a councilor whose face I vaguely recognize but whose name eludes me. Then—finally—Hadrian. I move to rise as soon as he's past us, but Luca presses me down with a hand on my shoulder.

"Wait," he says. "We can't risk him noticing."

"But we'll lose him," I protest, stirring restlessly.

"Not a chance," Luca says with a faint smile. "You forget who's on our side."

He whistles softly, almost under his breath, but Kirit hears him and pops out of a row of manicured shrubs like a wine cork from the bottle. He bounds over, his whole body wriggling with excitement.

"We need to follow Horrible Hadrian," Luca tells him. "You can find the scent, can't you?"

Kirit yaps once and races around for a few moments, his nose pressed to the ground. Then he pounces on something and performs a strange but adorable little dance, presumably to let us know that he's located Hadrian's scent.

"Well done, little brother," I say, rushing over to scratch his ears. "Good lad."

Kirit preens, his little toes tapping against the stony path. Then he dashes off, leaving us to follow as we can. It's all Luca can do to keep the fox from charging after Hadrian at full speed. Even so, we find ourselves using all the speed and elbows at our disposal to keep up with him. I can tell it's upsetting Luca, and even I become a little concerned at the attention we're drawing. But as long as Hadrian stays ahead of us, it won't be his attention, so I suppose we'll be alright.

"It's not that Kirit doesn't understand the need for secrecy," Luca tells us, a little apologetically. "It's just that he gets—"

"Excited," I finish for him, grinning at the sight of Kirit hopping up and down at the end of the street.

As we move into the Lower City, though, the streets become more sparsely populated, and a leaping, wriggling, hopping fox becomes far more obvious, even in the gathering darkness of nightfall. Luca is obliged to be quite stern with Kirit, who returns with his tail and ears drooping to walk quietly at Luca's side.

"Don't sulk," I tell him. "You're a good boy, and you'll have a little cake all your own when this is over."

"And you'll play with him until the sugar storm blows out, will you?" Luca mutters.

"Certainly, I will," I say stoutly, with a fond smile at Kirit. Luca rolls his eyes.

Deeper and deeper into the Lower City we plunge, past the familiar shops and homes of Pia's neighborhood, through the nameless, dingy streets that aren't quite the Midden or Honey Row but not part of the safe and respectable neighborhoods either. Those streets seem deserted entirely, and as we approach the Midden, it becomes clear where the missing inhabitants might have gone. The sounds of laughter and debauchery spurt intermittently out of dimly lit taverns, along with the occasional drunk. Kirit's nose wrinkles as he conducts another search for Hadrian's scent, and whatever he smells makes him release an enormous sneeze that lifts all four paws from the ground. But he perseveres, noble little lad that he is. Once Kirit finds the scent, he leads us unerringly to a tavern named—I blink—The Tippling Goose.

After a brief negotiation, Rowan enters first, then me with my hand on his back so he can hide both of us with his Gift, then Luca and Kirit close behind us. Anyone looking will very likely only notice Luca, who should be safe enough with his face hidden by his hood. Kirit, having flatly refused to be left outside, slips through the door and immediately into the shadows with strict instructions to stay out of sight.

As soon as we're inside, Rowan tows me immediately to a small table in the darkest corner of the room, while Luca drops into the nearest seat at hand and calls for the barkeeper. I scan the room and find Hadrian almost immediately. He sticks out like a poppy in a field of asphodels with his fine clothes, shining golden hair, and general air of smug complacency. Everything from his shoes to his perfume seems to suggest, "I could own this—and you—if I chose."

The man talking to him looks like a slightly shabbier, greasier version of Hadrian. His hair is slicked back with oil, and a sneer lingers around his mouth even when he pauses to toss back his ale. Neither of them bothers to keep his voice down, and so I hear every bleeding word.

"A promising enterprise, to be sure," the greasy man says. "By the time the chits realize their folly, they'll be good and ready to take whatever work is on offer—none will be fit for marriage, I'm sure we're all agreed on that score. Supplement with a few thralls, and you'll not lack for customers. But that princess seems an interfering sort. Will she not object?"

"She won't have the chance," Hadrian declares. "I intend to keep her busy."

Rowan stiffens beside me as the two share a hearty laugh. I, too, am rigid and brittle as old bones. My ears have gone soft, and all I can hear for a moment is a distant, tinny ringing. I swallow once, twice, then three times before I can speak.

"Tell me I misunderstood," I whisper hoarsely. "Tell me Hadrian isn't planning to turn my school into a brothel."

"I can't tell you that," Rowan says softly, but there's murder in his eyes.

"Well, then." I nod and take a breath. "*Well, then.*"

As if in a dream, I rise and walk to Hadrian's table with small, graceful steps that would make Ismeni proud. I don't have to look to know that Luca and Rowan are behind me.

"Hello, Hadrian," I say.

He leaps to his feet, his eyes wide. For a moment, he looks stricken. Then his eyes narrow in simple annoyance, and I can't tell whether the expression is genuine or not. I wouldn't put it past him to really believe that I'm the one who's out of line, that he hasn't done something utterly foul.

"My dear Arismendi, what are you doing here?" He flicks a glance at his associate. "My deepest apologies, sir—"

"This is *your best*, is it?" I ask, my voice thick with rage and disgust. "I knew you for a liar, Hadrian, but I never took you for a whore-master. This is going to break your father's heart."

"My dear, you have misunderstood." Hadrian smiles, but there's a ripple of fear underneath his usual patronizing. "You are overwrought."

"I am indeed," I agree, my fists clenching. "But I assure you, I understand your intentions quite well. Allow me to explain something to both of you, very clearly, so that we all understand."

"What's that, Princess?" the oily man asks, the sneer becoming more apparent.

I look him in the eye. "I am the executor of my bride-price. My brother the king has granted me the authority to decide where and how the gold is spent."

"Too late, love," the man says with a smirk, "The deal has been struck."

I nod. "Very well. If Hadrian has agreed to pay you, then pay you he shall. But it won't be with my money, I promise you that."

Hadrian goes purple and seizes my arm. "How *dare*—"

"How dare I?" I succeed in jerking my arm away, but only just, and I know I'll see bruises there later. "How dare *I?* Like this."

At my gesture, Luca and Rowan stride forward. Luca kicks Hadrian behind the knees, shoving him down. Rowan hauls Hadrian's despicable associate out of his chair and throws him onto the rough dirt floor at my feet.

"You will receive no gold from me," I say clearly. "Not a single. Blessed. Flake."

"I'll take you to court for this, you bitch," the man snarls. "I'll go to the king himself if I have to."

Rowan clouts him across the head, but I startle everyone, even myself, by laughing. "Please do. He'll only tell you exactly what I have. Did you not hear what I said? He granted me the authority to allocate the funds from my bride price. *Me*, not Hadrian. If my dear betrothed told you otherwise, then he's a liar twice over. Your contract, if one exists, binds you to Hadrian Prosper, not to me. And certainly not to the Crown."

"Let me go, bastard," Hadrian roars, struggling in Luca's grip. "I'll have you whipped—both of you—all of you—"

"Not until I have your purse, *my lord.*"

The oily man hurls himself sideways, catching Hadrian around the middle and bearing him to the ground. Luca leaps back, cursing, and nearly trips over Hadrian's vacated chair. The tavern's other patrons, who I now realize have been listening and watching with avid glee, erupt in a cacophony of cheers, jeers, and shouts of protest. Rowan hauls me backward as a few leap to join the fray. Others appear to be taking bets. Luca—now separated from us by a roiling mass of punching, scratching, kicking limbs—waves us away.

"Get her out of here!" he shouts at Rowan. "I'll catch up."

"Shouldn't we stay and help him?" I ask anxiously as Rowan hustles me out of the tavern.

"He'll be fine," he assures me, then whoops. He seizes me around the waist and spins me in a circle, laughing. "*Princess*. Whose horse did you geld to come up with balls that big?"

I smack him. "That is both disgusting and a poor analogy. Testicles are soft and delicate and easily crushed. It makes no sense."

"Who cares!" Rowan crows. "That was amazing."

I let a small smile of my own escape.

"It did feel pretty good," I admit, then my smile fades. "Though I'll probably regret it later."

"Later is later," Rowan says firmly. "Right now, I'm buying you a drink."

I sigh. "Do I have any say in this?"

"None."

Chapter Twenty-Two

The next morning, I am unsurprised to receive an invitation to breakfast at Villa Prosper. The note is signed by Norrin, not Hadrian. Unable to decide if this is a good sign or a bad one, I dress in a haze of sleepy trepidation, wincing as Sparrow pulls my hair into order. Rowan did indeed buy me a drink at the Honeysuckle Rose last night, but it was only cider, and we didn't stay long. Luca—or Kirit, anyway—would have known where to find us, but he never came. We searched for hours without success. We found nothing but our own beds, and by that time it was nearly dawn.

Sleep-deprived, angry, and still worried about Luca, the last thing I want to do right now is face Norrin. But I have little choice. Who knows what version of events he heard from Hadrian? The thought sharpens my attention to a knife's point even as my blood begins to race. *Hadrian.* That—that—I can't think of a vile enough word.

"Ari, are you ready?" Rowan calls through the door. Then, predictably, he lets himself in without waiting for a reply. "Let's get this over with."

"Any word from Luca?" I ask as Sparrow finishes tying the laces at my back.

Rowan shakes his head, looking worried. "If he doesn't turn up by the time we're through at Villa Prosper, I'll alert the king."

As it turns out, however, we needn't have worried. Cressen, Norrin's steward, leads me to the inner courtyard where Norrin likes to take his morning meal. And there he is—Luca. Bruised and somewhat rumpled, but whole... and looking quite comfortable with a goblet of something steamy. Kirit drowses at his feet, his little paws twitching with fox dreams. Hadrian sits beside them, much the worse for wear. The whole right side of his face is puffed and red, the skin stretched and shiny, with a nasty gash across his cheek. His eye is swollen nearly shut inside a spectacular bloom of purple and blue. His nose looks like a lump of raw meat.

"Hadrian hasn't yet seen the healer," Luca explains, clapping a hand on Hadrian's back. "He was just so determined to see justice done and tell Norrin all about what happened last night. Weren't you, Hadrian?"

Hadrian says nothing. He just glares into his cup and looks as if he'd clench his jaw if it didn't hurt so much.

"What *did* happen last night?" I ask, taking a seat opposite them.

"Let's wait for Norrin," Luca suggests. "I don't imagine poor Hadrian wants to tell the story twice."

We don't have long to wait. Norrin arrives moments later, looking uncharacteristically grave.

"I know there was a brawl in the Lower City last night, and I know you three—and young Rowan—were involved," he says. "Explain yourselves, if you please."

Luca gives Hadrian a meaningful look.

"It was my fault, Father," Hadrian croaks. "I tried to reason with my contact, as you suggested. It—didn't go well. Lucoran was kind enough to... help."

"I see," Norrin says, turning to Luca. "And you were there because your sister was there, I suppose?"

"Yes, my lord," Luca says. "She insisted, I'm afraid. I couldn't very well let her go alone."

"Certainly not," Norrin agrees. To me, he says, "My dear, what possessed you to take such a risk? Did you have so little faith in your betrothed that you felt the need to witness his effort with your own eyes?"

I don't know how to answer this. That is, in fact, exactly why I went. But I can't very well admit it if I want to keep Norrin's good favor, so I stay silent.

Luca answers for me, having no such reservations. "We thought he might require assistance. And we were right, weren't we?"

"Indeed," Norrin says with a sigh. "Foolish as you all undoubtedly are, you have my thanks. Were you successful, at least?"

At this, Luca motions for Hadrian. Though my brother has on his Serious and Responsible Guard face, I don't think I'm imagining the glimmer of satisfaction in his eyes.

"I was not," Hadrian says, his shoulders drooping. "I was obliged to promise payment from our own coffers."

"Ah, well," Norrin says philosophically. "It's a bit of a nuisance, but we can likely sell it at a decent price with a little time and work. Work," he adds, fixing his son with a stern gaze, "that *you* will do."

"Yes, Father," Hadrian mutters.

"And the Cloister building?" I ask tentatively. "That's still the one I want. It will be perfect once it's repaired. I—well, Rowan—thought that we might raise the funds with a banquet. I was going to ask for your help with that, before... you know."

"Of course, my dear," Norrin says, patting my hand. "None of this is your fault, and it pains me more than I can say that my son's foolishness has caused you such distress."

At this, Hadrian's jaw does clench, and he lets out a sound halfway between a groan and a yelp. I resist the urge to smile at the sound, but only barely.

"Actually," Luca interjects, smiling pleasantly, "Hadrian had an idea on that score, and I thought it was quite a good one."

Meaning, I translate silently, *Luca* had quite a good idea and bullied or blackmailed Hadrian into making the proposal himself.

"Oh?" Norrin asks, peering at Hadrian.

Hadrian, now very visibly in pain—and not just of the physical sort—takes a deep breath and says, very quickly, "I'll cover the cost of the school building's repairs from my personal coffers."

"We can still hold the banquet," Luca says reasonably. "To recoup the cost. Any extra can go to the school fund."

Norrin beams and claps his hands. "An excellent suggestion. Hadrian, of course, will plan the banquet."

"But that's women's work," Hadrian protests, then shrivels under his father's sharp look.

"Perhaps. But this is your mess to clean up, my son," Norrin says, but not unkindly.

"Besides," I add helpfully. "Do you really want *me* to plan the banquet that will get you your money back?"

Hadrian looks at me, considering, then sighs in defeat.

Our business concluded, we tuck into our breakfast—some of us with more enthusiasm than others. Hadrian winces with every bite and eventually gives up, choosing instead to sip on a goblet of warm spiced wine. I barely notice what I'm putting in my mouth. All I want to do is squeeze Luca until he bursts, and I intend to do just that the moment we're outside. With one stroke—I still consider blackmail most likely—he's not only secured the funds for my building's renovation but absolved me of planning that blasted banquet. The fact that it's now Hadrian's burden to bear makes it all the sweeter.

Stars, I have the *best* brothers.

After breakfast, Norrin walks us out. But just before we reach the door, he pulls me aside.

"I am not a fool, my dear," he says. "I trust you know that. And *I* know Hadrian didn't come up with that idea on his own—or agree to it on his own."

I bite my lip. "Do you really want me to tell you?"

"No, I don't," Norrin says, holding up a hand. "I absolutely do *not* want to know what Lucoran holds over him, or what really happened last night. But I do want you to be careful. You humiliated my son today. Not that he didn't richly deserve it, of course, and I will do my best to guide him toward a more, ah, charitable and humble frame of mind. As much as it pains me, however, I must admit that he very likely will retaliate—no doubt in some exceedingly petty and unpleasant way. I beg you, tread carefully so that we may limit his opportunities."

"I will," I say, my elation fading. "I'm sorry."

Norrin shakes his head, and for a moment he looks... old. Tired.

"It's not your fault," he says.

"It's not yours, either," I tell him softly.

"Whose, then?" he asks. "I'm his father."

I have no answer for that. But I shake off my guilt—and his—as I join Luca and Rowan outside. Both of them have enormous grins splashed across their faces, and I know Luca must have been telling Rowan about his little coup. Luca spreads his arms wide and bows extravagantly. I throw myself at him as he straightens up, and he catches me, laughing.

"You—" I kiss his cheek. "Are—" I kiss his other cheek. "The best—" I kiss his forehead. "Brother!"

"Ari, you're strangling me," Luca says, but I can tell he's pleased.

I slide to the ground, grinning. "I assume you threatened to tell Norrin what he was planning?"

"I wasn't sure it would work," Luca says, shaking his head. "But the little scat practically wet himself."

"He really does love his father," I sigh. "And Norrin would never in a thousand years condone something something so—so—"

"Repulsive?" Rowan offers. "Vile? Disgusting? Reprehensible?"

"Yes, all of that," I say. "I still can't believe he did it. He obviously knows what it would do to Norrin if it came out. What is Hadrian playing at?"

"Who can say?" Luca says with a shrug. "But now, foxling, you have your own work to do. You have—well, *will* have—a building. You have teachers."

"Not for everything," I protest. "I still need a Divine Arts instructor."

Luca waves his hand. "You have *enough* teachers for now. So what's next?"

"I suppose... " I consider this, and a grin to match Kirit's spreads over my own face. "Students."

"Happy hunting, foxling."

Chapter Twenty-Three

Pia spreads the word to her customers, inviting them to come to the Honeysuckle on the evening of the Corn Moon and hear what I have to say. No matter how much I pester her, she refuses to tell me who's coming, or even how many.

"I can't say, Princess," she snaps, swatting me with a dish towel. "Because I don't know. I'm not taking names. And what does it matter? You'll speak to whoever is there."

She's right, of course, but it still drives me mad. The summer is more than half gone, and I feel as if time is slipping between my fingers. I can't afford another delay or complication. I keep imagining an empty tavern, or maybe an angry, sneering mob. When the Corn Moon finally arrives, I'm a wreck of nerves.

"You should be pleased," Pia admonishes me when she sees my shaking hands. "I've never seen the Honeysuckle so full."

She's right—the tavern is packed with people, and they don't look angry or sneering. Yet.

But the noise is deafening. The children chatter excitedly to each other and play clapping games. The parents talk among themselves, some eying me with interest, others with suspicion and disapproval. Unease settles in my belly. I knew, of course, that not everyone would be happy about the school. I had hoped that those people would simply stay home, but no such luck.

But there could be an opportunity here. Maybe they just don't understand—maybe I can change their minds. Once they really understand what I'm offering, maybe they'll be pleased.

"I think that's all," Pia says, craning her neck to look over the crowd. "It's all we can hold, at any rate. Best get started."

I take a deep breath and clear my throat as I step onto the little platform Pia set up.

"Excuse me." No one pays me any mind. I try again. "Excuse—"

"Attention, please!" Pia shouts, her voice cutting easily through the din. "We're ready to begin."

"Thanks," I tell her weakly. She nods and steps away. I turn to the crowd. "Some of you know me, but for those who don't—"

"We know who you are, Princess," a man in the front barks. "Get on with it."

His neighbors shoot him disapproving glares and elbow him to the back.

"Sorry, Princess," a woman says. "Go on."

"Right." I give her a grateful smile and take another steadying breath. "I'll get right to it, then. I'm opening a school. I have the building, I have the teachers, I have staff, I have funding. Now I need students. I need girls." I wait a moment for the buzz of surprise to die down. "The girls of the Lower City are smart. They're capable—far more so than many in the Upper City and the Terrace. They start working the day they can hold a needle or stir a pot. But they've been denied any opportunity to better themselves—"

"What do you mean, better themselves?" a woman to my right demands. "There's nothing wrong with needlework, nor cooking. It's honorable work."

"Aye," another says. "Running a household and raising babies is no frolic in the daisies, and it's no work for fools. It takes know-how."

"I agree," I say. "But what if your daughter also knew how to work figures—to turn her needlework into a business? What if she knew how to conduct archival research and how to find methods or materials that could help her do her work better? What if she were taught how to think for herself, to come up with fresh ideas and create products that no one else is offering? She could bring a second income into her household to supplement her husband's—or even support herself. Until she marries," I add hastily at Pia's hard stare.

"That sounds grand," the woman says skeptically. "But what proof have we that they'll be able to actually do any of that?"

"You want proof that a woman can run a business? Look around you," Pia says with a snort. "But it's been hard, and I made plenty of mistakes, especially in the beginning. I almost lost the tavern in my first year. I found my way, of course, and I do well enough. But I'll tell you, Cora, I'd have done a lot better if I'd had some of the teaching the princess is offering. I'd be saving a pretty silver piece every month, too, if I didn't have to pay Perrin the Counter to keep my books for me. Not everyone has someone as trustworthy as he is, either. There's something to be said for knowing enough about numbers to tell when you're being cheated."

There is a hum of agreement at this. I shoot Pia a grateful look.

"Your girls *have* been cheated," I say bluntly. "Other families, they can hire tutors for their girls or send them to the Temple without fear of defaulting on a contingent contract. Here in the Lower City, your boys can at least work their way to independence through apprenticeship. But the girls have nothing to hope for—their futures depend on the generosity and industry of their husbands. Are there that many kind, hard-working, upstanding men available that you'd bet your daughter's life on her marriage prospects if you had another option?"

The women exchange thoughtful looks, but many of the men look affronted.

"That's a bit strong," one grumbles.

"Feeling caught out, are you?" someone calls, to a smattering of laughter. "If you're good to your wife and your little ones are fed and clothed and cheerful, she's not talking about you. If they're not, well, she's got a point then, doesn't she?"

The man turns beet red and subsides. He still grumbles, but now inaudibly. The rest begin talking among themselves, occasionally casting speculative glances my way. I wring my hands, my heart pounding. I don't really have much else to say—but I need them to hear me. To believe me. What else can I tell them? How can I convince them that this will change their daughters' lives?

Before I can decide whether I'm done or not, a vaguely familiar young man steps forward and makes the choice for me.

"Forgive me, Princess," he says, but his red face and puffed out chest steal any true humility from the words. "But I have something to say."

My stomach plummets into my feet. It's Yoren, the shelter guardian who keeps harassing Pia. This is just what I need! But Pia has never let him bully her, and neither will I.

"Speak, then," I tell him, my mind already spinning with potential arguments and counterarguments.

"I cannot allow you to lead these people astray," Yoren begins, but Pia cuts him off.

With, as it turns out, the simplest argument of all... and one I rarely think to use.

"It's not your place to allow the *Rose Princess* to do anything, Master Yoren," Pia says coolly, and someone snickers. "Or anyone else, for that matter. You have no authority here."

"I have the moral authority," he barks, "to speak out against wickedness and indecency."

"Indecency?" It's so ridiculous I have to laugh. "There's nothing indecent about a school."

"You cannot see the indecency in taking young girls from their natural place and turning them from their purpose? In thrusting them into the roles and realms of men? What then—will you ask them to take up arms? Take a wife?"

Yoren puffs up even further. I want to roll my eyes, but the men in the crowd are listening to him. They shift and cast each other uncomfortable glances. A flash of anger takes me by surprise. Would it really be so bad, so incomprehensible, if a girl grew up to wed another woman instead of a man? What harm would it bring anyone?

But this imaginary harm, whatever it is, has the crowd muttering darkly. I have to regain control, and quickly.

"No one is trying to turn these girls into men," I say, struggling to stay calm. "I'm only giving them the skills and tools to reach their full potential."

"These girls cannot—"

"No one can say what these girls can or cannot do," I say. "Not until we let them try."

A murmur of agreement rises from the gathered women. Even some of the men stop muttering long enough to look like they're considering the idea. But not all.

"This is a disgrace," Yoren snarls. "*You* are a disgrace. To our beloved City, to the royal family, to the Graces themselves."

I suck in a sharp breath. It's not so much that I'm offended. I couldn't care less what this toad thinks of me, frankly. But as a member of the royal family and representative of the Crown, I can't let such a blatant insult pass without comment. *Stars, I hate this,* I think, and force myself to speak.

"You forget yourself, Master Yoren," I say, trying to ignore the sweat pouring down my sides. "Shall I have my guard escort you to the palace to share your opinions with the king, or would you prefer to rephrase your comments?"

Yoren blanches for a moment, then scowls even more ferociously than before. But before he can speak, a high, clear voice rings out:

"Forgive my tardiness, Princess."

The crowd parts, revealing a woman swathed in the loose, flowing garments of a Temple dancer. She glides up the newly formed aisle, nodding graciously to the staring patrons.

"I am Sister Mora," she announces. "The Divine Arts instructor at the Rose Academy."

Surprised eyes flick my way, and I bite the inside of my lip to keep my own shock from showing.

"Welcome, Sister," I say gravely. "You honor us."

"It is my honor, Princess," Sister Mora says, bowing to me. "I offer not only my own good wishes but those of Temple Mother Wenla. She bids me tell you that you have her full support. We remember Queen Amari's good works and compassion, even if Yoren Silversmith does not. Which is curious, as our good queen founded the very shelters he oversees."

Yoren's face goes purple. "That is completely different."

Sister Mora speaks over him, her voice cutting effortlessly through his bleating protests. "The Temple smiles on this venture. And so, we believe, would Queen Amari." She looks at me, and her eyes soften. "Never doubt it, Princess."

Pia takes the opportunity to step up beside me, glaring at Yoren. He doesn't notice at first. He's too busy gaping at Sister Mora like a fish.

"Please leave, Master Yoren," Pia says. "You have no authority and no reason to be here."

His face grows dark. "I have been charged with the care of the Lower City!"

"You have been charged to provide a service to those in need," Pia corrects him. "And there is no need for you here."

"There is every need," he cries grandly. "These girls—"

"Are none of your concern." To my surprise, it isn't Pia who speaks but a rosy-cheeked, stout lady with an equally rosy cheeked girl at her side. "Do you count yourself wiser than the Temple Mother herself? More able to speak to the welfare of our daughters than we are ourselves? Be gone with you!"

Other women, perhaps heartened by the lady's courage, add their voices to hers. The rosy-cheeked woman gives her husband a look, and he gives her a short nod in return. He rolls up his sleeves, seizes Yoren's shoulder, and turns him firmly around. Another gives him a push. Yoren's face, already red, deepens to purple. He starts yelling something about perfidy and dishonor, but I can't hear him over the answering roar of the crowd. Then two more men seize Yoren's arms and frog-march him out of the tavern. Cheers drown out his furious protests. When the men return, the rosy-cheeked lady beams at her husband and kisses him, to riotous applause.

I smile too, heartened by the display of support—not only for the school, but for the man's wife and daughter. The little girl clings to her father's arm, chattering excitedly as she bounces up and down on her toes. I step off the platform and move to Pia's side. As unpleasant as Yoren's interruption was, it seems to have ultimately worked in our favor.

"What do you think?" I ask Pia anxiously. "Will anyone join us?"

"Oh, yes," Pia says. "More than we thought, if I'm not mistaken."

"I don't think you're mistaken," Sister Mora says, joining us.

"Blessed Sister," I greet her. "Well met. Your arrival was most timely."

"Dramatic," she corrects me. "Not timely. I almost didn't make it."

"How did you—I mean—well, why are you here?" I ask, shaking my head in wonder. "Are you really going to teach?"

"Certainly," she says. "Sadra told me you need someone for the Divine Arts. I owe her a favor, so here I am."

"Oh," I say, a little put out. I don't like the idea of someone teaching solely out of obligation.

Sister Mora must see the thought in my face, because she smiles. "I always loved teaching the little ones in Temple. This is the easiest debt I've ever discharged. Have no fear, Princess. I'll perform my duties well and with a joyful heart."

"Don't fuss, Ari," Pia says, pinching me. Then her face softens. "And don't worry. You did well."

Warmth fills me. Pia doesn't offer praise readily—at least, not without a bite of irony. Along with the warmth comes a dash of excitement. It's all coming together. I have everything ready, as I said. Money, teachers, curriculum, a roof over their heads—all the school needs now is students. Maybe these girls will grow up to change the world, maybe not. But they'll change their own worlds, and that's what matters. And they will, because *this is going to happen.*

The school will open.

The very next morning, however, Rowan pokes his head into my chamber with news that Costi needs to see me.

"Can't it wait?" I ask, groaning. I was having the loveliest dream with Sadra…

Rowan shrugs. "Maybe, but I don't think it should. Soren says it's to do with the school."

"But everything is going so well," I say, shooting upright. "Unless he's upset about that Yoren fellow? Perhaps we should have treated him more gently… "

"We don't know the king is upset about anything," Rowan points out. "Maybe he just wants to hear about your triumph last night. Let's go and find out, shall we?"

I throw on a gown and braid my hair quickly, not bothering to call for Sparrow. It's just Costi, after all.

Except it isn't. When we reach Costi's study, we find him with a man who looks vaguely familiar, with ruddy hair like Kirit's and a belligerent square jaw. He eyes me with dislike mingled with an odd kind of defiance. I frown, put off both by his demeanor and a tickle of recognition that I can't quite place. I'm sure I've never met him before, so why…

"Sister, this is Master Gerrin, of Midtown," Costi says, gesturing to the man. "He's come to speak to us about your school."

"I'm here to register a complaint," Gerrin clarifies. "On behalf of myself and the men of the City."

I blink, merely startled at first, but irritation sets in a heartbeat later. I frown at the man, my nostrils flaring, but I keep my voice mild. "On behalf of *all* the men in the City? Goodness, you must be quite a popular fellow."

Gerrin flushes and snaps, "On behalf of enough of them."

"And how much is 'enough,' exactly?" I inquire, still studying his face and trying to figure out where I know him from.

"Thirty," he says self-importantly. "From the Upper City and Midtown."

"Not the Lower City?"

He draws himself up, affronted. "I'd hardly have much to do with them, now, would I? My business keeps me north of the market."

"Interesting," I remark. "So, Master Gerrin, what is your complaint?"

"Your school." He puffs up like a frog, and recognition flickers again. "It cannot—"

"Master Gerrin," I interrupt as that flicker solidifies into certainty. "Are you acquainted with a young man named Yoren?"

His face, already as ruddy as his hair, deepens to purple. The resemblance is now unmistakable.

"Yoren?" Costi inquires.

"The shelter guardian I told you about," I tell him, trying for decorum's sake to keep the distaste out of my voice. "He was at the Honeysuckle last night."

"Ah. The... dissenter." He turns to Gerrin. "So? Are you acquainted with this person?"

Gerrin doesn't answer right away. He seems to deflate ever so slightly, then rallies and draws himself up again.

"My son," he says belligerently. "He brought the matter to my attention, and I was utterly appalled. This pet project of the princess's is a travesty, is what it is. Taking girls out of their homes, trying to teach them to do a man's work—it will surely fail. And on the off-chance it doesn't, it will ruin the girls for anything useful."

"And what do you consider a useful occupation for a girl?" I ask politely, choosing to ignore his prediction as to the school's likelihood of success.

"Marriage, of course," Gerrin bursts out, flabbergasted. "Keeping a good house, raising children—that's what girls are meant to do. Taking young, impressionable girls from their families, housing them all together, it's—it's insidious. It's dangerous."

I blink, truly confused now. "Dangerous?"

"Yes, dangerous." Gerrin glares ferociously at me from under his bushy, bristling red brows. "They'll form... unnatural attachments. Resist marriage."

"*Oh*." Realization dawns, and I snort derisively. "You think they'll all fall in love with each other and refuse to marry."

"Yes!"

"So, let me be sure I understand correctly," I say. "Girls are not permitted to go to school with boys due to the risk of sexual impropriety. But neither can they go to school with other girls, for the same reason. Is that right?"

"*Yes.*"

"So where are these girls to learn, then?"

"At home," Gerrin says coldly. "The only learning they need is what their mothers can teach them."

I hoped he would see the hypocrisy in his position, but I should have known better. To him, it's not hypocrisy; it's simple truth. His face is alight with righteous indignation and the conviction that these young girls are less worthy, less capable, less intelligent, just—less.

"Not every girl has a mother," I remind him softly. "And some mothers evidently want more for their daughters."

"You're messing about with the natural order, and we won't have it," he declares. "We won't let you put our girls at risk."

My gaze snaps back to him. "*Our* girls? Does Yoren have a sister, Master Gerrin?"

"I—what?" Gerrin eyes me suspiciously.

"Do you have a daughter?" I repeat patiently.

"No," he says.

"Then I fail to see how other people's daughters are any of your business," I say. I turn to Costi, who is hiding a smile with his hand. "If I may be excused, my king?"

"Wait just a blighted moment," Gerrin says furiously. "I'm not done yet. If you're so set on opening a school and teaching children for free, why aren't you teaching the boys? I paid the House of Light and Shadow a blessed fortune to teach my son, and now a bunch of snot nosed *girls* are getting an education for nothing at all? Tell me how that's fair."

A pang hits me. "It's not," I say gently. "But neither is it fair that the girls can't get an academy education even if they have the coin to pay. They can't apprentice, either. Your son has options. They don't."

"They don't *need* options!" Gerrin shouts. "You stupid cow!"

Costi stands. "That is enough."

Gerrin quails, seeming to come back to himself. "Forgive me, my king. I—"

"I will forgive you insofar as sparing you the whip," Costi says coldly. "But that is as far as my forgiveness extends today. The guards will see you out."

"This isn't over," Gerrin says, his face mottled purple. "The men I represent aren't happy about this, and our numbers are growing every day. You'd do better to heed my words."

"Certainly I shall consider your words—and your activities—most carefully," Costi says. "In the meantime, I bid you good day. Guardsman, please escort Master Gerrin to the Terrace Gate."

The guardsman at the door takes Gerrin's arm and tows him away. Gerrin goes willingly enough, though the look he casts me over his shoulder is as black as a rock worm's gut. I realize with a sudden chill that this man would hurt me if he could. And if I were anyone else—or even any*where* else, without my brother's protection—he would likely try.

With a shaky sigh, I drop into the chair opposite Costi's.

"Well, that was unpleasant," I say, rubbing my forehead.

"Indeed," Costi agrees. "I'm sorry, Ari. If I'd thought he would speak to you like that—"

I wave him off. "I don't care about that. As if I haven't heard worse!"

Costi's brows shoot up. "What—"

"What worries me," I go on, "is that he's right. Sort of. The folk of Midtown have their share of troubles. They have enough money to reach for opportunities, but not enough to take advantage of them without compromising their finances. It's *not* fair that they should sacrifice a quarter or a third of their income for an education when a richer man pays only a tiny fraction of his wealth."

"That's what I've been trying to make the nobles see," Costi says with a deep sigh. "If I can just get them to agree to the tax… but it's slow going. Even Norrin doesn't agree with me. He thinks the upper classes should contribute through philanthropy."

"If all the nobles were like Norrin, I'd agree," I say. "But only Norrin is like Norrin."

"Yes," Costi says with a weary smile. "We would all be much better off if there were more Norrins in the world. Unfortunately, what we have are a whole lot of Oreans, who look after their own interests first, their friends' second, and anyone else's not at all. Norrin thinks they'll come around if we lead by example, but… "

"But he's been leading by example all his life," I finish. "And they haven't come around yet."

"Well, that's not entirely true," Costi muses. "He has successfully shamed some into contributing. You've helped, too, as it happens."

"Have I?" I ask, astonished. "Really?"

"Really," Costi says with a smile. "I'm quite proud of you. But it's not enough. We don't have the time to bring enough of them in line to make the difference we need."

"So how can you get them to agree to the tax?" I ask, worried.

"Damned if I know," Costi says, scrubbing his face. "I might not be able to."

"And then what?" I ask.

"Tax them anyway," Costi says with a weary sigh. "And hope they don't murder me in my bed."

"Don't joke about that," I say sharply. "It's not funny."

"No," Costi agrees. "It's not. And I'm starting to think you and Luca were right about his captaincy. It's… not going well."

I frown. "So what are you going to do?"

"I'm not sure yet," he says. "Spend more time among the rank and file, I suppose. Take supper with the men, attend training sessions. If they don't trust Luca's worthiness as their captain, it means they don't trust my judgment as their king. I need to fix that. I need them to trust me."

"Perhaps they'll also feel better about Luca being in charge if they see him knock the king on his behind a few times," I suggest.

Costi raises an eyebrow. "Do you have so little faith in me?"

"Only a fool would bet against Luca," I say. "Just ask Rowan. He's lost enough wagers to know."

"We'll see," Costi says with a competitive glint in his eye that I haven't seen in a long time. "I was once a decent swordsman, you know."

I grin at him. "Well, don't say I didn't warn you."

But behind my smile, anxiety churns. I'm not naive enough to wonder why so many people object to Costi's plans, or my own. Wealthy men have been sitting comfortably on the backs of the less fortunate for decades, even centuries, and now any movement from those beneath them feels like an attack. They don't want change, even if it will benefit everyone, including themselves—why would they risk it, when they're perfectly happy with the way things are now?

My brother's councilors are among the wealthiest men in the kingdom. Their reluctance is driven by complacency and simple greed. I have more sympathy for those like Gerrin, who have just enough to be afraid of losing it. More sympathy, but not a lot. Not enough to back down. Certainly not enough to allow the girls of this city to remain shackled by fear and prejudice.

Costi won't back down, either. Nor should he, no matter how loudly his councilors scream about the new taxes or my school. He's doing the right thing, and so am I.

But Gerrin's murderous face flashes in my memory, and I pray *the right thing* doesn't kill us all.

Chapter Twenty-Four

Hadrian's fundraiser—it still gives me great satisfaction to remember that it's very much his, not mine—is held a week after the meeting at the Honeysuckle. We hold the banquet at the palace, not Villa Prosper. Hadrian is anxious to conceal the fact that he's the one in need of funds, not me. I certainly don't object, as any extra money raised will indeed benefit the school.

When I arrive, I find myself impressed by and almost envious of Hadrian's undeniable skill. Under his direction, the courtyards have been transformed into a veritable paradise. Though it's barely twilight, the Terrace is awash in shadows. Night comes early here in the ravine, and lantern flies both real and Crafted bob overhead, flickering and pulsing against the darkness beyond. Night blooming flowers hang from the latticed walls of the courtyard and float through the air to reach for one another through empty space, creating a shifting ceiling of blooms. Underneath, guests mingle and exclaim over the exquisite candied rose petals Kora and Perrin have prepared. Pairs of petals are fastened together on a narrow bed of spun sugar glazed with lemon, where they wave lazily like moths' wings. More delicacies are yet to come, and my mouth waters at the thought of them. I can only hope that Costi will deem it appropriate for us to be announced before the fig dumplings are served.

Hadrian appears beside me, absently tugging his tunic and sash into a more perfect complement to one another. Which is pointless, of course. He is, as always, impeccably dressed. But even so, he falls somewhat short of his usual lofty degree of manly beauty. He's slouching and sullen, his handsome face pulled into ugly lines of resentment.

"Everything is beautiful," I remark, trying to be conciliatory. "Well done, Hadrian."

He snorts. "I suppose it's a princess's prerogative to be condescending to her subjects."

"I wasn't trying to be condescending," I huff. "I just meant—"

"What, to congratulate me?" Hadrian asks, with a cynical edge to his voice. "As if *this* is what I wanted to spend my time on. As if I had a choice in the matter."

I roll my eyes. "Of course you had a choice."

"Obey you or lose the hand of the princess and disgrace my family," Hadrian says. "I suppose you could call that a choice."

"No one forced you to make that deal," I say. "You went behind my back."

"I was taking the initiative," Hadrian snaps. "Why is that so wrong? What gives you the right to make all the decisions, while I sit and wait for your commands like a dog?"

I let out a sharp breath through my nose. "You're my agent, Hadrian, and an agent doesn't make decisions or give orders. He simply carries them out. If you hadn't—" I break off and shake my head. "Never mind. This is my project, Hadrian, not yours. It's as simple as that."

"It was meant to be ours," he mutters, looking away with an oddly vulnerable set to his shoulders. "Father meant this to be a partnership."

I don't answer right away. It would do no good to point out his own domineering, decidedly un-partner-ly behavior. He simply wouldn't see it. I was a fool to ever think that we might be able to build a true marriage.

"We both know a partnership is impossible," I say sadly. "It's time we stopped pretending. I want my school, and you want a royal bride. Just remember all that you have to gain."

"I suppose indulging a woman's whims for a time is a small enough price," Hadrian says, though he still looks disgruntled. Then he brightens. "I suppose I'm getting the better end of this bargain. You'll be my wife far longer than I'll be your agent, after all."

"Indeed," I say through clenched teeth.

Finally, we are announced. Soren bows as we enter the courtyard arm in arm. Hadrian is, to all appearances, his normal self once more: handsome, preening, beaming toothily at anyone who looks his way. He drops my arm almost immediately and strides off to join a cluster of fashionably dressed young men and women.

I sigh and look around for Ismeni, my gaze skimming over the assembled nobles. But it's not just nobles. Gerrin lurks in a corner with some other men, presumably the other malcontents from Midtown. All of them are scowling and suspicious. I should probably make some sort of conciliatory gesture or effort to charm them, but I doubt anything I do could make a difference. Besides, their presence here was Costi's decision. As far as I'm concerned, they're his problem.

I find Ismeni near one of the tables, laughing at something another woman is saying. They both hold goblets, most likely filled with the spiced mulberry wine Hadrian ordered specially for tonight. I swipe a goblet of my own from a passing thrall and take a sip. Delicious. As distasteful as Hadrian himself may be, his taste in food and wine is unparalleled. I suppose it's something to be grateful for, that he has at least some useful skills.

"Here she is," Ismeni says merrily, taking my hand to draw me closer. "Princess, this is Lady Lanseli Silver. We've just been talking about how wonderful your initiative is."

"Truly, Princess," Lanseli says. "It's about time someone paid the girls of our City some attention."

"I'm so happy you feel that way," I say, meaning it with all my heart. "I must confess, not everyone does."

"Because not everyone is blinded by sentiment," a voice growls behind me.

I turn to see Councilor Orean scowling at me from behind his goblet.

Ismeni's smile flickers and stiffens, but her tone remains light and cheerful. "I hope you'll forgive him, Princess. My dear husband is something of a cynic, I'm afraid."

"Cynic," Orean says with a snort. "A realist, you mean. Your brother and betrothed might lack the courage to tell you, Princess, but I don't. This so-called school of yours is a waste of good coin. Teaching lowborn girls the intellectual arts? It won't work, for one thing. For another, what's the point?"

"To give them the tools to improve their lives," I say calmly. "And in turn improve the economy of the Lower City."

"They can't," Orean says flatly. "They're not built for it. A woman's purpose is to serve her husband and give him heirs, nothing more." He sneers at his wife. "And some can't even manage that."

He moves off, leaving a painfully awkward silence in his wake. Lanseli murmurs something vaguely polite and makes her escape. I bite my lip and look at Ismeni, whose face has gone deathly white. Tears glimmer in her eyes, and her breath is shallow and pained.

"Do you need some space?" I ask anxiously. "Or—or maybe some food? I think the fig dumplings are supposed to come out later, but I'll go get them for you. I swear, the dead would rise for just one bite, they're that good."

Ismeni smiles weakly, blinking away the tears. "Thank you, Ari, no. I'll be fine in a moment."

"Well, I want a dumpling, anyway," I say. "I think you'll change your mind once you see—and smell—them."

"I'm sure you're right," Ismeni says. She blows a long breath through pursed lips and straightens her shoulders. "Go on, Ari. You should enjoy yourself tonight. You've earned it."

"This is Hadrian's work, not mine," I demur, looking around at the dazzling display.

"I meant the school," Ismeni says with a smile. "Your hard work has born fruit. I'm just pleased that we have the opportunity to share in the experience tonight."

"How so?" I ask, frowning. "Do you mean this banquet?"

"Yes," Ismeni says, the tiniest wrinkle of confusion forming between her brows. "And your students. Hadrian tells me that they've been invited. I know all the ladies are eager to meet them."

"My students?" I say blankly. "But I don't have any yet. Not officially. We're holding registration next week."

"Then who—"

"Um." I take a gulp of wine and give the cup to a thrall. "I'll be right back."

I leave Ismeni with my heart pounding. What has Hadrian done now? The only girls already enrolled are Jessa and Calan's daughter Maia, and I know for a fact both of them are making honey biscuits and blanket fortresses at the Honeysuckle tonight, to make up for being excluded from the banquet. Jessa made such a scene when I told her that she couldn't attend. Not that I blamed her. I, too, thought it terribly unfair. But where is—there. Hadrian is drinking with yet another knot of laughing young men.

"Forgive me," I tell them as I take Hadrian's arm. "I must speak with my betrothed."

One waves a hand magnanimously and says, "We wouldn't dream of depriving you. Or him."

The others smirk and snicker, and I wonder what they could possibly find funny or inappropriate. But that doesn't matter now. All I care about is finding out what Hadrian is up to.

"I hear my students have been invited," I say. "But I don't *have* any students yet. Would you care to explain?"

"No," Hadrian says shortly.

"Hadrian, *what have you done?*"

Hadrian reaches out to pinch my cheek, and it's all I can do not to bite his finger off at the knuckle. "The school may be *your project*, my dearest, but this banquet is mine. You needn't trouble yourself."

I breathe hard through my nose and open my mouth to demand an explanation, but then nearly swallow my tongue as a line of little girls with plump cheeks and angelic faces file into the courtyard. Their eyes and hair spark with glamour, and the flowers in their hair glow. They smile and laugh and break into an endearingly clumsy little dance. A wave of applause and cooing admiration passes from lady to lady. Even some of the men smile.

"See?" Hadrian says smugly. "We want them to believe in our mission, do we not? We want them to be moved to open their purses. And now they are—the gold will be flowing like wine by the end of the night, just watch."

"But—but they're so young," I shake my head, as confused as I am appalled. "Too young to be at my school. What were you thinking? And after—"

"Yes, even after your little tantrum," Hadrian says with a sniff. "You require guidance, my dear Arismendi, and I will always be here to give it, even when you stamp your feet and cry—and when my father plays along."

"Hadrian." I grind my teeth so hard I'm afraid they might crack. "They are too young. These girls obviously can't be students, and your guests will surely find out, if they don't realize it already."

"It won't matter," Hadrian says, as if explaining something simple to a small, not very bright child. "No one cares about the school or its students. These people just want good food, good wine, and a good show. That's what they're paying for, and that's what I'm giving them. And they *are* paying. We'll make my money back with plenty left over for you and your precious students. You're welcome."

I want to scream. I want to rip the patronizing smile right off his face and dance on the bloody pieces. But I don't, because the damage is already done—and because it's working. All around, I see purse strings loosening and the glitter of gold falling into trays. Hadrian is right.

And I hate him for it.

Chapter Twenty-Five

I go to bed that night still fizzing with ire. Only the thought of seeing Sadra in my dreams soothes me enough to fall asleep. But she doesn't come. This isn't the first time she hasn't been able to join me, but it's close to it. I've come to rely on her company, her counsel, her comfort... and her ability to keep my nightmares in check. The fire girl dances through my dreams in a frenzied loop, burning the garden of our kingdom to the ground over and over again as if making up for lost time. And she seems angry, now, in a way she never did before. It makes me feel obscurely guilty, as if I've been neglecting her.

The next morning finds me sleepy and disgruntled. I'm in no mood to see Hadrian or even think about him, and so I decline Norrin's invitation to breakfast. Politely, of course, and with a promise to visit later in the day, when Hadrian is safely out of range. I join Costi and Luca instead and find them deep in discussion. They stop abruptly when I enter and rise to greet me, but I wave them down.

"Don't stop on my account," I say. "What are you talking about?"

"Luca had a bit of excitement on patrol last night," Costi says.

"I see," I say, taking in the bruise spreading across his jaw and the cuts on his hands. "What happened?"

To my surprise, a blush deepens the purple along his jaw and creeps up his cheeks.

"I just helped a couple of girls in a spot of trouble," he says. "It was nothing."

"Were they very pretty girls?" I ask, and his blush deepens.

"I didn't notice," he mutters.

Kirit yaps from under the table, almost like a laugh. I want to giggle as well, but I'm too intrigued. I haven't seen Luca blush over a girl since he was—I don't even know. Twelve, maybe? Thirteen? It's been so long that I've started wondering about him and Rowan.

"What's her name?" I ask. "Or is it both of them you fancy?"

"It's none of your business," he growls. "If I could return to my report?"

"Please, please tell?"

"I think he's right, foxling," Costi says—a little regretfully, I think. "We shouldn't pry."

I scoff. "Nonsense. It's a younger sister's prerogative—no, her duty—to nose into her brother's business. Especially when that business might possibly involve a girl. Or girls, plural."

"Of course it's not girls, plural," Luca snaps.

"So it *is* a girl," I lean forward eagerly. "I bet she *is* pretty. What does she like to do? Can we meet her?"

"Not telling, dancing, I think, and no."

"Ooh," I say, my eyes going wide. "She's a dancer? I'll have to ask—"

I break off, remembering that I haven't exactly been honest with him about my love life, either. I haven't told either of my brothers about Sadra, though that doesn't necessarily mean they don't know. I never exactly swore Rowan to secrecy, and I can't quite imagine him keeping such information from Luca, but Luca has never given any indication that he knows. If he's willing to pretend he doesn't, I want to keep it that way for as long as possible.

Especially in front of Costi. Luca darts a glance my way. He didn't miss my slip. He could put me in a very difficult spot right now, and he knows it. But I could continue my own interrogation in turn, and so we are at an impasse.

"Let us discuss more pleasant things," Costi suggests.

"Like what?" Luca asks, still eyeing me warily.

"Ari's birthday banquet," Costi says.

My head whips around so fast it cracks. "My what?"

What is he talking about? My birthday isn't for more than a month! And a *banquet*?

I take a deep breath and strive for a reasonable tone. "I don't need a banquet, Costi."

"Yes, you do," Costi says, as if it should be obvious.

"I've never had a banquet before!"

"You've never been betrothed to Hadrian Prosper before," Costi points out dryly.

"So *he* gets to decide how I spend my birthday?" I fume.

"Of course not," Costi says. "But you're a public figure now, foxling. You've entered society, and now society will expect certain things from you."

"So, to be clear," I say slowly. "My birthday isn't for me. It's for them."

"Well, of course it's for you," Luca says, rolling his eyes. "At least, it's for everyone to celebrate you."

"It has nothing to do with me," I insist, my eyes suddenly full of tears. "Anyone who actually knows me would realize that the last thing I want for my birthday is to be trotted out like a prized heifer. I'm so sick of all of this."

"I don't blame you, foxling," Costi says softly. "But it's the price we pay as royals."

"I *know* that," I snap. "And I've been paying it, and I'll go on paying it for the rest of my life. I'll play my part. But I don't have to like it."

"You're right," he says, and he goes quiet for a moment. Then, he offers, "But there will be cake."

"It had better be a big one," I mutter.

As my birthday approaches, I find myself spending more and more time in the kitchens. More often than not, I am joined by Ismeni, who has quite accurately surmised that I am utterly hopeless at planning any sort of social engagement. She is at my side through every minute decision, every debate, and every battle between Kora, the lead cook, and Perrin, the Lightcrafter who turns her food into the fantastical creations that have become standard at any event. The day before the banquet, we are in the kitchens before the sun rises, trying to keep the two of them from committing bloody murder.

Perrin is renowned for his unpredictable but delightful use of the Craft, and he's constantly pushing the boundaries of what Light can make possible. The trouble is that his zeal sometimes compromises the quality—and safety—of the actual food to be consumed, and this time Kora isn't having it.

"Come now," Ismeni says soothingly. "We must find a compromise. Perrin, surely it isn't necessary for the pheasants to actually take flight."

"They're birds!" Perrin cries. "Birds fly!"

"Not when they're roasted and glazed with ginger, they don't," Kora snaps. "The only flight these birds will take is on a roasting spit."

Perrin flushes. "Hear me, woman. I've been commissioned by the king himself to—"

"You'll poison the king and everyone else," Kora retorts. "I've said it before, and I'll say it as many times as I have to. Too much Light turns the meat, everyone knows that."

"An old wives' tale," Perrin scoffs. "Princess, surely you don't believe that. You're an educated lady!"

"I don't know enough to say, but flying food sounds a bit messy, in any case," I reply hesitantly. "What if they just—um—fluttered a bit, instead? With some gentle birdsong, perhaps? Subtlety sometimes makes just as big an impact. More, even."

I glance at Ismeni for confirmation, and she nods.

"Certainly," she says. "Understated elegance, that's what we need. The princess is a modest young woman, and this banquet should reflect her character."

"Hmph," Perrin grunts, unconvinced.

Kora casts us a grateful glance and tows Perrin away, filling his ears with the virtues of understated elegance.

"That was quite well done, Ari," Ismeni says. Then she laughs. "My goodness, what a pair!"

"I just hope they don't forget about our breakfast," I say. "Will you join us? You can tell Costi all about our plans."

"Oh, no," Ismeni says with a smile. "I wouldn't dream of depriving you of the credit you're due."

I groan. "I don't want any credit, and I don't want to talk—or think—about this anymore. I don't want this party, either."

"Come now," a voice says, and I turn to see Luca poking his head into the kitchen. "There will be cake, remember? Not to mention the outstanding present that I haven't technically gotten you yet but which will be in your hands by the end of the day."

"You don't have to get me anything," I grumble. "I'm not a little girl anymore."

"No, you're eighteen and about to get married," he says. "I think that calls for a present."

"Of course it does," Ismeni agrees. "I have something for you, too. Mind you don't outshine me, Lucoran."

Luca smiles politely. "I'll try. Will you be joining us for breakfast, my lady?"

"I'm needed elsewhere, unfortunately," she says. She touches my cheek gently in farewell. "I'll see you this evening, Princess. Try to enjoy your day, won't you?"

"I'll try," I sigh.

She sweeps away, leaving Luca and me in a flurry of skirts.

"Remember," Luca says, taking in my glum expression. "Cake and presents."

"I really don't need anything," I say.

"Well, you're getting something anyway," he says. "You might as well enjoy it."

"Fine," I say. "But no sweets. The last time you got me sweets, they ended up melted in my slippers."

"That wasn't my fault!"

We continue bickering all the way to breakfast, where Costi joins in the debate about suitable birthday gifts and, more importantly, suitable hiding places for birthday gifts. Not that he has the moral high ground here, having once hidden a new comb with very sharp teeth in my bed hangings. It fell while I was sleeping and stabbed me in the eye.

Of course Rowan feels the need to join in once he shows up, and I can't even banish him for his smugness, both because it's his rest day and he's off duty, and because he's the only one who hasn't left my gift to the last minute. He presents me with a set of scrolls bound together with twine.

"It's the Farwalker scrolls," he says, clearly trying to sound casual but unable to hide his grin. "I know you've been trying to get copies for Jessa."

"Rowan!" I squeal. "Where on earth did you get these? Only three copies have ever been made."

"Norrin helped me. But they're not copies." Now he doesn't even try to contain his glee. "They're the originals."

"*Rowan.*"

I throw myself at him, knocking several dishes over in the process. Marmalade splatters across the floor—and Costi's lap—as I pepper Rowan's face with kisses. Luca laughs, Costi pretends to sulk, Rowan complains that I'm strangling him, and Kirit hurls himself around the room in a storm of yapping and flying fur.

I have the very best brothers. For now, it is enough.

Chapter Twenty-Six

I spend the rest of the morning and afternoon devouring the Farwalker scrolls, entranced by Adin Farwalker's descriptions of the Wilds beyond the Garden and the Forest Folk who live there. The world he describes is full of risk and hardship but also unbelievable wonders. Wild cats the size of plow horses, trees large enough to build a house inside, a whole host of healing plants I never dreamed of or even imagined... I'm almost afraid to teach with these scrolls for fear Jessa will run off in the middle of the night to search for the Forest Folk.

Sparrow flits about the room like a ghost, clearing empty tea cups and pressing my wrinkled gowns. She has been well trained; I hardly notice her, and she proves no impediment to my wallowing. I'm still huddled under the covers when Ismeni arrives a full three hours before the banquet. I blink at her owlishly, my mind still spinning with visions of wilderness and adventure.

"It can't possibly be time yet," I protest. "It's only the third bell!"

"The fourth, actually," she says, already shaking out the gown she brought with her. "Listen."

Sure enough, the City bells are ringing in the distance. One, two, three, four. We have two hours until the banquet starts. I sigh and give the scrolls one last, longing glance before surrendering myself to Ismeni's well-meaning tyranny.

Just over three hours later (because of course I can't be on time to my own party), I am waiting in an antechamber. Ismeni is already mingling, I think. I have no idea where Costi is. Or Hadrian, come to think of it. Not that I mind that much. But it's odd that no one is around. Perhaps someone decided that as the night's honoree I should enter alone?

The door cracks open, and I know before the light falls on her face that it's Sadra. She slips in with a mischievous smile and eases the door shut behind her. I rush forward and throw my arms around her.

"What are you doing?" I demand, but I'm smiling so widely my cheeks hurt. "Someone could see!"

"Yes, you seem very concerned," Sadra says, extracting herself. "I'm here to steal you away."

My smile falters. "Oh, I don't know."

"You're the guest of honor," she says. "It's not as if they'll start without you."

"But if someone sees—"

"No one will see," she assures me, kissing my freckles. "I've fixed it all with Rowan. He'll get us out of the palace with no one the wiser."

I squeal and hug her again. Rowan appears, and I reach for him over her shoulder.

"You are an obnoxious rodent nine-tenths of the time," I tell him. "But that last tenth is really shining today. Thank you, Rowan."

"Don't get used to it," he says. "It's back to business as usual tomorrow."

Rowan takes our hands and sweeps us out of the room, down a hallway, and through a small side door without anyone seeing, as promised. We emerge onto a narrow path strewn with white pebbles, and Rowan immediately shoves us into a thicket of rhododendrons. Sadra lets out a surprised squawk that is most unlike her and stumbles into my arms.

"Shhh," I caution, stifling a giggle. "Don't you know where we are?"

"Certainly, I do," Sadra replies, taking the opportunity to trail her fingers over my collarbone. "We're in a steamy, tropical den designed solely for the pursuit of illicit pleasure."

"Yes, well, our den of illicit pleasure happens to be right under my brother's window," I say. "Costi made it for Luca and Rowan and me so that he could keep an eye on us while he worked."

"Well, it's ours now," Sadra declares. "If you're so concerned about noise, hush. We only have so much time, and I have a present for you."

Heat rushes to my face. "You didn't have to get me anything."

"I wanted to," Sadra says firmly, and presses something cool and smooth into my hand.

It's a delicate chain of rose gold hung with beads of polished jade.

"Mother Wenla gave that to me when I became an Initiate," Sadra says shyly.

"What?" I look up at her, my eyes wide. "Sadra, I can't accept this."

"Yes, you can," she says. "Let me finish. You know Initiates aren't permitted to marry or have children. We're meant to dedicate our lives and loyalty to the Temple. But Mother Wenla said that I might meet someone someday, someone who means as much to me as my faith. She said a bond like that deserves to be marked, even if it's not with a vow. So you see, this token was meant for you all along."

Warmth suffuses my chest, and a lump rises in my throat. I couldn't speak even if I knew what to say. I have no words, no voice. But I have lips.

I've kissed Sadra in my sleep too many times to count, but the reality of her is so much better than anything my mind can conjure in a dream. Her tiny gasp of surprise skates across my cheeks, then her hands are on my neck, my cheeks, my hair, and she's kissing me back with a passion that steals the strength from my limbs.

"I've been waiting for you to do that," she breathes against my mouth. "For so long."

"I don't know what I was so afraid of," I whisper, half laughing.

"Well," she says. "It was worth waiting for."

"Mm," I agree.

We sink to the ground and don't come up again until a sharp knock sounds from inside the window. We jerk apart, our eyes wide. Costi must have been in there the whole time—working, probably. Sadra's hand flies to her mouth, and I suspect she may be stifling a giggle. I give her a quelling look.

"It's not funny," I mouth.

"Lady Ismeni."

We both freeze. *Ismeni*? What is she doing in my brother's rooms? The impropriety... she must be dying. Or revealing a plot to murder the king. Something. I can't imagine her breaking decorum like this for anything less than treason. Probably Orean's, the snake. I can't help it—I have to see. Exchanging a quick, confirming glance, Sadra and I rise and peek through the shutters on the window. A guard stands in the doorway, babbling apologies.

"My king, I'm sorry, I—"

Costi's voice rings out, deep and calm. "It's quite alright. I *was* expecting the lady, but it slipped my mind. My mistake. Please, my lady, join me."

Ismeni enters the room with her head held high, but there's something fragile in her face and posture. Her little thrall, Cygnet, slips in behind her and settles into the background until she seems to disappear. Sadra goes rigid beside me. I look over, surprised. She's white as a sheet. I nudge her and raise my eyebrows in question. She shakes her head and motions to the window.

"What are you doing here?" Costi takes Ismeni's shoulders and shakes her a little. "Are you mad?"

"You're not even a little bit pleased to see me?" she asks. She sounds as though she's trying for a playful tone but just misses the mark.

Costi pinches the bridge of his nose and sighs. I can't help smiling at the all too familiar gesture. How many times has it been directed at me and Luca in just the same way? In this same room, even.

"Of course I am always happy to see you, my dear. But to come openly to my chambers this way—what were you thinking?"

What, indeed? I hadn't realized Ismeni and Costi spent any time together at all. I lean in, straining to catch everything as their voices lower. I only catch a few phrases, but it's enough to piece together the essentials.

"...couldn't be helped. My husband... exile... barren, you see."

Ismeni's words end with a small, gasping sob. So... Ismeni is barren, and Orean intends to exile her? But what good will that do him? He still can't take another wife, not while Ismeni lives. Cold washes over me. Exile would make it a lot easier to ensure that Ismeni *doesn't* live.

Costi moves then to take her in his arms, making me jerk in surprise. My mind reels. The two of them have obviously been having an affair. For how long? They seem so comfortable, so intimate. They sway together for a moment longer, their voices lost in indistinct murmuring until Ismeni pulls away.

"I don't care about that," she says, her voice growing stronger. "As a lady of my acquaintance once said, no one deserves to die childless more than he does. But I think—I am certain—he means me to die out there so he can marry again. And I will die, I will—I can't live without you. I *won't*."

Costi murmurs something and pulls her to him again, stroking her hair. "Of course I won't allow you to be sent away. You will remain in the palace as my companion. If he can have no heir from you, he has no grounds to deny an order of separation. I only wish... "

"What, my love?" Ismeni looks up at him, her face tear-stained yet still somehow radiant. "We will be together. What more is there to wish for?"

Costi's hold on her tightens. "I wish I could give you the position you deserve. I wish you could take your place as my consort—my wife."

Oh, Costi. I draw away from the window, my heart pounding. Oh, Costi, what have you done? Carrying on an affair with another man's wife is bad enough, but a *councilor's* wife? And to then take her as a concubine while her husband still lives and serves on the Council? They'll have his head!

Another knock on the door pulls my attention back to the scene inside.

"My king? It's time."

Costi bows and offers Ismeni his arm. "Will you allow me to escort you, my lady? I mean to make the announcement tonight. Why wait?"

"We can't, my love." I feel a pang of sympathy at the look of painful longing that passes over Ismeni's face. "Not yet. I must see Cygnet and Dove safely settled first. They belong to Orean, not to me. If I leave their sale to him, they'll end up as toys in a brothel, I know it."

"So sell them to me."

"And possibly give away our plans?" Ismeni shakes her head. "No. I have a buyer already who will take them both and treat them kindly. The transaction is nearly complete. We need only wait another two days, three at the most."

"And then you will be mine," Costi says, kissing her. "Your kindness does you credit, my love. But I must admit, I am most impatient for your business to be concluded. To have you here, always at my side... I never thought it would be possible. It pains me more than I can say that you will never know the joy of motherhood—of course—but what a stroke of luck!"

"I don't care," she says. "It's a price I would pay a hundred times over to be with you."

"You must send word as soon as the sale is complete," Costi tells her, kissing her knuckles. "I want you here with me."

"Of course," she says. "But for now, you must go. Your sister will be wondering where you are."

"Bother my sister."

I roll my eyes. Thanks, Costi.

Ismeni laughs. "Go. You don't want to hurt her feelings. It's her birthday."

Sadra tugs my sleeve. "You were right," she breathes in my ear. "We shouldn't be here. He'll be looking for you."

We back away from the window and out of the rhododendron fortress. I brush myself off and take a step toward the banquet hall, but Sadra pulls me back.

"You can't go like that," she says, her voice amused but her eyes troubled. "You have twigs in your hair."

"I have to talk to Costi." I pull absentmindedly at my twisted gown while Sadra picks the twigs from my hair. "What is he *thinking*?"

She looks at me quizzically. "Did you not know about them?"

"Of course not!" I gape at her. "Are you saying you did?"

Sadra looks like she's trying not to laugh. "Ari, everyone knows about them."

"I—what?" I flush, now embarrassed as well as appalled. "Everyone?"

"Everyone on the Terrace," Sadra says with a shrug. "Orean doesn't mind because he thinks he can use Ismeni to manipulate the king." As my eyes widen, she adds, "He's wrong, of course. Ismeni is smarter than that."

I let out a long breath through my nose. "Still. There's a difference between conducting an affair discretely and making a literal royal pronouncement. He can't do this—he can't!"

"Of course he can," Sadra says. "He's the king. He can do whatever he likes."

"Not without consequences," I argue. "The Council is already against him because of his tax proposal and my bride price, the school—this is going too far, I know it is. He's putting himself in real danger!"

"Have a little faith," Sadra urges. "He's been ruling for a long time. I'm sure he knows what he's doing. And they deserve a little happiness, don't they? I live in Orean's household, remember. I don't blame Ismeni one bit."

"I don't, either," I say quickly. "Of course I don't. And of course I want them to be happy! But throwing their affair in Orean's face is political suicide! Maybe even actual suicide. Don't tell me Orean isn't capable of murder."

"Maybe, but he's also one man," Sadra soothes. "There's a palace full of guards between him and your brother. They'll be fine."

I give her a look. "You didn't look so sure a few minutes ago. You looked like you'd seen a ghost. What was that about?"

"I don't know what you're talking about," Sadra declares, but she won't meet my eyes. "Go on, they'll be looking for you. And I should go get ready."

"Sadra—"

"Don't forget your gift." She smiles and gives me a lingering kiss, fastening the chain around my neck. "I'm fine, truly. Go, before someone comes looking."

I want to argue, but Rowan is motioning urgently to me from the end of the path. I sigh and squeeze Sadra's hand before hurrying to join Rowan.

"Cutting it a bit close, aren't you?" he asks. "You're getting sloppy. I can't keep covering for you."

"Oh, be quiet," I say irritably. "It's my birthday."

"The foxling bites! What happened?" he asks. "Did you quarrel with your lover? Poor little princess."

I give him a dark look and grasp my necklace protectively. "I did not quarrel with Sadra, and I'll thank you to keep your nose out of my love life. No, it's—it's Costi."

Rowan claps a hand over his mouth to smother a laugh. "He *caught* you?"

"What? No!"

In a low voice, I tell him what Sadra and I overheard. When I'm finished, I study his face for some sign of what he's thinking.

"So?" I demand. "Did you know?"

Rowan snorts. "Ari, everybody knows."

"Why didn't you *tell* me?"

"I didn't know I had to," Rowan says, rolling his eyes. "How in the world did you not notice? Even you can't be that oblivious."

I glare at him. "Maybe I am. Or maybe I had better things to do than gossip about my brother. But never mind that—what do you think?"

Rowan opens his mouth, then shuts it again. Finally, he shakes his head. "It doesn't matter what I think—or what you think, for that matter. He's the king."

"But he's making a mistake!"

Rowan shrugs and grimaces. "Even if it is a mistake, there's no one to forbid him from making it."

"*I'll* forbid him," I say fiercely. "I'll make him see sense."

"I don't doubt you," he says. "But you'll have to wait. Right now you need to sew on a pretty princess smile and greet your guests."

Chapter Twenty-Seven

I have never felt less able to put on a credible princess persona, but, as has been pointed out to me several times recently, it's the price I pay as the king's sister. And if Costi goes through with this idiotic idea of acknowledging Ismeni publicly as his mistress, it's more imperative than ever that I give our detractors nothing to criticize.

I enter the banquet hall with what I hope is a calm, gracious smile and make my rounds, greeting the guests I know by name and turning flawless social cartwheels around the guests I don't. For the first time, I find myself grateful for Ismeni's ruthless training regimen. Gone are the days of searching and floundering for something to say. My arsenal of conversational tidbits and stock responses is so robust that I hardly have to think at all.

Finally, I find Ismeni and pull her aside.

"I heard you," I say quietly, but I keep a bright smile pinned in place. "In Costi's study."

Ismeni pales, then flushes. "That's not the way I hoped you would find out."

I wave that away. "I'm worried for you—for you both. You must know Costi is already in a difficult position."

"I know." She looks away, pained. "But if you heard us, you also know what my husband plans for me. What choice do we have?"

"He could forbid Orean from sending you away," I tell her. "He could say it's because I need you. He doesn't have to expose your affair to the entire kingdom!"

"And what of me?" Ismeni asks softly. "Am I to continue living in Villa Glory, at the mercy of a man who wishes me dead? He is lord and master of his home, a king in his own right behind the villa walls. How long will I be allowed to live? And in what state?"

"You could have guards," I whisper. "You could have Rowan."

Ismeni shakes her head. "I thought your aim was to *conceal* our affair. Forbidding me to leave the City and assigning me guards in my own home could hardly make it plainer. Unless, I suppose, you wish to give the impression that I am under suspicion for—well, treason is perhaps a bit strong, but maybe conspiracy. It has some merit as a cover story, but I must confess, I find it far less appealing than a position of honor and safety at your brother's side."

"But—"

Ismeni takes my arm and leans in, laughing as if at a joke. "Do you think I don't know the risk Miocostin is taking? Do you think I welcome the danger it puts him in?"

"No, of course not! I just—"

"The only option that leaves Miocostin completely free of risk is the option that leaves me dead," Ismeni says, her smile never faltering for an instant. But her eyes snap and flash behind her mask of merriment. "Were I able to provide my husband with an heir, we might have continued discreetly, and I wouldn't have complained or asked for more. But I am not able. Am I now of so little value to the world that I should be disposed of like a faulty thrall? Am I of so little value to *myself* that I should choose death and misery when not only life but happiness is within my reach?"

"I don't know." I close my eyes, unable to pretend anymore. "I don't know."

This conversation hasn't gone at all the way I thought it would, and I find I have nothing more to say. Ismeni gives me a final, distant smile and moves off to join a group of ladies, leaving me reeling. I barely hear Costi's toast to my health. Nothing seems to reach me, not even Hadrian's smug face or the proprietary way he takes my hand, not even Sadra's performance. My birthday glow, small and tenuous as it was to begin with, has been snuffed out as thoroughly as a single flickering coal in a bucket of water. So many problems, so many injustices, so many dangers... and no answers. No solutions. Not for Costi, and especially not for Ismeni. Or for me, or any other woman in this rotting Garden.

What will my school accomplish, in the end? What chance can I really give my girls? What if all I'm giving them is enough rope to hang themselves? Enough vision to want more but not enough to get it? Even Ismeni—rich, beautiful, clever Ismeni—can be tossed aside like a rag doll. Like a thrall. Even I, a princess, could only get what I wanted by agreeing to marry a man I despise. And both of us would be utterly without hope were it not for our connection to my brother, the king. The girls of the Lower City will never have that security or anything like it, and no amount of education will change that.

"Darling Arismendi," Hadrian murmurs, squeezing my arm. "Do give us the honor of your attention."

"Hm?"

I blink, a prickle of irritation finally breaking through my despair. Perhaps, if I asked very nicely, Costi would add a clause to the marriage contract banning the words *darling Arismendi* from Hadrian's vocabulary.

"Darling, do you know these men?"

Hadrian motions to the red-faced, panting men before us. Luca and Costi stand a little distance away, whispering furiously to each other. Luca, too, is red-faced. Immediately, my mind clears and sharpens to a knife's point. Who are these people, and why does Luca look like he can't decide whether to murder someone or burst into tears? I narrow my eyes at the leader and recognize his ruddy hair.

"Master Gerrin," I say. "What an unexpected pleasure. Did my brother invite you to this banquet, as well?"

"No, Princess," Gerrin says, throwing his chest out as he swaggers toward me. "But we have a gift for you—for all of you."

"How kind," I say, resisting the urge to wrinkle my nose.

Gerrin raises his voice, his eyes flicking around the gathering crowd. "Some weeks ago, you engaged several young girls to put on a little performance for us. We would like to return the favor."

His cronies take a synchronized, evidently rehearsed step back, forming an aisle. With a grand sweep of his arm, Gerrin gestures to a group of horribly-familiar looking little girls. They skip up to me, beaming, and launch into a skit telling the story of Balia the Blessed. The littlest girl, barely five, plays Balia's infant son, crying and clinging to the leg of "Balia," who looks only slightly older. She, too, cries very prettily, begging the other girls—presumably the wicked rebels—to spare the life of her son. They pantomime Balia's Banquet and then parade around the banquet hall, pretending to whip Balia through the streets.

They're actually quite good, but I'm in no state to appreciate their talents. A knot of dread coils in my belly, tightening with every coo and peal of laughter from the gathered guests. It can't be coincidence that Gerrin chose the same girls Hadrian hired for his banquet—the same girls he passed off as my students.

"Oh, woe!" One of the wicked rebels is on her knees, weeping over Balia's prone form. "Oh, shame! What have we done?"

Another rebel wraps her arms around the infant king, who obligingly hugs her back. "We con—con—" The little rebel's face screws up in concentration. "We con-se-crate our lives to your service and your glory, young king! May the Graces forgive us and grant us wisdom. May we be worthy of you, O King, that we may guide you into manhood."

"May the Graces bless your good mother," another declares, her hands clasped beneath her chin. "And may we always remember her gentleness!"

"Her pure heart," says another.

"Her sacrifice."

"And above all," says the last, "her humility."

And all of them chorus together, "For this is a woman's highest virtue."

"Humility," Gerrin repeats after the applause dies down. "This is our gift to you, Princess. A reminder of Balia's sacrifice and our hope that you and your students will strive to follow the example of that blessed lady."

"Indeed," I say through gritted teeth.

"How lucky you are to have found such precious girls for your school, Princess," someone says.

I turn to see Lady Lanseli, whom I met at Hadrian's banquet. My stomach sinks. She was so kind about the school. What will she think when I tell her it was all a lie, that in fact I have no idea who these girls are or where they came from? And I do plan to tell her—but Gerrin beats me to it.

"Good lady, I'm afraid you are mistaken," Gerrin says, an ugly smile spreading across his face. "These aren't students."

Lanseli blinks, her gaze flicking between me and Gerrin. "They're—they're not?"

"Oh, no," Gerrin says. "These children were hired to perform tonight... just as they were hired for the princess's banquet."

"Is this true, Princess?" Lanseli steps back, a frown of confusion and disapproval marring her lovely face. Whispers and murmurs spread throughout the hall. "But why... "

"It's my fault, I'm afraid," Hadrian announces, and I'm so shocked I forget all about Lanseli.

Is he really...taking responsibility?

Alas, he is not.

"My beloved was so desperate to succeed in her little crusade," he goes on, smooth as silk. "I couldn't bear to see her disappointed. I allowed the deception to go forward, and I beg your pardon most sincerely, dear Lanseli."

Lanseli hesitates, then gives a short nod and fades into the crowd. I look around, fearful, but most of my guests have already lost interest. I should be pleased. If Gerrin hoped to stir the court against me, he seems to have failed—but only because no one cared about the school to begin with. Almost no one. Lanseli's face flashes before my eyes, her disappointment painfully evident.

I turn to Hadrian, my face flaming, but Norrin catches me by the arm.

"Don't," he whispers urgently. "Let it pass."

"But he—"

"I know," he says. "But these men want to make a scene. Don't give them one. You must rise above such pettiness."

My jaw clenches so hard it gives me a crick in my neck. My eyes bore into the back of Hadrian's head. He's laughing with Orean, without a care in the world.

"I'll speak with him," Norrin promises, seeing the direction of my glare. "You have my word."

"Fine," I mutter, then turn away.

I can't bear to look at either of them. I find Luca instead, still in deep conversation with Costi.

"What was that about?" I demand. "Why are they here if they weren't invited?"

"It's my fault," Luca says, his face still beet red. "I'm so sorry, Ari."

"It is *not* his fault," Costi says. "More than half the guards on duty deserted their posts. This is sabotage, Luca, and I won't have it. I'll sack the entire guard and rebuild it from the ground up if I have to."

Luca and I exchange a glance. Costi is a good brother. But sometimes being a good brother gets in the way of being a good king. When pushed to the limit, Costi will always put his duty to us above the practicalities of ruling a kingdom, and we can't let him.

"This isn't the time," Luca says finally. "Let's just—let's just try to enjoy ourselves."

I nod and return to my guests, floating from person to person and doing my best to laugh off Gerrin—and Hadrian's—little display. It's surprisingly easy, and I find my fury dissolving. Or changing, at least, morphing into something hard-edged and cold. Gerrin used Balia's story to shame me and put me back in my place. Hadrian, too, tried to cut me down and make me small and silly in the eyes of the court. Maybe he's succeeded, maybe not. Maybe he'll succeed in another year—or ten, or twenty. Perhaps I'll be just as bowed and afraid as they want me to be after a lifetime married to such a man. But it's a sacrifice I make willingly, just like Balia.

I sacrificed my future so that my girls could take charge of their own, and I will do whatever I must to give them what they deserve. An education won't magically change their prospects. It won't change the way the men of this city see them. If anything, it will likely make things harder in that regard. They'll be called sluts, whores, unnatural women, prideful and grasping. Many doors will remain closed to them, and some will close that would have remained open if they had been good girls. Quiet, compliant girls.

But, I swear to all three Graces, *my* girls will be able to smash those doors to splinters by the time I'm through with them.

The banquet drags into the night in an endless loop of noise and faces. By the time Soren murmurs that it's an acceptable time to leave, I'm numb and blank with exhaustion. All I want is a goblet of something that isn't wine, my bed, and Sadra. I squeeze Soren's hand gratefully and feel a weight lift off my shoulders.

But as I make my way for the door and freedom, Ismeni catches my elbow and flutters her fingers at Costi. He excuses himself from the cluster of councilors he'd been talking to and strides toward us, his gaze warm as he locks eyes with Ismeni.

"My lady," he says, bowing. His gaze flicks to me, and his mouth quirks. "Did you tell her?"

"I thought we might have a conversation together," Ismeni says. "Perhaps we can retire to your study."

"A splendid idea," Costi says, and beckons Soren closer.

After a short exchange, Soren announces the king's departure, and Costi bows to the room at large. He sweeps from the room, and Ismeni and I follow more discretely. We find Costi in his study, leaning against his desk and fiddling with a crystal pen, its tip glowing with Light.

When we enter, he straightens, beaming, and lunges forward to catch Ismeni in his arms. He spins her around, and my heart cracks to see how happy they are with each other when it's so bleeding *dangerous...*

"Ari," he says, finally coming to a stop. "We have something to tell you."

Ismeni lays a hand on his chest. "She already knows."

Costi's smile fades. "Oh."

"I overheard you in your study," I say. "I'm sorry."

"Sorry for eavesdropping, or sorry about what you heard?" Costi asks. "I hoped...well, I hoped you'd be happy for me."

"I am!" I reach for his hands. "Costi, I am. But I'm also worried."

"As am I, my love," Ismeni says, and I look at her in surprise. She seemed so set on her course when we spoke earlier.

"The princess has...concerns," Ismeni goes on. "And I find I agree."

"Ismeni..." Costi drops my hands and grasps hers. "What are you saying? You can't mean—"

"I have no intention of allowing my husband to kill me," Ismeni assures him with a short, hard laugh. "But that doesn't mean we should throw all caution to the wind. I will make my life here with you, but we will make no public announcements or declarations. We will keep separate rooms."

Costi frowns. "That's more than a little feeble as deceptions go."

"I know," Ismeni says with a shrug. "But we must at least refrain from publicly humiliating House Glory and rubbing Orean's nose in it."

"It's no humiliation," Costi argues. "There is historical precedent for taking a barren wife as a concubine. Ari, tell her."

I shake my head. "Father never did, nor his father. I'm not sure precedent matters if no one remembers it."

"It certainly won't matter to Orean," Ismeni says. "Nor, I suspect, to his fellow Council members."

"And when people inevitably wonder why you have established residence in the palace?" Costi asks.

"I need her here to provide companionship and support as I prepare for my wedding," I say promptly. "I can't possibly manage without her."

"Well, that's true enough," Costi mutters, then sighs. "I don't like it. My love...you deserve so much better."

"Maybe," Ismeni says, laying a hand on his cheek. "But I don't need what I deserve. I just need you."

Chapter Twenty-Eight

The next morning, I wake to the unusual but not unwelcome sight of my both my brothers entering my room. But my pleasure at seeing them dissipates as I register the dark looks on both their faces. Rowan follows them in and leans against the door with his arms crossed. Kirit leaps onto the bed and dives into my lap with an unhappy whine.

"What's wrong?" I ask. "What's happened? Is this about Ismeni?"

"No," Costi says, just as Luca says,

"Yes."

"This has nothing to do with Ismeni, and you know it," Costi says. "You're just using her as an excuse."

"Can someone explain, please?" I ask. "What's going on?"

"I can't be Captain," Luca says, ignoring me. "Costi, you must see that. The whole guard and Council thinks it was an abuse of your power to appoint me in the first place, and it will look even worse after you use your royal power to steal another man's wife."

"I let you share the Captaincy with Voss, didn't I?" Costi says, scowling. "It'll be fine."

"It's not enough," Luca bursts out. "It's not working. Which should come as a shock to no one, especially after what happened last night."

"That was not your fault," Costi says. "You're just running away because Voss is a massive—"

"I'm not running anywhere," Luca snaps. "And this isn't about Voss, or even Ismeni. Not completely. Has it occurred to you that I might simply want a place of my own for a change?"

"What are you talking about?" I stare at them, truly alarmed now. "Luca?"

"I'm going to live in my house in Midtown," he says.

I gape at him. "But... why?"

"Yes, do explain," Costi says. "The burden of our company has never bothered you before. If it's not Voss or Ismeni, then what?"

Luca turns away, but not before I see the real unhappiness in his face.

"Ari could have been in real danger last night," he says. "Those men could have had more in mind than simple rudeness. I can't be Captain—the men don't respect me. They don't follow me. Eventually, someone is going to get hurt."

"This isn't your fault, Lu," Costi says softly.

Luca twitches at the pet name, one he likely hasn't heard since he was a little boy. But he doesn't face us.

"I've told you," Costi goes on. "I'm not angry, it's not your fault, and I don't blame you. Nor does Ari."

"Definitely not," I agree.

Still, Luca says nothing.

"Unless... " Costi's face twists. "Unless *you're* angry, and it's my fault, and you blame me? For pushing you to be Captain?"

Silence.

"Well," Luca says finally. "The thought has crossed my mind. But I don't blame you. I just need to do this. Can we please not make it harder than it is already?"

Another silence, this time longer. Costi scowls miserably, and Rowan and I share a worried look. After several agonizing moments, Rowan clears his throat.

"I think I know," he says, with a creditable effort at a smirk.

"Oh?" Costi says dully. "Enlighten us."

"Luca's got a *girl*, remember?" he says, and his smirk grows as Luca goes red. "The dancer. And I'm guessing she's from Midtown."

Costi begins to smile, too.

"Oh, my," he says. "Well, now I feel like a real ogre. Stars forbid I should stand in the way of young love. Is she from Midtown, then? I hope I don't need to repeat the talk we had several years ago regarding appropriate courtship."

"I think you ought to, my King," Rowan offers. "I seem to recall you had some choice words for us regarding sexual restraint."

Luca glares at Rowan, apparently torn between relief at the release of tension and dismay at the turn the conversation has taken.

"She's not from Midtown, and I'm not courting her," Luca says stiffly. "She's not from the City at all—at least, not this City. She's from the City of Orchids. She's—she's a Companion, and she's accepted my patronage."

We all stare at him for a moment, then erupt into a cacophony of laughter, cheering, and jibes. Kirit joins in with a joyful yap, evidently glad that no one is scowling anymore. Indeed, the news of Luca's departure pales in comparison to *this*. Luca, in a relationship with a Companion!

"What's her name?" I ask, pulling at Luca's sleeve. "What's she like? Can I meet her? I've never met anyone from the City of Orchids!"

"No!" Luca growls, trying to shake me off with one arm and shoving at Rowan and Costi with the other. "She's very shy and still new to the City. I don't want—"

"She's not that new," Rowan disagrees. "Not if you've been sneaking around with her for as long as I suspect you have. And I find it difficult to believe a Companion is all that shy."

"Well, she is," Luca says. "Get *off*, Ari!"

"He just wants to keep her to himself," Costi says knowingly. "It's only natural. If she hasn't tired of him in another month or so, I imagine we'll meet her then."

"I'm leaving," Luca announces. "And I won't miss you at all. You are a ridiculous pack of halfwits, and I'm well shot of you."

He wrenches his sleeve free of my grasp and stalks out of the room with Rowan and Costi's laughter at his back and Kirit at his heels.

"He didn't mean it, though, did he?" I ask Costi. "He's not going live in town forever?"

"No, foxling," Costi says. "I very much doubt it."

"You said something about Luca sharing the Captaincy with Voss," I say with a frown. "What was that about?"

Costi's smile melts away. "Voss was meant to share the responsibility and prestige—a compromise to settle the unrest in the guard, but it doesn't seem to have worked. And now, I suppose, Voss is our Captain, at least until he gives me a reason to replace him. He used his authority to call the guards off last night. I'm sure of it, though I have no proof it wasn't a simple 'miscommunication between co-captains,' as he called it. Rowan, you will be our eyes and ears, I hope. I will continue to attend daily training, but I can't be everywhere."

"Of course, my king," Rowan says.

Costi nods and rises, clapping Rowan on the back. "I'll see you both for breakfast."

"I suppose Luca won't be there," I say sadly.

"We mustn't begrudge him that, little fox," Costi says. He sighs, shaking his head. "Perhaps he's right. If the men won't accept him, I can't force them. But I *can* replace them."

"That will take a while," Rowan points out.

"True," Costi says, then chuckles. "But Luca deserves a respite, and his recovery will evidently be a pleasant one. A Companion! Who would have thought? Luca, of all people... "

"Why not Luca?" I ask, forgetting my own shock and giving Costi a reproving look. "He's handsome. And smart and funny, too."

"And he generally likes animals far better than people," Rowan points out.

Costi just laughs, kisses my forehead, and heads for the door.

I wait until Costi is gone, then turn to Rowan with a conspiratorial grin. "You know what this means, don't you? If Luca's girl really is a Companion, Sadra must know her."

"Not necessarily," Rowan cautions. "Sadra has been in Villa Glory for months. If this girl is new to the City, their paths might not have crossed."

"But she must know *something*," I insist. "There aren't that many Companions in the City, and a transfer from the City of Orchids would be big news."

"You don't think we should give Luca his privacy?" Rowan asks.

"Do *you*?"

Rowan grins. "Not a chance."

I bounce out of bed, still grinning at the thought of Luca's Companion. Sparrow drifts to my side, hairbrush in hand. Rowan steps out while I dress—rather, while Sparrow dresses me. I find myself wishing, as I so often do, that I could talk to her. How pleasant it would be to giggle over Luca's romance or even my own while she dresses my hair.

Before the invention of thralls, princesses had human servants. Perhaps that's all they were, but I rather think—or maybe I just hope—they were also something like friends.

"I wish you were real," I say wistfully.

For a moment, I half-expect her to answer. But, like always, she just drifts away as soon as I'm dressed and ready. With a sigh, I join Rowan outside my door.

"Where are we bound?" he asks.

"Villa Prosper," I say. "I want Norrin's opinion on an idea I had."

"What idea is that?"

"I don't want to wait for the repairs to be completed," I say. "I want to start teaching now. Not the full curriculum, obviously, but at least something. We only have five girls so far—I'm sure we could hold lessons at the Honeysuckle for the time being."

Rowan nods. "And if it goes well and the girls tell their friends... "

I beam at him. "Exactly."

"So what do you need Norrin for?" Rowan asks. "It's a good idea. You don't need him to tell you so."

"I... " I frown. "I don't know. I guess I feel a bit beholden. It's his money, after all."

"No, it's not," Rowan says. "It's yours—your bride price."

"Until I'm married, it's a loan," I say grimly. "Anyway, I think it's only courteous to keep him informed. He's interested."

"That's true," Rowan allows. He shoots me a teasing smile. "Stars know why."

"I think you're interested, too," I tell him.

"Nonsense."

"I do," I say. "I have a strong suspicion."

"I don't know what you're talking about."

We continue bickering amiably as we stroll through the courtyards, but Rowan falls silent as we approach Villa Prosper. I roll my eyes but don't say anything. It wouldn't do to disrespect the Serious Guard Face.

"Master Norrin is in the inner courtyard with Lady Ismeni," Cressen, the steward, tells me. "Shall I announce you? I know they will welcome your company if you wish to join them for refreshment."

"Yes, please," I say, and follow him through the familiar corridors.

Cressen announces me, and Norrin and Ismeni both rise when I enter the tranquil courtyard where Norrin takes his breakfast. There's something stiff in the way they're smiling and a thick tension in the air between them.

"Sit, sit," Norrin says, ushering me to a seat beside Ismeni. "Your arrival is most fortuitous, my dear."

"Father," Ismeni says warningly.

"The princess isn't so delicate that she can't withstand a few questions," Norrin says.

"About what?" I ask, though I have an idea already. I suspect Ismeni has delivered the news of her relocation to the palace.

"I'm told you have come to rely so much on my daughter that the short walk to Villa Glory is too much to bear," Norrin says, peering at me over steepled fingers. "Is the thought of marrying my son truly so daunting?"

"The thought of marrying anyone is the most frightening thing I've ever faced," I say with perfect honesty, and I feel more than see Ismeni relax beside me.

"I sympathize completely," Norrin says. "But surely you must realize the impropriety in such an arrangement. Ismeni is a married woman. The king is an unmarried man. It is more than unseemly. It's dangerous."

Ismeni lets out a long breath through her nose. "Father, if anything is unseemly, it is this conversation. It is not for us to question the princess's decisions—or the king's."

"I trust Arismendi knows I speak only from concern for all involved," Norrin says. "People will talk—they're talking already."

"What are they saying?" I ask.

"I will not disrespect either of you by repeating it," Norrin says, scowling.

"Well, talk never killed anyone," I say, trying to keep my tone light.

"You are wrong." For the first time, anger creeps into his voice. "Arismendi, you should know better than most how easily talk can turn to action. To treason. The Council is already dissatisfied with Miocostin's handling of... various issues of state."

"My school," I supply helpfully.

"It's not just your school," Norrin says.

"Well, there's also the new taxes," I allow. "Which are the result of his debts, which could have been paid with my bride price, which is instead being used for my school. So, mostly my school."

Norrin winces. "You must agree, then, that demanding a prominent Council member's wife as an attendant, thereby forcing her to abandon her husband's household, will only exacerbate a situation that is already... tense."

I have nothing to say to that. He's perfectly correct, and I agree with him completely. But my brother is in love, and Ismeni's husband wants her dead. Not that I can tell Norrin that, if Ismeni didn't see fit to share it with him.

"It's done," I say instead. "I'm sorry."

Ismeni rises. "We should go. We have much to do, if I'm to earn my keep."

It seems now is not the time to tell Norrin about my idea to start teaching early, so I rise, too.

"Very well," Norrin says with a deep sigh. He kisses his daughter's cheek, then mine. "I hope you both know what you're doing."

"I do," Ismeni says, catching his hand. "Abba, I do. You'll see, I promise."

"Why don't you tell him?" I whisper as we walk away. "About Orean."

"I did," Ismeni says, and I stop dead in shock. Without breaking her stride, she snakes her arm through mine and pulls me onward. "The very hour I found out. He didn't believe me. He said I was overwrought, no doubt from the shock and shame of being told that I'm barren. A Lighthealer was on my doorstep within hours to put me to sleep."

"How could he not believe you?" I ask, confused and aghast. "He's your father!"

"And I'm his daughter," Ismeni says calmly. "A woman, and thus prone to fits and flights of fancy. Don't blame him, Ari. He reacted as any man of his station would."

"Costi believes you," I point out.

Ismeni slows, looking thoughtful. "I'm not sure he does, actually. But he wants me in the palace, so he acts as if he does. Maybe he even tells himself he does."

"You really think that?" I ask.

She sighs. "I'm not sure what to think, except that I need to get out of Villa Glory."

"It's not right," I mutter. "None of this is right. They should believe you, but more than that—it shouldn't matter if they believe you. You should be free to choose where to live, how to live. Things will be different, one day. It may be too late for you and me, but someday the girls in this kingdom will have *choices*."

Ismeni gives a wan smile and pats my hand. "I hope you're right, my dear."

Chapter Twenty-Nine

Though Norrin's preoccupation with Ismeni's situation prevented me from getting his blessing for my plan to start teaching early, I take it as a sign that Rowan is right that I do not, in fact, need his blessing. I put the idea to Pia and Jessa, and Pia immediately offers up her upstairs parlor for a classroom.

"It's not much," she says. "But little girls don't take up much space. I think four or even five other girls could join Jessa without too much elbow-knocking."

"You think there will be that much interest?" I ask.

"Don't look so surprised," Pia says. "You have students registered, don't you? They signed on because they want to learn."

"Maia will come," Jessa declares. "Channi and Taya, too. Maybe Cora. I only talked to her a little, but she seemed keen."

"Would you spread the word?" I ask them. "Extend the invitation?"

Jessa beams. "You can count on us!"

Jessa and Pia's enthusiasm does much to dispel the uneasiness of Luca's departure and Costi's dangerous games with Ismeni. By the end of the day, I've managed to put it out of my mind—well, most of it. I pounce on Sadra as she enters my dream, pulling her down with me into a bed of impossibly soft flower petals. Her breath is just as soft on my neck as she laughs, her arms snaking around my waist.

"Luca has a girl," I tell her without preamble, eager to focus on something light. Fun.

Sadra grins down at me as she props herself up on her elbows. "A handsome lad like him, I'm not surprised."

"Not just any girl," I say. "A *Companion*. From the City of Orchids."

Sadra's brows shoot up in surprise. "Really!"

"I think he met her some time ago. He helped her and her sister—or her friend, I can't remember—deal with some street toughs. He—" I stop abruptly at the look on Sadra's face. "What is it?"

"Nothing," she says quickly, rolling to her feet and seizing my hands. "Come on, let's do something silly."

"But this girl," I insist. "Do you know her? She's a dancer, apparently. I thought you might—"

"No," she says, her voice sharp. Then she smiles, tugging on my hands. "I don't know her, though I wish her well. I have a girl of my own, you see. *She's* the one I—"

Sadra breaks off, her eyes suddenly distant and distracted, her face slack.

"I have to go," she says.

"What? Sadra, wait!"

But she's already gone—and so am I. The suddenness of her departure from my dream jerks me into wakefulness, and I stare into the dark of my bed chamber with my heart pounding.

"Well, that wasn't quite the distraction I was hoping for," I murmur into the darkness, then punch my pillow and try to go back to sleep.

I tell myself that there's nothing to be worried over and that all will be explained when I see Sadra next. But her next visit doesn't come. Sadra is absent for three days, from both my dreams and our spot at the Mare's Tail. Though she has on occasion missed a night with me, she has never failed to appear when I leave the jade piece in the pool. Did I offend her somehow by asking about

Luca's Companion? Or—surely she can't be jealous! No, that's ridiculous. But *what*, then?

My doubts, combined with the resurgence of my nightmares, makes me so uneasy I often don't fall asleep until well after midnight—which in turn makes me worry that Sadra will look for me in my dreams and find me missing. Finally, though, I fall asleep on the fourth night and find her folded in the petals of an enormous rose. She curls in its center like a bee, dusted with shimmering pollen. When she sees me, she springs up in a shower of gold.

"Thank goodness," she cries, flying—literally—to meet me. "I've been desperate to see you. To explain."

"Why didn't you?" I ask, trying not to sound accusatory. "Didn't you see the jade?"

"No, I didn't. I've left the Terrace. Not because I wanted to," she goes on hastily. "I've been reassigned to the Cloisters. There was no time to tell you, and once I was here—well, they're very strict. I haven't been allowed to write or talk to anyone not initiated into the Temple. I can barely use the latrine without someone barking at me to get back to work. I've hardly slept since I got here. It's awful."

"I don't understand," I say, my half-formed suspicions and worries disappearing in an instant. "Are you being punished?"

"Mother Wenla says it's not punishment," Sadra says bitterly. "But I find that a little hard to believe. Stars, I hate it here. It's alright for some, but I don't give a rat's fart about the deeper mysteries of motion. I want to *dance*. I want to be out in the world, to see people—to see *you*."

"Well," I say, hope rising. "Maybe this isn't so bad. I'll soon be at the Cloisters rather often, you know. And now that you're free of Orean—I mean, you are free of Orean, aren't you?"

"Oh, yes," she says. "That's my one consolation in this miserable place."

"It's not so bad there," I say. "Maybe... maybe now you can teach. At the school, I mean. And we could—we could see each other in person. In public. Well, sort of public."

Sadra stares at me, eyes wide, then seizes my hands. "Ari, that's brilliant!"

"We can't get our hopes up yet," I say, as much for my benefit as for hers. "We don't know if Mother Wenla will allow it, and we'll have to be *so* careful... "

"She'll allow it," Sadra says eagerly. "She feels guilty for sending me here, I can tell."

I smile at her enthusiasm, but a prick of unease makes the smile fade.

"Will you tell me what happened?" I ask. "Why did the Temple Mother send you there if you didn't want to go, and why does she feel guilty about it?"

"I'm sorry," Sadra says, looking away. "I haven't... I haven't been honest with you. I've never lied," she adds hastily, "but there are things I haven't told you. Things I *can't* tell you. But I can tell you that I was doing something terribly important, and that it went wrong. I did my best, but it seems my best wasn't good enough."

She says this last with more bitterness than I ever thought I'd see in her. I raise her hands to my lips and kiss them.

"It's good enough for me," I tell her. "Whatever you have, whatever you can give."

"Even if all I can offer you is an illicit affair riddled with secrets?" she asks, trying to smile.

"Well," I say reasonably. "Secret affairs are supposed to be very romantic, aren't they?"

Sadra laughs, delighted. "That's the spirit. Now, come here and let me show you how much I missed you."

When I wake, I'm still buzzing with the thrill and relief of Sadra's presence, even if that presence is only in my dreams. But they're the best, most vivid dreams I've ever experienced. And... they're enough. For now.

On the morning of Jessa's next lesson—what I hope will be a group lesson—I wake up late. I've seen Sadra every night for the last three days, and each dream seemed to swing wildly from tenderness to troubled distraction. Which in turn drives *me* to distraction.

"What's wrong with you?" Rowan asks as I gather my things—the wrong things, for the third time in a row. "You're even more of a mess than usual."

I want to pretend that everything is fine. But I can't, both because I'm too tired to lie and because Rowan would see through me even if I did.

"It's Sadra," I say, and tell him about Sadra's strange behavior the last few days.

Well, mostly. I can't tell him about Sadra's Gift—it would be an enormous breach of trust. So I make it sound as if we've been leaving notes for each other. It's not much of a deception, but Rowan is more interested in the substance of my conversation with Sadra rather than the method. He listens carefully, and, when I'm done, he doesn't say anything. He just looks down at his crossed arms, thinking.

"Is my judgment compromised?" I ask anxiously. "Am I wrong to keep seeing her?"

Rowan frowns. "It *is* a bit... questionable. But even I have to admit she seems to sincerely care for you. I don't think she has any ill intentions, and I think she would do her utmost to protect you. I suppose that's what she's trying to do by not dragging you into her trouble, whatever it is."

"But we could help her," I say. "If she would just trust me... "

"We don't know that," he says, then sighs. "Even royalty can't solve every problem. You ought to know that better than anyone. She may be right to keep her secrets close."

"But if she doesn't trust me, how can we be... well, anything?" I ask miserably.

"Ari, you were never meant to be anything," he reminds me. "You're sworn to Hadrian Prosper, and she's sworn to the Temple. If you forget that, you're in for a world of hurt. I can't protect you from a broken heart."

I look away. "Do you think I should end it, then?"

"It's not for me to say," he says, and I give an incredulous snort. He shrugs, raising his hands. "I mean it, if only because I don't know *what* to say. I believe she cares for you, and I think you deserve some joy in the time you have left. But

I won't deny there are risks. If you want to continue on with her, you know I will protect you from any physical harm. But your heart... you have to look after that yourself."

Perhaps if Rowan had told me that I was being stupid and irresponsible, that Sadra's secrets were a threat to our security, I might have found the strength to take back my heart. Or perhaps if I had a mother's advice to lean on, rather than only my guardsman's. But he didn't tell me that, and I don't have a mother. And so I am helpless.

Yes, it hurts that Sadra feels she can't let me in, that she has secrets. Yes, it frightens me. But when I imagine leaving her, that hurts worse. And so I know that I will take whatever Sadra can offer me, even if it's scraps. I may come to regret it in time, but right now, I don't care. At least, not enough to do anything about it. I'm lost. I love her.

Much good may it do me.

At the Honeysuckle Rose, Pia is busy behind the bar, like always. I head right for the stairs, not wanting to bother her, but she waves us over.

"Don't go barging in there," she says. "Calan's teaching."

I goggle at her. "What? What do you mean?"

"He volunteered to do a lesson," she says coolly, but there's a smile playing around her mouth. "For the girls."

"Girls?" I repeat breathlessly. "How many?"

"Four, not including Jessa," Pia says. "Maia, Taya, Channi, and Cora. Just like Jessa said."

I squeal in delight. "Oh, Pia, this is wonderful! How is it going? Do they like it?"

Pia rolls her eyes. "How should I know? I've been up to my elbows in cabbage all day."

"I have to see this," I say, spinning around.

"Don't be a pest," Pia says, swatting at me with a rag. "Let the girls enjoy their lesson."

"They won't even know I'm there," I call back, already dragging Rowan toward the stairs.

To my surprise, he doesn't complain or even tease—much.

"Admit it," I tell him as we climb. "You're *interested*."

"Well, so?" He shrugs, trying—unsuccessfully—to disguise the defensive hunch in his shoulders. "I'm not allowed to be curious about the first girls' academy in the history of the country?"

"You mean the one you insisted would never happen and never work if it did?"

Rowan just rolls his eyes and shoves me up the last few steps. I shove him back and creep up to the door separating the tavern from Pia and Jessa's family quarters. Not much is audible through the heavy oak, but I can hear the low rumble of Calan's voice and a chorus of giggles.

"Do you think I can crack the door without anyone noticing?" I whisper.

Rowan sighs. "Ari, let the poor man teach in peace."

"Fine, then."

I drop to my knees and then my stomach. Ignoring Rowan's snickering, I press my ear to the crack beneath the door.

"You are ridiculous," Rowan tells me, shaking his head.

"Shhh," is all I say in reply.

I listen, enthralled, as Calan delivers a perfectly planned, perfectly executed lesson on the concept of ratios. His explanations are simple and elegant. Perfectly accurate, yet easily grasped. Even Jessa, who mastered the material ages ago, is laughing and chirping along with the rest.

I'm still lying on the floor, limp and dizzy with joy, when the scrape of chairs and rustle of skirts signals the end of Calan's lesson. Rowan seizes my waist and lifts me to my feet just in time. The door swings open and girls pour out, chattering excitedly. Several seize my hands and declare themselves dedicated to a life of scholarship. Calan and Maia are last to leave, the former brushing off my stammered praise with a pat on my shoulder and the latter darting by with a shy smile.

"That was fun," Jessa says once they're all gone. "You know what, Ari? I think this is really going to work."

"Yes," I whisper, tear-eyed. "Yes, I rather think it will."

Chapter Thirty

As autumn progresses, I find myself constantly swinging between overwhelming joy and equally overwhelming fear. I fall into bed each night buzzing with both exhaustion and anticipation. Even after so many weeks, the thrill of seeing Sadra in my dreams is so intense it keeps me awake far longer than I'd like. Sometimes we embark on fantastical adventures, each more impossible and ridiculous than the last. We make love in my dreams and pretend it's enough.

But most of the time, we simply talk. I tell her all about the school and my brothers and whatever ridiculous thing Rowan and I argued about that day. She does the same, sharing with me her upbringing in the Temple and her complicated feelings about being a Companion. When our talk turns to Cloister life, I have to laugh. Her hatred of the mundane and abstract work of the Cloisters is so passionate it borders on poetic.

My days have been growing increasingly busy as I attempt to balance my roles as princess, fiancée, school teacher, and school administrator. Hadrian, evidently still bitter, pounces on every available opportunity to diminish my efforts in front of Council members and social acquaintances alike, despite Norrin and Ismeni's pleas and outright injunctions. Those same Council members grumble and glare openly at me, and only slightly more discretely at Costi. I follow Ismeni's example and keep my head high and a polite smile firmly affixed to my face at all times.

My "parlor school" is my refuge. Jessa and Maia have developed an odd sort of friendship that's half soulful devotion and half bitter, rabid rivalry. I would find it amusing were it not for intermittent explosions over whose marks are higher on which assignment and the equally dramatic vows of undying love and friendship. The two girls seem to enjoy it, but I find it exhausting, not to mention disruptive.

Winter begins to creep up on the heels of autumn. Though the Frost Moon more than lives up to its name, I barely feel the cold as I hike up to the Cloisters every few days to monitor the school's renovations, familiarize myself with the grounds...and confer with my new colleague.

As Sadra predicted, Mother Wenla has allowed Sadra to take Mora's place as my students' Divine Arts instructor. It's both unbearably wonderful and horribly difficult. Though I see Sadra nearly every night in my dreams, having her so physically close, so real and solid and yet be unable to touch her...it's agony.

When I pass her on the Cloister paths or catch a glimpse of her through a window, and especially when we sit in the little office designated for our "curriculum meetings," I imagine how it would feel to reach out and twine my fingers through her curls. In my dreams, when I'm with her, I think of nothing but her—her lips, her scent, her skin under my dreaming hands, and when we're parted, she remains in my thoughts...her and her secrets. I sit across from Costi at breakfast and at Hadrian's side at banquets and wonder if I'm mad to continue on the path I'm on.

My heart is going to break, I know that. Once I'm married, Sadra will be lost to me. I can't go back to only seeing her in my dreams. Now that I've had a taste of having her in my waking life, I can't give it up, not by choice. But I'll have to! There's no way Hadrian could fail to notice if I continue to see her—really see her, I mean—and there's no way he would allow such a dalliance to continue. Some days, the thought fills me with despair and self-recrimination. I wake up furious with myself that I'm stupid enough to keep climbing a ladder that I know won't hold my weight.

Other days, I am desperate to burn every moment with Sadra into my memory and make the most of the time we have left. I savor every kiss, every touch. The Bear Moon comes and goes, and we sustain ourselves with clandestine meetings in hidden shadows of the Cloisters and love notes hidden beneath a loose stone in the Cloister wall.

But it isn't enough, not for either of us. So when midwinter comes and I find her note instructing me to meet her on the eve of the Chalice Festival, I don't hesitate. I send my regrets to Hadrian, Costi, Norrin, and the rest, saying that my blood is in and I won't be attending the festivities or vigils with them.

For the first time in my life, I give Rowan the slip. I use the tunnels to make my escape. I do regret the scare it will give him, but not enough to miss this chance. And I've left him a note. He'll survive.

Sadra's note directed me to the woods outside the Cloister gates, where a willow and an oak tree both grow close to the wall, but on opposite sides. Sadra pointed them out to me once, noting how well placed they were for just this purpose. She must have been planning this for some time, the sly little creature.

Sadra is already waiting for me when I arrive, a solitary figure clothed in starlight and shadows. I throw myself at her with a glad cry which is swiftly muffled by a kiss.

"I'm so happy you came," Sadra whispers. "Let's go! Before someone comes."

"Aren't you going to get in trouble for this?" I pant as we run headlong through the woods.

"Only if I get caught," Sadra laughs. "I don't care. Any punishment is worth a night with you."

My face and heart warm. "Well, let's make it a night to remember, then."

Sadra grins at me, her teeth flashing in the moonlight. "Oh, I plan to."

We continue downward, pulling on each other and giggling as we slide down the steep slope of the mountainside. The stars blaze overhead with silver fire, and moon shines even brighter. It's a picture-perfect night for the Chalice Festival. For once, I'm going to celebrate it the way I want to, the way it's meant to be celebrated: with good food, good wine, and good company. I'm going to spend my night dancing in the streets and bellowing songs along with whole city blocks full of people, not holed up in the palace, stuck at some stuffy banquet watching someone else sing and dance.

The festival is in full swing when we finally arrive, our finery somewhat worse for wear.

"Where should we go first?" I wonder, looking around eagerly.

Sadra throws her arms out and spins in a circle.

"Anywhere," she cries. "I want something smothered in honey and cream. And jam. And butter. And—"

"Alright, Sister Piggy," I laugh, towing her over to a food cart.

Sadra wasn't joking. She orders two cream buns, one with honey, one with jam, both drizzled with melted butter. And then she orders another two for me.

"I'll never be able to eat all this," I object, staring at the mountain of sugar on my tray.

"So share it," Sadra replies. "That's what we do in the City. Frankly, I've already broken the rules by buying this myself. We should have bought them for each other, or waited for someone to buy us something. But I'm just too hungry!"

"I won't tell if you won't," I promise, and moan as I take a bite of my pastry. "This is *so* good!"

"Oh, stars," she whimpers. "Oh, heaven. I haven't tasted sugar in weeks. I may die."

Sadra devours her bun in three bites, leaving me to choke on mine as I laugh.

"No," I say in disbelief, still coughing, as she starts in on the other one. "There's no way. That thing is enormous!"

"As is my appetite," she replies through a mouthful of cream and dough.

There's a smear of jam at the corner of her mouth. On impulse, I lean forward and lick it off. Sadra squeaks and drops her bun.

"*Princess!*" She looks at me, then at the bun, then at me again, torn between amusement and dismay. "You shock me."

My face burns, but I can't stop grinning. "It's not my fault you're so delicious. Even when you're stuffing yourself with sweets. *Especially* when you're stuffing yourself with sweets."

"Come have another taste, then," she challenges, and pulls me into a dark corner.

We emerge sometime later, flushed and disheveled. No one cares—what are dark corners for, after all? If we're in the minority, it's only because most people aren't bothering to be discrete. On an ordinary night, we might have risked stoning or worse with such indiscretion. But this isn't an ordinary night. It's Chalice.

"Let's find a tavern," Sadra says. She gives me a burning look. "I'm parched."

We find a likely looking tavern and squeeze in, by some miracle snagging a table for ourselves. I order cider, not trusting myself with wine. I already feel drunk. Can you get a hangover from joy? If so, I'm in for the worst morning of my life when this is over.

"Oh, no," Sadra says, her face going suddenly white.

"What is it?" I ask as she sinks down in her seat. "Are you sick? Um—here, take my cup."

"It's not that," Sadra says, though she does look ill. "It's him."

"Who?" I look around, bewildered.

"The singer," Sadra says. "He knows me—and knows I'm supposed to be in the Cloisters. *What* in the name of all the Graces is he doing here! I'd lay good money he's never celebrated a thing in his life. I'm not sure he even has any teeth, because I've never seen him smile."

"It looks like he's here to sing," I observe. "Look, he's got a lute."

"No," Sadra says, looking thoroughly shocked. "Bard? *Singing?*"

"Well, if his name is Bard…"

"I always assumed it was a joke," Sadra says. "Oh, I must see this. Here, scoot over a bit so he won't see me if he looks this way."

"Who is he?" I ask, shifting my chair slightly.

Sadra hesitates. "He's one of those things I can't really talk about."

My joy dims. I don't want to think about Sadra's secrets tonight.

"I'm sorry," Sadra says, seizing my hand and kissing it. "Someday, I promise—"

"It's nothing," I say, squeezing her hand. "Forget it."

She nods, but some of the euphoria has gone out of the night. We sip our drinks in silence as the man named Bard tunes his lute. But Sadra doesn't let go of my hand, and by the time the tavern keeper appears to refill our cups, the blunted giddiness has transformed into a soft sort of glow, something quiet and comfortable. The lights dim, and the crowd quiets as Bard's lute strings ripple with sound.

"Oh, I can't wait," Sadra murmurs, a smile tugging at the corners of her lips.

Bard begins to sing. I blink. His voice is rich and warm, like velvet. From Sadra's reaction, I expected something comical. I shoot a glance at Sadra and find that very something. Her jaw is hanging open, her eyes bulging.

"Shut your mouth," I advise, stifling a laugh. "Flies will get in."

"I just can't believe it," she whispers. "If you only knew..."

But she falls silent again, the better to listen to his song.

"Drink deep, drink deep
Of the Chalice of Grace
Drink deep, drink deep
Of beauty's embrace..."

The song is one I've heard many times before, or at least variations of it. It's the story of the Chalice of Graces, the source of all beauty and virtue in the world. The tale goes that in the early days, life was empty and dull and brutish, until a smith was visited by the three Graces: Joy, Passion, and Beauty. Upon waking, the smith forged a chalice of gold rather than pewter or tin, as he always had before. He took the chalice to the village vintner, who in those days brewed not wine but vinegar to cleanse wounds and preserve food. The vintner confided his own discovery, which he had never dared to share before. He told the smith that he sometimes sipped on the wine he used to make vinegar, and that it made him feel good—happy, even.

The smith and the vintner filled the chalice with wine and took it to the villagers. All who drank from the Chalice began to laugh and sing. Once the villagers knew joy, their work turned to play, and their playfulness grew into passion and genius and beauty. They discovered that they each had a special Gift inside of them that could make their lives better, fuller, more beautiful. Forever after, the folk of the Garden gathered at midwinter to celebrate the smith and his Chalice of Graces, or Chalice of Gifts, as it had come to be called.

As Bard's song comes to a close, I find myself a bit misty eyed. There *is* beauty in the world. I hope I will always remember that.

"That was very good," I say, clearing my throat. "Almost as good as Ismeni. Is he a Catchsong, do you think?"

"He's not." Something dark passes over Sadra's face as she looks at him. "That much I can tell you." She shakes herself, then smiles at me. "Let's get out of here before I push my luck too far. If he sees me, I'm done for."

"Where should we go?" I ask.

"Somewhere we can dance!"

I laugh. "That's everywhere."

"All the better, then."

She pulls me from the tavern and spins me into the street, where there is indeed a circle dance forming. We join in and let ourselves be carried away by the tide of hands and laughing faces amid cries of "Blessed be" and "Drink deep!"

Finally, I pull free of the grasping hands and slump against a nearby column, panting.

"I can't," I gasp as Sadra approaches. "I can't dance anymore."

"Your stamina is deplorable," she says with a grin. "We must work on that."

"That depends," I wheeze. "On how we practice."

Sadra laughs. "Oh, I'm sure we can think of something."

Dizzy with drink and shared passion, we collapse on a low wall and cheer on the other dancers. As midnight approaches, however, the crowds begin to fade away. Soon the streets and taverns will be empty, at least for a time. The midnight hour of the Chalice Festival is reserved for the sacred Contemplation, a time to watch the stars and reflect on what we're celebrating. Sadra and I make our way back through the streets and into the woods as the frenetic joy of the

City softens. But instead of leading me up the path to the Cloisters, Sadra turns onto what appears to be a narrow goat track.

"I know a spot," she explains as she leads me over boulders and through thickets dusted lightly with snow. "I stashed some blankets there a few days ago, so we won't freeze."

"Is it far?" I ask, squinting into the dark. I can't tell if the trees are swaying in the breeze or if it's my vision that's wobbling.

"Not very," she assures me. "Come on, I'll help you."

We stagger up the steep slopes, gasping and giggling, and finally collapse on a broad, moss-covered cliff overlooking the City.

"Oooh," I say, watching the lights wink out one by one far below. "This is beautiful."

"It certainly is," Sadra says, and I turn to find her gazing at me. She laughs suddenly, touching each of my freckles in turn. "You know, I never thought of it until now—your freckles look just like the Chalice."

"Do they?" I look up at the Chalice glittering in the sky and feel my lips curve in a smile. "You're right!"

"I think it's a sign," Sadra muses. "A mark of the Graces' favor."

"Good," I say wryly. "I need every scrap of favor I can get."

"No, no," Sadra admonishes me. "No talking about work or worry or anything unpleasant. Not tonight." She turns and burrows into a pile of blankets. "Get in here."

"There are enough blankets here for a whole regiment," I laugh as I slide under the blankets with her.

"I know. Isn't it lovely?" Sadra sighs against my neck. "I think this will be the best Contemplation I've ever had."

"I know it's mine," I reply. "I never really cared much for it before, or the festival. Luca always loved it, though." I smile fondly, remembering how we used to run away from the banquets and find the shape of the Chalice in the stars. "And he always made the best presents."

"I wonder how he's celebrating now," Sadra murmurs, nuzzling my ear. "If it's not like this, he's a fool."

I giggle. "I imagine he is. He's besotted with his Companion. Every time I see him—which isn't often!—he looks like a puppy, all soft and happy." Then my smile fades. "I don't know about tonight, though. He got a little jaded with the Festival the year our father died. It was slow, and Abba was ill for a long time. Luca was convinced that we could save him if we found the Chalice. He and Rowan searched all over the Terrace—and under the Terrace. Luca got lost in the tunnels once. Costi was so angry! And...so was Luca. He never found the Chalice, and Abba died. He never got quite as excited about the Festival after that."

"What were your parents like?" Sadra asks after a long silence. "I don't remember mine."

"I loved my father," I say softly. "But I'm not sure I know what he was *like*. I was six when he died, and I don't think a child can really know who a grownup is as a person, do you?"

"I suppose you're right," Sadra says. "But what do you remember?"

I think for a moment, then say, "He was...big. Everyone says Costi looks just like him, so I suppose they must be about the same size, but I remember Abba as a giant. A giant of love. He took love very seriously, my father. No matter what else was happening, he never missed a single supper with the three of us, and all the guards were under orders never to deny us entry to his study. Costi takes after him in that, too," I add.

"It sounds nice," Sadra says wistfully. "Having a family."

I smile. "It is. After Abba died, the councilors wanted to send me to be raised in the Temple cloisters. Costi never said what they thought should be done with Luca, but Costi wouldn't hear of it."

"A brave choice for a young man—and a young king," Sadra murmurs. "He must have been, what, twenty?"

"Eighteen," I correct her. "And it *was* brave. He was scared, even I could see it. When it happened...it's the only time I've ever seen him cry."

I fall silent then, remembering. When I was young, I knew my father was dead, but I didn't really understand what it meant. Everyone had said that he was gone, but he had gone places before and had always come back.

I still remember the moment that I finally grasped the truth of things. It was the day of Costi's coronation, and I went looking for him. I found him in my father's rooms, not his, and I thought that had to mean Abba was home. Memory takes me back, more than a decade passing in the blink of an eye. Just like that, I'm six years old and hammering on my father's door, certain that Abba has come home at last.

At first, my nurse denied my pleas to see my brother. Prince Miocostin was very busy preparing for the coronation, she said, and had no time for little girls. I looked on her with scorn and retorted that my brother was never too busy for me, and he would have her spanked if she tried to keep me from him.

I dodged between the guards at the door and pushed it open to find my brother sitting before the fire with his elbows on his knees and his head in his hands. He looked up at my noisy entrance and dismissed the guards, who were hovering nervously in the doorway. I ran to him and climbed into his lap, cuddling close.

"Why are you in here, Costi?" I asked. "Where's Abba?"

Costi, who had been rocking me back and forth, stilled.

"He's dead, sweetling. You know that."

I nodded impatiently. "I know. But when is he coming back?"

Costi leaned away so he could look at my face. His frown was no more than thoughtful, but it made me nervous.

"Ari, do you know what it means to be dead?" he asked.

"It means you're with the ancestors," I replied promptly. "It means you're gone."

Costi scrubbed a hand over his face. "Shadow and blight. Who told you that?"

I had to think about this. "I don't know. Nurse, maybe. Is it wrong?"

"Well..." Costi looked around, as if for help, but there was no one but us. His jaw tightened. "No, I suppose it's not wrong. Abba is gone, and he is with our ancestors. But, Ari... he's not coming back."

"Not today," I said. "But when?"

Costi closed his eyes, his throat working. "Never, sweetling. He's never coming back. We're never going to see him again."

I stared at him, dumbstruck. My horror increased tenfold when Costi's chest spasmed and he clapped his hands over his face. I leapt to my feet, terrified, and tugged at his wrists.

"Where does it hurt?" I cried, mimicking my Nurse, as if the words were a magic spell. "Where does it hurt!"

"Everywhere." Costi's voice was muffled and raspy. He sounded like a monster. "Everything hurts."

He lowered his hands and pulled me into his lap again, hiding his face in my hair. But I'd seen it already: twisted and pale, ravaged with pain. My heart hammered, my terror compounded by confusion.

"Why, Costi?" I whispered. "What's wrong?"

"Stars save me," Costi rasped. "Everything, little sister. Everything is wrong. Our father is gone, and I'm to be king, and I can't do it without him. He told me what it was like, before. When he had our mother. She helped him. She was so good, so wise... he told me, you know. He said he could do anything with her by his side, and when she was gone—he only had me. And I wasn't enough. I wasn't enough, and now he's dead, and I have no one."

I cupped his face in my tiny hands. "You have me. I'll help you."

Sadra's touch brings me back.

"I'm sorry," she says. "I didn't mean to make you sad."

"You didn't," I say. "You just made me remember. It's not a bad thing."

In reply, she tucks her head against my shoulder, and together we fall into silent contemplation of the stars.

Sadra and I part reluctantly an hour or two after midnight, and I float down the mountain in a cloud of sleepy contentment so thick I can hardly see despite the full moon overhead. I can't believe how lucky I am. Sadra is so beautiful—and this night is beautiful, the City is beautiful, and so are its people. *My* people.

I've never felt so connected, like I'm just another citizen and a part of the City's beating heart.

I was delighted by the City's extension of the custom of gift-giving—how everyone buys everything for everyone else. Just remembering it fills me with the urge to do one last thing for someone. But I can't go to Rowan, who will immediately puncture my bubble of joy. Neither can I go to Costi or Luca without giving myself away. Norrin? No, it's too late. Then it hits me—Sparrow. Maybe it's silly, but I suddenly can't bear the thought of anyone, even a thrall, going without some kindness tonight.

And then there's the fact that embarking on this little errand will delay the inevitable confrontation with Rowan, who is no doubt wearing a track through my rooms with his pacing.

I slip into Costi's study and scrawl a hasty note to Soren, then make for the storerooms. There are blankets in there, lovely soft ones that are perfect for my—rather, Sparrow's—needs. I let myself in and tuck one of the blankets under my arm. Leaving the note in its place, I head for the thralls' quarters, hoping I don't get lost. I've only been down here once, when Sparrow was delivered to me. Ismeni thought it was important to prepare the room and see to Sparrow's welfare myself. She also said I should conduct regular assessments, but I've been lax in that regard. Well, Chalice is a time of reflection and renewal. I will do better.

But, I realize as I reach Sparrow's chamber, I may be too late. Just as I turn the corner, a cloaked figure opens her door and stumbles in. I quicken my step. Whatever the stranger is up to, he's in enough of a hurry—or, perhaps, too drunk—to bother closing the door behind him. And so there is nothing to bar my view as he leans over Sparrow and lifts her skirts. In his haste, his hood falls, revealing—

"Hadrian!"

My shocked cry echoes in the empty corridor. Hadrian jumps, shame and alarm flashing across his face for the barest instant as he registers my identity. But then his usual complacent smile is firmly in place, clearly visible in the moonlight slanting through the window. He steps away from Sparrow and out of the room, closing the door firmly behind him.

"My dear Arismendi, what are you doing here?" he asks smoothly. "Did you need something from the thrall? You should have sent someone to fetch her. There was no need to trouble yourself."

"Never mind what I wanted with her," I say, fighting to keep my voice steady. "I'm more concerned at this moment with what *you* wanted. What were you thinking, Hadrian? You were going to—to—"

Hadrian laughs. "My sweet, are you jealous? I'm touched. I had no idea you cared."

"Don't be ridiculous," I snap. "I don't care about *you*. I care that you were about to rape my thrall."

"You can't rape a thrall," Hadrian laughs. "That's absurd, even for you."

"Whatever you want to call it, it's reprehensible," I say. "I won't have it."

He raises his eyebrows coolly. "Forgive me for trying to remain faithful to my future wife."

"Faithful!"

"Would you rather I find my pleasure with a real woman?" he asks, mocking me with his scrupulously polite tone. "I could, if you'd prefer that. But, silly me, I didn't want to dishonor you. I do apologize."

"I *would* prefer that, actually," I say. "At least a prostitute gets some say and a bit of silver for her trouble."

"Tut, tut," Hadrian admonishes me. "Spite does not become you. If you wanted my attentions for yourself, you had only to ask."

He reaches for me, and I slap his hand away furiously.

"You're vile," I say. "The last thing I want is your attentions, now or ever."

His smile is slow and slimy. "And yet you will receive them in time, whether you want them or not. An heir must be conceived."

A sick dread creeps into my stomach. He's right. No matter how long I try to ignore it or pretend it away, at some point I'm going to find myself in his bed. More than once, unless I am unspeakably lucky. Hadrian laughs.

"Not so high and mighty now, are you?" He smirks and reaches out to pinch my cheek. "I look forward to our wedding night. It will be such fun."

"Just stay away from my thrall." I jerk free and back away. "She's the property of the crown."

"Until we wed," Hadrian reminds me. "And then she'll belong to me... just like you."

Chapter Thirty-One

I bring Sparrow back to my chambers with me. With ruthless disregard for Rowan's need to lecture me, I make a bed of blankets for her on the floor. She lies down at my direction and seems to fall asleep immediately, seemingly unaffected by Hadrian's assault. But is that because she is as unaware and mindless as she looks, or does she not understand what happened? Or, lacking human emotions, is she simply unbothered by it?

But *I* am bothered. I am disgusted, furious—and afraid, both for myself and my thrall. I keep her close by me all the next day, and her presence is a constant reminder of what happened... what has *been* happening for who knows how long. In my dreams the next night, Sadra is concerned when I tell her what I discovered, but not surprised.

"I've seen it before," she says, her face hard. "Many times."

"I have to do something," I say, pacing the lavish chamber Sadra has conjured for us. "I have to help her. Would the Temple... ?"

Sadra hesitates, the shakes her head. "The Temple doesn't traffic in thralls."

"It's not *trafficking*," I huff. "She needs help."

Though she looks pained, again she shakes her head. "They don't keep thralls, either."

"Someone else, then," I say, thinking. "Pia. Or Calan, maybe. He could use the help, I'm sure."

"Not Calan," Sadra says quickly. "Maia is afraid of thralls."

"Rocks, you're right." I sigh. "I forgot."

"But Pia is a good option," Sadra says encouragingly. "You can ask, at least."

Unwilling to leave her in the palace alone, I bring Sparrow into the City with me the very next day. She carries a sack full of the gowns Ismeni supplied for her when she first arrived as well as some things of mine that I hope Pia will be able to sell or keep for herself. Sparrow follows after me like a ghost, moving so softly and smoothly it looks like she's floating. Whoever trained her did a good job.

Jessa is out when we arrive at the Honeysuckle. I breathe a sigh of relief. This will be difficult enough without Jessa's inevitable questions. Pia will have enough of her own, but she at least has the sense and tact to know when to stop asking them.

Pia is inside, busy as always. She looks up from the tankard she's filling and gives me a smile, though it turns into a frown of confusion when she sees Sparrow.

"What is that?" she asks, her tone too polite.

I sigh. "You know perfectly well what she is, Pia."

"Well, what's it doing here, then?" she asks.

"Why don't we talk in the kitchen," I suggest, casting a nervous glance at the patrons, who are watching and listening with interest.

"Well, that sounds promising," Pia mutters. "Come on, then."

I follow her back to the kitchen and motion for Sparrow to set down her load. She complies and settles into a corner to wait for further direction, as she always does.

"Why in the stars' names have you brought your thrall into my tavern?" Pia demands.

"To give her to you," I say simply, unable to think of a way to soften the words or dress them up.

"What for?" She's so surprised she doesn't even bother to put a bite in the words.

"To help you," I say, striving for a light and cheerful tone. "An extra pair of hands would be useful, wouldn't it?"

"Extra hands are of no use if they come without a brain," Pia says with a snort.

"She's very trainable," I say, still smiling. "If you keep commands simple and show her what to do a few times, she'll learn."

"It's a nice thought, Ari, but I don't need charity," Pia says. "You know that."

"It's not charity." I sigh, giving up the charade. "It's a favor—to me. I can't keep her."

Pia eyes me suspiciously. "Why not? I thought you said it's useful."

I flush with embarrassment and remembered fury. I fidget, reluctant to tell her that I need her to save my thrall from my future husband. Pia looks at me with her brows raised, waiting.

"It's... it's Hadrian," I finally say, my face burning. "He's been abusing her."

"What, hitting it? I don't see any bruises."

"Not hitting her," I say. "*Abusing* her. Like—like—"

"*Oh.*" Realization dawns on Pia's face, followed closely by disgust. "I've heard of brothels that offer that—particular service, but surely no decent man would—rocks, he might as well swive a sheep!"

"Yes, well, we both know my betrothed isn't a particularly decent man," I say bitterly. "She can't stay with me. And I don't want to sell her for fear she'll end up in one of those brothels. Won't you take her?"

"I don't know." Pia looks at Sparrow, dislike warring with pity on her face. "It could be bad for business. Folk might think I'm setting myself above them, keeping a thrall. Or they might even be afraid of her. Three Spiritwalkers have been discovered and arrested in just the last week. One was found trying to steal food."

"Food?" I frown. "Why would a Spiritwalker go to the trouble of possessing a thrall just to steal food?"

Pia shrugs. "Desperation? Maybe he meant to abandon it before he got caught. Leave the thrall in the dungeons and escape himself."

"Still, you'd think someone that powerful would be after something more than food," I muse.

"I don't know why it happened, and I don't care," Pia says, waving a hand irritably. "I care about keeping my customers happy, and a thrall is likely to get them riled. It might even keep them away entirely."

I wince. "I'm sorry. But—can't you just keep her out of sight? Please, Pia. I'll pay for her upkeep. I just need to get her out of the palace."

Finally, she sighs. "Oh, alright. I suppose she can sweep the floors, if nothing else."

"Thank you," I say, hugging her. "She can do much more than sweep the floors. You won't regret this, I promise."

"Don't make promises you can't keep, Princess," Pia warns.

Before I can answer, Jessa bursts in with Nettle on her shoulder and a basket of vegetables on her arm. When she sees me, she gives a glad cry and jumps into my arms. I catch her—and Nettle, who yowls and scrambles over my shoulder in a flurry of claws and fur.

"What are you doing here?" Jessa asks. Then she catches sight of Sparrow, and her eyes widen. "And why do you have your thrall?"

I look at Pia, who sighs and shoves her hair out of her face.

"She's our thrall now, apparently," she says.

Jessa gasps in delight. "Really?"

"Really," Pia replies, somewhat sourly.

"But... " Jessa turns to me, her excitement fading into puzzlement. "Why?"

Again, I look at Pia. She makes a face and pulls Jessa away.

"Ari's betrothed isn't treating the thrall the way he should," she says. "Ari wants to keep the thrall safe, and this—" She throws me a sardonic glance. "—is the best she could come up with."

Pursing her lips, Jessa peers at me, then her mother. I can see the questions tumbling in her head, but—for once—she keeps them to herself. Instead, her brows pull together, and she looks at me worriedly.

"Ari," she says slowly. "Hadrian isn't a very nice person, is he?"

For a third time, I look to Pia for direction. But she merely shrugs and moves to scoop up the vegetable basket. I sigh and turn back to Jessa.

"No," I tell her. "No, he isn't."

"But he's the reason you got the money for the school," Jessa presses.

"Yes."

Jessa bites her lip. "Did you know? When you agreed to marry him, I mean."

"I hoped I was wrong," I say bleakly. "I hoped he'd changed. Grown up."

"But you weren't wrong," Jessa says. "And now you're trapped. Because of me."

"No, sweet." I pull her into a hug. "I wanted this. I chose this. I was always going to have to marry someone. At least this way I could get something out of it."

"But you might have found someone wonderful," Jessa insists. "You might have fallen in love. You might have been happy."

Tears prick my eyes. I am in love. I did find someone to make me happy. But even without Hadrian, I could never have married Sadra. The thought sends a bolt of unexpected pain through my body. I shake it off.

"Or I might have ended up with someone like Hadrian anyway, with nothing to show for it," I counter. "Put it out of your mind, Jessa. I don't regret a thing."

Jessa hesitates a moment, then nods, her shoulders relaxing. I give her one last squeeze and hold her away.

"Now," I say. "Can I trust you to take good care of Sparrow?"

Her eyes shine. "Yes!"

"Good," I say, trying to smile. "I'm counting on you."

I leave the Honeysuckle with heavy steps. Did I do right? Will it work? As usual, Hadrian is awful, but he's not wrong. When we marry, Sparrow will belong to him. He'll be able to take her back and do whatever he likes with her... and with me.

As guilt ridden as I still am for Sparrow, I can't help feeling relieved at her absence. For the first time in months, I can enjoy true privacy in my rooms. But it can't last. There will be a thrall in my rooms again soon enough, if Ismeni has anything to say about it. Which she does. She has plenty to say, and ample opportunity to do so now that she lives in the palace.

Ismeni hounds me relentlessly for weeks. The subject pops up every so often at odd moments, and she keeps threatening to drag me back to the auction house by my ear. I ignore her, sure she'll eventually tire of pestering me. But as the winter deepens, so too does Ismeni's conviction.

"You are a lady," she says crossly one day as her seamstress measures me for yet another new gown. "A *princess.* How are you to manage?"

"The same way I did before Sparrow," I say with a shrug.

"But, you can't, you must see that!" Ismeni exclaims, and snatches up a gown from my bed. "You never dressed like a proper lady before Sparrow, but now you do. Now you must. Who will tie up your laces? Who will fix your hair?"

"I could learn to fix my own hair," I suggest. "And Rowan can help me tie a few bows if it really comes to it."

"Stars save me," Ismeni mutters, then glares at me ferociously. "As I refuse to consider the possibility that I have taught you nothing, I will choose to believe that you are merely teasing."

"I am teasing." I sigh. "But would it really be so bad to employ an actual human?"

"Yes," Ismeni says succinctly, and that is that.

The seamstress is finished with her business, but Ismeni is not finished with me. I've been wondering when her patience would expire, and today, apparently, is the day. She drags me—gracefully, somehow—to Villa Prosper and all but throws me at her father.

"Abba," she says. "Talk sense into the princess, if you please."

"What sort of sense?" he asks, blinking owlishly at us over a scroll.

"*Common* sense," she cries. "She needs a thrall and refuses to buy one."

Norrin sighs and sets down the scroll. "And why do you need a new thrall? What happened to the old one?"

"I gave her away," I say, lifting my chin. "To someone who needed her more."

"That was foolish in the extreme, my dear," Norrin says, frowning. "As is your continued aversion to thralls. You must move past this. You need a thrall, Arismendi. It's simply a reality of your station."

"So we will find you one," Ismeni says with a smile, her composure restored by her father's support. "Abba, when will the next auction be held?"

Norrin winces. "Not for some time, I'm afraid. Our supply is limited at the moment."

"What?" Ismeni leans forward, concerned. "What do you mean?"

"There was some trouble with the last shipment," he says. "More than half the thralls were compromised by Spiritwalkers."

"So many?" Her hand flies to her breast. "And the rest?"

"Safe, so far as we can tell," Norrin assures her. "But it was a blow, to be sure."

"Is there anything suitable left for Ari?" Ismeni asks, her brow furrowed.

Norrin grimaces. "Perhaps, but none are available. The thralls that remain are all spoken for."

"I don't understand," I say. "Why did this happen?"

"What do you mean, why?" Norrin asks, giving me a quizzical look. "Thieves steal, my dear."

"But why thralls?" I insist. "Surely there are easier things to steal?"

"But fewer things more valuable," Norrin replies. "There is, unfortunately, a well-established and robust black market for thralls and other House goods. Which is a problem—beyond the obvious immorality and the drain on our profits, of course. When thralls arrive in the City under the auspices of the House of Light and Shadow, they undergo a rigorous screening process and multiple protections against tampering. Black market thralls are far more susceptible to possession. Which puts everyone at risk, and it's getting worse."

Ismeni's eyes are wide. "Is anything being done about it?"

"The House is increasing security for our caravans, naturally," Norrin says. "And Joram tells me they will be conducting investigations throughout the City and outlying villages, with a focus on the Lower City. Which brings me back to your predicament, my dear." He turns to me. "If, as I suspect is the case, you have given the thrall to your friend Pia, I urge you to reclaim it immediately. The inspectors' orders are to confiscate any thrall who seems even slightly suspicious or out of place."

"And if I'm too late?" I ask, my heart fluttering.

Norrin waves that away. "We'll get it back. But it will take time—more time than my daughter will tolerate, I'm sure."

"Indeed," Ismeni says severely. "Ari, you must go and retrieve poor Sparrow immediately."

"I can't," I say, flushing. "It's—I don't—"

How on earth am I going to explain why I can't keep Sparrow myself? I can't very well tell Norrin the truth.

"My dear," Norrin says, and something about his half amused, half pitying tone reminds me of his son. "Come now, I thought you were made of sterner stuff. Your Sparrow was a legitimate purchase, with all requisite safeguards. No harm will come to you."

My flush deepens, irritation mingling with embarrassment, and I decide the truth is a viable option after all. I didn't want to speak of Hadrian's perversion in front of Norrin, but if he insists...

"It's not Sparrow who worries me," I say, trying not to sound—or feel—spiteful. "It's Hadrian."

"Hadrian?" Norrin asks, puzzled. "What do you mean, child?"

"I caught him in her room," I say, my nostrils flaring in anger at the memory. "I'm sure I don't need to tell you what he was doing."

Norrin goes pale. "Hadrian wouldn't—how dare you suggest—" He takes a deep breath. "My dear, you must be mistaken."

"I am not," I say clearly. "He was quite open about it. He seemed to think I should be grateful that he had taken a thrall to bed instead of a woman."

Norrin stands abruptly, shaking his head. His hands tremble as he gathers up the scrolls scattered across his desk. One of them falls to the floor, but he doesn't retrieve it.

"I will not hear this," he murmurs, and leaves the room without another word.

Ismeni looks at me, her eyes tight.

"Was that really necessary?" she asks.

"I'm sorry." My eyes drop to my hands. Shame pools in my belly, cold and clammy. "I didn't mean to hurt him."

"But you did," she says, and her voice wobbles just the tiniest bit. She rises and moves to leave, but then she pauses at the door. "And I warned you about buying a beautiful thrall, do you remember? I told you what could happen, and now both you and the thrall must live with it. Go and get her."

I leave Villa Prosper feeling like an utter villain. Norrin's attitude bothered me, but he is not his son. Norrin might tease me, but I know he respects me. I didn't need to throw Hadrian's faults in his face. I didn't need to hurt him—and Ismeni, too. Both of them have done so much for me, and I might as well have spat on their kindness.

"What's wrong?" Rowan asks when Cressen closes the villa's doors behind me. "You look ill."

"I said something I shouldn't have," I tell him. "About Hadrian."

"What, that he's a disgusting deviant and you won't marry him?" Rowan says lightly. At my pained look, his jaw drops. "No!"

"Not in so many words," I say. "But—yes, I told them what he did."

"How did they take it?" Rowan asks, looking more fascinated than concerned.

"Not well," I say shortly, then sigh. "We need to go see Pia."

"What for?"

I wrinkle my nose. "I need to get Sparrow back before she's confiscated. Norrin said the House is tightening security measures because of all the Spiritwalker activity."

"And you're... open to that?" Rowan asks slowly.

"I'm not sure I have a choice," I sigh. "Norrin says we can get her back if they take her, but who knows in what condition? If they take her, they'll test her."

Rowan doesn't argue with that. And so we head straight for the Honeysuckle Rose, hoping that we're not too late.

Chapter Thirty-Two

When we arrive at the Honeysuckle, Rowan immediately slides behind the bar and takes a tray of empty mugs from Pia's hands. He nods in my direction, murmuring something.

"I need to talk to you about Sparrow," I tell Pia, leaning over the bar so I can keep my voice low.

Pia gives me a sharp look. "You know, then."

"About the raids?" I frown. "Yes, Norrin told me. Have they already come, then?"

"What are you talking about child?" Pia asks. "Have *who* come?"

I furrow my brow at her in confusion. "The House raids for compromised thralls. What are *you* talking about?"

Pia winces, then sighs. "You're right. We do need to talk."

She nods toward the kitchen, and I follow her. Jessa watches us with an avid gaze, hungry as always to be involved. But she doesn't leave the customer she's attending, which is a surprising but not unwelcome reminder that she *is* growing out of childhood fecklessness.

"So," Pia says once the door swings shut behind me. "Sparrow."

"I need her back," I say, and wince at the bluntness of my statement. "It's not safe for her to stay here."

Before Pia can say anything, I launch into an explanation about the recent thefts and the House's crack-down on illegal thralls. She listens in silence, her face growing more and more troubled as she peels potatoes.

"So I need to bring Sparrow back to the palace with me," I conclude. "For her own safety."

Pia doesn't say anything at first. She just stares down at the potato in her hands, her paring knife flicking steadily. When she finally looks up at me, it's with an expression of vulnerability I can't remember ever seeing before.

"I owe you an apology, Ari," she says. "I should have told you sooner. But I was ashamed and—and afraid."

"What do you mean?" I ask, my heartbeat picking up speed.

"It happened weeks ago," Pia says quietly. "That's why I'm so ashamed. Sparrow... Sparrow is gone. Forgive me, Ari. I should have told you right away."

"But... I don't understand," I say, shaking my head. "What do you mean, she's gone? What happened?"

"She just disappeared," Pia says. "She must have run away in the night."

"That can't be," I say. "Thralls don't just run off. They can't. They have no desires, no independent will. She must have been stolen. Unless... unless she really *was* a Spiritwalker!"

"I—maybe." Pia turns back to her potatoes, looking strangely flustered.

The door slams behind me, making me jump.

"She wasn't," Jessa says hotly. "You know she wasn't, Mama."

Pia's head snaps up. "Jessa, out. This isn't—"

"Isn't what?" Jessa demands. "Isn't important? Isn't my business? It's both of those things! You aren't the only one who lied to Ari, Mama, and I'm sick of it."

"Jessa—"

"We should have told Ari the truth *weeks* ago." Jessa crosses her arms, her jaw set stubbornly. "The least we can do is tell her now. Tell her *everything*."

Pia stands, white-faced, scattering potato peels in her haste. "Jessa."

"Sparrow wasn't a Spiritwalker," Jessa tells me. "I know because—"

"*Jessa.*" Pia lunges for her daughter, but Jessa dances out of the way.

"Because *I* am a Spiritwalker," Jessa finishes, shooting Pia a triumphant look.

Silence reigns. Pia gives me one stricken look before covering her face with her apron, her shoulders shaking with what look disturbingly like sobs.

All I can think to say is, "No, you're not."

Jessa smiles a little. "Yes, I am."

"But—but you're a Beastspeaker," I say helplessly. "You and Nettle… "

"He doesn't speak to me, not like Kirit speaks to Luca," Jessa says. "But we are… connected. That's why it was so easy to let people believe that I'm a Beastspeaker."

"Connected? Connected how?" I ask, shooting a glance at Pia. But she seems to have surrendered. She sits in the corner with her head bowed, tears streaming down her face.

"He lets me ride with him," Jessa explains. "My spirit."

"Ride with him… you mean you need another body to house your spirit? You don't walk on your own?" I ask, my mind whirling with questions. I pace around the kitchen, too shocked and galvanized by Jessa's news to sit still. "And you said Nettle *lets* you ride with him. Do you need his permission?"

"Yes," Jessa says. "I mean—I *can* walk on my own, but not very far or for very long, and I can't touch anything. It's hard to even hear or see anything very clearly. And, yes, I need his permission. That's how I know the House has been lying about thralls and Spiritwalkers. They can't be possessed."

"Because they can't give permission?" I ask. "Because they're not really alive?"

"I'm not sure why," Jessa says. "Not exactly. I just know that they can't be controlled by Spiritwalkers like the House mages say. I can't ride with another person. I've tried. It's like… I can ride with Nettle because I'm a girl and he's a cat. There's room for me. If I were a cat, I couldn't do it. Because Nettle's already in there. You can't have two cats in one cat. Does that make sense?"

"You can't possess a real person," I press. "But—"

"I don't *possess* anyone," Jessa says sharply. "I can't force Nettle to do anything he doesn't want to do. I just… visit, for a bit."

"Yes, fine," I say, waving a hand. "But have you ever tried—ah, visiting—a thrall?"

"Yes," she says. "It doesn't work. I told you, there's no room. There's already a person in there."

I cease pacing and put a hand on the wall to steady myself. My heart pounds in my chest so hard it feels as though it's pushing the air out of my lungs with each beat. My head swims, making me feel a little sick, but I also feel strangely... joyful. Excited. Exhilarated, even. Vindicated.

You were right, a little voice whispers. *They are alive. They aren't empty. They're... people.*

"Wait," I mutter. "Wait."

I need to get a hold of myself. Just because *Jessa* can't do these things doesn't mean another, stronger Spiritwalker can't. And the House... The House of Light and Shadow can't have been lying about this, not for four hundred years. How could something of this magnitude have remained a secret? Surely there must be more to the story, intricacies of Light that Jessa or I couldn't even guess at.

But something in me balks at this perfectly reasonable line of thought. I've always resisted the accepted wisdom peddled by the House. Something always felt *off*, rang false. What Jessa says, on the other hand, rings absolutely true. No matter how I try to argue myself out of it, I believe she's telling the truth. I believe she's correct.

And if she is—stars, what does this mean for Sparrow? She was a *person*, and I made her a slave. Hadrian raped her, who knows how many times. And now where is she? Could she have escaped the city and found some safe haven, or is she starving somewhere, all alone? Or has she been recaptured by the House?

"We need to find her," I say, almost to myself. "Oh, stars, we need to help her!"

"That's enough," Pia says, having finally gotten hold of herself. "*If* Jessa is right, and if Sparrow has any sense, she's long gone by now. It's over."

Jessa opens her mouth to make some reply, then uncharacteristically checks herself.

"Jessa?" I ask, trying to keep my voice steady. "Is there something else?"

"My daughter has said quite enough," Pia says, grabbing Jessa's arm. "It's time for her to go do—something. Anything else. This conversation is over."

"Pia," I say softly. "I would remind you of your place—and mine."

Pia rears back as if slapped. Jessa's eyes widen.

"I'm sorry," I say, feeling sick. "This is too important. Jessa is right. I placed Sparrow in your care, and you lied to me. You owe me this much, even if I weren't asking as your princess."

Pia's face closes like a fist.

"Very well, *Princess*," she spits, and slams out of the kitchen.

"I'm sorry," I say again, to Jessa this time. "But I need to know. Is there something else?"

Jessa bites her lip, then takes a deep breath. "Maybe. I'm not sure. I could be wrong, or I might have misunderstood. And it might not mean anything, anyway."

"Just tell me," I say. "Please."

"You have to promise she won't get in trouble," Jessa says.

"I promise," I say impatiently. "Just tell me."

"I... I heard Maia talking to Sparrow," Jessa says, looking deeply unhappy. "The day before Sparrow disappeared. They were in the storeroom before lessons. I couldn't hear what she was saying, but she sounded... I don't know. Not like herself. And then I saw them both come out. At the time I just thought it was strange, but then later, when Sparrow left and I started thinking about it... I don't know. I guess it still just seems pretty strange."

"You didn't hear anyone else?" I ask. "You didn't hear Sparrow speak?"

"No," Jessa says. "Just Maia."

"Did you ask Maia about it?" I ask.

"Later, yes," Jessa says, her voice sad. "She said she wasn't even in the store-room, but I saw her. She lied to me."

Tears fill Jessa's eyes, and I pat her awkwardly on the shoulder. My mind is elsewhere, spinning with possibilities. I don't hear it at first when Jessa speaks to me.

"What?" I shake my head to clear it. "Sorry. What was that?"

"Is Maia going to be in trouble?" Jessa asks.

"No," I assure her. "No, of course not."

"What are you going to do?" Jessa asks.

"Honestly?" I sigh. "I have no idea."

Chapter Thirty-Three

That night, it takes me even longer than usual to fall asleep, troubled as I am by everything I learned today. Thoughts of Jessa, Maia, and Sparrow swirl around each other until I lose the thread of each mystery. And, to make matters worse, it isn't Sadra waiting for me in my dreams. Just a beautiful garden consumed by flames.

It's just a dream, I tell myself. *I have nothing to fear. Sadra can't save me every night, but she'll return. She'll come to me, and we'll fly away on feathered cats or float across the Sweet Sea on a turtle's back. She'll come back.*

She doesn't have to. She's *here*, stumbling toward me through the chaos.

"Ari," she calls, half-choking on the acrid smoke. "Ari!"

"Here," I cry, running to meet her. "What are you doing here?"

"I didn't mean to," she says, coughing. "I didn't mean either of us to be here. Your dream is too strong—rocks, I knew you had nightmares, but I never imagined *this*!"

"Just wait," I say, resigned. "*She'll* be here any moment."

"She?" Sadra asks. "Who…"

Then her eyes go wide as the fire-girl materializes before us, twirling into being from a twist of flame. She dances around us in a circle, bending and turning with ethereal grace. Sadra gapes at her, white-faced. Her lips move, shaping a word, but I can't hear her over the roar of the fire.

"We have to get out of here," she says, seizing my arm and drawing me close to shout in my ear. "You shouldn't—we shouldn't be seeing this."

I frown. *We shouldn't be seeing this...* Did she mean simply that she should be able to control what we see, or did she mean something else? It almost sounded as if the fire-girl is something dangerous—forbidden. But what can Sadra know about my fire-girl?

"Come on," Sadra says, coughing. "Let's go."

I shrug helplessly. "Where? There's nowhere to go."

"Let me try," Sadra says. "If we can just get away from the flames... "

There's no escape from the flames. I know that well enough by now, but Sadra is a newcomer here. She drags me around and around the burning remnants of the garden, choking on ash and smoke. The fire-girl follows, doggedly spinning and twirling in our wake.

"You should go," I tell her at one point. "There's no reason for us both to be here."

"No reason?" She shoots me a disgusted look. "As if I'm going to leave you here alone. Is that what you think of me?"

"No, I just meant—"

"I'm not leaving you," she snaps.

"Can you wake us both up, then?" I ask, trying to hold onto my temper as we pass a burning rose bush for the fifth time. "You've done it before."

She chews her lip. "I don't know. This dream has such a strong hold on you... I don't want to risk it. What if you don't wake up and then I can't get back in?"

I let out a small huff of laughter that ends in a cough. "Then my friend and I will pass the time until I wake."

I almost wouldn't mind. The more familiar misery of my burning garden is in some ways preferable to the mess that awaits me in the waking world. But I can't explain that to Sadra. As much as I trust her, I can't tell her what I've learned without also telling her about Jessa, and that's not my secret to tell.

Sadra darts a glance back at the fire-girl, her shoulders tense. "Definitely not."

"Sadra—"

"*No.*"

I hold my hands up in surrender and let her tow me along as she resumes her search for a way out. The fire-girl brings up the rear, and we proceed in a bizarre little parade through the wreckage until, finally, the dream fades into the soft pre-dawn shadows of my bed chamber.

Groaning, I drag myself out of bed. My limbs are heavy, my fingers clumsy. My thoughts are like mud. Even so, they return immediately to the same patterns that tormented me last night. Sparrow and Jessa—and Maia. Does she know, too? Or was she merely tormenting poor Sparrow out of fear, as children sometimes do? I don't know. I don't know anything.

And Sadra was behaving so oddly last night! Now that I'm awake and free of the raging flames of my nightmare, I find myself growing more and more uneasy. Sadra looked at the fire-girl with a sort of shock that seemed almost personal. As if she wasn't horrified merely to see a girl on fire, but *that* girl in particular. As if Sadra somehow recognized her, even faceless and on fire. And what did she say—or, rather, what did she start to say? *You shouldn't be seeing this.* She was so determined to keep me away from the fire-girl...

I shake myself, snorting at my suspicions—and of what? What, exactly, do I suspect? That Sadra knows something about the girl in my dreams? The thought is as ridiculous as it is irrelevant. What, then?

Something niggles at the back of my mind, something that instinctively makes me shy away, but I force myself to confront it.

What if Sadra knows about the thralls? What if she's involved? She was Orean's Companion. She's all but admitted that she's involved in something nefarious, or at least dangerous. What if it's the thralls?

My heart leaps. What if she's working *against* the House? The Temple has always been vehemently opposed to the use of thralls. What if it's because they know the truth? What if I'm not alone in this? With the Temple's resources, I could do so much more for Sparrow than I can on my own.

I spend the whole day sunk in my own head, debating whether—and how—to broach the subject with Sadra. If I'm right, I could gain a powerful ally. If I'm wrong, I could be betraying Jessa and Sparrow, and perhaps Maia, too, to the enemy.

But this is *Sadra*. I would stake my own life on her trustworthiness. And if I'm right... I have to try. I'll be careful. I won't just spill the whole thing. I'll tread lightly, and if the slightest thing feels wrong, I'll stop.

Luckily, I'm already scheduled to see her today for one of our weekly "curriculum consultations." I drag myself up to the Cloisters with Rowan in tow, and it occurs to me to wonder if I should feel guilty for giving him an edited version yesterday of my conversation with Jessa and Pia. It's not the only time I've lied or kept something from him, but it's close, and I don't like it. I'm also not sure if it's a mistake.

But, one thing at a time. Sadra first. When we reach Sister Tilla's office, Rowan takes up a position outside the door. I let myself in and drop into a chair to wait, utterly exhausted. The moment Sadra arrives, a weight lifts from my heart. Her eyes sharpen as they flit over my face, and her brows draw together in worry.

"What's wrong?" she whispers. "You look awful."

I give a soft laugh. "I'm sure I do."

"Is whatever this is—" She waves at me and my general dishevelment. "—the result of last night's...excitement? Or is it the cause?"

"The cause, I think," I say. "Something happened, and it's... it's bad."

"How can I help?" she asks instantly.

"I'm not sure," I say. "Do you... what do you know about thralls?"

Her face closes like a door slammed in my face. "Nothing. The Temple prohibits their use."

"But you haven't... you don't... "

"I'm not interested in thralls," Sadra says. "They're unnatural perversions of beauty, and those who rely on them for Light or labor are too lazy to cultivate their own abilities and Gifts. It's a disgrace—literally. An affront to the Graces."

"I just—"

"Ari, I don't want to talk about thralls," Sadra says, taking my hand. "If that's what's upsetting you, put it out of your mind. Nothing good can come of it."

"Alright," I say, defeated. "I will."

I still don't know where Sadra stands or how much she knows, but she's made one thing abundantly clear: I'll find no help here.

"Go home," she says gently. "You're in no state to work right now. Go and rest, and I'll see you later. Somewhere marvelous, I promise."

I want to rest. I want to lean against her and just let her hold me. But I can't, of course. I can't even touch her hand. All I can do is try not to cry as I leave her.

Chapter Thirty-Four

As if Jessa's revelation was some signal to the universe, everything speeds up. The renovations come to a close. Calan and Sadra declare their curricula and lesson plans complete. Norrin declares mine complete for me, knowing that I'll continue to tinker with them until I'm an old woman if left to my own judgment.

The school will open a week before the Festival of Lights, to coincide with the birth of spring. The fruition of all my dreams and struggles is so close, and yet I find I can't enjoy it. Mere moments after the school's opening date is announced, Hadrian all but beats down Costi's door demanding that our wedding date be set as well. I sit silently as the negotiations play out and merely nod in agreement when they settle on the Festival of Lights itself. This was always the price for my school, and it's time to pay.

With my wedding now only weeks away, Ismeni flies into a frenzy. My every waking moment, it seems, is packed with fittings, menu planning, shopping, and lessons. Always, lessons. A Companion—not Sadra, sadly—is hired to explain to me the mechanics of consummation and advise me on how best to please my husband and find some pleasure of my own. Afterward, I can't decide whether I want to gag or laugh.

Amid all the chaos, I have little time and less opportunity to search for Sparrow. Pia flatly refuses to make any sort of inquiries for fear of drawing attention from the House of Light and Shadow. I have to admit that her fears are not without merit. But still, I can't let it go.

"There's nothing you can do," she tells me the fifth time I try to draw her into my attempts. "Short of physically turning over every stone in the City, and even that is impossible without raising awkward questions. Just stop, Ari. She's gone. And for all you know, she could be perfectly safe."

"But—"

"But nothing," Pia says firmly. "Your precious school opens tomorrow, and you promised me it would be a success. If you want to worry about something, worry about that."

She's right, of course, and so I reluctantly take her advice. I spend the rest of the day and much of the evening obsessively sorting and re-sorting my supplies, making sure everything is in perfect order. I fall asleep with my fingers still twitching with the urge to reorganize my quills just one more time. Sadra laughs herself silly as we find ourselves in a dream version of my room doing exactly that, at least until she takes control.

The next morning dawns bright and clear, and I can't help but feel it's a sign of the Graces' favor. It rained all week, and the sun has finally broken free of the clouds just for my special day.

Ridiculous, of course, but I'm not about to turn down whatever encouragement I can find. My stomach is a tangle of nerves. Today the months of hard work, the tears, the arguments, it will all come to fruition—provided nothing goes wrong. But no, something is bound to go wrong, that's just life. But as long as nothing irreparable goes wrong, it will be a success. Validation, vindication, and victory.

I've done it. At the thought, a tiny bubble of pride blossoms in my chest. It doesn't grow too big, not yet, but it's there, a tiny flower frosted with hope. I look out the window and pray that this day will go smoothly for the girls' sake, if not for my own.

"Ari?" Rowan calls through the door. For once, he remembers to knock, even if he doesn't wait for a response before letting himself in. "Oh, good, you're ready. Will you be joining the king for breakfast?"

"I suppose," I say, biting my lip. "But I don't have much of an appetite."

"You should eat anyway," he says. "You have a big day ahead of you. It won't exactly add to the grandeur of the experience if you faint in the middle of it all."

"Vomiting on my students probably won't, either," I reply. "But I'm sure a compromise can be found. A little bread and marmalade, maybe."

"Orange and lavender?" he guesses. "With some clotted cream?"

I snort. "You just want the leftover cream."

"But am I wrong?"

"No," I admit. "You're not wrong. That sounds lovely."

He nods briskly. "I'll see it's done."

Rowan disappears, and I hear him giving orders. Such things aren't technically his job as my guard, but Rowan considers anything to do with my wellbeing his business. Though it's precisely this attitude that makes him so obnoxiously free with his opinions, it also means no task is too menial for him to attend to, including the particulars of my breakfast.

I take a deep breath and turn to the clothes I carefully laid out the night before. I put a great deal of thought into this ensemble, which is something I'm not sure I'll ever get used to. Ismeni has drilled into me over and over again that my appearance matters, that everything I wear sends a message whether I intend it to or not.

Today, I want that message to be one of confidence, but not arrogance. Beauty, but not vanity. Simplicity, but not meekness. But now, everything seems wrong. My silver necklace disappears into the pale blue of my gown, and it sits awkwardly on the draped fabric of the neckline. I take it off and drop it onto the vanity, then inspect the slippers I chose last night. These, too, seem completely wrong in the light of day. I throw them into the corner and rummage in a trunk until I find a pair that look right. And a sash—do I need a sash?

With every decision, a little more of my hopefulness slips away, leaving me tired and anxious before I even leave my room. I pick at my breakfast and barely manage a few words to Costi and Luca. But neither presses me except to insist that I finish my bread. I leave nearly all the clotted cream for Rowan, but even he seems too preoccupied to enjoy it. We leave it on the table and make our way in silence out in to the courtyard, where a full complement of guards awaits me.

"Is this really necessary?" I ask glumly as the guards take their places about me. There will be even more waiting in the City, ready to escort my students up to the Cloisters.

Luca shrugs. "Costi's orders. And I agree with him. It shows the people that you have the Crown's blessing, and that the king takes it seriously."

"Or makes it look like I'm setting the girls above their neighbors, which is exactly what that Yoren and his pack of cretins keeps accusing me of," I fret.

"Too late now," Rowan says. "Come on. Do you really want to risk what Jessa will do if you're late?"

I shudder at the thought. She'll probably come find me, or lead her classmates to the Cloisters herself and get into who knows what trouble along the way.

"Let's go," I say.

People stare as we enter the Upper City, and I shrivel under their gaze. I can't remember the last time I went among the people with more than just Rowan or, occasionally, Rowan and Luca. To the people, it probably looks like a rare event—the royal princess descending among the common folk. They don't know the princess spends more time in the Lower City than on the Terrace—or, at least, that she used to, before... all this.

Jessa squeals when we enter the Honeysuckle, her eyes shining as she takes in my guards with all their finery. She clasps her hands together and all but vibrates with excitement.

"Behave," Pia warns her. "Remember the princess has done this for your sake, and she paid for it dearly. Don't dishonor her."

My stomach sinks a little at the reminder that my triumph today was bought on credit, and soon I'll have to make good on the debt. My wedding is just ten days away. Ten days, and I'll belong to Horrible Hadrian Prosper. The thought makes me want to vomit all over again.

But I can't think of that today. There's too much to do, and I want to at least try to enjoy it. More students are trickling in. Some are unfamiliar, but others I've met already: Taya, with her flaming curls; Cora, small and plump and pretty, with her mother's rosy cheeks; Channi, the only girl from the Upper City; and Maia, who I've discovered has an uncanny knack for calculating sums in her head... like her father, Calan. I wondered if perhaps her Gift has begun to manifest itself, but only time will tell. My heart lifts a bit as I watch the girls greet each other shyly and begin to mingle. I'll get to watch these girls grow into their Gifts and talents, help guide them. They'll have the tools they need to care for themselves and flourish on their own.

I have eight years to teach them what they need to know. It seems an impossible task. But then, opening the school once seemed impossible. And I've done it.

"One step," I murmur to myself. "Then the next."

Finally, all ten girls are gathered outside the Honeysuckle. My nerves jangling, I motion to Rowan.

"I think we're ready," I say. "Let's round them up and start walking."

"Oh, we're not walking," Rowan says.

I frown. "What do you mean?"

"You'll see in a moment," he says cryptically.

And I do. Just then, a massive litter born by six—no, *eight*—thralls rounds the corner and comes to a halt in front of us. The girls cheer and clap their hands, chattering excitedly to each other. I turn to Rowan.

"What is this?" I demand.

"Hadrian insisted, and Norrin backed him up," Luca says. "So did Costi. I told you, he wants to show that the Crown approves of the endeavor."

"And this is how he wants to show his approval?" I fume. "I won't have it."

"You already do, I'm afraid," he says, for the girls are being helped into the litter by a cheery little man. The thralls' owner, I think, or perhaps an overseer employed by the owner. But he looks far too pleasant to be an owner or an overseer. I chide myself for the thought. Not everyone mistreats their thralls. In fact, very few do. Thralls are too valuable to neglect, if nothing else.

But still, the idea of getting into that litter makes my skin crawl. If Jessa is right, these are *people*. Not dolls. Not tools.

"Your turn, Princess," Rowan says.

I stiffen. "I'll walk, thank you."

"You'll do no such thing," Luca says, though he gives me a sympathetic pat on the shoulder. "How do you think that will look?"

"Like I enjoy walking?" I offer. "Or like I get motion sickness?"

"It looks like scorn," he informs me. "It would give the impression of scorning your betrothed, the king, and even the girls."

I groan. "That's so stupid."

"But that's the way it is."

I stare at the waiting litter, and the thralls waiting beside it. They stare at nothing, docile as sheep.

"Why couldn't we have a carriage with horses?" I ask, struck by inspiration. "Or donkeys, even."

Luca scoffs. "What did I just say about scorning this gift? And, anyway, it would take hours for a team to arrive."

He's right, of course, and it makes me grimace. Livestock of any kind—any kind but thralls, of course—are prohibited in the City. There just isn't enough room. Not enough need, either, with thralls to pull and carry.

Rowan lays a hand on my shoulder. "I know you don't like it, but they're here, and they're waiting for you. Just think of the girls."

I soften, my eyes falling on Jessa. She's so excited, and she looks so proud to be sitting in a litter, likely for the first time in her life.

"Fine," I say, defeated.

Rowan hands me into the litter, and I settle myself between Jessa and Maia. Rowan nods to the cheery man, who nods back and takes his place at the head of the litter. He taps one of the thralls on the shoulder. A small flare of Light pulses briefly in the air, and the eight thralls rise as one. I close my eyes as the litter lurches upward, my hands clasped tightly in my lap. What is so wrong about walking on one's own two feet? Why does respect for one person have to come at the expense of another person's degradation?

"Ari, are you alright?" Jessa asks, not bothering to keep her voice down. "Why aren't you smiling? This is marvelous! Look, everyone has come to see us off. Even... " Her smile falters. "Even Yoren Silversmith."

My head whips around, and I follow her gaze. It is indeed Yoren Silversmith, and he has a contingent of House guards at his back. I bite back a groan.

"What now?" I whisper. "For Grace's sake... "

I look around for Luca, but he's already moving to intercept Yoren. The crowd around us thickens as more people are drawn by the spectacle of thirty House guards and Yoren's voice, ringing with triumph.

"These thralls have been compromised," Yoren announces. "And must be recalled."

"Compromised?" The thralls' driver, no longer cheery, glares daggers at Yoren. "Says who?"

Yoren gives him a gentle smile that calls Hadrian to mind so strongly it makes my blood boil.

"That information is confidential," Yoren says, smoothing his ridiculous little wisp of beard. "Have no fear, my good man. They will be returned to you as soon as we ensure that they are free and fettled against Spiritwalker interference."

At the mention of Spiritwalkers, a low, ugly hum rises from the crowd. Some back away, but more press forward, emboldened by the shimmer of Light that surrounds the House guards.

"Take 'em," someone shouts. "Take 'em and beat the evil out!"

"But—but—" The driver looks at Luca for help and finds none.

Luca scowls at Yoren. "Take them, then, and be quick about it. Ari, get the girls down."

At the driver's direction, the thralls lower the litter to the ground once more, and I shoo the girls back onto the street. None of them ask what's happening, or why. Jessa glares at Yoren with narrowed eyes, partly, I suspect, in dislike, but also in calculation. Perhaps she finds the timing of this little emergency a bit suspect, as I do. But she appears to be the only one. Most of the others simply sigh and shrug—disappointed, but not surprised or suspicious. And Maia—I frown, concerned. Maia has gone bone white, and her trembling shoulders jerk with each shallow, labored breath. Now that I think on it, she was pale and quiet even before the House guards arrived.

"Do thralls upset you, Maia?" I ask quietly, bending so I can speak into her ear.

She nods and whispers, "Yes."

"Me, too," I whisper back, and she gives me a startled look. "Perhaps now we can use donkeys, instead. Or cavalry chargers. Wouldn't that be grand?"

She smiles shyly. I grin in return and pat her shoulder before straightening up to look for Rowan and Luca. They're deep in conversation with the thralls' driver, who, though scowling, appears to be making a great effort to speak calmly. Finally, he takes a deep breath and strides away with a determined air.

"What's the plan?" I ask Rowan when he returns to my side.

"He's going to borrow some thralls from a friend," Rowan says, giving me a commiserating sort of grimace when I wrinkle my nose. "There's just not time to fetch animals from outside the City. And I think thralls might be uniquely suited to the task."

I frown. "What do you mean?"

"Look around," Rowan says, nodding to the muttering, buzzing crowd. "If this continues, it could get ugly—or at least loud. Thralls don't spook. It's safer this way. For the girls."

I sigh. I can't argue with that, so I don't. The driver is back within the hour, with a new team of thralls plodding behind him. It's the work of only a few minutes to get everyone back into the litter and into position. The crowd, which had begun to disperse, reforms as we set off. Anxiety roils in my belly as I scan the sea of faces. A few are merely curious, but the vast majority are set in lines of suspicion, derision, anger, even fear. The mutters and chatters of the crowd grow into a buzz like a swarm of angry hornets. The girls huddle together in response, their shoulders hunched. Here and there a hand creeps out to find a friend's.

"Whores!" a woman suddenly cries out. "Shame on you. On all of you!"

Another woman shakes her finger at us and shouts, "The queen weeps in her grave!"

Ice floods me. I look for Rowan, but he's busy. So is Luca, so are all the guards. But am I imagining—no, I'm not. We started with a company of twelve, and only five remain. Each one of them is fully occupied with the crowd, which has begun to press in on us from all directions.

"Princess?" a small voice asks, but I'm too flustered to notice whose. "Are we safe?"

"Yes," I say firmly. "Ignore it, girls. These people are ignorant and small minded, and they deserve our pity, nothing more."

"That's my neighbor," one of the girls murmurs. "He buys our bread."

"Ignore them," I say again, trying to keep the rising fear out of my voice.

"Get back in the kitchen where you belong," a man calls. "Your father is waiting for his breakfast."

A smattering of laughter follows, along with a few other, coarser suggestions. Tears begin rolling down Maia's face. Cora and Channi are huddled into each other, arms linked and foreheads touching. Taya's face and neck are as red as her curls. And Jessa... Jessa looks ready to launch herself from the litter. I grip her arm, ready to haul her back if she tries.

She never gets the chance. Something dark and wet flies out of the crowd and strikes Jessa in the chest with a wet splat. She recoils in surprise, her head colliding with my jaw. I wince but shake off the pain. Whatever the missile was, there are more of them coming, flying from all directions. The girls duck and cower on the floor of the litter, their heads tucked together, their backs to the crowd. I stand, clutching the rail of the litter for support. One of the things—what *are* they?—lands on my shoulder, leaving a sticky red streak and the smell of blood.

"Rowan," I cry. "Do something!"

"I'm a little busy," he shouts back, struggling to fend off a pair of red-faced old ladies without hurting them.

Something flashes—sunlight on metal. I gasp as I catch sight of a skinny, mean-faced man elbowing the old ladies aside.

"Rowan—*the knife!*"

Too late. Rowan shouts in pain as the knife bites into his shoulder, but his attacker is down in the next moment with Rowan's boot on his neck. Rowan shouts something, and the scent—or touch?—of Light drenches the air. The crowd falls back, knocked off their feet by the blast.

"Fall back to the litter," Luca barks to the other guards. "Rowan will keep the crowd off of us."

Rowan shoots Luca a glance that's half irritated, half amused and mouths something that looks like *Thanks a lot.* But he raises his hands before him, muttering, and leads the way. Light pulses with each step he takes, pushing the angry mob back and away like a wedge. His stride never falters, but I can see the sweat beading at his temples. After two blocks, his hands begin to shake. After three, he gasps for breath. After four...

"Is Rowan alright?" Jessa whispers, her hand creeping into mine. "How long can he keep the wards up?"

"He's fine," I say, and I can only hope I'm not lying. "Everything will be fine. We just have to be brave and believe in him."

"I can do that," Jessa says fiercely. She gets to her feet and leans over the rail of the litter to yell at the crowd. "You dung beetles can't scare us! Don't you have anything better to do? Dung to eat?"

I choke, torn between laughter and horror. "Jessa!"

"I had a big breakfast this morning with plenty of oats," she bawls. "Toss me a chamber pot and I'll serve you a meal you won't soon forget—with extra sauce!"

The Light throbbing around us fizzes for a moment as Rowan's step falters. But then it's back, stronger than before, and a wide grin spreads across his face. The other girls began to giggle. Even Maia, once she recovers from her shock. She stoops and picks up one of the mysterious bloody blobs.

"Is this the best you can do?" she cries. "You had to cut the balls off some poor donkey because you had none of your own?"

She hurls the blob—could it really be a donkey testicle?—and hits a portly, bristle-jawed man square in the eye. Jessa and the other girls cheer and start scooping up more missiles to return fire. Soon the air is thick with flying blood and insults, and I can't decide which is more disgusting—the testicles or the epithets.

But I don't stop them. They're having entirely too much fun, hopping up and down and shrieking like the monkeys Father once brought home from the City of Orchids. Their antics seem to have breathed new life into Rowan's wards.

Or maybe good cheer and courage are their own sort of ward. The crowd seems to lose interest in antagonizing them now that they're no longer cowering in fear. Some have even begun to laugh as the girls' taunts grow more and more outrageous. By the time we reach the Cloister gates, the mob has dispersed entirely, and the girls are congratulating each other and picking bits of donkey testicle from under their fingernails.

When the litter comes to a halt, they leap to the ground and charge Rowan. Jessa hurls herself into his arms and kisses his cheek. The other girls begin a sort of war dance in a circle around him, cheering and singing their congratulations. I descend more decorously, allowing the litter driver to hand me down.

"They've got spirit, I'll give them that," he remarks, watching Rowan wrestle free of Jessa's grip. "But you sure do have your work cut out for you, Princess."

I laugh, and it comes out a little wild. "I'm aware."

Today's little adventure was just the beginning, I'm sure. I'll have to work myself to the bone, not only to keep the school running but to fend off our detractors. It's going to be the hardest thing I've ever done. Maybe the hardest thing I'll ever do.

I can't wait.

Chapter Thirty-Five

Sister Tilla—bless her—is on hand to greet us and help me corral the girls. It takes some effort and time to settle them into my classroom, but not as much as I feared. I let them spend their still-fizzing energy in a game to get to know each other, then begin with a lecture on the fundamentals of composition. Soon they're happily practicing with chalk and boards, drafting letters to their families. I settle behind the teacher's desk with a deep sigh and try to let my shoulders relax. Though the day is far from over, I am cautiously optimistic that it will be a success despite this morning's dramatics.

The girls seem happy, anyway, scratching busily at their boards. It's peaceful, despite the sounds of Calan singing to himself in the next room. I smile. It isn't loud, and it isn't hurting anyone. There's no need to chastise him or ask him to stop. In fact, if I'm not mistaken, it's Rowan's favorite drinking song. I look up to point that out to Rowan, but he isn't at his post. I frown, a prickle of unease tip-toeing up my spine. Where has he gone? I move to the door and look out.

"Rowan?" I call down the hallway.

"He went somewhere," Jessa says, looking up from her board. "I saw him slip off when he thought we weren't looking."

"That's not right," Channi says with a prim sniff. "He's a guard, and you're the princess. He's supposed to follow your orders."

"Yes, well, when your guard is also your brother's best friend, you'll find that it doesn't always happen that way," I say dryly. "I'm sure he's just gone to make sure you girls chased off all the rabble, do rounds, that sort of thing. That's part of a guard's job, too, you know."

"I suppose," Channi says dubiously.

"Back to work," I say. "Take another few minutes, and then we'll share our work."

They bend their heads back to their boards, but look up again in confusion at the sound of a commotion outside. I move to the window to see who's shouting. It's Sister Tilla. She seems to vibrate with a fury that I never imagined she could possess. She's shouting at guards clothed in the black and white of the House of Light and Shadow. Rowan is with her, and it looks like he's trying to mediate the dispute.

"Oh, rocks, what now?" I mutter, pressing my nose against the glass.

Whatever Rowan is saying to the guards' captain doesn't seem to be having much effect. After a moment, he turns and strides into the building and out of sight. I meet him in the corridor. His face is calm, but the lines of his shoulders and jaw are tight and anxious.

"Come with me, Ari," he says. "Bring the girls outside."

"What's going on?" I ask, my heart fluttering. "What are House guards doing here?"

"They won't say," he says. "Only that they have business with you... and your students."

I gape at him. "My students? What could they possibly—?"

"I don't know," he says, shaking his head. "I just know I don't want them to find the girls in here, where there's nowhere to run."

"Fine," I mutter. "Fine."

I take a deep breath and school my features into something that—I hope—looks like calm composure. At Rowan's nod, I turn to the class and call for attention.

"We need to go outside for a few minutes," I tell them. "Come, now, quickly—and quietly, please."

"What's going on?" Jessa asks, never one to let something out of the ordinary pass without explanation.

"The House of Light and Shadow has some business with us," I say. "Let's go and get it over with, whatever it is, so we can return to our work."

Maia, already pale, goes deathly white and sags into her chair. Jessa and I exchange a look. I think suddenly of what Jessa told me about Maia speaking to Sparrow and wonder uneasily if I should have confronted her, or perhaps Calan, about it after all. But it's too late now. I hurry to her side and kneel beside her.

"Don't be afraid," I say. "They probably just have some questions for us, that's all."

"I want my papa," she whispers. "Where is he?"

"I'll fetch him," I promise. "He's just in the next room."

Maia nods and gets to her feet shakily. Jessa tucks her arm around Maia's waist, and they follow the other girls out into the hall. I move toward Calan's classroom, but Rowan stops me.

"He's not there," he says. "I checked."

"I heard him, though," I say. "Just before you came in."

Rowan shrugs. "Whether he was or wasn't, he's not there now. And we don't have time to look, Ari. We have to go."

"Alright," I say, and shake him off when he reaches for me. "Alright! I'm coming."

Together, we hustle the girls out of the school building and into the chilly serenity of the Cloister grounds. Sister Tilla faces the contingent of guards with her fists clenched, tiny but fierce. I join her and fix the captain with my best royal glare.

"What is this?" I ask. "Why has the House of Light and Shadow seen fit to trespass on Temple property and disrupt our lessons?"

"You have our deepest apologies, Princess," the captain says with a bow. "It couldn't be helped. We have reason to believe there is a Spiritwalker in your midst. Please remain calm."

"And what reason is that?" I inquire, though I heartily doubt they have one. This is simple harassment. That weasel Yoren is behind it, I'm sure.

"Again, I ask that you remain calm," the guard says, puffing his chest out importantly. "We're here to help."

"We don't need your help," I say firmly. "There are no Spiritwalkers here."

"I'm very sorry to disagree with you, Princess," the captain says, not looking sorry at all. "But there are. Two, in fact."

"Who?" I demand. "Who are you accusing?"

"A man known as Calan Skinpainter and the girl he calls his daughter. You know her as Maia." The captain's eyes rove over my assembled students, now whispering and clutching each other in terror. "We'll be taking them into custody."

My heart stops.

"No," I say, and I'm surprised at how calm and reasonable the word sounds. "No, you're not. You're not taking them anywhere."

Rowan is suddenly at my side, thrusting me back toward the girls.

"Take them," he says. "Run, Ari!"

Rowan throws up his hands, and Light explodes outward, knocking the whole contingent of guards backward. Sister Tilla and I hustle the girls away, but they're frightened and confused and tangled in their skirts, and Rowan is one man against twelve. We make it no more than a stone's throw before we're surrounded and on our knees.

"Maia Skinpainter," the captain barks. "Declare yourself."

Silence.

"*Declare yourself*," the captain roars. "Which of you is Maia?"

"I am," a quavering voice replies. It's Jessa, her face screwed up in fury.

"I am," says Channi, rising to her feet.

"I am."

"I am."

"I am."

One by one, the girls stand and clasp their hands. My heart swells at their courage, then breaks at the slow smile that spreads across the captain's face.

"Well," he says. "I suppose you'll all be coming with me, then, won't you?"

Chapter Thirty-Six

I don't spend long in the House's custody. In fact, we've hardly set foot on the valley floor before Luca arrives with a contingent of royal guards and orders our release—at least, mine and Rowan's. The House captain flatly refuses to release the girls until Maia is identified. Immediately, the girls start shouting and spitting, each insisting that *she* is Maia Skinpainter. Luca's eyes flick to me. I shake my head dazedly, at a complete loss.

Simple logic dictates the sacrifice of one to save many, but logic is useless in matters of the heart, and the situation is anything but simple. If I identify Maia, she will never forget that I gave her up, that she was less important to me than her friends. She'll never forgive me, and neither will the other girls if I undermine their sacrifice. They'll never trust me again. I can't. I *can't*. I have too much respect for them, and Maia *isn't* less important. She isn't expendable. But if I don't speak, all of them will end up in the House dungeons, at least until their parents retrieve them. And I shudder to think of what the parents will have to say about *that*.

Before I can make a decision, the parents themselves arrive with Pia at their head. Sister Tilla must have sent a message. Without a word to me or even the guards, Pia marches over and hauls Jessa away. Taya's mother looks nothing like the cheery, rosy-cheeked lady I met at the Honeysuckle. She looks like a tigress, and her husband a bear. The look she gives me chills my blood. Mercifully, it only lasts a moment before her husband scoops Taya into his arms and all three of them hurry away. Next to escape is Channi, then Cora, then Zenna, Sima, and Nonna until, finally, only Maia remains. She has no one to speak for her, no parent to claim her. I don't know whether I'm disappointed at Calan for abandoning his daughter or relieved that he escaped. I just know that the look on Maia's face as they take her away will stay with me forever.

"We should go," Luca murmurs to me after sending his guards back to their posts. "Rowan needs a healer, and there's nothing you can do for the girl now."

"Maia," I say sharply, my focus returning to me with almost painful force. "Her name is Maia. Which you would know if you hadn't—"

"If I what?" Luca asks, his brows raised. "Go on."

"If you hadn't abandoned us," I say, my voice thick. "If you weren't so wrapped up in your Companion's bedsheets that you've forgotten you have a family. If you cared about anyone's business but your own."

I expect him to snap at me—part of me *wants* him to snap at me. But he just sighs and shakes his head. "That's not fair, Ari. You know it isn't. I'm here, aren't I?"

"Yes, I'm very grateful you could spare the time," I say nastily, and I push past him to stalk through the Terrace Gate.

"Where are you going?" Luca demands. "Rowan needs—"

"A Healer," I say. "Which I am not. So stop wasting time and send for one. I need to see Costi."

"You can't," Luca says. "He's meeting with the councilors."

"I don't care!" It comes out almost a shriek. I lower my voice and try again. "I don't care. Please, Luca. Just help me."

"I will," he says. "I promise. Give me a moment to get Rowan sorted and we'll go together."

"I'm fine," Rowan says from the ground. "Go. Do what you need to do to get Maia back."

"Yes, you look the picture of health," Luca snorts. "No cause for concern here at all."

I ignore this byplay as a flash of blue catches my eye. It's Soren, striding toward us in his usual sober yet elegant robes. I rush forward, barely noticing the flare of Light blooming in Luca's hand as he calls for a Healer.

"Soren," I say, seizing his hands. "Thank the Graces. Rowan has been badly hurt. Will you stay with him until the Healer arrives? I must see Costi right away."

"Certainly, Princess," Soren says. "But the king is—"

"I know," I say. "I'm sorry. It can't be helped."

Soren gives me a troubled look. "I think this is not wise, Princess."

"Necessity does not presuppose wisdom."

"Very elegantly put, Princess. Councilor Norrin has taught you well." Soren gives me a wry smile. "Do as you must, then. But, Princess... tread carefully. *Speak* carefully, I beg you."

"I'll try," I promise.

Luca appears at my side and touches my elbow. "Ready?"

I swallow and nod. Soren moves to Rowan's side and crouches beside him, his hand on Rowan's shoulder. As Luca and I hurry away, I realize I have no idea what I'm going to say to Costi. Part of me wants to simply throw myself at him and cry as I did as a little girl. Which, in defense of my inner child, has proven quite effective in the past. Costi has always had a knack for quickly grasping what's wrong (even with a minimum of coherent input from me), then taking decisive and effective action. It's what makes him a good king and an even better brother.

But I'm not a child any longer. I need to present the situation—and myself—in a manner befitting a princess. How, though?

I have no idea.

"So are you going to tell me what that was all about?" Luca asks. "A runner from the Cloisters brought word that House guards were dragging you through the streets in chains."

"That's a colorful interpretation," I say, a flicker of amusement flaring briefly in spite of myself. But I sober quickly, wondering how much I can safely tell him without revealing Jessa's true Gift. "I wish I could tell you. It makes no sense at all—they wanted to take Maia and Calan into custody on suspicion of Spiritwalking. I can only assume they'll also be accused of tampering with thralls. Being a Spiritwalker isn't illegal in itself, after all. But it doesn't make *sense*. Why them and not—"

I stop myself just in time. No one can know about Jessa, not now. I steal a glance at Luca to see if he noticed my slip and find him staring at nothing with an odd, tight look on his face.

"Luca?" I say uncertainly. "What's wrong?"

"Nothing," he says, his face smoothing. "I just—you're right. That makes no sense. It must be a mistake."

"That's what I thought," I say, trying for confidence. "Costi will be able to sort it out."

Luca doesn't reply.

Inside the palace, the corridors are empty and hushed. There's a strange tension in the air even before we reach the Council chamber, heavy and ominous, like thunder that has yet to break. As we approach the chamber, a rising wave of angry voices greets us.

"Wait here," Luca says when we reach the door. "I'll announce you."

I wait, resisting the urge to pick at the loose thread on my sleeve or chew on my nails. I probably already look a fright with my disheveled hair and mud on my hem and knees. No need to make matters worse.

Luca returns moments later and beckons me forward, his face grim.

"I hope you know what you're doing," he murmurs.

"Me too," I whisper back, and square my shoulders.

I walk into the Council chamber feeling like a mouse in a room full of cats. Every eye is on me, angry and haughty and so weighted with maleness I'm surprised I don't simply sink into the floor. In truth, I might prefer that to standing up under their gaze.

"My king, forgive me," I say to Costi, willing my voice to remain steady. "But I come with grave news that cannot wait."

Costi nods. "Speak, Princess."

I take a breath, grateful to Costi for his subtle reminder to his councilors—and to me—that I outrank them all.

"There has been a breach," I begin, thinking fast. "An egregious breach. Of honor and decency, but, more importantly, of jurisdiction and due process. The House of Light and Shadow trespassed on Temple grounds and abducted one of my students without any evidence."

"What is this?" Orean cries. "You would allow *this* to interrupt our work, my king? A girl's trivial complaints over an even more trivial—"

"There is nothing trivial about the abduction of a defenseless child," I return, striving for calm. "I am sorry for the interruption, gentlemen, but this simply cannot wait. A young girl, no more than twelve, is being dragged to a dungeon as we speak. The House has already acted unilaterally and violently in taking her captive, and I have no reason to believe they won't subject her to further violence without the Crown's immediate intervention. The House of Light and Shadow does not delay, and it doesn't hold back in its interrogations. The child's very life could be at stake."

"This is ridiculous," Orean says, slamming his fist on the table before him. "Someone remove this—female—from our presence."

"Lord Orean, you forget yourself," Costi says softly. "You do not give orders here."

"Someone must," Orean cries. He turns to the assembled councilors, spreading his arms wide. "My lords, how much more abuse must you endure before you take action? Before you realize that your king no longer has your interests at heart? For too long, your needs have been ignored, your opinions discarded like offal. Over and over again, your king has shown where his true allegiance lies—with bastards and commoners and women."

I gape at Orean, completely thrown by the abrupt turn the situation has taken. How on earth did we go from Maia's abduction to what sounds horribly like treason?

"How much longer will you allow this to continue?" Orean demands. His voice is thick with passion, but his eyes remain cold and calculating. "How much longer will you reason with a fool who throws away what coin he has and then demands your own? How much longer will you allow yourself to be ruled by a man who is himself ruled by the whims of women?"

He's making a move, I realize. Whatever he's been planning, he must have been waiting for an opportunity. And I've just given him one. What's more, it seems to be working. Though many councilors fidget uncomfortably in their seats, more are nodding and murmuring to each other in apparent agreement. A few, Norrin included, look to Costi. I do the same and find him simply watching Orean with an almost imperceptible smile on his face.

"I will not have it," Orean bellows. "Someone must stand for decency and simple common sense. If that one must be me, so be it."

Orean whirls and jabs a finger at me. I jump, startled by this sudden return to the spotlight.

"Guard Captain Voss," Orean says coldly. "Remove the princess and the king from this chamber and keep them under guard while the Council deliberates."

There's a moment of stunned silence, then my eyes widen incredulously as Voss steps forward. He hesitates, licking his lips, his face pale and sweaty. But then he throws out his chest, and his voice rings out as he gives the order.

"Seize them."

Nothing happens. I suck in a breath and wait, my eyes darting to the guards posted around the room. One or two take an uncertain step forward, then back. They glance around at each other once, twice, three times, then settle on Luca.

"Well, I'm certainly not going to," he tells them with a snort.

"Neither am I," Sammon says, braver now that Luca has spoken. "Seize the princess? The *king*? That's—that's plain treason, that is."

"Indeed," Costi agrees, his smile becoming more pronounced. "Thank you, Sammon. Would you do me the favor of escorting Lord Orean and Guard Captain Voss to a holding cell? Torrin, Morrick, and Carr—you, too. Sammon, you have the command."

Sammon bows. "Yes, my king."

"Tyranny!" Orean shouts, now paler and sweatier even than Voss as he appeals to his fellow councilors. "My lords, the time has come to take action. I call on you now to honor the vows we made one another. Stand with me! Against tyranny, corruption—"

"Corruption," Costi remarks. "What an interesting choice of words. I imagine Voss will have quite a lot to say on that subject, won't you, Voss? How disappointing this must be for you. I imagine if you had shared some of Lord Orean's coin, your fellow guards might have in turn shared in your corruption and proven more obedient. But, then again, perhaps not. They have far more honor and discipline than you do, as I have good cause to know."

"You should have spent more time training and less time drinking with rich nobles, Voss," Luca says with a grin.

"And Orean should not have been quite so eager to see what his coin bought," Costi says, his face going hard. He stands and addresses the councilors. "My lords, this Council meeting is adjourned. I look forward to speaking with each of you—at length—about what vows you have made, and to whom. Until then, farewell."

Not five minutes later, I'm sitting, dazed, in Costi's study. Luca leans against the wall, watching Costi as he tilts back in his chair, rubbing his temples. Now that the drama has concluded, he looks wan and tired.

There's a soft knock on the door, and Ismeni slips into the study. Costi's chair hits the ground with a thump. He smiles at the sight of his lover, the deep lines in his face relaxing.

"It's done," he tells her, taking her hand as she reaches him. "Thank the Graces."

"*What's* done?" I demand, unable to stay silent any longer. "What in the nine hells just happened?"

Costi raises an eyebrow at me. "Foxling, Orean just attempted a coup and failed. Surely you noticed."

"Well—yes," I say, struggling to find words. "I suppose I meant how, or why. Mostly how."

"That's exactly what I mean to find out," Costi says grimly. "He can't have believed he would be acting alone. We'll find out who he thought would be joining him, never fear. As for why—well, you know the broad strokes. The wealthy and powerful are not pleased with me. They like their rulers biddable and accommodating, and I have been neither. It was only a matter of time before someone did something... drastic. Orean in particular."

"So you knew," I say, looking from him to Ismeni. Her relationship with my brother suddenly takes on new significance.

"Not that exact ploy at that exact moment," Costi allows. "But then, I doubt it was meant to happen that way. Orean saw an opportunity and lost his head. Perhaps he was simply too eager, or perhaps his nerve failed him and he couldn't wait any longer. Either way, he made his move too soon."

"But you knew Orean was going to try to depose you." I shake my head, aghast. "Why didn't you *say* something?"

"Because I'm the king," he says gently. "And your elder brother. It's my job to protect you, foxling. Not the other way around."

"I'm not the one who needs protecting," I say with a wince. "I was telling the truth before Orean's—interruption. They took Maia."

Costi sighs, the lines of worry returning to his face. I plow ahead.

"I'm sorry," I say. "I know it's not... um, the best timing. But they're saying she's a Spiritwalker. They're going to test her, interrogate her—they'll torture her, Costi. They could kill her."

Costi nods wearily. "I know."

"So you'll order her release?"

He hesitates. "I'm afraid it's not that simple, foxling."

"But—"

"Ari, one of my councilors just committed open treason," Costi says, a hint of warning entering his voice. "I'll need to investigate not just Orean but my entire Council. I won't insult you by asking whether you understand how complicated, not to mention dangerous, our position is at this moment. Once you take a moment to think, I'm sure you'll see that I can't afford to antagonize the House of Light and Shadow."

I chew my lip. He's right, of course.

"So what will you do?" I ask in a small voice.

Costi sighs. "My best, Ari. That's all I can promise."

Chapter Thirty-Seven

Dismissed from the royal presence with nothing but Costi's lukewarm promise, I make my way to Rowan's chamber, itching with the need to do something. As I told Luca, I'm no Healer. I won't be able to assess his condition or the quality of the Healer's work. But I can at least assure myself that he's still breathing, and perhaps my presence will bring him some comfort. At the very least, I can thank him for what he did—or tried to do—for Maia.

Rowan is asleep when I arrive. So deeply asleep, in fact, that I nearly call for another Healer. But he isn't dead or dying. After a moment, his chest rises and falls, though slowly, and his heartbeat is strong and steady under my fingers.

"I'm sorry," I whisper to him. "And I'm grateful. Please be alright."

He doesn't answer, of course. I pull a battered but cozy chair next to the bed and sink into it, letting myself slump sideways in a manner that would make Ismeni pinch me. I should leave. There's nothing I can do here, and Maia still needs me. But there's nothing more I can do for her, either. Nothing except wait and hope that Costi's best, whatever it is, is enough.

I'm still slumped over Rowan's body when the door opens to reveal Lord Joram, the Premier of the House of Light and Shadow. I blink in stupefied surprise, then in alarm. I straighten unconsciously, Ismeni's training taking over. This is perhaps the most powerful man in the kingdom after the king.

"Lord Joram," I say. "What a—a pleasant surprise. What brings you to a humble guard's chamber?"

"I've been with the king," he says, closing the door behind him. "He said I would likely find you here. I thought we might talk, and I might also look over your guard. Rowan, is it? I was the royal Lighthealer before I became Premier, did you know that?"

"No, I didn't know that," I say. "I... that's very kind of you. Thank you."

I rise and take a step back, both to escape his overpowering presence and to give him room to work. Joram seems too big for the room with his broad shoulders and bulging stomach, his thick robes and imposing height. But his face is calm and serious as he extends his hands over Rowan. After a moment, he lowers his arms and turns to me with a slight smile.

"You needn't worry, Princess," he says. "The Healer did good work. Young Rowan will wake in the morning as good as new. He will suffer no lasting harm from his foolishness."

I stiffen at this but bite my tongue just in time. I school my features into a mask of polite interest. I wait in silence, not trusting myself to speak.

"You must allow me to express my regret at how today's events transpired, and how they must have affected you," Joram goes on. "The news of a snake among your lambs will have come as quite a blow, I'm sure, both to you and your guard. Though I must confess, I find myself surprised that Rowan didn't recognize the girl for what she was, skilled as he is in our craft."

"He is skilled," I agree. "Skilled enough to recognize innocence when he sees it."

Joram smiles. "I find your own innocence charming. Refreshing, in fact. When you have lived as long as I, seen as much as I... I hope you will never be so burdened."

"Yes, knowledge can indeed be a great burden," I say. "I presume the king made our requests regarding Maia's release?"

"Indeed, he did," Joram said. "But I'm afraid that wasn't the only topic of discussion."

"Oh?"

"Lord Orean is dead," Joram says, his voice matter of fact. "As is the treasonous guard—Voss, I believe his name was. Their bodies were discovered not two hours ago. I was asked to conduct an examination, resulting in my unfortunate delay—for which I apologize, of course. It is never seemly to keep a lady waiting."

I ignore that. My heart and mind are racing, both from his news and its implications.

"Lord Orean is dead?"

"Yes," Joram says. "And the king's investigation with him, I'm afraid. Without direct testimony... "

"But there must be others," I say without thinking. "Orean said as much. Either they were killed, or they killed Orean themselves. Either way, Orean and Voss's deaths served somebody." I look at Joram. "Why are you telling me this?"

"It is... relevant," he says. "To what happens next."

"What happens next?" I'm getting a very bad feeling about this.

"Consider the situation," Joram says, linking his fingers over his paunch. "An investigation into these deaths will take all the king's time and attention. His safety and yours will be compromised. Your wedding will almost certainly be delayed until the situation is resolved to the king's satisfaction. Which, unless I miss my guess, is not an altogether unpleasing prospect to you. However—" Here he holds up a cautioning finger. "Such an investigation would delay *our* investigation of the Spiritwalkers' activities. The more time passes, the more gossip will spread and grow. I shudder to think how the truth might be distorted. *I* know, of course, that you had no idea you were harboring a Spiritwalker in your midst—"

"Maia is *not* a Spiritwalker!" I snap, my heart pounding.

"I say she is," Joram says gently. "And you—forgive me, Princess—are in no position to contradict me, having no skill in the Craft yourself. Knowingly or not, you exposed innocent children to the machinations of not one but two

Spiritwalkers, whose only aim could be to corrupt our youth. For what other purpose would the fiends have placed themselves thus, among young girls? Your school may never recover from the scandal. Not without help."

"Surely you aren't suggesting that *you* would help me," I say, incredulous.

"But I would," he says. "I would happily pledge my public support, along with a sizeable donation."

"In exchange for what, exactly?" I ask suspiciously.

"Nothing," he says. "Do nothing, and urge your brother to do the same. Stop worrying about things you don't understand, marry Hadrian Prosper, and put all this behind you. The traitors are dead. Let all talk of conspiracy and treason die with them. Have pity on my poor wife, who has born the shame of her brother's treason and now must also bear the grief of his death."

"And you also would appreciate such pity, I'm sure," I say cynically. "Treason in the family can't bode well for your continued leadership in the House."

He spreads his hands. "Orean's treachery hurts us all, it's true. But you don't have to compound the hurt. You could use your influence to sway the king."

"And if I don't?"

Joram smiles sadly. "Then the king's investigation will continue, as will ours. No doubt your young friend Jessa will be taken for questioning regarding her association with the two Spiritwalkers. With such serious stakes, the questioning would of course be... rigorous. If she survives, her good name will be forever ruined. Your name, too, will be dragged through the mud. Even if the school manages to survive a second scandal, your marriage to Hadrian Prosper will be postponed. Perhaps it will be called off entirely. I imagine, in that case, House Prosper would cease to fund your little passion project."

"What about Maia?" I ask after a long moment.

"There *is* no Maia," Joram says, as if speaking to a child. "The girl you thought you knew does not exist. Grieve for the loss if you must, but then turn your mind to the true young ladies in your charge. You can still finish what you set out to do. You can give them the education you were denied yourself. All you have to do is forget all this."

His eyes bore into me, black and unyielding.

"Do nothing, Princess, and all will be well."

I lock myself in my room for the rest of the afternoon and evening, refusing food or company. Costi comes and tries to tempt me with cake and apologies—and news—but I don't let him in. I can't. He probably thinks I'm angry with him, but my disappointment pales in the face of my new predicament. It hurts me to send him away, but I can't let him see me like this. He'll know something is wrong, and I won't be able to resist if he presses me.

I want to confide in him more than anything, but that is the one thing I absolutely cannot do. If Costi learns that Joram is trying to bribe or threaten me, he will act first and look for evidence later. And when he does go looking for evidence, what will he find? Joram will be able to say with perfect honesty before a Truthseer that he only laid out the facts as he knew them.

The snake! At best, Joram is willing to let the other conspirators, whoever they are, go free in order to prevent any further damage to his family's reputation. But what if it's more? As I'd told him, Orean's death benefited somebody. Protected somebody. And if anyone could arrange a death with no witnesses or evidence... What if Joram himself is one of the conspirators? What if they intend to try again?

I can't let that happen. The investigation *has* to go on. But that means condemning Maia and perhaps also Jessa to the House's own investigations. I don't believe Joram's was an idle threat—both could very well die under the House's questioning.

I sequester myself in my room the whole of the next day, wracking my brain for a solution. This is too big for me. I need to talk to someone. But Rowan is still recovering, and Luca has been so distant, so erratic. I don't know what to do, and time is against me. I know perfectly well whom I *want* to talk to, but can I? Is it safe to bring Sadra into this? For her, for Maia, for me? Maybe not.

But I can't do this alone, and Sadra has the Temple behind her. She has people, resources, that are beyond Joram's reach.

I fall asleep feeling better for having a plan. But when I dream, I find Sadra standing on a vast, bleak expanse of stone with storm clouds boiling overhead and a freezing wind whipping around her. I squint, clawing my hair back from my face, and struggle toward her against the wind. She turns, and I can see bloody tears streaming down her cheeks. Her face is ravaged by grief, her eyes solid black like empty pits. She flickers in and out of my vision, as if struggling to retain her hold on my dream.

"Ari," she cries. "Ari, I need you."

"I'm here," I shout, seizing her hands. They feel cold and insubstantial. "What's happening? What's wrong?"

"I can't hold the connection," she says. "I can't stay—but I need you. Will you come?"

"To the Cloisters?"

"The willow tree behind the school," she says. "I'll be there. Please. Please come."

Then she's gone, and I'm lying in my bed once more, even more scared and confused than I was before. Without stopping to consider, I roll out of bed and whip a cloak around my shoulders. For a fleeting moment, I'm grateful that I don't have to try to sneak past Rowan or try to convince him to let me go. But then a thousand recriminations stab into my belly, my back, my heart. Rowan isn't around to get in my way because he's deep in a healing sleep, recovering from wounds won protecting me and my girls.

But I can't think about that now. I race through the tunnels and emerge in a cave about halfway up the steep slope that leads to the Cloisters. I scramble up the rest of the way as quickly as I can, blessing the moon for its light. Guilt over Rowan wars with worry over Sadra. What's happened to her? I've never seen her so broken, so out of control. What could have brought her to such a state?

The wall surrounding the Cloisters is sturdy and tall, but there's a massive, gnarled oak tree very near the willow Sadra spoke of. The two trees reach for each other across the wall, their leaves tangling together in a twiggy embrace.

This is where Sadra made her escape on the night of the Chalice festival, and it's how I'll reach her tonight. I pull myself into the oak and over the wall, sliding down the willow's branches like a rope.

Sadra is there the moment my feet touch the ground, throwing her arms around me and burying her face in my neck.

"You came," she breathes. "You came!"

"Of course I did," I say, and hold her away from me so that I can look at her.

Even in the moonlight, I can see the strain there, the shadows under her eyes. I have the feeling that they might be red-rimmed, as well, though of course I can't see the color. There's a raw, ragged look about them, as if she's been weeping.

"What happened?" I ask softly. "Is it... is it Maia? Had no one told you?"

I bite my lip. If Maia's situation has put her in such a state, perhaps it isn't right for me to add to her worry. I was relying on her to be strong for me, but maybe she needs me to be strong for her. Or maybe... maybe I was a fool for pretending her secrets didn't matter.

"No," Sadra says. "I mean, yes, but it's not just that. It's everything. I can't stand it, Ari."

"What everything?" I ask cautiously. I bite my lip, hesitating, all the questions I never asked her swirling in my mind. Then I ask her, "Why were you really sent here, Sadra? I'm sorry. I wish I could simply trust in your word, your intentions. But Maia has been taken, my brother's Council is plotting against him, and Rowan... " My throat closes. I take a breath, then go on, "Orean was arrested for treason, and now he's dead. You were his Companion for months, and now I see you like this—I can't believe it isn't all connected somehow."

"I want to tell you," Sadra says, her eyes filling with tears. "I want to tell you everything, Ari. I want it more than you can possibly know. But I can't."

"I won't say I understand," I tell her. "Because I don't, and I don't like it. I'm begging you, Sadra."

Sadra goes silent, and I know she's not going to tell me what I want to know. But she looks so lost, so heartbroken, that I can't be angry with her. I sigh and wrap my arms around her.

"You said you needed me," I murmur.

"I do," Sadra says, and her voice breaks. "Oh, Ari, I do. Something terrible has happened."

"But you can't tell me," I say, trying not to let my anger creep into my voice. I have secrets, too, after all. How can I blame her for hers, or leap to conclusions?

"No."

"You can't tell me everything," I say. "But does that mean you can't tell me anything? Please, Sadra, give me *something*."

Sadra sniffles against my shoulder for another moment, then nods. We sit at the base of the willow tree, our bodies pressed against each other. I loop my arm around her knees, while her hand runs up and down my calf. Finally, she begins to speak, her curls tickling my ear as she leans her head against mine.

"I was there to help someone," Sadra says. "In Villa Glory. Orean was hurting her, and I was there to help her get away from him."

My mind flashes to Ismeni, trembling and white in the door to Costi's study. I open my mouth, then close it. Bombarding her with questions will only delay the real answers I seek. So I just squeeze her hand to go on.

"I succeeded," Sadra says. "But things got ugly, and Mother Wenla said I got too involved emotionally, and she sent me here. But how could I not be involved? How could I not *feel*? The things I've seen... I'm so tired, Ari. Of all of it, all the ugliness in the world. I'm so tired."

She cries in earnest, then. First, it's a tremble, just a tiny quiver in her shoulders. But the shiver grows into a wracking sob that bursts from her chest like a thunderclap.

"And I miss her," Sadra says, her voice choked. "They didn't even let me say goodbye before locking me up here. She came to see me tonight, and I was so happy, and then—she's going to die. That's what she came to tell me. She's going to die, after everything that's happened."

A spark of surprise shoots through me, mixed with jealousy and confusion in equal measure. I had no idea Sadra and Ismeni were so close. In fact, I always had the impression they didn't much like each other. Was it all just a ruse?

And was—is—there more than friendship between them?

Stop it, I tell myself firmly. Now is not the time.

"Sadra, no one's going to die," I say. "Ismeni is fine, she's at the palace with Costi."

"I don't care about Ismeni," Sadra says, blinking in surprise.

I frown, too. Something is wrong. She isn't making any sense. There's a wild gleam in her eyes, speaking of something—unhinged.

"I only care about you. I'm so glad you're here," Sadra murmurs, taking my face in her hands. Her lips taste of tears. "If I didn't have you… "

"Of course you have me," I say, warmth chasing away everything else. I kiss her deeply. "You always will."

"That's not true," she says, pulling away suddenly. "You'll be *his* soon."

I wince. "Sadra… let's not… I mean, that doesn't matter right now."

"Yes, it does," Sadra insists. "You're going to marry Hadrian, and you'll leave me. You'll have to. He'll demand more of you—your time, your attention. Your body."

"I don't want to talk about Hadrian," I say, trying to reel the conversation back to more pressing matters. "I want to talk about everything we've been trying not to talk about for the last year."

"Well, *I* want to talk about Hadrian." Sadra pulls away and stands up, beginning to pace. "The thought of you in his arms, in his bed… I can't bear it, Ari, I can't! I want you to be with me. There, I've said it. That's what I want. I want it more than anything I've ever wanted in my life. You and me, together. Always."

"I want that, too," I say carefully. "And we can be together. We'll find a way. But not without honesty, Sadra. I have things to tell you, too. Can we just—"

"You don't understand," Sadra cries passionately, ignoring my attempt to bring the conversation back into line. "I don't want him to have you. Ever. At all. I don't want to share. Maybe it's selfish, but there it is. I want us to belong to each other, and *only* to each other."

"But we can't, Sadra," I say softly. "I'll be making my vows to Hadrian in a matter of days, and you already made your vows to the Temple."

"I'll break my vows," Sadra declares. "And you don't have to make yours. We can run away. We'll go somewhere no one will ever find us, to the City of Orchids or the Northern Reaches. To the Salt Islands if we have to. Wherever we have to go to be together." She takes my hands and presses them to her lips. "Can't you just see it? Us, growing old in a little cottage by the sea, with no one to tell us how to live our lives? We could do it, Ari. We could both be free."

"Sadra… " I stare at her helplessly, at a total loss. "Sadra, we can't do that. You can't mean it."

"I do mean it," Sadra says fiercely.

"But what about Costi? Maia?" I shake my head. What is she saying? She can't be serious. She can't. "I can't just *leave*."

"Why not?" Sadra demanded. "Miocostin is a grown man and a king. He's been ruling on his own for over a decade. He can keep doing it. And your school is finished. I'm sorry, but it's true."

She doesn't know. She doesn't realize—she'd never say such things if she knew the truth. So I tell her. About Orean's treason, about Maia and Jessa and Joram's threats against them. I tell her everything and wait to see understanding appear in her face, as it surely must. But with every word, Sadra's face only grows harder until she is as still and cold as marble. Her face is terrible, devoid of the laughter and life I've come to cherish so deeply.

"I can't leave them," I finish. "You must see that. Joram will kill Maia, I just know it."

"People die," Sadra says, her voice flat and cold. "People die, and we can't save them. The best we can do is save ourselves."

"No." I shake my head, unable to believe what I'm hearing. "*No*, Sadra, you don't mean that. Listen to yourself! I can't leave my family. Don't you have—what about Mother Wenla? She raised you, loved you like her own. You can't abandon her."

"My beloved *Mother* threw me away like a used rag and left me to rot," Sadra spits. "Just like my real mother. She took away the only person besides you who meant anything to me. So, yes, I can. And I will, if you'll go with me. Ari, *please.*"

"Let's talk about this another time," I suggest. She can't be serious. She just can't. She isn't in her right mind. "You're upset right now, and unwell. Maybe if you get some sleep—"

"I don't need sleep," Sadra explodes. "I need you. I've never asked you for anything, Ari. Not a single thing. And all the while I've helped you with your school, with Hadrian, with your brother—I've helped you do things for everyone else, and I've never asked you for anything in return. And now I ask for this one thing—"

"You're asking for the one thing I can't possibly give," I snap, getting angry now. "You're asking for something you would never dream of asking if you really loved me, or even knew me at all. Leave Maia to die? She's just a child—an innocent, helpless child! How could you suggest such a thing? How could you think I would even consider it? And even if Maia weren't—how could you ask me to leave Costi and Luca and Rowan? They're my brothers. If you had a family, you'd understand."

"But I don't, do I?" Sadra says. She's shaking—with grief or anger, I can't tell. "I don't. I don't have anyone but you."

"Sadra, please," I beg. "I can't. I *can't*. Let me speak with Mother Wenla. Maybe she'll let you return to the Terrace."

"Return to the Terrace?" Sadra scoffs through her tears. "For what? So I can watch you pledge yourself to that pig, Hadrian? No, thank you. If you want his money more than you want me, I suppose I'll have to accept that. But I don't have to be there to watch."

"That's not fair," I say. "You know it isn't."

"Life isn't, though, is it?" Sadra says. "Someone pointed that out to me recently, and she was right. Go back to your palace, Princess. We're through here."

"Sadra—"

"I have nothing more to say." Sadra lifts her chin, a hint of a sneer tugging at her lips. "Except, perhaps, that I wish you well. I hope you'll be very happy with him—or with his money, at least."

"This is ugly, Sadra," I say in a low voice. "This is beneath you. Or maybe it isn't. You never let me in, never showed me who you really are. I thought you were the kindest, bravest person I'd ever met, but all I see here is a bitter, twisted child who doesn't know a thing about real love."

"Go on, then, leave me if I'm such a child," Sadra says hoarsely. "Go!"

"Gladly," I snap.

I leave her there beneath the willow. As I stalk away, I can't help glancing back, hoping that she'll call out to me to stop. With every step, I imagine her footsteps behind me, her hand on my shoulder, her lips on mine. We'll murmur apologies between kisses. Of course I didn't mean it, she'll say. Of course I love you. I want to be with you any way I can. We can be together, even if it isn't perfect. I love you.

I love you. That's all I really want to hear. But she can't—she can't truly love me, not if she wants me to leave my family and forsake my duty not only to them, but to my people.

That's what hurts the most. Not her words, not her bitterness, but the knowledge that the love I thought we shared wasn't love at all. It was just a dream—and who better to weave such a dream than a Dreamwhisper?

Chapter Thirty-Eight

I pass the rest of the night lying rigid in my bed, breathing through gritted teeth, refusing to give in to tears. Dawn brings some relief. There's something about sunrise that makes even the darkest shadows recede, though they don't disappear. I drift off shortly after, only to be awoken by a knock at my door.

What time is it? I peel my eyelids apart and squint at the window. Late morning, I think, perhaps noon. And who is knocking at my door? I hope Rowan is fit for duty again soon. He would know I shouldn't be disturbed. Then again, even Rowan wouldn't turn away the king, and it most likely is Costi at the door.

Luckily, I *can* turn away the king. But I find I don't have to, because it isn't Costi.

"I beg your pardon, Princess," comes Soren's gentle voice. "But you have a visitor, and she insists that she must see you."

"Please convey my apologies, Soren." I roll over in bed, turning my back to the door, and even that small motion feels as though it takes all my strength. "I'm in no state for company, I'm afraid."

"Ari, please," another voice cries, and I sit bolt upright without thinking.

"Jessa?"

I scramble out of bed, taking the tangled sheets with me in my haste. I kick them away and stumble to the door. I wrench it open and find Jessa standing beside Soren. His hand is on her shoulder; hers are buried in her skirts, twisting the fabric so hard her knuckles are white. Nettle prowls back and forth at her feet, growling and yowling in discontent.

"This brave young lady stood up to a dozen guards to get to you," Soren says softly. "Won't you allow her an audience, Princess?"

"Of—of course," I say, blinking rapidly. "Thank you, Soren."

"Mama says I can't go back to school," she bursts out. "She says there *is* no school anymore. She says it's over, and that Maia... she says Maia is lost to us and that all we can do is pray to the Graces for her soul to find peace. Is that true?"

Soren, tactful as always, bows and slips away. Jessa pushes past me and stands in the middle of my room with her hands on her hips, looking around with a disapproving frown.

"I thought a princess's quarters would be nicer," she says.

"Sorry to disappoint you," I murmur.

"You look awful," she says, and her face crumples. "Tell me my mama isn't right. Tell me you haven't given up."

"I'm not sure I can tell you that, rosebud," I say softly. I attempt a smile and add, "You know me—I can't lie for anything."

"But you *can't* give up," Jessa cries. "You can't!"

I sit and stare at my hands. "I don't want to. I want to say I haven't. But Jessa, I... I don't know what to do."

I've never felt so wretched, or so helpless. But Jessa seizes my hand, and I look up, startled.

"I do," she says earnestly. "Or Calan does. You need to come see him."

"Calan!" My hand tightens on hers, and I sit up straighter. "You've seen him?"

"He's at the Honeysuckle," she says. "He says he needs to see you, that you can help Maia."

"Jessa," I hiss. "The House is after him. The danger—"

"He needed help," Jessa says simply. "What else could we do?"

What, indeed? Jessa's courage both shames and steadies me. I take a deep breath, and the spike of fear in my chest eases slightly.

"You're right," I tell her. "Forgive me."

"So, you'll come?" Jessa prompts.

"Yes," I say firmly. "Let's go."

With Rowan still recovering, I have no choice but to sneak out. Again. Sammon, earnest and loyal though he is, is still mostly a stranger to me. There's no way I can trust him—or anyone who isn't Rowan—with something like this. So we scramble through my window into the courtyard, evading the guards with Nettle's help. For the first time, I see Jessa use her Gift. It makes me shiver to see the light leave her eyes as her spirit walks. She looks like a thrall.

The Honeysuckle Rose is closed when we arrive, with a sign on the front informing patrons that those within are observing a three-day vigil to commune with the Graces, as is sometimes necessary in times of acute stress or grief. Well, this is certainly one of those times. No doubt more than one of my students is doing the same with their families after being arrested and marched publicly through the City.

Jessa and I enter through the back garden, which is little more than a few patches of shade-loving herbs—Pia grows most of her vegetables and spices on the roof. When she's not there to greet us, I wonder if that's where she is, either taking comfort from routine or taking out her frustration on weeds. But when I head for the stairs leading to the upper quarters, Jessa shakes her head.

"Down here," she says tersely, and leads me to the cellar stairs.

"Jessa?" Pia calls sharply, appearing at the bottom of the steps with a lit candle in her hand. "Is that you?"

She catches sight of me, and her mouth tightens. She turns away without another word. Calan replaces her, his huge form filling the doorway.

"You came," he says, his voice thick with relief.

"Of course," I reply. "But Calan—what's going on? Where have you been? How—"

I choke off what I'd been about to say: *How could you leave Maia?* I can only imagine how he must be suffering. No need for me to add to it.

"Come and sit," he says, nearly yanking me off my feet has he pulls me down the stairs.

I settle on a crate of potatoes, trying not to notice how Pia studiously avoids looking at me. She glares at Calan instead, her arms crossed.

"So will you finally tell us what this great mystery is all about?" she demands. "I know you're no Spiritwalker, Calan Skinpainter, and neither is Maia. So why does the House want you?"

"Because what we are is far more dangerous," Calan says heavily. "We are—we *were*—thralls."

I blink, sure I must have misheard him. "Did you say... did you say *thralls*?"

"Yes."

"Which is a metaphor for what, exactly?" Pia asks. "Get to the point. I want to know why I'm harboring a wanted man in my cellar."

"It's not a metaphor," Calan says. "The House has lied to you. To everyone. Thralls aren't what you think they are."

"They're real," I breathe.

"They're people!" Jessa exclaims in the same moment. "Mama, I *told* you. There are people already inside! That's why I can't walk with them."

Calan nods approvingly. "Thralls aren't created—at least, not in the way the House claims. They're stolen, body and soul, from another world. They're slaves, called here against their will and bound by Light. The House calls it the Pall. A deep magical working to keep the victim silent—absent, mindless, so that all the energy from the thrall's mind and spirit can be converted into Light. The House brand concentrates and emits the Light for mages to use."

Calan unties the sash holding up his trews, ignoring Pia's alarmed protest. My focus only sharpens. As he lifts the edge of his shirt, my memory flashes on Sparrow with her skirts hiked up over her hip to reveal the star-burst of her brand. On Calan's hip, however, is a sprawling design of what looks like interlocking wheels or suns, each inked in bold, precise strokes. But underneath, I can see the warped skin of an old scar on his hip, exactly where the House places its brand.

"They cut it out," Calan says quietly. "The people who rescued me. Later, I painted over it. To take my freedom for myself and make it my own."

"Does Maia have... that?" Jessa asks. "Did they brand her, too?"

"No," Calan says. "*Alhamdulillah.*"

"What?" I ask, diverted. "What did you say?"

"Praise the Graces," he says. "Something like that, anyway. In my own language."

"Your own language," I murmur. "Stars! Your own *world*. What— "

"What about Maia?" Jessa cuts in, her voice shrill. "Are they going to make her a thrall again?"

"Maia never served as a thrall," Calan says. "She was too young when they pulled her into this world. They were going to do... something else." He pauses, looking sick. Then he takes a deep breath and goes on. "She told me one of the caravan guards helped her escape the camp during the—the harvest. She wandered the Deadwood for days until a woodcutter and his wife took her in. She said they were kind enough, but she was too frightened to stay so close to the House's facilities. She ran away and made her way south. She'd been on her own for two years by the time I met her. I knew what she was the moment I heard her speak. It was the first time I'd heard my language in over ten years."

"What did she say?" Jessa asked, eyes wide.

Calan gives a faint, wry smile. "She told me I looked like a *ghurilaa.*"

"A—a what?" Jessa stares at him blankly, as do I. Pia's mouth pinches even tighter, and I wonder if she believes him.

Calan waves it away. "An animal that—never mind. I told her that I would keep her safe. And I did. We kept each other safe—the two of us together were less suspicious than we were on our own. Until now." He shakes his head, his face crumbling. "I still don't understand how they found us out."

It comes to me in a flash. Ice spreads through my chest. "Sparrow."

Jessa and Pia understand immediately. Pia curses. Jessa starts crying.

"What?" Calan asks, looking around at us all. "Who?"

Quickly, I explain Sparrow's history and what Jessa told me about her disappearance.

"Maia must have told her who—and what—she was," I say. "Jessa overheard her talking to Sparrow just once, but Maia could have spoken to her any number of times. She probably did, trying to earn her trust. And when Sparrow left... "

"She was recaptured," Calan finishes. He shakes his head. "Oh, Maia. My brave, foolish girl. If she had only *told* me."

"That's how they knew about me, too," Jessa says. "Sparrow would have known all about me. We never thought to hide anything from her. We thought..."

"We thought she was a thrall," Pia says, turning her furious gaze on me. "We thought she was safe!"

"I didn't know," I whisper. The horror of all that I've just learned crashes over me. "I didn't know anything."

For a moment, no one speaks. Then I realize that the situation is even more dire than they know.

"Pia, Jessa," I say. "You need to leave. Get out of the City. I was going to tell you to do that anyway, but now I'm even more sure. The House Premier came to see me yesterday and made threats—nothing direct, of course, but he made his meaning clear. And now... if he knows you know all this—if he even suspects—I think it won't matter if I do what he wants. He won't risk letting you go free."

"What does he want from you?" Pia asks sharply.

"He wants me to influence Costi," I say. "Get him to stop his investigation into Lord Orean's treason. I can only imagine it's because that trail will lead to the House eventually." I shake my head. "Treason seems tame compared to what they've been up to all this time."

"So what can we do?" Pia demands. "Calan? You didn't put all of us at risk just to tell us a story."

"There is a man who once called himself a Lightcrafter, one who might have become Lord Premier. But he renounced the House of Light and Shadow,"

Calan says. "He is an outcast. I'm told the House has forbidden any mention of him, even his name. He's known simply as the Apostate. They tell their acolytes that he's dead, but he's not… and he can prove that Maia is no Spiritwalker. He can bring down the House of Light and Shadow itself."

"And where is this Apostate?" I ask.

"He'll meet our agent outside a village in the foothills of the Crown's Teeth. Once he's safely in the City, the plan is to arrange for him to give testimony against the House."

"Who is this agent?" I ask. "And why do you need me?"

Calan winces slightly. "Because the agent is your brother. Lucoran."

I suck in a sharp breath. "*Luca*?"

"He's been helping us for quite some time," Calan says. "Since the Harvest moon."

The Harvest moon… that's when Luca started pulling away last fall. He wasn't abandoning us for a Companion's attentions. He was protecting us from—all this.

"You keep saying *us*. Helping *us*. *Our* agent. Who are you talking about?" Pia asks, while I try to recover from my shock. "Not just you and Maia, I presume."

Calan looks away, troubled. "I can't tell you everything. There's too much at stake, too many people whose lives depend on secrets remaining secrets."

"How about something, then?" Pia says impatiently.

"An organization," Calan says with a helpless shrug. "Dedicated to finding and freeing thralls, wherever and however we can. That's all I can say." He mutters something in that strange language of his. "If only Maia had come to me, confided in me about your Sparrow, we could have helped her. Both of them."

"She didn't know, then?" Jessa asks. "About this organization?"

Calan shakes his head. "It was too dangerous."

"You didn't trust her," Jessa says. "So you can't blame her for not trusting you."

"Yes," Calan says sadly. "Yes, I see that now."

"What about Luca?" I ask. "Is he in danger?"

"Yes," Calan says. "His plans have been discovered. The House knows, and they will do everything in their power to prevent the Apostate's return. Please... the Apostate is Maia's only hope. *Our* only hope. He could change everything. No more hiding in the shadows, spiriting thralls away one by one. With his help, we can bring a real case against the House of Light and Shadow. We can change *everything*... and bring Maia home."

"Why does Ari have to do it?" Jessa asks, her hand creeping into mine. "Why can't you go after Luca?"

"The same reason I escaped when the House guards took her in the first place," Calan says, looking stricken. "I know too much. If I'm captured, they would learn enough to wipe out our entire network. And Ari is a princess. The beloved sister of the king."

Jessa's brow furrows. "So? You don't think Luca would listen to you?"

"No, rosebud," I say. "He means that I have a better chance because the House would hesitate to attack a group that I'm a part of. If he went, they would just kill him. We're more likely to succeed if I go."

"More likely, but not definitely," Calan says, as if forcing himself to speak the words. "It's still dangerous. A secret like this... we can't be sure. The House may take the risk regardless."

I don't speak for several long moments. The wedding is less than a week away. If I leave now, I lose any hope of resurrecting the school and delivering on the dream I promised ten young girls. Not to mention the fright and humiliation my absence will inflict on Costi while he's already embroiled in a treason investigation.

An investigation, I remind myself, in which Norrin is his only true ally, the only one we know he can trust. Norrin, whom I would be spurning alongside Hadrian if I don't go through with the wedding. I could ruin everything, and not just for myself. I could cost my brother his throne.

"Take a few hours to think about it," Calan says, seeing the dilemma play out on my face. "I'll need at least that long to make arrangements. I'll send word at midnight."

"How?" I ask. "You can't send Jessa again."

Calan hesitates, then says, "Sadra. She says she has a way to contact you without entering the palace herself."

Shock hits me like a fist.

"Sadra is a part of this?" I whisper, my breath all but gone.

But then the pieces fall into place. Her secrecy, her presence in Villa Glory, her refusal to talk about thralls.

"She took on Lord Orean's patronage so she could help thralls," I say.

"Yes," Calan says. "One in particular, who we thought could be saved. It takes time, you see, to combat the Pall's influence on the mind."

"But it went wrong," I say, remembering. "She was removed from the Terrace."

"Through no fault of her own," Calan returns with a slight frown. "She risked her life to save Sasha."

"Sasha?" Jessa asks breathlessly, looking fascinated. "Is that the thrall's name?"

"Yes," Calan says. "She's with Luca now, trying to reach the Apostate."

"The Temple must be involved," I murmur, my mind still on Sadra and the revelation of the secret she's kept from me all these months. "It was Mother Wenla who sent her to the Cloisters."

"Please," Calan says, looking pained. "Don't ask me anything more. This mission is not a sanctioned one. Sadra and I are acting alone. Please don't ask us to betray our vows any more than we already have."

"I understand," I assure him, though I'm not sure I do. I want *answers*.

But more than that, I want to help Maia. And Jessa and Pia and Calan—and, yes, even Sadra, though my shock has morphed into a seed of anger that flickers and grows with each breath.

"I don't need to think about it," I tell Calan. "Of course I'll help. But I should go now and make my own preparations. Send word through Sadra where and when I can find you."

"Thank you, Ari," Calan says, taking my hand in both of his, covering it to the wrist. "You don't know what this means to me."

"Don't thank me yet. I don't know what... if I can... " I sigh. "I just hope this works."

"Yes," he says. "Yes, I hope so, too."

Chapter Thirty-Nine

I leave the Honeysuckle and make my way back to the palace as discreetly as I can, but distraction makes me clumsy. Sammon catches me before I can make it to my window, and the relief in his face pierces my heart. I almost wish he would scold me, as Rowan would. But that's not Sammon's way. He would never speak out of turn. In fact, Rowan could stand to take some instruction from him. Sammon's wounded silence makes me feel far worse than any tirade of Rowan's.

Safe in my room once more, I gather together everything I can think of that might be useful for several days on the road and send to the kitchen for hard cheese, bread, carrots. Portable, hardy fare. I wish Rowan were here to advise me. He would know far better than I what's suitable. But I can't send for him, not yet. He needs all the rest I can give him, for one thing. And, for another, I can't give him any time to argue with me or talk me out of this. I'll tell him where we're going when it's time to go.

I write a note for Costi in the vain hope that it will ease his mind. It's short and simple, almost offensively so: *There's something I need to do. I'll be back as soon as I can. Rowan is with me—don't send anyone else. I'm sorry.*

Then I lie in bed, grappling with fear and doubt, until I finally fall into a fitful sleep. When I do, I find myself in a sparsely furnished room that looks something like Sparrow's old quarters. The stone floor is bare and cold, the walls unadorned, with a single window so small it only allows a sliver of moonlight through. A narrow cot is tucked into the shadowy corner, and on that cot—

"Sadra," I say, my voice surprisingly calm. "What news?"

"Everything is ready," she says. "Calan will meet you two miles from the City Gates. There's a small sanctuary and spring just off the King's Road, on the southern side. You'll find him there with Pia and Jessa. They've already left, so they'll be waiting for you."

"Alright," I say. "Is that all?"

She shrugs. "What else is there?"

"Oh, I don't know," I say, my heartbeat loud in my ears. "You could tell me how long you've been lying to me. How long you've known the truth about the House of Light and Shadow and said nothing."

Sadra doesn't answer.

"*How long*?" My shout echoes, bouncing off the stones. But still, she doesn't answer. So I answer for her. "You've known the entire time, haven't you? This is the big secret you've been keeping. You've been working against the House—against Orean? You and who else? Are you truly working with the Temple's blessing, or does your true allegiance lie elsewhere? How many lies have you fed me, Sadra?"

"I have *never* lied to you," she snaps, her composure finally breaking. "I kept secrets, and so did you."

"I told you my secrets," I return. "And they were nothing like—Sadra, this changes everything! The truth about thralls, the House? People will die for a truth like that. They'll kill for it. Nearly half the Council owns shares or holds contracts with the House of Light and Shadow, and the other half relies on House products to maintain their lifestyles and businesses. This secret will change the whole world, Sadra, and you just sat on it!"

"I had to!" she cries. "What else could I have done?"

"You could have trusted me," I say. "You knew how I felt about thralls, you knew I already—everyone said I was ridiculous. They said I was crazy. And you knew I wasn't, and you never said a thing. I would have understood. I would have helped! And maybe if I'd known, if Costi had known, we could have investigated the House and their allies sooner, and Maia would never have been taken. Maybe if the House had been under investigation for the thralls, they wouldn't have had time to kill Orean and obstruct the king's justice. Maybe Joram wouldn't be threatening Jessa's life as well as Maia's. You could have stopped all of this, and you said *nothing*. Every time I tried to talk to you about thralls, about anything *real*, you shut me out!

"And you've decided *now* is the right time? My wedding is days away. What if I'm too late? What if I can't find Luca? What if I warn Luca and the House kills or captures this Apostate anyway? I'll lose everything and humiliate Costi in the middle of a treason investigation. Half the councilors think he had Orean assassinated, most think he's a tyrant for imposing new taxes, and nearly all of them think he's an utter fool for giving me control of my bride price. What are they going to think of him if he takes the money but fails to produce the bride?"

Sadra opens her mouth, but I plow on, my fury mounting. "And even if I do deliver the Apostate safely to the palace, what then? How do you think those councilors are going to respond to being asked to prove their loyalty to a king for whom they have lost all respect—and then have that same king accuse them of slavery and worse? How open minded do you think they're going to be when that king asks them to consider that their wealth and livelihoods, their very sense of reality, have all been built on brutality and lies?"

"If they can't accept it now, they never would have in the first place," Sadra snaps. "It's *true*. That's all that matters."

"It is *not* all that matters," I say, struggling to hold onto my temper. "This could have happened differently. If the Council could have been a part of the investigation from the start, if they could have had time to get used to the idea, to explore it for themselves and come to the light of conclusion of their own accord rather than be attacked with the truth on the heels of conspiracy and scandal—"

"Ari, stop!" Sadra cries, throwing her hands up. "I appreciate that your circumstances right now are... difficult. But, I'm sorry, political problems and broken betrothals really aren't the point, are they?"

"You're right," I allow. "The point is the secret. The point is that Maia was taken and Jessa is at risk because the House needs to keep its secret—a secret that will change the world, a secret that threatens my brother's reign and his life. A secret *you knew*. The point is that you had ample opportunity to tell me the truth, and you chose not to. And now it's all coming down on all of us, including Maia and Jessa. Their lives are at stake, and it's—"

"And what about my life?" Sadra demands. "What about Sasha's life? Are we less worthy of protection and safety? You're betrothed to *Hadrian Prosper*. His family is the largest distributor of thralls in the country, and you were—*are*—destined to share his bed, his life, his business. It was too dangerous, surely you must see that! You aren't the only one with people to protect, Ari. I had an obligation."

"One you were more than willing to leave behind," I remind her. "Have you forgotten why we parted? You wanted to leave all this behind and run away, and you wanted it so badly you broke our bond when I wouldn't go with you. So you'll forgive me if I'm a bit skeptical of this great burden of responsibility that forced you to lie to my face for months."

Sadra's face is bone white. "We don't have time for this. Calan is waiting for you. If you don't go, he'll do his best to find Luca himself with Pia and Jessa in tow, and he'll do his best to protect them. But it will be safer for them, for everyone, if you go. So you can believe me. You can forgive me. Or... not."

"Forgiven," I say, forcing my face into smooth serenity, as Ismeni had taught me. "And forgotten. Of course I'm going."

"Forgotten," she murmurs. It's a low, bitter sound. "How lucky for you, that you can forget so easily. Good luck and good travels, Princess."

But I will forget nothing. Not her lies, not her rejection, not my own broken heart. Certainly I will never forget the sight of her turning her back on me for the second time, or the way she fades into the dark of my dreams.

But neither will I forget the scent of her skin or the music in her laughter or a thousand other tiny, miraculous details that torture me still with their beauty. Each one will remain, a shackle on my heart, and I will never be free of her.

Chapter Forty

I open my eyes in darkness. What's the hour? After midnight, surely. The night is deep and still, and the Terrace is quiet. But the guards on duty will be wide awake and ready. Luca trained them well.

Luca. Alternating jabs of shame and resentment stab me as I dress. I thought—Costi and I both thought—he was angry about his captaincy falling apart, or that he was simply in love, or both. But all along, he's been working in the shadows with Sadra, fighting an injustice I knew nothing about. I had no idea they even knew each other! What else don't I know? What else has been going on right under my nose?

I have spent my life in pursuit of knowledge so that I could protect myself, and it seems it was all for nothing. For all my studying, all my intellect, all my skill, I know nothing. I don't know whether Sadra has finally told me the whole truth or whether it will make a difference if she has. I don't know if I can find this Apostate or if he can save Maia if I do. I don't know what I will say to Costi upon my return or how he can possibly weather this latest blow to his reputation.

But it's time to go. I flit through the halls of the palace like a wraith, making for the guards quarters, where Rowan shares—shared—rooms with Luca. Luca, who I thought had abandoned me, who has indeed been keeping secrets from me. Luca, who is walking into a trap.

Not wanting to wake anyone else, I ease Rowan's door open and slip inside—only to find myself slammed against the wall with Rowan's forearm across my throat.

"Rowan," I croak. "It's—*me*—"

Rowan lets me go with a curse. The Lightglobes scattered around the room flare to life, illuminating his sleep-ruffled hair and the pillow-lines on the side of his face. He scowls at me as he yanks on a pair of trousers.

"Ari, what in the name of—"

"Hush," I say. "I'm sorry, I know you're recovering—"

"I'm perfectly fine," he says, his scowl deepening.

"Good," I say. "Because I'm leaving the City, and I need you to come with me."

For a moment, I think he's going to haul me off to bed or demand an explanation at the very least. But then he merely nods, pulls on the rest of his clothes and weapons, and follows me out.

"That was easy," I remark as we hurry along. "I expected an argument. Or questions, at least."

"If you've finally seen sense, I'm not going to complain," he says. "I'd rather see you on the run and living in exile than shackled to that pig for the rest of your life."

"Oh," I say, realizing what he must be thinking. "I'm not running away from Hadrian."

"Of course not," he agrees equably. "We're running *toward* a new and beautiful freedom. Much more poetic."

"No, you ass! Listen to me... "

As we make our way to the tunnels, I tell him everything: my dreams with Sadra, Joram's threats, Calan's confession, Luca's supposed involvement, and, finally, Calan's—and Sadra's—plea for help.

"I know it sounds crazy," I finish. "But—"

"It doesn't, actually," Rowan says, and I'm surprised at how calm he sounds.

"Really?" I shoot a glance at him and immediately trip on the uneven ground of the tunnels.

He reaches out to steady me. The touch, or maybe just his belief, makes me want to hug him. But there's no time for that. Jessa is waiting for me. She needs me. Maia needs me. And I need to focus on where I'm putting my feet, or I'll break my leg and finish our mad quest before it starts.

"Really," Rowan says. "I've always known there's something odd about thralls. Once you know enough about the principles of Lightcrafting, you come to realize that thralls don't make any sense. Not the way the House explains them, anyway."

"So why has nobody discovered the truth?" I wonder.

"They probably have," Rowan says. "Though not many. Most Lightcrafters are more interested in practice than in theory. They likely don't see the inconsistencies, or, if they do, blame their own lack of understanding when things don't add up. I know I did. And those who *are* interested in theory... Well, all Lightcrafters know that the secrets of the Pall come with a price."

"You know about the Pall?"

"Of course," Rowan says. "We all learn about it, at least in general terms. It's the enchantment that brings thralls to life and lets us command them—that's what we're taught. Only a very, very few are invited to learn the secret of producing thralls, and fewer still choose to do so, despite all the honor and gold that comes with the invitation. There have been rumors for years of Lightcrafters going mad or missing, or dying under questionable circumstances. I think we can make a good guess as to why, now."

I shiver. "But... Rowan, it *is* crazy. To think we can challenge the House this way—to think we can win."

"Maybe," he says, and gives a soft huff of laughter. "But it's too late to turn back. So we'll just have to be very, *very* crazy."

By the time we find Calan and the others, the night has faded into false dawn and farmers from the surrounding countryside are filing through the city gates with their wares. I can see them as hazy, dark blotches against the glow of the City from the stand of trees where Calan, Pia, and Jessa have been huddled all night. Jessa throws herself at me with a cry of relief, but Pia turns away. She blames me—for Sparrow or the danger from Joram's threats spilling over to her daughter, or both. I don't blame her.

"Let's go," Calan says without preamble. His face is pale and drawn, but determined. "Luca and Sasha have two days' head start. We have a lot of catching up to do."

"Who is this Sasha? Sadra—" I pause, biting back a wave of pain. "Sadra mentioned her, too."

Calan hesitates. "You may know her as Lucoran's Companion, but it's a ruse. Sasha isn't a Companion. She isn't even a Temple Initiate, not officially. She's... like me."

I gasp. "She's a thrall?"

"Not a thrall," Calan says sharply. "Thralls as you know them don't exist, Ari. Sasha *was* a captive, but no longer. She won her freedom, and it cost her dearly."

"And Luca loves her," I murmur.

Calan shrugs. "As to that, I can't say."

"Oh," I say. "Sorry. It sounded like you know her."

"Only as well as any fellow survivor can," he says, then falls into brooding silence.

That silence continues for hours, broken only by the occasional grunted query or direction. Even Jessa is quiet, her usual exuberance wiped away by fear and the demands of the road. I don't mind. I'm lost in my own troubled thoughts, grappling with doubts and fears both old and new.

I think of what I've learned about Sadra and the thralls, about what it will all mean for the Garden. I think of the fire-girl of my nightmares, who burns my kingdom to the ground and dances over the ashes.

What if Sadra and the fire-girl are one and the same? What if my Gift, silent for so long, hasn't been silent at all? What if my dreams weren't punishment but premonition? What if they were a warning—what if I'd listened?

What if I could have stopped this?

By the time we make camp for the night, I'm desperate for a respite from my own mind. I wait for awful silence to lift as we gather around the fire, but no one speaks. Pia hustles Jessa through her meal and then all but stuffs her into her sleeping roll. Calan, too, goes right to sleep—at least, he lies with his eyes closed and his arms crossed, breathing steadily. Rowan and I make our beds on the other side of the fire, giving the other members of our party the privacy they so clearly desire.

"It'll be alright," Rowan whispers to me. "We'll make it right. We'll find this Apostate."

Unable to speak, I simply nod and close my eyes. But I don't sleep. I spend the night tossing and turning, plagued both by doubts and the cold, unforgiving ground beneath me. I rise stiff and sore and more profoundly miserable than I ever imagined possible. For a moment I think, *No, I can't do it, I changed my mind.* But I take one step, then another, and another, and I go on putting one foot in front of the other for five days before Calan finally stops at a crossroads.

"That way lies the village of Twin Oaks," he says, indicating the southbound road. "You'll reach it by sunset if you hurry."

"And you?" I ask.

He shakes his head. "It's safer if you don't know. Just in case."

I shiver as I finish the thought in my head. Just in case we're caught. Just in case we're tortured.

"Goodbye, then," I say awkwardly. "And... good luck."

"I'm surprised you're not coming with us," Rowan says, speaking directly to Calan for the first time. Though his face is impassive, he somehow still conveys disapproval. "Even if Maia isn't your true daughter, surely she has some claim on you still."

Calan turns and takes one long, swift step in Rowan's direction. I find myself all too aware of the sheer size of him, which I'd become so accustomed to that

I rarely thought about it anymore. The cold rage in his eyes only amplifies the effect—stars, his fists are the size of small hams. But Rowan stands firm, regarding Calan with a faint frown.

"Maia *is* my daughter," Calan says, his voice deadly soft. "She has every claim on me. But so do hundreds of others who will die if I'm captured and the House learns what I know. You're a Lightcrafter. Don't try to tell me they don't have ways."

Rowan nods, his jaw flexing. "You're right. Forgive me."

"I'll forgive you," Calan says, his stance relaxing a hair. "If Maia lives. Go—find Lucoran and the Apostate. Bring them home."

The words are harsh, but Rowan only nods and reaches out to clasp Calan's hand. I look to Pia, hoping for some sign of reconciliation, but she won't meet my eyes. Jessa sniffles at her side and mouths *Goodbye*. And then they leave. Rowan and I watch them until they disappear around a bend in the road—their road—then we set our feet on our own path.

It occurs to me that Calan ordered us to find my brother and this Apostate, with no mention of Sasha. Then Sadra's words come back to me: *She's going to die. That's what she came to tell me. She's going to die, after everything that's happened.* She had been talking about Sasha, not Ismeni. But why? Is Sasha ill? From the—what did Rowan and Calan call it? The Pall? Or is it a natural illness? That could make sense. There are some things even Light can't fix, and a girl who lived as a thrall would likely never allow a Lighthealer to lay hands on her, anyway.

I hope we find her. I hope we find them all. Rowan sets a brisk pace, and we reach Twin Oaks just as the sun dips below the trees. Two oak trees guard the village gates, towering and ancient. A ring of torches surround the base of each tree, casting eerie shadows over the faces carved into the massive trunks. On the left, a man with a flowing beard. On the right, a woman with kind eyes and wild hair.

The Festival of Lights... I've been so consumed by exhaustion and our journey that I lost track of anything else. Today is the spring equinox—my wedding day. If I hadn't left, I would be Hadrian's wife by now. I might even be in his bedchamber carrying out my first duties as his wife. Oh, Graces, he must be furious.

Hadrian won't be the only one. Norrin, Ismeni, Costi, the Council. Everyone must be cursing my name. And Joram… Is he doing more than cursing me? What if he kills Maia out of spite? What if he's killed her already? I push the thoughts out of my mind. It's too late to think about any of that now. I have to focus and find Luca.

The gates of Twin Oaks are wide open, welcoming anyone who wishes to join in the celebrations. Despite the gravity of our situation, I find myself amazed by the dazzling displays of light—natural light. I've never seen anything like it. In the City, we mark the birth of spring with a lit candle in the window. But here in the countryside, or in Twin Oaks, at least, spring is welcomed with exquisitely carved torches blazing at every door, every corner. And, at the center of the village, a massive bonfire that soars into the night sky.

Goosebumps ripple over my arms and shoulders. My mind flashes to the fire-girl, who is never far from my thoughts these last few days. A wave of certainty rolls over me like the heat of that bonfire: Something is coming. Something bright and hot and terrible.

The tide of villagers surges toward the fire, pulling us along with it. At first, I resist, both out of instinctive fear of the flames and a growing urgency to find Luca. If he's here and in danger, surely he won't be in the thick of everything. We should be looking in the shadows, in the fringes. But—I nearly trip over Rowan in my surprise—Luca *is* in the thick of everything. He's right there, sheltering a slight young woman against the crush of people. Their backs are to me, but I would recognize my brother anywhere, even without the flash of fox fur at his feet.

"There!" I grab Rowan's arm and point. "There he is."

We push our way through the crowd, ignoring the annoyed mutters of those who catch a bit too much foot or elbow. Once we make it to the bonfire's edge, however, we find ourselves trapped. There are too many people behind us pushing us forward, and those on our sides have nowhere to go.

I've lost sight of Luca. He could be anywhere—right across from me, even, and I'd have no idea. I can't see anything through the roaring flames.

"Rowan!" I cling to his arm with both hands. "We need to get to Luca. Use Light if you have to, just get these people out of our way."

"I can't," he yells back. "I haven't got an amulet, and there aren't any thralls here. Haven't you noticed?"

I tear at my hair in frustration. "Then—I don't know, hit someone! Just—"

The words die on my lips as the women begin to dance. They whirl around the fire, leaping and ducking with the drums' beat. My heart answers, a pounding counterpoint rising on a tide of dread.

She's here, a voice inside me whispers. *She's HERE.*

My fire-girl. I scan the line of dancers, straining to see their features. But their lithe forms are silhouetted against the fire, black and faceless, like ghouls. Then they turn, completing their circle around the fire, and I can see. A face stands out from the crowd. It draws my eye with such strength and immediacy, I think at first it's Sadra.

But she's not Sadra, doesn't even look like her. Though dark haired, she's pale and slight, graceful as a young swan. Her delicate face is animated by high spirits and firelight... and something more.

I follow her gaze and find my brother, and the love in his eyes tells me who the girl is. Sasha. Luca's false Companion. Sadra's... *friend*. The one I thought must be dying of some grave illness. She doesn't look ill. She's beautiful. A crack runs through my heart as I remember Sadra's wild grief at the prospect of this girl's death. Were they really just friends, or something more? Sasha is so lovely—and a *dancer*.

Stars, what a dancer she is. Hoots and cheers rise from the crowd as she spins like a top and slaps the ground, mimicking the men's dance.

My breath comes short. *She's a dancer*, the voice inside me insists. *She's a dancer. She's THE dancer. Sadra isn't the fire-girl. It's her, it's her, it's HER.*

Sasha laughs along with the crowd, a blush mingling with the firelight on her face, her dark hair flowing around her slender form. Then her head turns. Her eyes meet mine... and the world ends.

Chapter Forty-One

Doom. Doom and ruin, the end of everything. My soul buckles under the weight of a crumbling city, shaken to pieces by this girl. She will destroy our country—*destroy* it utterly, as if it never was. She will be the death of us all.

Dimly, I hear Rowan calling my name. But his voice is fractured, distorted, as if he's underwater—or I am. Yes, that's it. I'm drowning. But—but not in water. In feeling, in knowledge, in death. I see faces. So many faces. Some bloated and black, hardly recognizable and half hidden in a mountain of dead bodies. And then a sea of wailing, crying faces, pale and skeletal, covered in pustules and horrible black swellings.

"Ari!"

Rowan has me by the wrists, and it hurts. But still, my arms jerk and flail as if by themselves, and with a strength I never knew I possessed. My legs, too, drum against the ground beneath me. I can't control it. I can't control anything. But I try.

"Rowan," I rasp. "Help—"

"You need to put her under," a voice says, and it isn't Rowan's. "She'll do herself an injury."

Who is that? I can't see. I can't see anything but death. Men and women brawling in the Terrace, in the City—in all the Cities. Soldiers hack down wave after wave of citizens dressed in rags beneath the white towers of the City of Lilies and among the sprawling temples of the City of Orchids. The City of Sage burns, the roar of flames mingling with howls of misery. Shrieking shadows stagger through the flames, still fighting, still determined to draw blood even as they burn.

And through it all, my fire-girl dances, leaping and twisting in agony—or ecstasy. But now she has a face. She has a name. It stays with me, stuck deep inside like a blade. She is the spark. She is the flame. She is the beginning of the end of the world.

Sasha.

I drift in darkness punctuated by waves of fire and disjointed images. At first, they all blur together—just scene after scene of chaos and suffering. In most of them, I can't tell where or when I am. But then, slowly, I begin to make sense of what I'm seeing. At least enough to realize that they're not all visions of future turmoil but of the present.

I see Market Square burn as men and women flee, staggering, through streets. And yet in the same moment I'm watching as Luca stands shoulder to shoulder with Rowan and a craggy-faced man, arguing with someone—Yoren! What on earth...

I'm with my brother as he and Rowan escort the craggy-faced man into the palace, but I'm also riding into battle beside a young man with dark curls and gray eyes.

Then those same gray eyes are staring back at me from a different face, wreathed in flames.

"*Little princess lost in time, on the edge you mustn't lie,*" she sings.

"What do you want from me?" I cry.

"One day a little wolf will come and on the wicked dine. Free the ghosts from chains and runes, underneath the willow root."

"Please," I beg. "I don't understand. Why are you doing this to me?"

New flames blaze to life and swirl around the fire girl until a new shape emerges. A fox stares back at me with glowing eyes.

"I *am* you," the fox says in Sasha's voice. "Don't you know your own Gift?"

"I can't change it," I sob. "Why—"

The fox flickers back into a girl, and this time it's not Sasha's but my own face burning against a backdrop of stars. Fire flickers across her brow like a crown, then spreads until my strange twin is engulfed in a plume of gold.

"Don't you know your own Gift?" Sasha demands again, stepping out of the inferno.

No, I realize. *I don't.*

I always believed my Gift was to foretell death. Why, then, am I also seeing things that must be happening now? How do I know that Sasha—the real Sasha—is in this very moment shivering in a dark cell, naked and afraid?

And why do I feel as though something is still trying to break in—or break free? Like there's more to see.

Sasha's blazing form dances in circles around me, a shooting star in an endless sky. Her voice echoes around me as the Garden blooms out of the darkness then burns away to ash, over and over again.

"Little princess, lost in time... "

"Wake," Sasha says, and seizes my face. *"Wake."*

There are voices—angry voices. This is nothing new and not particularly troubling after who knows how many days drowning in the roar of fires and angry mobs. But something about the voices catches my attention. They're different, somehow. Closer. More real.

And I realize that I'm awake. Truly awake, for the first time in what feels like years and yet mere moments.

Without opening my eyes, I focus and try to make sense of what I'm hearing. I recognize my brothers first. Luca's voice, perfectly controlled but with an unmistakable undercurrent of hostility. Costi's, melodious and warm, soothing. And another, measured and calm—Norrin. Which means the petulant, slightly nasal drawl bordering on a whine must be Hadrian.

" ... the moment she wakes," Hadrian is saying. "We delivered what we promised and were repaid with scandal and humiliation. We'd be well within our rights to seek reparations for that alone. You ought to consider yourself lucky we only want what was originally owed."

"Hadrian," Norrin warns. "Mind your place."

"I have been robbed of my place," Hadrian snaps. "I would be a member of the royal family by now if Arismendi hadn't run off."

"She evidently had good reason," Norrin says. "If even part of this business with the House of Light and Shadow is true—"

"None of it is true!" Hadrian explodes. "You can't possibly take the word of a crackpot old man and a bastard over the House Premier's."

"That bastard is my brother," Costi says quietly. "And we have more than enough evidence to warrant a hearing—a hearing that must be held while also investigating Lord Orean's treason, if you recall. This is no time for a wedding."

"I agree," Norrin says. "The wedding can wait."

"The wedding can*not* wait," Hadrian cries. "The princess gets her school, we get the princess. That was the deal. I have a right—"

"Hadrian," Norrin says urgently. "Be silent!"

"No!" Hadrian's voice cracks with passion—or is it desperation? "I will be paid what I am owed. I have *rights,* hells take you! I demand that the contract be upheld."

"Are you sure about that?" Luca asks, and I could swear I hear a smirk in his voice. "Perhaps you should read the betrothal contract again."

"I—what?"

"A certain clause," Luca goes on smoothly. "Specifying the requirements and expectations of any man who seeks to join the royal family. Such a man must come from a family in good standing, with a spotless reputation and unquestioned loyalty to the crown."

"So?" Hadrian demands. "House Prosper—"

"Is tainted," Luca says. "Your family is bound by marriage to House Glory, whose head is the subject of a—sadly posthumous—treason investigation. Or had you forgotten?"

Silence follows. Evidently, Hadrian hadn't considered this.

"Not to mention your own unsavory personal habits and associations," Costi finally adds, his voice deadly quiet. "Did you think I wouldn't have you followed? Did you imagine I was unaware of your financial stake in the Midden's brothels and gambling dens? I didn't break this sham of a betrothal already only because it would break Ari's heart to lose her school. Do not speak to me of your contractual rights, Hadrian. You have none."

"Please," Norrin says. "Miocostin, I beg you, make no decisions in haste or anger. There is another who must be consulted. You said it yourself—it would break Arismendi's heart to lose the school. Until she awakes and can tell us her wishes, I beg you, stay your hand."

"You speak wisely," Costi says after a moment's pause. "As always. What a pity your wisdom skipped a generation."

"Wisdom comes with age," Norrin says. "Age, experience, and—and guidance. My son is young and foolish, but he has time. Please—give him time."

"Very well," Costi says. "I will wait until Ari wakes and the trials are concluded. Then we will see whether Hadrian Prosper is a fit match for the Rose Princess. I would advise you to use the time wisely. Clean up your son's messes and *help* me, Norrin. We must get to the bottom of Lord Orean's schemes and this business with the thralls, and quickly."

"We will," Norrin promises.

There's a small grunt, then Hadrian mutters, "Thank you, my king. I will not waste the time you've granted us, I assure you."

A moment later, the door bangs shut. Someone sighs, and a weight settles beside me on the bed, making the mattress dip. Another, smaller weight presses against my side. Warm, canine breath puffs against my face.

"Ari, I know you're awake," Luca says. "Kirit can hear your heart galloping like a racehorse."

Someone—Costi—smooths a hand over my hair. "Time to rejoin the world, foxling."

I open my eyes and squint at my brothers.

"Where's Rowan?" I croak.

"I'm here, Ari," he says from his place at the wall. His face is haggard and drawn, his shoulders tense.

"How long?" I croak. "How long have I been... you know."

"Nineteen days," Luca says.

"Nineteen," I whisper, shivering.

For me, it's been a single moment since I fell—a single, century-long moment. But I'm awake now, truly awake, with Costi and Luca sitting beside my bed and Kirit in my lap.

I look out the window and find that spring has bloomed in earnest while I was—absent. Freshly cut crocuses and candytufts sit in a vase on my windowsill, arranged in a clumpy, haphazard manner that suggests a man's touch. Costi's perhaps, but more likely Rowan's. I shiver, both at the eerie sense of time lost and the fact that my condition was dire enough that Rowan felt the need to bring me flowers.

"Costi, about the wedding—"

"Don't worry," Costi says. "There won't be a wedding."

"But if there's no wedding, there's no school," I whisper. "It will all have been for nothing."

"Ari, the school is finished," Costi says gently.

"It's not! I can fix it—I can—" My throat closes.

"The school is the least of our problems," Luca says, and I can see that he's making an effort to be kind. "We need to focus on bringing down the House of Light and Shadow and freeing the thralls."

Part of me wants to argue. I've been fighting for this school for so long, and I was so *close*. Give up? Now, when I've finally tasted victory? I can't! The young girls of this kingdom need help, too. They are no less deserving of our aid. They, too, are downtrodden, oppressed, limited… owned.

But it's not the same. I know it's not the same. Lack of education and opportunity cannot be equated with the horrors committed against thralls. My own cause, no matter how worthy, no matter how cherished, must wait. So I force my wedding and my school from my mind and pull Kirit closer, trying to remember that awful night at Twin Oaks. But it's all a blur of terrifying visions and doom.

"What happened?" I ask, giving up.

Costi smiles faintly. "You'll need to be more specific, foxling."

I think for a moment, and the effort sends a bolt of pain through my head like lightning. But I persevere and eventually land on the most important question.

"Where is Sasha?"

Luca twitches, and his face darkens. "She's here. Finally."

"Luca," Costi says in a warning tone.

Instantly, I forget the thralls' plight and my own convictions. Terror seizes me, and all I can see is Sasha's face, ghoulish in the firelight.

"No," I whisper, starting to shake. "No, you can't, she's—she's—"

"Foxling, breathe." Costi leans over and takes me by the shoulders. "You're safe, and so is she. She's been unwell, like you."

Luca's jaw works, and he looks away, as if he can't bear to look at me. Like it's my fault. The thought startles me enough that the terror recedes to something manageable, only to be replaced by guilt. It *is* my fault. I remember that much. If I hadn't gone after them… but what actually *happened*?

"How am I here?" I ask. "Why—how—"

"We were followed," Rowan says, coming to kneel beside the bed. "Or Pia was, perhaps. It was that weasel, Yoren. He had an amulet. He helped me—quiet you. But he also called reinforcements to Twin Oaks. They captured Sasha."

"And then they confined her in darkness and starved her until she succumbed to the Pall again," Luca says in a low voice. "It's a miracle she returned to herself."

He shoots Costi an accusatory look, which Costi meets with his own glare.

"I'm still in the middle of a treasonous plot, if you recall," he says. "And I need the House's cooperation. I'm doing my best, Lucoran."

"The rocks-cursed House is a snake pit and should be burned to the ground, *Miocostin*," Luca snaps.

"It's not that simple," Costi sighs, massaging his temples. "Even if you're right—"

"I *am* right!"

"Even if you're right," Costi goes on doggedly, "I can't make that kind of decision unilaterally."

"You've been making all kinds of decisions unilaterally for months!"

"And my councilors plotted behind my back to take the throne," Costi snaps, his composure finally breaking. "And what's more, Ari's Gift has reawakened. I can't ignore that."

"Ari is out of her mind." Luca shoots me a look of apology but doesn't take it back or try to soften his words. "You can't trust her judgment right now."

"Ari is not insane," Costi says firmly. "She's Gifted, just like any of us. And her Gift has never been wrong."

"Ari's Gift has only surfaced twice," Luca says stubbornly. "That's hardly a basis for—"

"Ari is—"

"Sitting right here," I remind them through gritted teeth.

Their sniping has given me a vicious headache. And they've reminded me of my fear. My heart flutters like a caged bird at the thought of Sasha in the palace. I see her face in my mind and the doom crashes over me once more, darkening the edges of my vision. Costi is right. My Gift has never yet been wrong. But Luca is right, too. An unbroken record doesn't mean much when that record consists of two entries in the ledger. Unless it *wasn't* only two, unless my dreams and my Gift are indeed intertwined.

I don't know. I don't know what my Gift is telling me, or even what my Gift truly is. But I *do* know that Sasha is a girl like me. Rather, a girl like Maia.

"Maia," I whisper. "Is she safe?"

Rowan looks away, his face pinched. Luca and Costi exchange a glance.

"We don't know," Costi says. "The House of Light and Shadow has declined our requests for information on her case."

"So insist!" I say. "You were willing to storm in and take Sasha by force, but for Maia you'll only ask nicely?"

He shakes his head. "That's different."

"*How*?"

"We need Sasha's testimony," Costi says. "I'm sorry, foxling. Joram and the other House elders have agreed to a formal hearing on this business with the thralls, but they're not happy about it. I'm lucky I got Sasha out without starting a civil war."

"And if the allegations against the House are proven to be true?" I ask, my heart pounding.

"Then I'll have grounds to seize the House itself and recover any prisoners," Costi says. "Which I will do the moment the trial is concluded."

It's a staggering thought... the House of Light and Shadow seized? Lord Joram arrested—neutralized. With his authority gone, his reputation destroyed, he is no threat to me, nor Maia, nor Jessa... nor my school.

Freeing thousands—more likely millions—from abject slavery is paramount, of course. But this trial holds the key to my girls' futures, as well. Is it wrong to want both?

Perhaps. Defeating the House of Light and Shadow means saving Sasha, the harbinger of my country's destruction. I clutch at Kirit, making him squeak. Luca gives me a look and reaches for Kirit. I force a long, slow breath into my lungs and let it out again, forcing myself into calm.

"So when is this hearing?" I ask, handing Kirit over. "Did you find the Apostate?"

"Porr is here and ready to testify," Luca says with considerable satisfaction. "As is Mother Wenla."

"The hearing is in two days," Costi says. "So get your rest, foxling. You'll need your wits about you."

"You mean… " I look at him, hardly daring to hope. "You mean I can be there? I can sit in?"

He nods solemnly. "At my right hand."

I throw my arms around him, unable to say anything more. He returns the embrace, holding me tight. "I'm not sure I've done you any favors, little fox. It's going to be a grim affair."

I don't doubt that, but I can't be sorry that he's giving me this chance. Between my fear of Sasha, guilt over my role in her capture, and my desire to see justice done, I'm afraid I'll go mad. I need to know why my Gift spoke to me—what it's trying to tell me, what it all means. I need to know if I've condemned an innocent girl or my country… or both.

Chapter Forty-Two

Two days later, I put on my best gown with Ismeni's help. Though she is as efficient and capable as ever, all the warmth has gone from her face and manner. She barely speaks to me. I suppose I can't blame her. I've broken a betrothal contract worth twenty thousand gold pieces and humiliated her whole family.

The hearing is to be held in the Council chamber. Costi is already there, seated at the head table with Luca and Rowan standing guard behind him. Ismeni leaves me to sit at his left side. The seat to his right is empty and waiting for me. A hint of warmth eases the cold sickness in my belly. Rowan pulls the chair out for me and I sit, smoothing my skirts over my knees. Costi smiles and leans over to kiss my cheek.

"Are you ready?" he asks.

"More than ready," I say, though my hands are clenched in my lap.

Norrin and the other councilors arrive soon after and take their seats to our left and right along the high table. Norrin doesn't so much as glance my way. My throat tight, I watch as Soren directs the final preparations for the hearing. Chairs have been set out for the witnesses and their own counsel. They are permitted to enter only after the Council has been seated. Mother Wenla walks through the double doors, followed by a man who looks vaguely familiar, then one whom I've never seen but I suppose must be the Apostate. Porr, Luca called him. And... Sadra. The sight of her face hurts so much that I have to look away to compose myself.

Next come the House representatives. Lord Joram, of course, and Yoren. Joram's wife, Cimari, is also in attendance. To give testimony? Or does she simply not want to be kept in the dark? If so, I can't blame her. She has as much—or as little—right to be here as I do. More than one councilor shoots me a resentful glance as we wait for the proceedings to begin.

And then Sasha enters. Kirit yaps, his bushy tail whipping back and forth at the sight of her. My heart warms, just a little, though I can barely feel it under the weight of my dread. I grip the arms of my chair so hard my knuckles turn white. *Be brave*, I tell myself. *You must be brave. You must be better than this.* But I'm still sweating and trembling when Costi beckons to Sasha.

"Come forward, child," he says in his king voice. Serious, measured, a little distant, with none of the laughter that Luca and I have always known.

Sasha approaches, studying Costi's face even as I study hers. What is she thinking? She seems impassive, almost cold, as Costi introduces her case to the gathered Council. But it's not just her case—it's Maia's and Calan's and thousands of other victims'. Does she feel the weight of all those lives? I look closer, taking in the slight tremor in her hands and the shallow, quick rise and fall of her chest, and I think she probably does. Her thin shoulders seem terribly small for such a burden.

When the time comes for Sasha to explain herself in her own words, she hesitates. She opens her mouth, then closes it, then takes a deep breath. But when she finally does speak, her voice is low and clear.

"I'm sorry," she says. "I just—I don't know where to begin."

"Tell us your name and how you came to be here," Norrin says kindly, and I wonder what he must think of all this.

All his wealth comes from the thrall trade. If—no, *when*—the truth comes out, he will be ruined. But none of that shows in his voice or manner. He is the same Norrin I've always known: calm, curious, measured, with none of his own desires or opinions in the way. He just listens intently as Sasha tells her story.

Her name is Sasha Nikolayeva. It's a strange, foreign name, fitting for a girl who says she's from—somewhere else. Another country, another world where she had a life and a family... until she didn't. She lost her grandmother and began to go mad. Or she thought she did, for she was plagued by visions of herself here, in Kingsgarden.

Is that how it was for Maia? Did she lose someone? Did she, like Sasha, fear she was losing her mind? Did she wake, alone and afraid, in a nightmare? But Maia was far luckier than Sasha.

Sasha was branded. Sasha was sold. To *Ismeni*.

"What?" I whisper.

Sasha's face changes as she speaks of her enslavement, growing still and distant—blank, empty, like a mask. Like a *thrall*. And, all at once, I know her. My stomach heaves. This is *Cygnet*. Ismeni's pretty little swan. *She'll look so sweet with my Dove.* That's what Ismeni said that day at the auction, as if she were matching a necklace to a gown. I wrap my arms around myself, trying not to vomit.

"I had forgotten who I was," Sasha is saying. "I had forgotten a lot of things. I couldn't speak. I had trouble understanding and thinking. Sometimes I didn't think at all. I was... gone. Absent from my own body. I'm sorry, it's—difficult to describe. After a time, though, I remembered how to dance, and the more I did it, the more I came back to myself. Then Sadra found me and started teaching me your language. She—well, she bullied me into waking up in the end."

Of course she did. I can't tell if it's laughter or grief or sickness bubbling up inside me. My eyes turn to Sadra before I can stop them. But she doesn't look at me. Her face is turned to Sasha, and the look I see there makes me want to die—fond, tender, and worried all at once, with a hint of the sparkle I always thought was just for me. But Sasha is still speaking, telling us how she spoke her name and knew herself again, how Sadra taught her about our world and the Pall that afflicted her.

At this, a wave of whispers roll over the councilors. Norrin speaks softly to the man beside him, in the middle of some detailed explanation of Light theory. Costi sits motionless, his face rigid. Finally, he calls for order and leans back, looking at Sasha over his steepled fingers.

"Certainly you are not the empty shell we have always believed thralls to be," Costi says. "You speak with an accent, yes, but you speak—something we have long thought beyond the ability of a thrall." He turns to Joram. "How do you explain this? Do you deny that Sasha is—or was—a thrall?"

Joram rises once more from his seat. "No, my king. A thrall is not a hollow vessel, as many believe—"

"As you and your House have led us to believe for generations." Costi's voice is steady, his face stern and controlled. But I know him well enough to see what lies beneath. He is *furious.* The corner of his mouth is pinched, like he's trying not to vomit—or hit someone. As he continues, the anger in his voice grows more pronounced. "And neither are they prey to Spiritwalkers, as you have stated explicitly—and untruthfully. But go on."

"As I say, they are not—completely—empty," the Premier allows. "But neither can they be considered complete, sentient individuals. In short, they are not people."

I stiffen. How in the world can he have come to that conclusion?

"How so?" Costi asks, his tone dangerously mild.

Joram folds his hands over his paunch and settles into a lecturer's stance. I grit my teeth at his smug, complacent air but force myself to attend to what he's saying.

"There lies in the northern forests a certain singularity," Joram begins. "A catalyst, of sorts. Early members of the Temple of Graces discovered the singularity some four hundred years ago. They studied it for many years and found that this catalyst attracts various... essences, shall we say, and concentrates them until those essences coalesce to form a body. A living, breathing body, yes, but not a *person.* What lives inside the body is—if anything—merely an echo, an imprint of a mind long dead."

"And how did these investigators come to such a conclusion?" Norrin asks, echoing my thoughts.

"Every attempt was made to communicate with the creatures," Joram says, spreading his hands. "Each attempt, however, was met with incomprehensible babble at best or violence at worst. The creatures proved incapable of—or even interested in—caring for themselves, and so we did it for them. We cared for them and studied them. And, yes, we made use of them. We found a way to harness their energies through the Pall, as the creature says. Light was born, and with it the first Lightcrafters of the House of Light and Shadow, who helped the first king of the Garden build the very kingdom you rule today."

He nods to Costi, who narrows his eyes but says nothing. Norrin frowns at Joram with a look of mingled offense and distaste.

"The King's Chalice—" he begins, but Joram interrupts him, waving a hand dismissively.

"Is a tale for children," Joram says. "Or at best a highly sanitized edition of the Garden's history. The first king conquered and united the Cities with armies strengthened by Lightcrafters."

I glance at Costi. Though his jaw was tight, still, he says nothing. He simply nods to Joram to continue.

Joram smooths his robes fastidiously. "By itself, the singularity is not particularly prolific, producing perhaps two or three thralls per year. House mages developed methods to amplify and concentrate the singularity's effects so that more thralls could be cultivated among the roots of the trees."

"And will you tell them what these methods are?" The interruption comes from Porr, the Apostate. "Will you tell them how you water your foul garden with the blood of innocents?"

A hush falls over the room, then dissolves in another wave of chatter. What can he mean? Sacrifice of some kind, I'm sure, but—my mind jars to a halt, refusing to consider the possibilities, each bloodier and more horrific than the next. I can't afford to fall into the dark grip of my Gift again. Not now. Instinctively, I look to Sadra. And, once again, I wished I hadn't. Her hand is on

Sasha's shoulder, solicitous and comforting, and the sight of it makes me dizzy with pain.

"Order, please," Costi says. He lets out a sharp breath through his nose, then turns to Porr. "You will have your turn to speak. Until then, I must ask you to remain silent." Then, to Joram: "But do elaborate, if you please."

"Life must be fed with life," Joram says. "This truth cannot be disputed. We grow our wheat and barley in soil comprised of the once living flesh of other plants and animals. We harvest living plants to make our bread and ale. We raise livestock and hunt beasts of the forest and field that we might eat. What we of the House do is no different."

I close my eyes, sickened. No different? *No different?* I force myself to open my eyes and look at Sasha. Even as my heart breaks at the way Sadra is holding her close, even as my Gift screams at me to fear her, I can't see her the way Joram clearly does. She isn't a cow or a sheep. She is a girl—a girl like Maia, who still languishes in the House's dungeon.

Joram smiles gently. "I can attempt to explain the exact mechanics of our processes, but I think it is not necessary. Do not let the words of a malcontent and oathbreaker sway you, my lords. What we produce is livestock, nothing more, to be used as we see fit. That which proves unsuitable to serve as a thrall is used in other ways. We are not wasteful."

"What my former colleague means," Porr interrupts, "is that thralls fall into a fairly narrow range of age and physical ability. Those who are too young, too old, too weak, or too unlikely to sell are slaughtered wholesale, their blood and bone harvested for amulets and other workings."

Maia. At this, I truly think I will faint. Maia is young. Maia is small. If the House prevails today, they won't sell her as a thrall. They'll kill her and grind her blood and bones into mortar. I want to believe that Porr is lying, that even Joram couldn't be so cruel, but I can see the truth written in the man's craggy face.

"You have seen this?" Costi demands, his face pale.

"I have, my king." The other man stands and bows, and now I remember—he's Bard, the singer Sadra and I saw at the Chalice Festival, the one she was afraid would see her out of the Cloisters. "I have seen children as young as three years old bled like pigs—but more slowly."

"Like pigs," Joram agrees. "My point exactly. Do you object also to the meat we serve at our tables? Do you contend that the ox should be relieved of the plow? Thralls are no different from any other beast raised for food or labor. They are property—*our* property."

I glance at Ismeni and find that she is already looking at me. Orean treated her like chattel for years, even plotted to have her killed once it became clear she was no longer useful to him. Hadrian very likely would have treated me the same way if I'd married him. Women, like thralls, have always been the property of men.

"That's not true." Sasha is deathly pale, her hands shaking. But she stands firm, and her voice is steady. "I am not a piece of meat. I'm a girl, just like her."

She points at me, and I feel it like a physical blow. It's my fault that she's here fighting for her life, trying to defend herself to a group of men whose wealth and livelihood rest on the premise that she isn't a real person. A lesser soul might have crumpled under the weight and given up or tried to escape. But not this girl. Her gray eyes blaze with fury, and I see why my brother loves her so.

"I have—I had—a family," she says. "The House of Light and Shadow stole me from them. They pulled me into this world against my will and turned me into a *thing* to be used by whoever had the coin to pay."

"My lady," Costi asks a small, mousy woman I didn't notice before. "What is your word? Who speaks the truth?"

She's the court Truthseer. I've only met her a few times before, and only in passing. What is her name? Talla, I think. She's been hovering a few paces behind his chair, but now she steps forward, her watery brown eyes tight and nervous.

"I am called a Truthseer, my king, but in reality, I see deceit. All I can say is that neither of them lies." She holds up a cautioning finger. "But believing a thing doesn't make it true."

Costi sighs, rubbing a hand across his forehead. "Then we must proceed and do our best to uncover the truth for ourselves."

"My king," Joram says. "Might I question the thrall?"

"You may," Costi says through gritted teeth.

Joram turns his oily smile on Sasha and begins questioning her. With each query, a new flame of anger bursts to life inside me. His questions are misleading, his logic flawed. The way he frames his case is simplistic and manipulative. He again likens thralls to livestock in the fields, poses carefully phrased questions that cast doubt on Sasha's experience, her very existence. He claims that she died in the world of her birth, that her body here in Kingsgarden was created by the House of Light and Shadow—and therefore is the property of the House of Light and Shadow.

Joram calls Ismeni and Cimari as witnesses, posing carefully chosen and even more carefully phrased questions to elicit the answers he wants. The holes in each testimony are obvious. The Truthseer is silent, though her jaw and fists are clenched, her eyes snapping. Half-truths, then. But you can do a lot with half the truth, so long as no one asks for more. And no one does—save Norrin, but even he barely touches the surface of Joram's deceit.

Poison has grown deep roots in our Garden. I understand, now, what the fire-girl was trying to tell me. And I'm starting to agree.

"Make no mistake, my lords," Joram says in closing. "This is a *thrall* we're discussing, not a young woman, not the equal of your wives and daughters. It is a semi-functioning brain inside a body that was not born but *created*. Furthermore, it is a valuable commodity which has been stolen and subverted from its intended purpose. It—"

"That is enough." Costi cuts Joram off with a gesture, barely containing his distaste. "Have you any witnesses who can confirm that any such training has taken place?"

"No, my king. However—"

"Then I think it's time we heard from the Temple Mother and her witnesses," Costi says. "Please be seated, Lord Premier."

Joram gives an exaggerated bow and takes a seat beside his wife. He should look cowed, or at least angry. Despite the drama of the testimonies, his case wasn't particularly compelling, riddled with holes and gaps of logic. But he is perfectly calm. In fact, the smug tilt to his lips is more pronounced than ever. Dread trickles into my stomach, and I reach for Rowan.

"Something isn't right," I whisper. "Warn Luca."

I turn back and find Sasha slumped in her chair with Sadra and Bard hovering over her.

"My king," Mother Wenla says. "I fear that my young friend is overwrought by these misrepresentations and half-truths. Might Sasha retire for a short time and begin once she has had a chance to compose herself?"

"Of course." Costi nods, then sighs. He looks as if he's aged ten years in the last hour. "We could all do with a bit of a break and some refreshment, I think. Go, then. We will reconvene when we are recovered."

Immediately, Costi and Norrin fall into deep conversation while the other councilors call for food and wine. Rowan tries to offer me some, but I can't even look at it. I watch, sick with misery, as the girl I love frets and coos over someone else—someone who I am absolutely positive is going to destroy the world. But I can't hate Sasha. Yes, this strange girl is going to destroy everything...but only with the truth. Our idyllic Garden, so full of joy and justice, never existed. I rub my eyes. It's all so *huge*. The enormity of the truth presses on me like a mountain. Everything will have to change—where will we even begin? All the prosperity and opportunity enjoyed by our citizens is possible because of the Light and labor provided by thralls. Without them...

"It's time," Costi says, standing. "We can't put this off any longer. Where are the girls?"

"In the antechamber," Mother Wenla replies. "I'll fetch them."

"No, I'll go," I say quickly.

Here is one thing, at least, I can try to mend. I accused Sadra of treason, conspiracy. I can't even remember all the things I said to her, and all the ways I'd been wrong. I have to tell her so.

"Don't take too long," Costi warns me with a knowing look.

I nod, unable to speak, and cross to the antechamber door. It isn't far, but it feels like running a gauntlet. The eyes of the assembled councilors and witnesses seem to burn into my back.

"*That*'s the princess?" someone mutters.

"Running errands like a thrall," someone else says. "It's fairly typical."

"I heard she's the reason we're all here."

"It's all nonsense, if you ask me—first that school, now this."

I tune out the rest, hunching my shoulders against the stares and whispers. But my discomfort at least serves to propel me through the door when I might have hesitated. I close it behind me and lean against the cool wood, closing my eyes. When I open them, I find Sasha looking at me with an expression of painful hope on her face. My heart squeezes. She must be waiting for Luca. Stupid—I should have asked him if he had any message for her. But it's too late—I have my own piece to say.

"You shouldn't be here," Sadra says harshly. "You're on the trial council."

"I know." I give Sasha one last look, then, reluctantly, focus on Sadra and take a deep breath. "I've come to fetch you both. But first—can we talk?"

Sadra turns away, her face stiff and cold. "This isn't the time or place."

"Sadra." I take a step forward, reaching for her. But she doesn't see, and I'm too much a coward to actually touch her. I let my hand drop. "Please, let me explain—"

"How could you possibly?" Sadra whips around, her whole body an accusation. "I loved you. I pledged myself to you. I would have broken my vows for you. I betrayed my cause in trusting you, and you betrayed *me*. Sasha might die today because—because—I don't even know. If you want to talk, tell me that—tell me why."

I gape at her. Yes, she would have broken her vows to the Temple and forsaken her duties, and she asked me to do the same. She asked—practically demanded—that I abandon my family. She can talk all she likes about her love for me, but she was keeping secrets all along, secrets that are going to tear down the kingdom. I came here to explain that I *didn't* betray her, I *didn't* summon the

House of Light and Shadow, I didn't do anything but fall into madness for a time.

But, as so often seems to be the case, my good intentions crumble in the face of her unfairness. She betrayed me, too. How quickly, how conveniently she forgets that small fact. I should stay calm, I know. She's hurt and confused. She deserves an explanation. And I'll give her one. Eventually. Right now, with the blood pounding in my ears and my every nerve alight with anger, I just can't.

"*You* dare to speak to me of trust?" I demand. "You've been lying to me since the moment we met!"

Sasha shifts in her seat and whispers to Sadra, "Maybe I should go."

I turn to her, blinking away tears as I struggle to regain control. "Yes. They're waiting for you in the council chamber."

I swallow and steel myself. Sadra can wait for her explanation, but Sasha... No apology could ever be enough, but I have to try.

"I'm sorry, Sasha. My Gift is unpredictable, and it took me by surprise." I look her in the eyes, praying that she will understand. "When I saw you, I was terrified. I forgot everything Sadra told me, everything I promised. I knew—I *knew*—that the world was going to end because of you. Now I understand that the world as I knew it *must* end, because I didn't know it at all. And now that I do... it will end. Of course it will."

Something inside me stirs. Is it my Gift, or intuition? Or simple fear? I hesitate, then speak once more.

"I can tell you that my brother isn't very impressed with the Premier's arguments. But you must be wary. I don't think convincing him is the Premier's primary aim. He relies more on spectacle than logic, and I think he's hoping to make a spectacle of you."

Sasha lifts her chin. "Well, I'll give him one. I'm ready."

She stands, resolute, hand in hand with Sadra. I smile a little. I like this girl, in spite of my jealousy. She will be a perfect match for my brother... if she survives.

Chapter Forty-Three

Joram and Porr are at each other's throats when we return, barking at each other like hounds. Costi looks as if he wants to order them both out of the room—or perhaps run away himself. But he can't, and neither can I. I reach him and lay my hand on his shoulder, offering what support I can. He spares me a swift smile before turning back to Porr and Joram.

"Sit down, both of you," he snaps. He looks at Sasha with troubled eyes. "Welcome once again, Sasha. I trust you are recovered?"

"I am." She looks at him with steady gray eyes. "For months, I lived in fear for my life. I hid the only way I could—with a mask. But I'm not afraid anymore. I don't need my thrall's mask, and I won't ever wear it again. I'd like to show you something, please."

"And what will you show us?"

Sasha speaks softly, but with conviction. And, I think, with real faith. "The Temple of Graces teaches that the soul withers without knowledge of the beauty in oneself and in the world. I want to show you that my soul is present, complete, and entirely my own."

Costi nods, and his eyes soften. He likes her. Hope surges in my chest. Costi will fix this. Everything will be alright. Sasha will go free, and so will Maia. The

House of Light and Shadow will fall, and Calan and Pia and Jessa will come home.

"So may it be, child," Costi says. "Show us."

There are a few moments of bustling as Mother Wenla directs the audience to stand and clear their chairs from the center of the room. Joram and Cimari move away only reluctantly, their faces flushed with indignation. Mother Wenla pays them no mind. She sits with a harp on her knee and Bard at her shoulder. He stares at Sasha with an odd intensity. Something in me stirs. It feels like my Gift, but I'm looking backward, not forward. My father is looking at me with the same expression I now see on Bard's face—longing, despair, fear.

I shake the vision out of my eyes. What is this? My Gift is premonition. The future, not the past... isn't it? But my vision is flickering again. I see my father once more, so clearly I almost reach out to touch him. I squeeze my eyes shut. What is happening to me?

I don't have time to wonder. Mother Wenla begins to play, and Bard sings, the foreign words and melody sending a wave of prickles over my skin. Nothing like that ever came from Kingsgarden. And Sasha—Sasha is amazing. Her dancing is exquisite, pristine. Otherworldly, in the most literal sense. She dances on her toes—on a *single* toe, even—as if she weighs nothing. Her motions are fluid, ethereal. She defies logic, defies nature itself.

No one can believe anymore, if they ever did in the first place, that she was coached to imitate humanity. It's simply not possible. Unschooled though I am in the Divine Arts, even I can see that Sasha is as good as any Temple dancer. That kind of skill takes years of training, dedication, passion, and raw talent. It's beautiful. It's art. It's... divine. The Graces come alive in Sasha's body, her soul on display for all to see.

The music rises, and Sasha's dance grows broader, stronger. My Gift surges with it, first pulling me backwards into flickers of memory, then pushing me forward into the terror of the future. Something is pushing at me, stoking the fire of my Gift like a blacksmith's bellows.

Sasha spins on one leg, the other pointing straight at the ceiling. My breath comes short. Something, some force, pulses from Sasha, battering against me, trying to get in. Visions flicker, coming faster and faster as the music reaches its climax until, finally, a bolt of power explodes from Sasha. It pierces the bubble of my Gift, breaking it open like an egg.

Past and future crash together in my mind. I drown in it, unable to separate visions from memories—and some of those memories are not my own. The searing pain of a brand on my hip, the waves of helpless fury and despair—those aren't mine. Are they Sasha's? No, the shackled hands I see in my mind's eye are a man's, coarse and calloused. My gaze flickers to Bard. His eyes are closed, his face a paroxysm of pain. These are *his* memories. His testimony. He, too, was a thrall. He's sharing his story with all of us.

This is his *Gift*, I realize. His Gift is memory, and somehow Sasha has broken whatever tether kept it bound inside him. Bard's history, his memories, stream out with this song, and I live it all with him: the death march from the northern forests, the auctions and sales and whippings. The years of back-breaking labor and starving night after night. His escape, his freedom, and his infiltration into ranks of caravan guards escorting merchants and their thralls from town to town.

I see the faces of children both dead and alive, and I feel the anguish and hope battling in his heart as he whispers in the ears of some to lie still, then run. I feel his shame and horror as he burns the dead and delivers the rest to the House mages' knives. Face after face flashes before my eyes, and I gasp as I recognize Maia. Calan told me there was a man—*this* man—who spared Maia's life. *Graces, hear me,* I pray. *He saved her once. Let him save her again.*

Bard's miraculous testimony continues, playing out in my mind, in my heart. It seems like an age and an instant both at once, blazing forward to the present. For one sickening moment, I'm watching Sasha dance through Bard's eyes and my own. My vision swims, and I think I might faint. But then Bard's strange power recedes, leaving me alone in my own mind. The music fades, and Sasha sinks into a strange sort of obeisance with her head bowed and her leg gracefully extended. Then she stands, breathing hard, with her chin up and her eyes ablaze.

"I am myself," she says. "I am my own person. You don't have the right to decide for me what I am."

"I think we are all satisfied on that point," Costi says gravely.

"However," the Premier cuts in, "the point is moot."

My Gift flares in warning, and I find myself reaching back for Rowan before I can stop myself. This is the Gift I thought I had, to feel Death's approach. Joram is about to do something—someone is going to die.

"Seize him," I whisper frantically. "Stop him. Do something!"

Rowan looks stricken. "Ari, I can't."

"Moot?" Norrin asks, politely confused. "The girl's status as—well, as a girl—is what we are here to decide, is it not?"

I need to say something, I realize. If no one else will speak, I must. But I can't—I can't catch my breath. Darkness swarms at the corners of my eyes; my head swims.

"Stop," I wheeze, almost inaudibly. "Don't—"

Joram bows. "With respect, my lord, it is not. We are here to decide if the House of Light and Shadow has the right to continue manufacturing and selling thralls. And I say we do, regardless of what sort of mind lives inside the body. While it is admittedly a bit, ah, *uncomfortable* to consider, the fact of the matter is that the body in question was not born but created *by us* and as such belongs to us to do with as we please."

"Ari, what's wrong?" Rowan demands. "What do you need?"

"*Stop him,*" I gasp, clutching at his hand. "Help me—I'll do it."

"Ari, no," he says, his voice low and soothing, barely audible over Joram's pontificating. "Calm down. It's just talk—filthy talk, but just talk. Costi knows that. Trust him."

I want to scream at him. "You don't understand."

Joram's voice is like a knife in my side, talking, talking, *talking*. His voice is poison. And, like any good poison, it hides behind what we want to see and taste and feel. He's so reasonable, so fair—surely it is not only acceptable but *right* to use these thralls. The kingdom depends on Light, and Light depends on thralls. They are not people, not like the citizens of the Garden. They are bodies. Livestock, dependent on their caretakers for survival and shelter. It's their fate, their purpose, to serve our needs. It's as simple as that.

I try to rise, but my knees are weak. My heart flutters in my chest. Rowan's hand is too heavy on my shoulder, pressing me down.

This time, I'll do it. I'll scream. I'll...

"My king," Joram is saying. "You most graciously allowed this—girl—a demonstration. I beg leave to present my own."

"Granted," Costi replies, his shoulders rigid.

"No," I whisper.

"Ari, *stop*," Rowan hisses. "You can't contradict a direct edict from the king. If you want to help him—and Maia and Luca and this Sasha—just be *quiet*."

Joram motions to his wife. "My dear, if you would."

Cimari nods and disappears, returning moments later with a wispy figure clad in a plain, cream-colored gown. The strength drains from my body. Rowan frowns.

"Isn't that... "

"Yes," I say dully. "It's Sparrow."

The fragile ghost before us is my thrall—my captive. My failure. Her skin is corpse-white, a stark contrast to the dark hollows under her eyes. Her face is skeletal, the bones of her cheeks and jaw so sharp against her skin I almost expect them to slice through. I assumed she was dead... and she is. She just doesn't know it yet.

I was a fool to think I could stop this. My Gift never lies.

Nausea floods my belly as Joram reaches for Sparrow. Everyone gasps—everyone but me—as Sparrow screams. Joram is unperturbed; he tears something faint and rippling out of her chest, like a mist, or a ghost. The Pall, I realize. It confuses the senses, much like Light. It ripples as Joram gives a final, vicious yank and rips the Pall away. Sparrow screams once more, and I know the sound will haunt me to the end of my days.

"Stop," Costi shouts, leaping to his feet. "Stop this at once!"

Joram ignores him. It's already over. Sparrow lies at his feet, broken and sprawling like a discarded doll. The floor seems to tilt beneath me. Darkness flutters at the edge of my vision. This is my fault. I gave her up; I gave her to Pia.

I thought I was protecting her, but I just rejected my responsibility for her. And here she is, dead, the victim of who knows how many horrors.

Everyone is shouting now, in anger, in surprise, in horror. If I had any breath in my lungs, my voice would surely be among them. But I have no breath—nor blood nor beating heart, it seems. I'm cold, so cold, and the darkness is creeping from the corners of my eyes, threatening to blind me completely.

I fight it, clinging doggedly to consciousness as Costi demands an explanation from Joram. I manage only the barest scrap of understanding: The House contends that thralls cannot survive without the Pall—as we all just witnessed from Joram's grisly demonstration. Thralls are here; they exist. What good would it do to kill them rather than make use of all they can offer us? The Apostate disagrees. But what alternative does he offer? I can't understand, can barely hear them over the pounding of my own heartbeat.

My Gift is coming for me again—no, no, not now, not here. I don't want to make things harder for Costi, I don't want to make things harder for Sasha...and, more importantly, I don't want to *know*. Whatever my Gift has to tell me, I don't want to hear it. It's too much, too terrible, too everything.

I dig my nails into my palms as the Apostate raises his hands, forcing myself to focus. He reaches for Sasha. What—surely he can't mean to remove the Pall from her, too? After what we just saw?

I clutch at Rowan. "I don't understand. Why is he hurting her? Why... "

"To prove that it can be done," Rowan replies softly. "That she can live without the Pall."

I close my eyes and pray. But for what? If Sasha lives, the Garden will die. But if Sasha dies, so will the truth.

The Apostate reaches for Sasha—rather, *into* Sasha, and yet he never touches her. He pulls the Pall out of her in a slow, smooth motion, obviously trying to be gentle. For a moment, she seems alright, and I feel a flicker of hope. But then she drops like a puppet with cut strings.

Flames flicker to life from Sasha's eyes, her hair, spreading until they consume her as she thrashes in agony. But is it real, what I'm seeing? A ghostly, blazing figure rises from Sasha's body, leaving it behind as easily as I might shed a cloak. My fire-girl has come for me, no longer content to beg my attention in nightmares. Now there will be a reckoning. Now there is no escape.

The fire-girl strides toward me, her hand outstretched. I cling to the arms of my chair, powerless. I couldn't flee if I wanted to—and I don't. I will give this strange phantom what she is owed, whatever that may be.

She wears Sasha's face, but her features ripple, smoldering like the heart of the Blacksmith's forge. And in her hands, suddenly, is a chalice. *The* Chalice. The rest of the room—the rest of the world—falls away. The Chalice glows before me, filling my vision.

Take it, the fire girl says, many voices layered into one. *And drink deep.*

I take the Chalice in my hands, peering into its fathomless depths.

"Drink deep," I whisper.

And raise it to my lips.

For a moment, I think I'm back in the Council chamber. Colors burst in my vision, shot through with flashes of motion. My stomach heaves, then settles as the swirling fragments reform. I blink, but the chamber I see isn't the same one I was sitting in. Neither are the people in it the same ones I entered with.

Robed Lightcrafters huddle around a bed, chanting in synchrony as Light pulses around them. A woman shrieks, and the chanting redoubles. One of the Lightcrafters shifts to bend over the bed, and I gasp. It's Joram. But he's younger, stronger, and the woman in the bed... my stomach swoops. I know her, despite the pain and fear contorting her features. Because those features are my own. How many times have people told me I look just like her?

My mother.

She wails and thrashes in the bed, hunching over her enormous belly with a grimace of effort. My father bursts in, shaking off the robed mage who clutches at his sleeve.

"Amari!" He falls to his knees beside the bed and seizes her hand. "My love, have courage."

"No," she pants. "You need it for yourself. All my courage, all my love. Don't forget... when I'm gone."

"Don't say that," he says softly. "You'll be alright. Everything will be alright."

She shakes her head. "She's not going to come out. Not while I live."

"Amari, what are you saying?" Father looks lost, confused, stupid with grief. "I don't understand."

"She speaks the truth, my king." Joram lays a hand on my father's shoulder, and I note with some shock that his sorrow is genuine. "We cannot save both mother and child. You must choose."

"*I* must choose." My mother's voice snaps like a whip. "The choice is mine, and I choose her. I choose my daughter."

"A daughter!" Joram's sorrow dissolves into disdain. "My queen, you are overwrought. Trust in your husband. Your king." To my father, he says, "She can yet recover from this. You will lose this child, yes, but you can have another. A son."

"I have two sons," my father says faintly. "I have only one wife."

"A wife who will never forgive you for killing this baby," Amari pants, her eyes bright with fury and pain. "Never."

"Leave us, Master Joram," Father says. "I must speak privately with the queen."

Joram looks as though he wants to protest, but he nods and gestures for the other Lighthealers to vacate. He follows with one last look at my mother. Once everyone is safely out of the room, Father slumps forward, pressing his forehead into Amari's—Mother's—hands.

"I can't do this without you," he whispers.

"You can," Mother says. "You are strong. And wise and brave and good."

Father raises his head, his face serious and focused now. "That's not what I mean, and you know it. You are the Chalice. Without you, my Gift is weak. The Healers are weak. The illness will return, and it will outstrip their power. I won't place my life in the hands of the House of Light and Shadow. They already have a choke hold on the kingdom's wealth. I won't give them control over whether I live or die. And so I *will* die. In a year, or five, or ten. Miocostin is barely twelve. He's not ready to rule. He's not ready to lose us both." Now his face crumples again. "*I'm* not ready."

"But I am." Mother strokes his cheek. "Forgive me, my love. I've given my life to you, but now I must take it back. For her—for this little girl inside me. She will live. She *must* live. I love her, Costi."

A pang strikes my heart as I hear her call Father by the same call-name as my brother. It makes them feel real to me in a way they never were before. They were just people. They were in love... and in pain.

"Do you love her more than you love me?" Father closes his eyes but can't hold back the tears trickling onto my mother's fingers. "More than you love our son?"

"You have each other," she says, her voice faint and tired. "You have little Luca. You have Norrin and Janna. My Arismendi has only me. I must do this for her, Costi. I must. Call Joram, call Wenla. Tell them you want to meet your daughter."

"Mari—"

"Please. I don't have much time." Tears leak from her own eyes as she reaches for Father. "Forgive me, Costi, please. I can't bear it."

He kisses her tenderly and leans his forehead against hers. "I will bear it for you. Don't be afraid, my heart. If you need my forgiveness, you have it. And if this is what you want, I will stand with you."

She looks afraid for the first time. "You'll stay with me? To the end?"

"To the end."

Father calls for healers, both Gifted and Lightcrafter, and sits on the bed at Mother's side. She leans into him, tears now flowing freely down her face. Mother Wenla takes my mother's hands and looks into her eyes.

"You are certain?"

Mother nods. "I am."

"Are *you* certain, my king?" Joram asks. "Again, I urge you—"

"The decision has been made," Father says, and his voice is strong and kingly once more. "Save the baby."

"Arismendi," Mother whispers. "I give you your life. It's yours, my love. Take it and drink deep."

Her eyes close, lulled to sleep by Mother Wenla's Gift. My father presses her fingers to his lips and whispers his farewell into one last kiss.

And then they cut her open.

There's blood everywhere. Streaming from me, my mother... and Costi. Costi? My brothers' faces flash before me, both stricken, splattered with red. What is happening? What has been going on while I was—elsewhere? I don't understand—I don't believe it, even as Costi falls into Luca's arms with a knife in his throat. Another strikes his chest. I cry out, reach for them—but in their place now is another man, another knife.

That man bares his teeth as he presses his blade against the throat of a young boy. A woman cries out, falling to her knees.

"Yes," the man sneers. "Kneel. That is your place. That is your purpose." His voice shakes with suppressed fury. "You dare to sit on your husband's throne. You dare give orders to *us*, his Council? You bitch. You *bitch*. Kneel!"

That last comes out as a roar, spittle flying from the man's mouth. The woman lifts her chin, looking him square in the eye, then slowly lowers herself to her knees.

"I will kneel," she says from the floor. "I will die. But so will you. You see it, don't you? No? Let me help you."

Power flares, and the man staggers sideways, freeing the boy to run to his mother. She regards the man steadily.

"Now you know, Farseer," she says.

"Chalice," the man whispers.

"Yes," the woman says. "There will be another. The Chalice and the Crown always find each other, if the Crown's rule is just. You may take the throne and the crown, but you will have no Chalice, no blessings."

My mind reels. The Chalice of Gifts. Of power. The source of the king's blessing and virtue. Not a cup but a woman—two women, at least. My mother and... Balia. Yes, this woman can only be Balia the Blessed.

Balia's blazing face morphs into Sasha's. Sasha is my fire-girl. My Chalice. She touches my face, and together we fly forward into an explosion of vision and knowledge.

The kingdom will fall, as I foresaw. There will be war, famine, disease, upheaval like we've never known or even imagined. And there's a boy. A little boy with Luca's face and Sasha's gray eyes, a boy who will be king of a broken country. But he's a Healer in every sense of the word, and he will heal the land.

"So there's hope?" I whisper.

"Always," Sasha says, and in her voice I hear the echo of my mother's. "But now it's time to go back."

"No," I say, suddenly frantic. "I'm not ready."

Her eyes are as hard as diamonds. "Neither was I."

She places her burning hands on my chest and shoves, sending me screaming into the void.

Chapter Forty-Four

Rowan throws me against the wall, where Ismeni and Mother Wenla lean over Costi's blood-soaked form. I gasp, trying to make sense of the influx of sight and sound. Everywhere I look, swords and knives flash. Screams mingle with the clash of steel and the sickening sounds of impact. Sasha kneels over Bard, tears streaming down her face as she holds his bloody hand to her cheek. Luca directs a handful of guards who form a semi-circle around us, holding off a seemingly endless wave of attackers. I don't understand. Who are they? What do they want?

Besides my brother's death. That much is clear. Horribly, sickeningly clear. Costi lies beside me with a knife in his throat and another in his chest. His eyes flutter, his lashes like ink against the deathly pallor of his face. The sight of him brings me back to myself with awful clarity. Shaking the last shreds of my vision out of my eyes, I clutch at Costi's hand and look desperately at Mother Wenla.

"Can you save him?" I ask. "What can I do? How can I help?"

"Pressure," Mother Wenla instructs. "Put pressure on the wounds while I work."

I nod and join Ismeni, pressing down on the hole in his chest the moment the knife is removed. His eyes are squeezed shut, his jaw tight. He's still alive, still fighting.

Before I can speak, a shadow falls over me, and I find myself jerked backward by my hair. I scream in pain as my assailant drags me away from my brother. I clutch at his hands and pull, trying to relieve the agony in my scalp, but he shakes me off. Something tears, and I cry out in pain. Finally, the man flings me down. My hands shoot out as I try to catch myself, and they land on a severed arm.

I lunge backward with a gasp of horror and collide with my attacker's legs. He kicks me aside, sending me sprawling face-first into the carnage painting the floor. I push myself to my knees and try to turn, but my skirts are tangled and heavy with blood. My hands scrabble as if with a mind of their own and land on the hilt of a knife stuck low in the gut of the body beside me. I jerk it out and then freeze as my eyes fall on the body's face. Then my shock breaks, and I throw myself forward, cradling his head in my hands.

"Norrin," I choke. "*Norrin.*"

"Yes," a soft voice says, and I look up to see Hadrian looming over me. "My father is dead. And it's your fault."

Hadrian advances, tossing aside a dark, knitted mask—the same mask, I realize, worn by those battling Luca and his guards.

"Hadrian, what have you done?" I whisper, tears streaming down my face and onto Norrin's.

"I have done what is right," Hadrian says, his voice still calm and distant, with no hint of his customary condescension. "I have done what was necessary."

"How?" I croak, my voice thick with grief and horror. "How can you think any of this is right? Hadrian, *you killed your father.*"

His foot lashes out, catching me in my side. I grunt at the impact but don't let Norrin go. Hadrian glares down at me, his eyes wild and glittering with unshed tears.

"*You* killed him," he snarls. "You and your arrogance, your ambition, your unnatural intransigence. You are a disgrace to our beloved Garden, Arismendi, and so is the fool we called king. Many spoke to me of his incompetence.

Lord Orean, of course, and many others too timid and shrinking to stand up and speak. But it was you—*you*—who made me see the truth in the end. Your willfulness made me see that something needed to change, that *I* had to change. What kind of man allows a woman in his care to behave as you do? To *think* as you do? Your brother failed you, my dear Arismendi. He allowed you to ruin yourself and squander my family's gold. Miocostin refused to take responsibility, but I will not be so weak. *I* will take responsibility. *I* will take control."

I shake my head wordlessly, unable to speak. Hadrian takes a breath, and I can see him force himself into calm. He smiles down at me, his face alight with righteous certainty.

"It's all arranged," he tells me, "Our betrothal contract still stands. We will wed. Lord Joram will support my regency, as will the councilors loyal to our cause. The others will fall in line, or simply fall. As your husband and guardian, I will be king in all but name, and one day my son will ascend the throne."

Still, I shake my head. Vomit burns in my throat like acid—or like flames. Hadrian cocks his head, and now his smile is the one I remember: amused, patronizing, complacent, and utterly insufferable.

"Even now, you deny the truth," he says. "Look around you, dearest. It's over. You are defeated. Your brother lies dying as we speak. The renegade thralls will soon join him, as will the vile Apostate. Your little friend in the House's dungeons will die—or perhaps she won't. Perhaps they'll keep her alive until she's old enough to bear the Pall. Perhaps she'll be sold to me, for my wife's use and my own pleasure. Yes, I rather like that idea."

Hadrian leans down and seizes my jaw, forcing my face toward his. He doesn't seem to care that the knife is still clutched in my hand. He must think I lack the courage to use it, or perhaps only the strength.

"Do you understand yet, my dear?" he whispers against my lips. "I will be master of you both, master of all. I will be your king."

"No," I whisper back. "You won't."

I whip my hand up, burying the blade in his armpit and pulling it back toward me. He jerks back, surprised, and I wonder if he knows that a major artery lies just beneath the skin. It doesn't take much strength to reach that artery, to sever it and release the blood inside. It only takes knowledge—and the willingness to use it.

At first, Hadrian merely seems annoyed. He doesn't know, doesn't realize that he's a dead man. He shakes his head, like a dog shaking off flies. But then his gaze falls on his dangling arm, drenched in blood. His lips part, and he falls heavily to his knees. He lifts his good hand weakly, trying to stem the flood of red. He sinks to the floor and lays his head on Norrin's chest. I can't believe the amount of blood... and neither, it seems, can he. Hadrian dies with his eyes wide.

I stand and stagger away, my whole body shaking so hard I nearly fall with each step. Hadrian is dead, and so is Norrin. But what about Costi? Mother Wenla was with him, and so was Ismeni. They were working, they were try-ing—Graces, please, let them save him.

My legs give out as I approach. There's something about the line of their shoulders, their bowed heads. I drag myself the last few feet, my breath coming in short, whistling, whimpering gasps. Mother Wenla helps me kneel beside my brother, her eyes glistening with tears.

"Costi?" I ask, my voice small and broken.

An awful gargling noise comes from his throat. He's trying to speak. But there's a knife in his throat. My stomach heaves at the sight, and I look instead at his face, ghastly pale beneath the splatter of blood. His eyes are open—wide open, more frightened than I ever thought possible. My heart breaks for him. He should die an old, old man, surrounded by his family and safe in the knowledge that he did right by his people even when it was hard. But he won't. I don't need my Gift to tell me that. He's going to die here, in blood and fear. Because he's a good man and a good king. Because he wanted to do the right thing.

"I love you, Costi," I tell him. "I love you so much."

He tries to smile, tries to speak again, and fails at both. But around a grimace of pain, his lips move, form words. *I love you.* And something else, something harder to understand—and harder to do.

Take it.

His crown lies beside him, the gold and silver roses painted with his blood. His fingers scrabble against it, pushing it toward me.

I have spent my whole life living in fear. Fear of exposure, fear of failure, fear of judgment. I thought myself unworthy, sinful, a murderer. I was sure, deep down, that Costi and Father must resent me. I lived because my mother died, because I took her life. And so I promised myself that I would live for my brother and my people, never for myself. I wanted atonement. I wanted absolution. I never thought about what my mother wanted. But I know, now.

She gave me my life, and now Costi is giving me his crown. Two parting gifts given with the same command:

Take it.

I've been told all my life that a woman is meant only to *accept* things—the rules, her place in life, whatever scraps this world deigns to give her—without ever taking anything for herself. I've been told that it has always been this way and always will be, that the perfect woman is silent, meek, compliant. Like Balia.

But it wasn't that way. Balia the Blessed was neither silent nor meek. She was fierce, proud, capable... and, above all, willing to rule. She saw what needed to be done, and she did it. She knew she was worthy of the crown, and she took it.

The women of this kingdom have been told her death was noble, generous. Glorious, even. But it wasn't. Her death, like Costi's, was murder. It was betrayal. Treason, and at the hands of her own councilors. She died defiant, not humble. She wanted to help her people, to *do* things. So she did, without waiting for a man to do it for her. She didn't apologize, either. Rather, she promised that another would rise to take her place.

I want to help my people. That's what my school was about. I wanted to give the girls of my kingdom tools and opportunities. But my dream—my real dream, the one I never let myself look at too closely—is bigger than one school. There are so many more in need, so much more I could do if only... if only what? If someone would let me? If I had the power? My eyes fall on the bloody crown.

Take it.

The voice in my head is so clear. My eyes fly to Costi's blood-spattered face and find it empty. He's gone.

"I almost had it," Mother Wenla murmurs. "I almost saved him. My Gift is so strong, stronger than I've ever felt it. And it still wasn't enough."

Ismeni chokes, curling in on herself. A high, thin sound escapes, like she wants to scream but doesn't have the breath.

"Don't blame yourself, Mother," I say, my voice curiously steady. My skin ripples with waves of hot and cold. I feel ill, and yet stronger than I ever have. "Blame *them*."

Hadrian is behind this, I'm certain. But he couldn't have done this alone, and Orean is dead. Who else? I have my suspicions, but I need... I look around and spot the Council's Truthseer hunched against the wall nearby, her arms wrapped around herself. I scoot toward her and shake her arm.

"Who did this?"

She looks at me with wild eyes. "What do you mean? I can't—my Gift isn't—I don't just *know* things."

"Things have changed."

I have to yell over the noise. It's hard to hear, hard to focus. Perversely, this is the thing that breaks the fragile wall between me and my anger. I look out at the few combatants still standing—and the carnage they left behind. Broken bodies litter the room, swimming in a sea of blood. My mother's voice comes to me, mingled with Costi's. The same wish, spoken years apart.

Take it.

My Gift flares, and I see that I will. I will take the crown, and I will keep it. I scramble back to my brother's side and seize the delicate ring of thorns and roses. I push myself to my feet with the crown still clutched in my fist and walk through the line of guards surrounding us.

"Stop this."

Everyone freezes. I move forward, into the middle of the room, heedless of the steel still flickering around me. No blade will touch me. I know it. I've seen it. And, though our attackers are masked, I see their faces in my mind. So many faces, bloated and black and swinging at the end of a noose. I pause beside one of them and speak softly.

"Are little girls really so frightening, Gerrin?" I ask. "Were your *concerned citizens* so concerned that they would rather commit murder and treason than accept that things change?"

Gerrin gulps, licks his lips. "We fight to protect our country, our way of life. We will die heroes."

"You are a fool," I tell him. "And you will die a fool."

"Princess."

Rowan has Lord Joram by the throat. He throws the quivering, bleating man down at my feet and steps back, his face grim. I give him a fleeting look of distaste and then speak to the room at large.

"You are defeated," I say. "Lay down your weapons and you will be granted the mercy of a painless death. Resist and I will order my men to take you alive, that you may be publicly flayed before you die."

I stride over to the Truthseer and pull her up.

"Who is responsible for this attack?" I ask her again.

"I don't know." The Truthseer shakes her head frantically. "I told you."

"Try," I say. "I believe you may surprise yourself."

She closes her eyes, then gasps and points at Joram, staring at him like she's seeing clearly for the first time.

"He is responsible," she says. "He ordered the attack."

"I thought so." I glare at Joram. "The trial was a sham. You only needed time and a distraction to move your thugs into place."

Joram raises his hands in a pleading, placating gesture. "Princess—"

"Queen." Luca steps to my side, his hand on his sword and his eyes on the crown clutched in my fist. "You are addressing your queen."

I close my eyes. I didn't want this. I *don't* want this.

Joram flinches. "My... queen."

His tongue flicks at his lips, and his eyes dart about like a cornered animal's. There ought to be some satisfaction in seeing him so humbled, but I find none.

Joram reaches for me like a supplicant. "I know nothing of these men. I—"

"He lies!" The Truthseer shrieks. "He *lies!*"

Joram flinches away from me, his whole body shaking. He pleads with me in whispers that grow softer and softer, until he's only mouthing the words. His lips form the shapes, but he has no breath to give them life. Just like Costi. A wave of dizzying rage overtakes me. I think I might fall, but I don't. Somehow, I keep my feet and keep talking.

"This man is guilty of treason and regicide," I hear myself saying. "Kill him."

I never even see Luca's sword. I only see Lord Joram's head at my feet, staring up at me in disbelief. Disbelief at what, I wonder? That his plot failed? That I would order him slain? Or that my order would be obeyed? So surprised, just like Hadrian.

"It's over." I take a deep, shuddering breath and look around. "Soldiers, put down your arms."

They obey me without question. All but Luca. He kneels and holds out his sword, the blade laid flat across his palms.

"Hail the queen," he says softly.

"Hail the queen," Rowan echoes, going to one knee beside Luca.

Sammon follows. "Hail the queen."

One after another, Costi's guards become mine. Once again, a thought slips across my mind like a shadow.

I didn't want this.

But it doesn't matter if I want it or not. These men are offering me their loyalty, their service, and I will serve them in return. Costi is gone, but his work is unfinished. I will take up the task in his stead. I touch Luca's shoulder.

"Rise, Captain."

Luca rises in one smooth motion, and I pull him into an embrace. The gesture is a formal one, to honor and accept his fealty. But once I'm in his arms, I'm just his sister, and he's just my brother—my only brother, now. I hide my face in his shoulder. I can't cry, not yet. I step away and steel myself.

"Come," I tell him. "There is work to be done."

My first—no, I suppose my second—task as queen feels familiar, almost easy. Organizing and delegating tasks, directing workers, giving encouragement and critique wherever each is needed. Soren and I work together, as we have for years.

Mother Wenla takes charge of the injured, Luca and his guards take the surviving rebels into custody. Luca returns, and he and Rowan carry Costi's body away. I don't go with them. I can't bear to watch them wash the blood from his skin and hair, to see them handle his body like the empty shell it is now.

The other bodies are removed by the palace guard. Most are faceless, hidden behind their masks. But some I know. Joram, Bard, Yoren—Cimari. What happened to her? Though clearly dead, I see no wound. Her eyes are wide and vacant in death, and I wonder what she was thinking, what drove her to participate in this madness.

Not everything goes smoothly. There is much to do, and we have fewer hands than we need. And there are complaints, mostly from my brother's councilors—former councilors. If they can't understand why I will not use thralls to clear the mess, they have no place in the new government, or the new reality. I keep Porr at my side as the beginning of my new Council, advising me on what our next steps should be. He tells me that there are likely hundreds of thralls in the City who are secretly awake and aware, as Sasha was. And as Sparrow was—no, not Sparrow. But I don't know what else to call her. I never knew her true name, and now I never will.

"It will be slow going if I am the only person removing the Pall," Porr says, drawing me back to the grisly present. "I must teach other Lightcrafters how to do it safely. It will mean an initial delay, but I believe it will benefit us in the long run."

"The delay may not be as great as we think. It will take time, after all, to locate and organize the—the—" I stumble, wondering what to call the poor folk I once called thralls. Then I see Sasha, rolling her eyes at Luca with a small smile, and I have it. "The survivors."

I move to join my brother and his love. As I approach, I catch the end of Sasha's reply to what I suspect is his fussing.

"I'm free," she says. "My strength is mine to keep, now."

"And to share," I add. "You're the Chalice, Sasha."

Her eyes widen. "The Chalice... "

"It was never a cup," I tell her. "The Chalice was a person—a person like you, with your Gift. You make the Gifts of others stronger. I have seen... so many things. I was right, you know. You will tear down the kingdom."

My throat tightens, and I can't go on. Sasha reaches for Luca, then, tentatively, for me.

"I'm sorry," she whispers.

"So am I." I try to smile, but a tear falls instead. "Costi would have done it, you know. He would have tried to... to put things right. He was a good king, a good man. And he died for it."

"And you?" she asks. "What will you do?"

For a moment, I can't speak. I think of my mother, and of Balia the Blessed. Both Chalices, both strong, brave women who shared their strength and courage with the kingdom. Like Sasha. I take Sasha's hand and squeeze it.

"What will *we* do," I correct her. "I'm going to rebuild my kingdom... with a Chalice at my side."

Chapter Forty-Five

The death ceremonies begin the very next day, beginning with the pyres. Despite a few raised eyebrows, no one questions me when I decree that the dead should be burned in Market Square rather than at the Terrace Gate. The field separating the Terrace from the City is big enough, but nearly every one of the guards who died had been from Midtown or the Lower City, not the Terrace. Joram had recruited discontented, fearful men like Gerrin, desperate men just looking for coin, and power-hungry men like Yoren. All men who felt they didn't have enough, perhaps that they *weren't* enough.

Nearly everyone. Hadrian and the treasonous councilors will not be honored today, though their bodies were found among the dead. Did they see themselves as patriots, like Gerrin? Did they see themselves as the brave few resisting tyranny? Or were they simply taking their last chance to save themselves?

Either way, they have no place in the games, which are held on the second day. That honor is for those loyal soldiers and councilors like Norrin who died protecting the king, protecting me, protecting the truth...and Maia, who I've learned was already dead by the time Joram came to me with his vile proposal. He was bargaining with Maia's ghost as coin the entire time.

Costi, Maia, Norrin, my brother's guardsmen—they were true patriots. They died trying to do what was right. They should be honored in the City's heart, among the people. Hadrian would have thought it all terribly uncouth, but I don't give a damn what he would have thought. He's dead... and I am queen.

But there is one other person whose opinion I want. I seek out Sasha in the little courtyard abutting the rooms I've designated for her use. She's at a long wooden rail, which Luca constructed for her immediately after taking up residence together. The craftsmanship is exquisite—surprisingly so, for he's always been a middling woodworker at best. But then, perhaps it's not so surprising. He loves her.

I stand for a moment, enjoying the peace of the moment and the knowledge that she and my brother are safe and happy together. Sasha's arms and legs move in smooth, practiced patterns that seem to have no direction but are nonetheless full of grace and power. Her face is serene, though I know that grief lurks just beneath the surface.

"Hello," she says after she comes to rest. "Did you need me?"

"Just your opinion," I say, resisting the urge to wring my hands. I'm still not completely comfortable with my brother's beloved, though she seems to bear me no grudge. "The funeral pyres will be set this evening. I thought—I wondered—"

She smiles faintly. "Just say it. Whatever it is."

She reminds me so much of Luca that I smile too and relax a little. "I wanted to talk to you about the man Bard. I never knew him, but he once helped someone dear to me. I never got to thank him... I want to honor his passing appropriately, at least. I hoped you could tell me if there are any customs in your land that we can incorporate into the ceremony."

She bites her lip and doesn't answer right away. But when she does, it's with certainty. "He had a choice, a long time ago. He chose Kingsgarden. I think he would be happy to be honored your way, to be treated like he belonged. Like he was a citizen."

I nod. "Our citizens are offered a tribute by their families—a song, a dance, a trinket. It can be anything so long as it's from the heart of a loved one. He didn't have any family here, obviously, but—"

"He did have family," she says, shocking me into silence. "He was my grandfather, and I will stand for him."

She doesn't only stand. On the third day, Sasha dances. It's even more beautiful than her dance at the trial, when her very life was on the line. Or perhaps that's why—she dances now out of love, not fear. This dance is deeper, gentler. There is nothing of the fierce desperation I saw at the trial. This is more familiar, too. Her dance at the trial demonstrated two things: that she was whole, and that she was not of this world. Her dance for Bard evokes their dual identity, the marriage of the world they left and the world they chose as their own. The result is something more beautiful than has ever been seen in either realm.

"I still can't believe he's gone."

I freeze in shock. My heart stops, then begins to race. Sadra stands beside me, the torchlight flickering over her face. Tears cling to her lashes as she watches Sasha, making her eyes glitter like they're dusted with frost. These are the first words she's spoken to me since we fought at the trial.

"And yet... is it terrible of me to be happy?" Sadra wonders, her face tight and pensive. "Am I a horrible person for thanking the stars? Sasha is safe and free, but only because he died protecting her."

"You're not a horrible person," I say. "You love her. That isn't something to apologize for."

"I don't know what I'll do now." She heaves a sigh and rubs a tear from her cheek. "I did my job. And now she doesn't need me anymore."

"Because she has Luca?" I ask, my heart aching with grief—and, yes, jealousy.

Will I never be free of it? Sadra offered herself to me and I refused her, no matter how good my reasons. I can't blame her for giving her heart to someone else.

But Sadra only looks at me quizzically. "Luca?"

"It must be hard," I say, forcing the words out of my mouth. "To see her with him. I... I know what that feels like."

She stares at me for several long moments. Then she huffs a soft breath of laughter and touches the freckles on my cheek. "Ari, you are an idiot."

And she walks away. I gape after her and then turn to Rowan, who has appeared at my left shoulder without warning, as is his custom.

"I don't think she's allowed to speak to the queen like that," he observes. "Shall I have her whipped for her insolence?"

I pat his arm. "That won't be necessary, but thank you."

"You could do it yourself," he suggests. "Some people enjoy that, I've heard. In bed."

"Rowan!"

He smiles. "She's right, you know. You *are* an idiot."

"I should have *you* whipped," I grumble. "You just said that's no way to speak to the queen."

"I said *she's* not allowed to speak to you like that," he corrects me. "I helped Nurse Maja change your nappies as a babe. I have privileges."

I snort. "You stole my dirty nappies and hid them in the Council chamber. I don't think that counts."

"Not the point. The point is, she obviously still loves you."

"She doesn't," I say sadly. "She loves Sasha."

"Certainly," Rowan allows. "But it's the way you love me. And—do pardon me if I'm wrong—that's a very different sort of love. Unless you do want to go to bed with me, in which case I must humbly decline. You're not my type."

I smack him, but a fizzle of hope tingles in my chest. "Do you really think…"

"I really do," he says, serious now. "I think she's just too proud to say it. Or too scared."

My first instinct is to chase Sadra down and demand an explanation. But I can't do that. Because it would be unseemly, because there's simply too much to do, too many people who need my time and attention. Because I'm queen. I greet the families of the dead and offer my gratitude and condolences. I listen to them as they cry and tell me about the ones they lost. I speak to survivors of the Pall who have come out of hiding, about who they were in their former lives and who they might be in this new one.

They leave me in awe... and in hope. The skills and knowledge they've brought with them from their old world will go a long way toward filling the gaps the loss of Light will leave behind. There are architects, healers, natural philosophers, and mathematicians, all eager to make Kingsgarden a better place. There are even teachers, whom I have every intention of putting to work at the girls' school and in the academies.

Jessa, Pia, and Calan arrive at sunset on the third day, just in time to present their tribute to Maia: the silhouette of a young girl surrounded by blooming roses, inked over each of their hearts by Calan's needle. I ask Calan for one of my own, right on the spot. Sasha and Jessa hold my hands as Calan marks my left shoulder with the same image. But to mine, he adds a bird in flight. A sparrow.

The day is difficult and painful for everyone. Through it all, I catch glimpses of Sadra watching me from the edges of my vision. I can't go to her, not yet—I can't indulge my own desires when my people need me. But when we return to the Terrace at dawn, I sneak away to Balia's Bridge and tuck a piece of jade among the stones of the pool.

Chapter Forty-Six

Sadra comes to me in a dream, the night before my coronation. We meet in a meadow filled with wildflowers, under a sky so blue it makes my eyes and heart ache with the beauty of it. Sadra stands hip-deep in flowers, the buds and petals bumping gently against her thighs as she moves toward me.

"I am a coward," she says without preamble. "I couldn't face you awake."

"I could have been braver myself," I admit. "I was too afraid to believe you might still love me, and far too afraid to ask."

"You can ask me here," Sadra says. "It's much safer than the waking world."

"Do you love me, then?" Even in the dream, I struggle to keep my tone light, to keep the pain of longing out of my voice.

"With all my heart," she says. But when I move to embrace her, she holds up a hand. "I need to tell you something first. Rather, I need to ask you something."

"Ask me what? If I love you? You must know I do."

"No," she says. "I need to ask you for your forgiveness."

I shake my head. "Sadra, there's nothing to forgive."

"There is," she says. "I should never have asked you to run away with me. You were right—about everything. Of course you couldn't leave your family, nor I break my vows. It would have been—there aren't words for how wrong it was for me to even think it. And it wouldn't have done us any good. We could never have been happy with that knowledge following us for the rest of our days."

"You were distraught," I say. "You weren't thinking clearly."

"Not at all," she agrees. "I think I went a bit mad."

"Why?" I ask tentatively. "What happened that night?"

"Sasha and Luca came to see me," she says. "I was so happy... until I realized Sasha had come to say goodbye. She said she was going away to find the Apostate and have the Pall removed."

"That seems like a good thing," I say, confused. "I know it's dangerous—we all saw that—but it's much safer with the proper procedure and enough time, isn't it?"

"It wasn't that." Sadra shakes her head. "There's more to it. Bard told her that he and other thralls who had been through it had been offered a choice—to return to the world of their birth or here, to Kingsgarden. The ones who survived had all chosen Kingsgarden. The ones who didn't... did they choose to go home, and it was only their bodies here that died? Are they alive now and happy in some other world? Or did they just die? There's no way to know."

Realization dawns. "And Sasha wasn't planning to choose Kingsgarden."

"It was the only thing she wanted, the only thing keeping her going," Sadra says. "She had people waiting for her, people who loved her. I shouldn't have blamed her for wanting to go back—but I did. I thought she was being an idiot. I was furious at her. After everything I'd done to keep her safe, she was going to just throw it all away. I felt like she was throwing *me* away, too, which wasn't fair at all, I know that. But all I could see was that she had a choice and wasn't going to choose us. It was stupid and selfish, and it all fell on you. I wanted—I wanted to be chosen. So I asked you to run away with me. To choose me."

"And I didn't," I say sadly. "I'm so sorry, Sadra."

She shakes her head. "*I'm* sorry. I should never have asked you to abandon your family. It's just—you and Sasha and Luca, you all have people in your lives who are more important than anything, who you'd do anything for. I suppose I wanted to be one of those people."

"You are," I say, taking her hands. "You *are*. You always were—but running away wasn't going to solve anything."

"I know," she says quickly. "I know that now. But, like I said, I went a bit mad. I realized how ridiculous I'd been within minutes after you left. But I was too scared and too proud to come after you."

"I should never have left," I say. "I should have stayed with you. Forgive me?"

She smiles crookedly. "If you forgive me."

"I forgave you a long time ago," I say. "I just wish... "

"Yes," she says. "Me, too."

We remain silent for a long time, just holding each other's hands and listening to the rustle of wind in the blooms. My hands drift up her arms, and hers go around my waist. We move together slowly, so slowly I almost can't tell the exact moment our lips touch. And then we're pulling at each other, wild and clumsy with need. We sink into the meadow in a tangle of limbs and lips and tears.

"I love you," she murmurs in my ear afterward.

I trail my fingers up the smooth skin of her back. "As I love you. And I want you to stay with me. Forever. I'll speak to Mother Wenla. You don't have to break your vows. You can still teach at the school, and you can be my Companion. If you want."

Sadra props herself up on an elbow to stare down at me incredulously. "Companion to the queen?"

"Why not?" I ask with a shrug. "There have been royal Companions before."

"Yes," Sadra says with an exasperated laugh. "To *kings*."

"It's a change," I agree. "But with everything that's happened and everything that will happen, I don't think anyone will have the time or energy to argue about who shares my bed."

"But—the succession," Sadra says. "You'll need an heir."

"And I'll have one," I assure her. "Luca and Sasha will have a child within a year, maybe two. I've seen it."

"You do recall that neither of them is actually royal," Sadra points out.

"Sasha is the Chalice," I remind her. "She already has a growing following in the City. She's... mythic. She'll be perfect."

Sadra cocks an eyebrow. "And have you told her of your plans for her womb?"

"Not yet," I say. "I think she'll agree, but it doesn't matter, really. Her son will one day reign. How it happens, though... I don't know. I just know that, whatever does happen, I don't want to face it without you. I need you, Sadra. I choose you."

Tears fill her eyes. "I choose you, too. Whatever happens next, we do it together."

I sigh, joy filling me like—well, like a chalice.

"Let's wake up," I say. "I want to do this again with real bodies, in a real bed."

Sadra kisses me, long and lingering.

"As my queen commands."

My coronation is held the next day, on the eve of Balia's Banquet. I kneel before her statue, newly carved and erected in Market Square. She is not the Balia that we knew. Though she kneels, her head is unbowed. Her face is defiant, triumphant, and her eyes are fixed on something far in the distance.

Another will rise. That was Balia's promise. Am I that one? Perhaps. But I hope not. I hope there will be another girl, another queen. And another, and another. But, for now, it starts with me. I will rise and do my best to bring my people with me.

Tonight, the City will come together and share their arts, their Gifts, their grief and their joy. Pia has already led the effort in the Lower City to welcome the Pall's survivors by taking several into her own home and bullying the shocked and hapless Yoren Silversmith into opening the House's shelters. Whether he regrets his father's involvement in the attempted coup and his own role in the House's great deceit or he merely wants to save his own skin by cooperating, I don't know. All I can say is that he provides thorough and competent care to newly freed thralls as they recover from the Pall's removal and find work in the City.

It's a season of both upheaval and renewal, and a time for second chances. I feel the weight of the crown as Mother Wenla settles it on my brow, and I don't need my Gift to tell me that death is coming for the Garden. There will be storms of blood and fire and thorns, of fury and hate. We will burn to the ground. There is nothing I can do to change that; I can only meet it when it comes and trust that this kingdom, this Garden, will rise from the ashes and bloom again.

Today, my people are united. Today, they want to heal. Rose petals tossed from balconies dance on the wind like snow flurries, fluttering down to land on the heads and shoulders of those below. The square rings with laughter and shouts of exultation, and the swell of a thousand voices lifted in song. They're singing for each other as much as for me, and that's as it should be.

"Rise, Queen Arismendi," Mother Wenla says, her voice full of pride. She turns to the gathered crowd and shouts, "People of the Garden, I give you your queen!"

Cheers erupt. More rose petals and shouts of "The Rose Queen!" and "Balia's Blessed!" rain down on me. I see Jessa and Channi clinging to each other and jumping up and down like squirrels, their faces ablaze with excitement. The sight gives me the courage I need to take one step forward, then another, until I'm surrounded by people.

Once, I would have run. But I can't, now, and I find that I don't want to. These people are mine, and I am theirs. When an old woman reaches for me, I return her embrace. When a father presents his infant daughter, I bestow a kiss on her tiny hand. When Soren hands me a goblet of honey wine, I take it.

And drink deep.

Not ready to leave Kingsgarden?

Don't miss *The Chalice and the Crown,*
a companion to The Fox and the Flame.

"The thrall's eyes bore into mine, willing me to understand. She draws her hand across my face and her finger across my throat. Pretend, she's saying, or they'll kill you.

I believe her."

All Sasha ever wanted to do is dance. But just when she lands a role that could launch her career, she finds herself trapped in a nightmare kingdom where the wealthy harvest labor and magic from their mute and —supposedly—mindless servants.

Sasha is one such servant, a thrall. The family she serves has no idea she's anything more than what she appears to be: a living doll enchanted to do their bidding. But the slavers who stole Sasha away from her own world know the truth, and one misstep in her fight for freedom could cost Sasha her life... or her soul.

Even as she endures the pain and indignity of captivity, Sasha can't help being drawn to the beauty of her nightmare world and the underground rebels who offer her friendship, shelter, even love. Before Sasha can break her chains for good, she'll need to choose between the life waiting for her at home and the countless lives she could save if she stays.

To choose a nightmare over her real life, her future, would be madness... but maybe a little madness is just what it takes to change the fate of a kingdom built on lies.

Available now!

Acknowledgments

Full disclaimer: I hate writing the Acknowledgments for my books, because how in the world are you supposed to fit everyone? So many little things go into making a book what it is. A conversation with a stranger that made me think, a word of support from a friend...even the random internet troll who left a barf emoji on my reel and gave me the push I needed to keep going out of sheer spite. But there isn't enough room to list everyone and everything, so I'll limit myself to the biggest players:

First and foremost: my parents, for reading to me every night without fail until I was old enough to do it myself; my husband, for his unwavering love and support; and my baby girl, for just existing.

My writer friends: PJ, who read more drafts of this book (and every other book I've written) than anyone should be subjected to; Jessie, who turned into my loudest and most unexpected online cheerleader; and all my beta readers, whose invaluable feedback made this book 1000% better than it would have been otherwise.

Last but not least, huge thanks to my Kickstarter backers who made all this possible, and to you, dear reader, for picking up this book when you could have watched Netflix instead.

A graduate of the Sunderman Conservatory at Gettysburg College, Kassandra Flamouri grew up telling stories through both music and prose. She currently resides in Pennsylvania, where she juggles writing and motherhood. Her other novels include *Magissa* and *The Chalice and the Crown,* a companion to *The Fox and the Flame.* For more information, visit her online at www.kassandra-flamouri.com.